La Espina

(THE THORN)

A STORY OF FRIENDSHIP, LOYALTY, LOVE, SEARCHING, AND HEALING

CAROL ALFORD

Gratuity
Direct Number: 2134389957
(888) 290-0987
9350 Wilshire Blvd, Suite 203,
Beverly Hills, CA 90212

Published by Gratuity: 01/17/2025

ISBN: 978-1-965386-18-7(sc)
ISBN: 978-1-965386-19-4(e)

This book is lovingly dedicated to my parents Jacqueline
Rose Michie and John Alexander Michie who shared
their joy, laughter, strength, and unconditional love.

And to my husband David Alford who championed our
motorhome travels and opened the door to our explorations
of this awesome world, may you rest in peace.

Contents

Chapter 1 1
Chapter 2 8
Chapter 3 19
Chapter 4 27
Chapter 5 32
Chapter 6 38
Chapter 7 45
Chapter 8 54
Chapter 9 65
Chapter 10 74
Chapter 11 84
Chapter 12 94
Chapter 13 104
Chapter 14 116
Chapter 15 125
Chapter 16 130
Chapter 17 135
Chapter 18 147
Chapter 19 156
Chapter 20 166
Chapter 21 178
Chapter 22 192
Chapter 23 203
Chapter 24 215
Chapter 25 231
Chapter 26 242

Chapter 27 255
Chapter 28 266
Chapter 29 275
Chapter 30 280
Chapter 31 289

Acknowledgements

Between the years of 1963 and 1995 it was my good fortune to enjoy multitudes of students who enriched my life as together we studied a variety of subjects in the discipline of Family and Consumer Studies. Since that time, I have not given up my love of teaching and continue to journey in and out of the classroom as a substitute.

I was touched by many of the stories of my students—as one might guess, those in the educational field grow quite possessive 'our' students. Pieces of those stories have made their way into the novel, *La Espina*. Though they will never know how they inspired me, I did share with them my desire to write novels when retirement came. I have done so. Thank you, dear students, for your inspiration and wherever you may be, I wish you well.

Much of this writing took place in Mexico where I immediately tasted the spirit and flavor of her people. Thank you, Mexico, for sharing your wonderful neighborhood of contrasts with me. I am indeed grateful to my Mexican friend, Veronica, who introduced me to her own story of *la espina* and expressed her enthusiasm for this work. I am also indebted to Manuel, who is reflected in the character by the same name in *La Espina*.

Dixie

Freedom at last! In reality I deceive myself. I will never be free of the dirty secret I carry, like a spine that never leaves, but festers, then oozes, tainting all it touches. I have been lucky so far, however. No more than five miles out of town I was picked up by a trucker heading to his home in Colorado. I've never hitchhiked before. Some say it's too dangerous evil things may happen. But hey, it can't be worse than the past thirteen years in the presence of a predator that I couldn't escape.

Charlie—that's the trucker—doesn't know that I'm not yet eighteen. I told him I'm a college student looking for an adventure and summer employment. I'm not sure he bought it. He assures me that the place to go is the "cozy tourist and summer place of Estes Park"—those are his words—where there are all kinds of jobs at resorts, campgrounds, hotels, you name it.

I'm leaving a few friends. But they didn't know about my dirty secret, so it was hard to get really close. They will be shocked out of their skins about my disappearance. I do miss Snowball. But my kitty is nearing twelve and may not have too many more years. She was the best listener I ever had. I considered bringing her on the road. All I have that ties me to back there are six pairs of underwear, two pairs of jeans, three shirts, three pairs of socks, hiking boots and sandals. I'm traveling light.

I doubt they will report me missing. They know I will talk. I made that clear in my note. Once I'm hidden away in some resort, they won't find me. They won't dare to try. I gave them enough hell this last year anyway, they are probably celebrating my absence.

Hey world let me tell you. I'm ready to go it on my own. I don't need anyone.

CHAPTER 1

Joanna Johansen slid her thumb across the one-hundred-year-old box. The flaxen finish had the same high gloss she remembered. She examined the intricate inlays of red and brown tones. *What an exquisite piece.* Smooth as the day it was finished by an unknown wood worker, it had been in her mother's family for three generations. Allison, the only mother she had ever known, had lovingly stored three items in this family heirloom. They were the only link to that 'other' Mother, the one Joanna pictured as cowardly and weak.

Slumping to the floor, Joanna leaned against the bed that had been her mother's and crossed her legs in front of her. Using the corner of her shirt, she attempted to dry the splotches of tears that rolled from her cheeks onto the heirloom cradled in her lap.

Thoughts of the past coiled through her mind like the smoke of a smoldering campfire. The last time she remembered opening this hand-hewn treasure, she was fourteen. There would come a time when she acknowledged the sharpness of the spine in her heart, when it plunged deeper and threatened to fester, yet today her memories were both tart and sweet.

It had been one of those nights when Joanna and three friends sat cross-legged amid pillows and sleeping bags, crackers, and cheese puffs, giggling, and swooning over the new boy in school. The foursome had become fast friends in Mrs. Patterson's sixth grade class when they labored over a Colorado history project. They chose as their theme the colorful character, Molly brown, one of the survivors of the Titanic disaster and created a play depicting several scenes in Molly's life. In their research they toured the Molly brown house in Denver and gathered dresses of the period to use in the play.

Performing it several times in the community brought some notoriety, and the group was featured in the *Loveland Daily*. Thus began an important and unceasing friendship.

Joanna was probably the most rounded of the four, a composite of tomboy and femininity spawned by unknown genetic makeup. She was one not one to talk about being adopted but her friends knew and tonight the subject would be opened.

So, there they were. Miss self-reliant, Janene, sprawling Lauren, and that mite of a thing Amy, making memories in the Johansen home as Joanna played hostess to her teenage friends.

"Jo you never talk about your other mom. What's the big deal? Why are you so secretive?" Janene Santini clearly portrayed her Italian heritage with dark hair and eyes. Confident, bright, and outspoken, school bordered on boring for her. With her typical bluntness she spat the words toward Joanna, daring in her attitude.

Joanna's belligerent glare stifled the chatter on the tongues of her friends. Waiting and wondering about her reaction, they watched the glare soften. Then Joanna rose and motioned the three to follow. With a sense of mystery, Joanna led the wide-eyed friends to the linen closet at the end of the hall.

She *did* have something to show her friends. Some of Janene's questions could be answered. On tip toes, the honey blonde stretched to grasp the hand-hewn box, embellished with red and brown inlays from the top shelf. The young teens could hear the monologue of *The Tonight Show* from the bedroom on the right.

Lauren leaned her coppery head toward Joanna. Ordinarily easygoing and unshakable, uneasiness crept into her whisper. "This looks like some special box. Are you sure it's OK with your folks?"

Tossing her head to the side, Joanna insinuated the tone of her answer, "It's my box and I can do whatever I want with it. In fact, I was the one who wanted to put it away. For years it was on my dresser.

It really wasn't part of my life, and I didn't need it there staring me in the face every day."

The trio followed her back toward the family room. Amy smoothed the rumpled sleeping bag and made herself comfortable. Pint sized and freckled, she was the athlete of the group. Despite being the youngest Snider and the only girl in her family, she had no trouble keeping up with her three brothers. Too busy to be bothered with hairstyle, two dark pigtails with escaping frizz became her Insignia. "Come on, don't keep us in suspense! What's inside Jo?"

Cautiously Joanna lifted the lid. She fingered a faded cloth doll. A pinkish bonnet framed the painted face—now barely visible—and matched a puff sleeved dress. The whole thing was rather flat and flimsy but had been well-cuddled.

"As you can see this poor old thing has been through the ringer. I slept with her till I was nearly three, and mom put her in my 'birth box' so that she wouldn't waste away to nothing. It was one of three things that my birthmother left me. Mom and I always called it my Cara Dolly since Cara was the name my birthmother had given me."

Janene spoke out again, "Aren't you curious about her? Wouldn't you like to find her someday?"

"Naw, she really means nothing to me. I know all I want to know. Besides, I *have* parents. They are the ones who raised me and the only ones I will ever have."

She fished a ring from the bottom of the box, held it out to her friends, then slid it on her finger. "It almost fits. Just a little too big. Kind of old fashioned with this filigree design, don't you think?"

"Geez, is that neat. And that ruby—what a rock. Was it your other mom's?" Lauran's drawl had a singsong to it.

"Well, not really. If I read this, it will explain." Joanna unfolded a three-page, yellowed letter. It was handwritten in blue ink. "It's from her. She left the doll, the ring, and this letter. It's all I have from her."

Three pairs of eyes stared, then darted. What did it say?

Joanna turned away and heaved a sigh. Why was she so reluctant? They were her best friends, so close that her mom had once called them the Quad Squad and the name stuck. Looking down at the artful script she began.

"April 25"

"This was written when I was only three days old," Joanna interjected.

"My dearest little Cara,

You are so pink and soft. As all babies you have a wonderful fragrance. When I touched your nose you sneezed and opened your blue, blue eyes so wide. I can tell that you are going to be a snuggler. You like to nuzzle against my face. Your little mouth and nose already scrunch into all kinds of expressions. I would say that you will be an expressive the little gal.

I want you to have every opportunity possible in this sometimes-harsh world. I know that I will not be able to give you those opportunities, at least not now. I am barely out of high school, and I don't think I'd make a good mom.

You need to know that I am not married. I knew your father for a few weeks. He was out of my life before I knew I was carrying you. He was one of those blue-eyed blondes who tans well and has a dazzling smile. He was a charmer and seven years older. He had a wife and family of his own. So, he doesn't know about you, my little one.

I grieve that I will not be able to know if your eyes stay the deep blue that they are now. Will you inherit my olive complexion and dark brown hair or your father's glow? Nor will I be the one to rock you or dry your tears or mend your skinned knees and scrapes.

Joanna paused from her reading. So far, her voice had not wavered, but Amy detected a quiver when Joanna read, *"Your new mother and father will do that for you."*

Softhearted Amy fought the brimming tears threatening to spill. Lowering her head, she knew if she saw Joanna's eyes, the sob caught in her throat would not stay there. How could a mother give her child away? Where would she be if her mother had not wanted her? How awful it must be.

Joanna looked up at her three friends and their somber reactions. Gaining her composure, she flashed her blue-green eyes. "Hey guys don't be so serious. Do you want to hear the rest?"

Lauren pulled her knees close and gave a definite nod.

"My parents and I have never been close. They will never understand

that I feel betrayed by them. And somehow, I have always seemed to disappoint them. I am afraid as your mother I would always disappoint you as well. Think of me as this far off friend. One you never see but one who has you in her heart every moment, one who watches in the night.

I want you to have this little Dolly I had something like this when I was young. Since I can't be beside you as you sleep, Dolly will be there in my place. The ruby ring I wore only once. It was my grandmother's engagement ring. When grandpa died and grandma remarried, she gave it to me. I treasure the ornate work. I hope you will, too.

Remember to taste and smell and feel all that flows around you. Know that we see the same moon and stars. You are my special little one. I love you, my little Cara.

Your far away Mommy"

"Well, that's it. That's all I know about my far away mommy. Joanna did not try to keep the bitterness from her voice.

Lauren's drawl broke the silence. "Geez, Joanna, she sounds neat. We love your mom, but you have to have some compassion for your real mom. Imagine holding you and cuddling you and handing you over to someone else. Then writing that letter to a baby she knows she'll never see again."

Joanna cut in. "She's *not* my real mother. I have a real mother in the bedroom down the hall."

Amy ignored Joanna's retort and blurted, "yeah and just think she was probably only a few years older than we are. No offense Jo, but I don't think I could give up my child at any age. And what do you think about that part—be sure to smell, taste and feel the whole world…and be sure to remember you both see the same stars and moon?" Amy paused to take a breath. "It gives me the shivers." She rose and peered into the night through the nearby window. "She may be looking at that moon out there this very minute."

Janene's practicality took over. "Well one thing we know. You got your dad's coloring. Blonde, with that golden tan. Your eyes came out with a hint of green though. 'Spose that came from your mom?"

Joanna shrugged.

Lauren unfolded her lengthy, lean body and stretched out on her stomach. A long thick braid flipped to one side as wisps of Auburn fuzz framed her bait maturing face. With those high cheekbones, slender nose and generous lips, no one would deny that Lauren was a beauty blooming. "Did your folks ever want to adopt a brother or sister for you?"

"Well, when I was about five, they talked about it and asked me if I wanted one."

"Well, didn't you?" With three brothers Amy thought everyone should have siblings.

"It never really mattered to me. I guess I still feel that way."

"How did your folks get together anyway?' asked Janene. "

"Mom and dad met in college. Mom was studying physical therapy or occupational therapy, whatever. Dad was in business. He dropped out when a sales job with a medical company came up."

Amy added, "You could tell he was meant to be a salesman always joking around and being Mr. Social."

Joanna twisted her dangling ponytail. "Yeah at least he puts on a good show in public. Anyway, Dad was making some pretty good money. They got married and Mom got her degree and did her internship before she started her physical therapist job at the orthopedic clinic."

"So how old were you when they got married?" Lauren asked, trying to do some arithmetic in her head.

"I guess they were twenty-one."

Janene had it figured out. "I bet I can finish this story. They didn't start a family for a few years, so your mom could get a start in her career. Then once they wanted children, nothing happened, so they adopted you."

"You got it. It took about a year and a half to get me. When they did, Mom was thirty and Dad was one week away from thirty. So, he always said I was his favorite birthday present. As time went on, I think they thought they were getting too old to start the adoption process again."

Janene continued the probing. "What would you do if you got a phone call one day and on the line you heard 'I found my little Cara. This is your mom'?"

Joanna bit the left side of her lip before her voice came out—like stretching taffy. "Hmm! The woman can stay out of my life." She shook her head vigorously. "Today I'd probably hang up."

"No! Not really! How could you? I mean cripes Jo, she gave you your life. Don't you owe her something? How come you're so mad at her?" Janene's attitude was challenging.

Every word was punctuated as Joanna shot back, "Don't you dare accuse me and give me that crooked look! I don't owe her a thing! My loyalty goes to my folks who raised me. It wasn't my fault that she screwed around with some married man and got banged up." She wondered if she used the right expression, but she thought that's the way she'd heard it.

"Jo…Janene didn't say anything was *your* fault. Of course, you are loyal to your parents." Amy, the peacemaker, hoped to smooth things out. This was certainly sensitive territory. But one could walk the fence and be respectful of both sides. It seemed logical to her. She grinned. If I know your mom like I think I do, I bet she gives thanks to your birth mom every day for sending her such a delightful daughter."

Joanna cooled a smidgen. "Delightful, you call me? You think you're funny, don't you?"

Amy continued, "And I bet your mom wouldn't be one bit jealous if you found your birth mom someday."

"I suppose you're right. We've talked about it, and she said she'd help me if I wanted her to. I just don't care about my birth mom. I'd probably be disappointed. I've heard too many horror stories. And it feels like it would be a slap in my parents' faces." Joanna continued to cool down then added. "I do know I was born in Estes Park."

Janene's eyes mimicked those of a night owl. "Cripes Jo, that's only thirty miles from here. It should be a cinch to get info in our own county."

"Yeah, but I still say no way." Joanna shook her finger toward Janene.

"Well if you change your mind, it'll be a Quad Squad joint endeavor all the way. Right A and L?"

"Right on." Amy and Lauren agreed.

"Even if you say to no tonight, let's shake on it. It's our pact," Janine insisted, "you never know the future." And the Quad Squad sealed their pact.

CHAPTER 2

Pushing the past behind, Joanna took one last swipe across the heirloom, ridding it of her salty tears and lifted the front latch that released the lid. That smell. The same one. Do smells last that long? Cara Dolly was on top. The letter and the ring were still there. This time when she mouthed the words she read, she didn't feel so brave. Her tears left blotches on the dry brittle pages.

The horrible news was still sinking in. Her mother, the indestructible Allison Block and her stepfather Steve, had lost their lives on I-25, four miles north of Northglenn. It was one of those late June Colorado cloud bursts. Joanna had been in one about the same time last year coming back from Elitches fun park with three of Steve's grandchildren. It was scary for the kids, and it was scary for her, too. Lots of banging thunder and flashing lightning. Everyone was going too fast and hydroplaning.

It was probably the same for her mom and Steve. He was a solid and excellent driver. He had to be to handle the RV rig, a 36-foot motorhome he and Allison traipsed all over the country with. But with impossible visibility and a small tornado threatening to touch down, there was no avoiding the SUV that crossed the median and slammed into their four-door sedan. Allison and Steve died instantly, and the driver of the SUV would be recuperating for quite some time after being wired and pinned back together. But he was alive. It was so unfair.

Just yesterday morning she had talked to her mom. "Hi Mom."

"Hi Hon. You're back early. I thought you were coming in tomorrow."

"Finished early. I'm getting pretty speedy at putting these travel packages together. I followed up on the lead you gave me about the Mexican hotel in Rincon de Guayabitos."

"Oh yes, that one being built next to the RV park. The workers kept us up all night with their pounding."

Allison and Johanna's stepfather liked to spend their winters RVing in Mexico. Joanna had no way of knowing that she would winter in Mexico this year.

"I liked the hotel, a beautiful place. I wrapped up a good deal and hit the road. Got in last night."

"Tell me about it."

"Not on the phone mom. Too much detail. Maybe I'll stop by this afternoon for a visit."

"Gee Hon, that would be great, but Steve and I have tickets to the Rockies and they're on a winning streak. That new pitcher they're raving about is on today."

"Sounds good Mom."

"Before we hang up—tell me. How were things between you and Paul when you got back? I know it was rocky before you left."

"OK I guess, but that is part of what I want to talk to you about. I'm beginning to think thar you were right. I'm not sure he's the right one for me or maybe I'm not the right one for him."

"Joanna honey, I didn't exactly say you were wrong for each other."

"No, but I can feel your vibes, Mom."

"I'm sure. Um…I just don't want him taking advantage of you. He moved in with you, what, six weeks ago?"

"About that."

"Anyway, I bet he has yet to help pay the electric, phone, or whatever bill, not to mention the other part of being a thoughtful companion."

"He's kind of getting back on his feet."

"As assertive as you are in your work, you're much too easy on friends and boyfriends."

"Yeah Mom. Well, I don't like to hurt people. But I think I'm ready to tell him it's over."

"I can't say that I would be sorry. I know there's someone better out there for you."

"Talk more later, Mom. You two have fun at the game. OK?"

"Bye Hon."

"Love ya, Mom." Click.

At least she had told her mom she loved her. They always told each other how they felt and never held back, and Joanna could always count on her mom for a good hug. There would be no more mom hugs.

Why hadn't her dad called by now? Of course, he would expect her to be at her condo and not her mom's house. *I bet he hasn't even tried to call.* She couldn't understand him. Surely, he knew about the accident. It was on the front page of the *Loveland Daily.*

Paul. He was still at the condo. The restaurant didn't open till 4:30. Shay's Steakhouse was the new restaurant in town and as assistant manager he went in at 3:00 to supervise the pre-prep. Joanna punched in the numbers and Paul picked up on the 3rd ring. "Hi Paul, it's me. Has my dad called?"

"No, but Amy and Janene both called. They are bringing supper over at 6:00. They thought they would hang out as long as you needed them."

At thirty-one the Quad Squad treasured their close bond. In fact, before Joanna left her condo this morning, she had a call from Lauren. Lauren's mom had e-mailed her, so she knew immediately about the tragedy. Lauren was devastated and would fly out as soon as she could get a flight. Her costume designs for the TV movie had been well received and shooting at High Seas Studios had finished up last week. Don't do a thing till I get there," she had said. And tonight, Amy and Janene wanted to come by. What friends.

Haltingly she started, "It will be good to be around people who really care about me."

"Hey, I care, but you know I can't miss work. I'm just getting started in this job. I'd be there if I could."

"No, no. I'm not referring to you. Besides you already missed a night's sleep last night. You were an angel. Thank you, Paul. I thought maybe my dad would call for once. Maybe he'd want to give me some comfort."

"Jo, you know his wife wouldn't put up with an any contact that involved your mom."

"Probably not. But he and mom were married for 27 years, and I thought he might have an idea or two about the arrangements. Mostly I guess I need some family right now."

Paul let the topic drop. "How did the meeting go with the funeral people?"

"I need to go back this afternoon and finalize things for the memorial. It will be Saturday morning since Mom's brother Dave and his family can't get here till Friday. Uncle Dave said to do whatever I thought mom would want. They didn't see each other much after Mom left Oregon to come here for college. There isn't much to do. The funeral people have everything pretty well organized. I suppose the cremation was today I try not to think about it."

"It's tough Jo. Are you over at your mom's and Steve's?"

"Yes. Had hoped to sort through papers, the mail and stuff, but never really got to it. Found some things and the memories flooded back. Well, I gotta go. Hope all goes well at work today and thanks for being there last night."

Many times, she had tried to figure out her dad. He had been very successful in sales for a pharmaceutical company, though now he was semi-retired. He played golf and tennis with a few male friends and was often a little cocky and funny in social and work settings. He knew how to put on a show. Joanna pictured his relationships as superficial and the toughness he displayed as a cover for deep insecurities.

Her mom had been the one to handle the finances, income taxes, insurance and decisions about furnishings and appliances, wallpaper or whatever. Joanna believed that he could have done these things but somehow, he ended up taking a helpless role in the home. Yet Clay had the say on most things. If he didn't want to go to the neighbor's cookout or any social function, they didn't go. And at supper time he was the big cheese. He relished the praise that followed the stories of his latest big deal at work. But most often he complained and blamed someone for a recent crisis, personnel problem, or worry, and they heard every detail. When Joanna 's mother had an idea or suggestion, it was immediately shot down as being ridiculous or impossible, followed by a 'You think you have all the answers, don't you?' in a sarcastic tone.

Several years after the divorce, Allison talked to Joanna about her take on her dad's infidelity. Allison blamed herself for allowing him to continue that helpless feeling at home. When depression set in, she tried harder to please him.

"Maybe," Allison said," if I'd slammed my fist and said 'Clayton Johansson what in the hell is going on with you? You're crotchety and nasty with me most of the time. We never talk, much less have any tenderness or love making. You walk around half the time mumbling to yourself. You refuse to let me have any friends over for dinner or to see any of your coworkers and their spouses...' If I really leveled with him instead of trying to keep peace and picking up the loose ends, if I recognized the depression for what it was, things might have been different. Perhaps your dad would not have been so vulnerable and his much younger secretary, unhappy in her marriage, would not have made him feel important, youthful, desired, and needed."

Allison had been willing to get counseling and work on the relationship if he could give up this fling. After all one doesn't easily throw 27 years of marriage to the wolves. But her father was determined that his happiness was with Cindy. Her father's last speech was not meant for Joanna's ears, but she had listened through the upstairs window as her parents talked on the patio below.

"You want me to be happy, don't you? She really needs me. Her kids need me." That part continued to sting for Joanna. "She's had a rough life and I can show her so much in the world that she's never experienced. You will be all right, Allison. You can do anything. You could build a house. She can't even use a screwdriver."

Was that supposed to make her mother feel better? To Joanna it seemed that her father traded a strong and capable wife for a much younger, yet helpless and controlling one. Go figure. The ink was barely dry on the divorce papers when Clay and Cindy made their promises in the local Loveland wedding Chapel. From that time on Clay was pretty much out of Joanna's life, since Clay was so tied up with his new wife and new family. Joanna expected to take the back seat in the beginning, but she also expected things to change once he settled in. They didn't. Clay refused to call Joanna if he thought her mom might be around. Even when Joanna moved into her own condo five years ago nothing changed.

Joanna tried to keep in touch with him, so she made the calls. However, the response went something like: 'it's not a good time today, JJ.'; 'I'll try to get back to you by next week; 'I'll call you for lunch.' The gap between them grew wider and wider and though it was generally a polite interchange when they did see each other, there was a subtle tension between them.

Dammit. She needed him now. If Cindy didn't like her talking to him about her mom, tough.

She would give it one more ring. It had already been five.

"Hello." Cindy was breathless and sharp. In the background Joanna heard a baby crying.

"Hi Cindy, it's nice to hear your voice."

"Who's this?"

"It's Joanna, Cindy/" Joanna couldn't believe that after 13 years she still didn't recognize her voice or maybe she didn't want to. "I hope you are fine. Do I hear that little granddaughter in the background?"

Then Cindy's speech became sticky sweet, "Oh Joanna it's nice of you to call. Yes, I took the day off so I could watch little Cody. Diane has just been worn out since the baby was born and needed a day of rest. Now I'm the one getting worn out. You know how it is."

No, she didn't know how it was. She guessed she remembered right, and that Cody was a little girl. These days Codys were sometimes girls, sometimes boys. At least Cindy hadn't corrected her. To be sure, if she made a mistake, she would have been corrected. "I bet she is really growing up. Is she about five months?"

"Oh no, she's six and a half months now. Can you hold on a minute? She needs her bottle. Let me get it and I'll be right back."

The crying in the background changed to a whimper and Joanna could hear clinking and clanking and then the ding of the microwave.

Could she just talk to her dad instead of all this chitchat? She would bide her time until the right moment. She had vowed to be polite to all her step relatives. Really, they were good people. Even Cindy had her virtuous moments, but she seemed to rub Joanna the wrong way most of the time.

"Whew, I'm back. This little thing is a handful." Joanna could hear gulping and gurgling sounds. "I was so sorry to read about your mom and her husband in the newspaper. I know you must be devastated. It's just terrible. Drivers these days are a menace. We prefer to stay home rather than take chances on the highway. And the weather. You can never count on it being a good day."

"Thank you, Cindy." Joanna cut in before she rambled on. "Is my is my dad there? I'd like to talk to him."

"Well, not at the moment. Since he retired, he's in charge of the cleaning, shopping, and cooking. I told him that he couldn't expect me to work all day and keep up the household and watch the baby when Diane needs me, while he putters in his shop or is out on the golf course. Anyway, it's shopping day. You'd think he'd have it done. If I weren't home to prod him, he'd be procrastinating as usual. He should be back soon though cause he's bringing something for my lunch.

Joanna knew that he still worked part-time putting in three to four hours a day although he had retired a while back. The health and medical sales business had expanded. The territory had broadened, and Clay was needed to fill in the gaps. It was good for his ego, added to the pocketbook and kept him from boredom "I'll call back in fifteen minutes. Do you think he'll be back by then?" Joanna knew she could not expect him to return her call.

"I certainly hope so. I'm getting really hungry and he's bringing the baby some baby food. She's pretty hungry too."

Joanna hung up trying to picture her dad in the kitchen and laundry room. He did his part with the laundry when she was growing up. However, the kitchen was definitely out of his league. Her mom always made sure that meals were in the refrigerator if she needed to be gone during supper time. No encouragement or directions from her mom could motivate Clay in the kitchen. He would persuade Joanna to prepare something, they would order pizza, or go out for fast food.

The thought of food produced several rumbles in her stomach. Yet the thought of eating was like 'yuck.' Her mom would have said that twenty-four hours of empty stomach was too long. She opened the refrigerator. Ham slices waited to be put into a sandwich. A somber half-full gallon of milk, part of a pecan, and a freshly prepared Mandarin orange gelatin salad stared at her. All should have been devoured last night when Steve and her mom returned from the Rockies game. Her stomach caught in her throat. Oh mom. There was so much to do, so many decisions to make. She hadn't thought of the refrigerator. Much of it could wait, but the refrigerator couldn't wait too long.

She had half a notion to toss the food planned for last night's meal. Seeing it knotted her chest. The reality of losing her mother cut deeper.

Mechanically she arranged a plate. Her mom would be proud at the artistry of it. "Each meal should have an inviting experience and should be planned to have variety in color, shape, texture, and flavor, and it should be nutritious." She could hear her mother's words. The first bites felt and tasted like cardboard. By the fourth, her taste buds were beginning to work. Each mouthful gave the nourishment she supposed she needed, for both body and soul. *Thank you for the good food, Mom.*

Her hand caressed the patina of the round oak table as she sat in the spacious kitchen. How many times had she and her mom felt the comfort of this old friend? They were always sipping something here. She remembered sipping one of those fresh fruit blender drinks and the thrill of that day. "Your dad and I have decided to consider that horse you've been dreaming about. He's found a Morgan. She's three. Pretty well trained and the owners claim she's mighty speedy. He said we can see her this afternoon when he gets back from golfing."

Joanna was eleven when Sprint came to live in the Johansen's pasture. How she loved that pony. It was Sprint who taught her all about competing, winning, and losing. Somewhere there was a box of medals and ribbons earned from weekends of gymkhanas, drill teams, and parades. Her horse days came to an end when seventeen-year-old Joanna swapped Sprint for driving and boys.

The vivid image of getting ready for the ninth grade Halloween party came with an elusive chuckle. In her fantasy she had wanted to dress in a red, satin, slinky go-go outfit and imagined looking sexy and flashy. Some ninth graders were already sex bombs, but not her crowd, the Quad Squad.

"Hey, there's some spiced cider on the table. Let's toast 'I dream of Jeannie' before you leave," her mom had called to her as she put the last-minute touches on her face. She actually did feel a little sexy in her silky long sleeved peasant blouse, snugged at her waist with a bright turquoise cummerbund. The billowy soft pantaloons pulled tight at her ankles, silver sandals and a ponytail perched on the top of her head, gave her the look of authenticity. Together the Quad Squad had painted the 'magic lantern.' She felt ready as she sat to sip the hot spice cider. Her mom toasted and claimed, "You're the most awesome genie I have ever seen. There will be some eyes turned to night."

It was then that Joanna fell off her chair in hysterics. Her mom was behaving perfectly proper, sipping with grace, all the while wearing the most gosh awful Billy Bob teeth Joanna could ever imagine. It was five minutes before either could talk without giggling.

Another night there was hot chocolate. It was meant to soothe. The night her dad left. Joanna was facing college the next year and was counting on support from both of her parents. "I guess we've both been dumped, Mom, but at least we can have each other."

The sipping took a questioning mood another afternoon. This time it was wine. "Hey, Mom what's the occasion? On a Saturday afternoon at that!"

Joanna had moved into her own condo but most of her things were still in her old room. Every few days she was back rummaging for some piece of clothing that she decided to wear. This afternoon it was for a wild oversized shirt to be worn over black tights for a party at her condo complex. She was excited to be meeting new people. It had been a good decision to move out, though she felt guilty leaving her mother alone.

"What did you think about your own mom getting hitched?"

"Mom, you're not kidding? You and Steve are getting married?"

"We've been talking about it for a few weeks, but I told Steve I needed to talk to you. I know I don't need your approval, but I'd like to know your opinion."

"Gee, I don't know him too well. But he seems nice, nothing flashy but…"

"Honey, at my age I don't need flashy."

"No, I'm just kidding. He's a fine man and nice looking. This is pretty sudden, isn't it? You've been seeing him about two or three months, haven't you?"

"Before we went out, I spent six months getting to know him as his physical therapist."

"Oh yeah. I guess you ought to know about every bone in his body then. Right?"

"Very funny."

"Hey Mom, go for it. You deserve it. I wish you the best."

Well, my friendly oak table, you may remember I barely made it to my party that evening. It was one of the few times I saw mom tipsy.

Joanna took in a deep breath, dialed her dad's number, and waited. She didn't know what she was going to say or exactly what she wanted from him.

"Hello."

"Hi dad. I'm going to meet with the funeral people again this afternoon and wanted to talk to you beforehand."

"It's hard to realize she's gone JJ." There was no mistaking the lump in his voice. "But I don't know what I can do."

"Will you be able to be at the memorial? It's going to be Saturday morning at Mom's church. It was the church that her parents were married in. During Joanna's youth he attended a few times a year, but he hadn't been there since the divorce.

"I don't know. It's awkward and I don't think Cindy would like it."

"It's time to stop thinking of mom as the enemy. Mom always treated Cindy decently. Besides, you and Cindy are the only family I have left. I need your support." Joanna surprised herself, referring to Cindy as family.

She had flashes of her dad's anger when she and her mom attended his niece's wedding after the divorce. Cindy and Clay were late, and he was fuming when they arrived. He scowled every time he glanced their way. Allison was not invited to the next wedding. Clayton and Cindy refused to go if Allison was there. Joanna's cousin was sorry, but she was determined to keep the family's peace. Her mom understood and sent a gift anyway.

Joanna suspected that guilt and regret prevented him from facing her mom. In recent years, things had been less tense when her mother's name came up. When grandpa Tom, Clayton's father died last year, her mom was shattered. Grandpa Tom and Allison shared a special bond from the time they met. Nothing would keep her from attending the funeral and the graveside ceremony.

All had gone well. In fact, Cindy had walked up to Allison, all gushy with, "Oh, it is so nice of you to be here. It means so much to the family. Please come to the dinner afterwards." As if she had the authority to invite Allison, anyway. It was almost funny because Cindy never attended the Johansen family gatherings. During picnics and barbeques, Joanna watched her dad arrive with some excuse. 'Cindy has a headache.' 'She's in bed with the flu.' 'Work is getting her down these days and she's tuckered out.' Unfortunately, it was a family joke and before her dad arrived bets were taken concerning the excuse for the day.

The hesitation in her dad's voice continued. "JJ, I don't think it will work out. I'm sure your aunts, uncles, and cousins will be there. You have lots of friends and you are a strong gal. I'll call you. We'll have lunch next week. OK?"

Back at her condo Joanna stretched out on her cushiony couch and closed her eyes. Lunch next week with her dad? Sure. It would never happen. She guessed everything was set for the memorial. A few people from the choir would sing three of her mom's favorite hymns. It would be tough for them as well. Her mom was well loved and had been a part of the choir since her college days. A poem rolled around in her head. Joanna hoped to write something in tribute to her mom. It would never say all that she felt she knew it would be insignificant in comparison, but she would do her best.

CHAPTER 3

Ding-dong. Thump, thump. Joanna was having difficulty getting out of her web of dreams. "Joanna, it's Amy and Janene." She couldn't cut through the fog. She hated it when she wanted to wake up and couldn't. Joanna saw herself roll off the couch, push herself to a stand. But no, her eyes would not open. She could not claw out of it.

Janene opened the door and glimpsed her longtime friend sprawled on the couch clutching a flowered pillow to her chest. "Maybe we should let her sleep. Poor Jo. I'm sure she needs it."

Joanna heard the click of bottles and wanted to say, "No, wake me please, shake me out of this." Instead, a mournful moan was all she could muster.

Pizza smells followed Janene into the kitchen. "I'll stick these in the oven to keep warm till she comes around."

Amy unloaded the bottles, ice, blender, and frozen limeade before they slipped to the floor. "Boy, that was close. I couldn't hang on much longer. Something was gonna go." Amy took no chances. She wasn't sure if Joanna had a blender and maybe there wasn't enough ice, so she brought everything. "You aren't going to put those pizza boxes in the oven, are you Janene?"

Janene twisted the knobs on the stove. "Well, yeah. I'm not turning it very high. They won't burn, will they?"

"The boxes might scorch a little, besides heating them up makes the pizza taste like cardboard. Just put the pizzas on some foil. It'll save messing up pans."

"OK. OK." She never thought her pizza tasted like cardboard, but Amy had a sensitive taster, so she began searching for the foil.

"Look in the drawer to the left of the stove."

Sure enough, she found the foil, plastic wrap, and potholders in the suggested spot. Amy, now a Ford and the only one of the Quad Squad who was married, knew her way around the kitchen. Janene marveled at her energy and her homemaking skills. Her floors were ever glistening, the counters clean and uncluttered, the beds neatly made. Her sewing machine ran into the night stitching up clothes for four-year-old Andrea and six-year-old Jonathon. She operated her own business from the hair salon her husband had added to the garage and, from time to time, she filled in for her mother-in-law who did the bookwork for the family construction company.

Janene thought about her own piece of real estate in a pricey part of town. Each townhouse had its private, walled courtyard, immaculately groomed, and cared for as part of the homeowner's fee. Beyond the carved double door entry was a comfortable, cluttery shambles. The bed got made when she changed the sheets, which was definitely not on a timetable, but occurred possibly once every few months. It didn't matter much. She was the only one to see it. Her social life and business life were somewhat of a blend and certainly didn't occur in her home. No husband. The moocher, drinker had been dumped five years ago before she quit teaching in Gillette, Wyoming. When she finished college, teaching jobs were easier to get in Wyoming, but three years with high school kids and two years with 'the husband' led her to the conclusion that both had been a mistake. She took her Santini name back and headed home deciding to try real estate. That was no mistake.

She liked being back on the Front Range between the Wyoming border and Denver. The real estate market was booming. She paid her dues during the first couple of years listing and selling small stuff and now Janene was making a name for herself in the commercial venue.

Amy scooped half of a large can of frozen limeade into the blender bowl, added a couple spoonsful of sugar, crushed ice and topped in off with water. The blender whirred a while. "I'll add the Tequila and Triple Sec when Joanna is able to join the living."

Amy and Janene both jumped as the kitchen phone rang. On the third ring, Janene managed to grab it from its hook. "Hope this doesn't wake Jo." She spoke into the mouthpiece. "Hello."

A familiar voice responded, "Hey Jan, you're at Johanna's?"

Then there was a click and a clunk, clunk.

"'Llo, is there anyone there?" Joann had picked up the phone from the end table in the other room and was awake, kind of.

The voice on the phone burst out, "Now that sounds like Jo…It's Lauren. I'm on my cell, about two miles from town. I didn't wait for the shuttle, rented a car. Are you up for another visitor?"

"You bet. Come on over."

"Can I pick up something? Food? Drinks?"

Janene cut in, "We're all set. I have the pizzas in the oven keeping hot and Amy has a pitcher of margaritas ready."

"Amy's there, too? I can't wait."

Despite the somber mood, all made grave attempts at being upbeat and much of the table talk involved happy, and what ordinarily would be, hilarious moments.

Two pitchers of margaritas later, the aroma of Italian spices and pepperoni wafted about the kitchen. Amy sighed as she rose and moved the plates to the counter. Her voice missed its usual lilt. "It's like old times, isn't it? Feels good to remember those days. I wish we were sitting here together for another reason, though." Each felt the heaviness of sorrow, and silence ebbed around them.

Janene stretched and patted her mid-section, interrupting the stifling cloud. "Cripes, we sure put those pizzas away. They really hit the spot, especially since I missed lunch again. And if I have one more margarita, I'll have to be put away, too."

"Hey guys, let's leave this stuff and get comfy in the living room." Joanna motioned with a sweep of her arm. She needed to get out of the kitchen. Now. Too many reminders from her mom—splashes of Mexican tiles in blue, yellow, and gold and hand-woven treasures, the blue tablecloth, and sunny yellow napkins—all brought from Mexico.

Amy remained in the kitchen. In a few minutes it would look like the untouched kitchens of the local builders' *Tour of Homes*.

Janene and Lauren spotted the watercolors Joanna had been working on. Thumbing through a spiral notebook, they paused at each bird, flower, fruit, and antique pitcher. "I didn't realize you knew how to paint, Jo. These are quite good." Lauren, the fashion designer, had an eye for art.

"They seem pretty primitive to me—I don't have the vaguest idea what I'm doing. Still experimenting."

"Have you been doing this long? Don't be so hard on yourself. You have talent, Jo." Even though Janene would not spend a cent on anything that was unnecessary, which she deemed paintings of any type to be, she appreciated talent.

"I've always wanted to try painting, but never got around to it. With Paul here, I've had a lot of evenings alone. He manages that new Shay's Steakhouse restaurant, you know, and doesn't get home until after eleven. Anyway, last month I bought a bunch of stuff and started piddling around. I don't even know if I have the right brushes, but…"

Lauren turned to the last watercolor. It was unfinished. "Hey Jan, look at this Mexican courtyard—the colors and the deep blue shadows. Hmm, this is going to be something."

"Thanks Lauren. I did that in Mexico. Hard to believe that was only a few days ago." Her voice was wistful. "I don't have much desire to finish it now. It reminds me of my mother's unfinished life." There was an awkward pause, then Joanna barked, "Amy, get out of my kitchen and join this group, or your ears will be burning."

"Sounds like I'd better obey." Amy poked her head through the doorway, then plopped on one end of the leather couch, pulling her bare feet beneath her. "Jo, tell us, what do you need from us?"

"Nothing, really, just a good visit." Joanna sank into the matching leather chair, the color of cinnamon. It was new furniture that she had saved and saved for and was proud and pleased with her purchase. A change in carpet was on her list. She wanted something to sink her toes into. Everything was on hold now. "It seems like our times together are too few these days, with Amy's two jobs and a family, Janene finding property for Walmart superstores and our own Lauren off in California designing fashions for Mel Gibson movies."

"Sure." Lauren rolled her eyes. "I'm not in the big league yet, Jo. And you down in Mexico. Tell us about that."

"Nothing much to tell. I put some travel and resort packages together for the travel agency. I've done four of those here and there in my last three years at International. I like the travel and the challenge. Probably will do some more, but it's on hold for now. My boss says to take a few weeks off, but you know me, probably won't."

Joanna's effort to be spirited eased out of her like the last bit of air from a balloon that got away. Her face slack and her eyes expressing an unusual blankness, she admitted, "I'm not as strong as I thought I was. I don't know if I can face all that needs to be taken care of."

Amy threaded her fingers through her short, natural curls, gone the long braids of her youth. "Need some help getting all the finances in order? Sometimes it's had finding insurance, investments, bank accounts. I know sorting out that stuff."

Joanna leaned forward and wrapped her arms around the softness of her brushed denim jeans. "Mom kept me informed about her finances, even after she and Steve were married. Everything is carefully spelled out. I have no idea what my dad and his wife have agreed to. Well, I could guess.

"The house is mine; the motorhome will go to Steve's kids. Mom worked hard and put chunks of her earnings into investments since Dad left. It's not millions, but she left a good nest egg. I feel cheated though. No amount of money can make up for losing her."

Janen's voice was tentative. "Even if everything is well organized, handling an estate is no easy task. If you decide to sell and want to list the house with Mountain Peaks, I'll do everything I can to help you."

Joanna shook her head. "I don't know yet. At this point I can't bear the thought of selling the place where I grew up. There is no hurry, except I don't like things hanging over my head. I'm *not* looking forward to going through what's left of Mom's and Steve's life and disposing of it."

"Surely Steve's kids will help with his things." Janene expected people to do their part.

"Oh yes, but it's not Steve's personal items and tools that I'm dreading. Mom has lived in that house twenty-five years. Can you imagine the junk in the basement?"

Lauren absently scratched a few squiggles on the notepad beside her. "We can help. I'll be here at least ten days. Gotta stay for my folk's fortieth and spend some quality time with them. Are you two available to help Jo dive into the house while I'm here?"

"I can shuffle my schedule at the office, besides half of selling in the real estate business is after the regular workday. How about you Amy? Is your schedule flexible? I know you have kids, your salon, and Dan's books to worry about."

Amy couldn't bridle her enthusiasm. "Not a problem. Dan will help out. When he's checking various construction sites, the kids often ride along and during the summer I use the high school neighbor when I'm in the salon all day. Anyway, we can work it out. So, it's set. The Quad Squad will whip this project in no time." The squad reference was a little cory, yet none of them was willing to leave it in the past. Amy's cadence became less fervent. "Do you want to do this after the memorial: Will there be a double one?"

"That's a tough decision." Joanna looked away from her friends, hoping to suppress the tears. She had done well, so far. "Steve will be buried in a casket and of course Mom wanted to be cremated. They knew different people and Steve's kids probably have different ideas than I do. So, everything will be separate. Steve's memorial will be Thursday and Mom's is Saturday."

Her voice trailed off and she turned toward Amy, a glow of affection in her eyes. "Let's stop all this talk about my stuff. Don't you think it's time we heard about Lauren's movie?"

Lauren refused to accept any fame. "I just did my job and it's not *my* movie. But it's my first time to be in charge, not an assistant this time. I designed some pieces that I'm proud of. However, most of the job involves coordinating and obtaining clothes for all the main characters, and of course, supervising the assistants. It's a lot of running around, and of course, research. *The Folly of Angela,* that's what it's called, will air in a couple of months on Sunday Night at the movies. That's about it."

"Your job sounds important to me, and we can say we grew up

with the famous Hollywood Designer, Lauren McBride. Right, Amy and Jo?" They both nodded.

Amy folded her arms and gave Lauren a saucy look. "There must be some man in your life; those movie-star looks must be attracting them in packs."

"Are you kidding" With all that competition in Hollywood? Besides no one interests me, and when you're climbing that ladder, there's no time for men. What about you, JJ? You're still with Paul, aren't you?'

Joanna smiled at the JJ part; a knick-name coined in her youth by her dad. "Honestly, it's a tough situation right now. Just two days ago, I told Mom that I was ready to ask him to move out. Yet, he's been such a sweetheart since the accident. I don't know what I would have done without him. So, how can I tell him I want to call it quits?"

"If you're sure that there is no future for you two, it's not fair to have him hanging around. For either of you." For Janene, it was either black or white, no gray.

"You *would* think it is easy, Ms. Logic. In real life, two and two don't always make four. He has feelings you know. And I keep having second thoughts."

"You were having second thoughts in the other directions two days ago. Obviously, he's not the one."

Why did Joanna feel pushed into a corner by Janene? It happened often. This was none of her business, but she was too drained to put up a defense. "Let's change the subject."

Janene did. Looking Joanna square into her eyes, she said, "Jo, what would you do if you knew the name of your birth mom? If you knew where she was living when she had you?"

The green of Joanna's blue-green eyes flashed and Jo glared back. I can't believe you asked that. My mom just became ashes and…You can be so perverse. What's going through your head, anyway?"

Janene's face shadowed. "Sorry, Jo. Foot in mouth again. My mistake. I just wondered."

"Yeah, it was a mistake. Where's your respect anyway?" The words shot like bullets. "I think I'd better get some shut-eye. Hope you don't mind if we call it a night." Her tone softened, "Thank you for your thoughtfulness. It was good to see you all."

Eyes shifted toward Janene as if to say *except for Janene's big mouth.*

Later, Joanna pondered why Janene's question hit her so hard. Maybe it *was* an innocent expression of curiosity. No. It was insensitive and indignant. Did Janene know something? No way. Anyway, she had a right to be ticked.

CHAPTER 4

I t was not your typical June day in Colorado. Usually, the morning sun stretched into Joanna's kitchen. Today was gray and somber, like her mood as she poured another cup of coffee. How could she bury her mom on such a day? It should have been bright and cheerful, a noisy and chirping day. Silly, *she* wasn't being buried. Steve was the one who was buried, two days ago. It had been a cheery event, if they can ever be so. Oodles of flowers, crowded rows, lively songs, a real attempt at celebration. At least when one dies young there are still many among the living to attend the service. No doubt her mom's service would be well attended, as well.

Oh, why did Mom want to be cremated? At least Steve was there at his own memorial. It wasn't too late. She had the cremains and could put them in a vase or jug or something and take them to the service. What was she thinking? Good God, they were both gone. The body was of no importance. The memory of a person's life was what was important.

Did she choose the right songs? What about her poem? The words she had written seemed trite. Thoughts kept whirling. Would the spike penetrating her heart ever leave? As alone as she felt, she was glad that Paul was sleeping, and she didn't have to make conversation and could have her own stupor.

Joanna entered the church an hour before the service. She had expected to have some quiet time in prayer and meditation. If only this emptiness would melt out of her. The first pew was designated as the family pew. Sitting there alone it seemed much too spacious for her, her uncle, and his family. The gloom of the morning softened the brilliance of the stained-glass windows extending from the altar to the towering ceiling. Even the deep blues, blazing yellows and crimson reds took on a duskiness. They seemed to comfort. Instead of praises, thanksgivings and supplications, there was quiet and peace.

Soon, the sanctuary was alive with activity. Candles were placed. Flowers arrived in succession. Her mother would have wanted her friends to give to the church or the local safe house. Yet, they knew she loved flowers. And they sent flowers. Brilliant color flourished in every available space at the front of the church. The organist practiced a few bars and set some stops. The minister marked Biblical passages at the podium. Joanna continued in her own quietness, unmoving.

A hand touched Joanna's shoulder and she turned to look into her uncle's bearded face. She was surprised to see that the sanctuary was filling up. They shared greetings and hugs. Her aunts, uncles, and cousins from her father's side of the family slid into the pews behind her. They had not abandoned her. She felt tears gathering.

The minister saw that Joanna's quiet was finished and approached her with his sideways grin. "Joanna, is there anything you need from me?"

Having known each other for ten years, Joanna felt comfortable with Pastor Bill. When they visited earlier in the week, she felt some guilt because she had not attended church regularly the last couple of years. His warmth and understanding dissolved the guilt.

Thank you, Bill. I only want everything to go well. My mother deserves that tribute."

"It will."

The organist played a dramatic toccata that was one of Allison's favorites. Her mother had chosen it when she and Steve were married. It was such a powerful piece, full of vitality and life. The voices of the choir blended in a song of joy and praise. Yes, it was fitting for her mother.

Pastor Bill *could* read scripture. It seemed easy to grasp the meaning when he spoke. Today, he chose verses that celebrated life and avoided dwelling on death. Joanna was glad for that.

His tribute to her mother was witty, yet reverent, as he spoke of her life with verve. Joanna's chest tightened at the first chords of the final choral work. Doubt pervaded. She rose and took her place at the podium but was unable to quiet the stirring created by the tranquil melody and promising words. *Help me do this, Mom.*

The soft dusky glow of the sanctuary warmed and brightened. The sun had not forgotten the morning. Joanna smiled, gazed thoughtfully and began.

My beloved mother

What wonder the journeys in life,
We know not always where they may lead.
One footprint in one direction
Brings something so varied and new
And transforms a path forever.
A miracle, a blessing, you chose me
And left footprints in my heart
Loving, teaching, affirming.
With such swiftness are the days
Are there ever enough?
So many moments, joy, sorrow,
Some we cherish, others pass without notice.
Our time cannot be ended, I want more.
In my sadness, I smile remembering,
Completing the thought of the other
Laughing at words misspoken
A clever smirk and twinkle of the eye
Catching me in some misdeed.
And now, dear Mother, I say not goodbye.
Brimming with joy and pride
I hold you to my bosom, forever.
I cherish the gift of you and had *I* had the choice,
Even knowing you would leave so soon,
Unceasingly my choice would be you,
My beloved mother

Her voice had not wavered. Stillness faced her as she stood smiling with glistening eyes. No one disturbed the moment. Joanna locked on another pair of glistening eyes far back in the room. He *had* come. She knew her father would be gone before she made her way to him. Yet, his presence warmed the piercing of her heart and filled the emptiness that had engulfed her. She envisioned a page of her life turning. This chapter was at an end.

More luck. I have a job. The resort is off the beaten track, rustic and surrounded by lush grasses and gigantic pines. It's hard work. I've done about every job possible, scrubbing everything from toilets to floors, making beds, peeling potatoes, leading hikes, throwing hay to the horses. What animals, those horses. This riding thing is a new experience, but I vowed no one would label me a greenhorn. I look like the real thing and those magnificent beasts, and I have a real connection. When I'm in the saddle and up in the high-country leading trail rides, I can forget some of my pain—for the moment, anyway.

The couple that owns the resort are young and energetic. I can see that they have great visions for this place. A new stable is in the works and the cabins are being remodeled. They're good parents, too. Don't know how they keep up with a two-year-old plus the business. Kids like me OK, but I don't want any. With my background I'm not parent material.

Except for weekends, when we have cookouts, campfires and entertainment, our evenings are free. Most nights we head to town to do some partying. Of the ten, I'm the only one under 21. But nobody seems to care if you're underage, and the liquor flows freely. Things get a little wild sometimes and I got stupid entering chugging contests. Both times I won but went back to my room sicker than a skunk each time. No more of that, but I'm learnt to live it up. No more feeling sorry for myself.

CHAPTER 5

Seven-fifteen. Time to get up and get at it. Was this a big mistake? She looked out of the bedroom that had been her mother's and into the morning sunrise. It was hers now. This was home, even though she rattled around in it. Someone had suggested that she take in some starving grad student. Maybe she would. Colorado State University was twelve miles up the road. It would provide some company and the student could watch out for things when Joanna was out of town on assignment. The basement could make a nice apartment with its bathroom, bedroom, and cozy room with a fireplace.

Paul had rented her condo. She had to hand it to him. He paid all his bills and rent on time. Splitting up didn't seem too difficult, so it must have been the right thing. Both kept busy and though their schedules clashed they continued to have lunch together on occasion. Neither one was seeing anyone. Joanna was without a man again. Not unusual. She wasn't looking, but on occasion the notion of her biological clock wormed its way into her thoughts.

Moving had been a pain and Joanna couldn't understand those who moved every year or two. This would definitely be her last move for a long time. Once her mother's and Steve's things were sorted, boxed, and disposed of, her own things packed and moved, she was certain her biceps had expanded. Then there was the lifting and moving of all that furniture. Paul was a godsend. But that was Paul. Often, he was off helping every Tom, Dick and Harry instead of doing the things he needed to do. This time Joanna was grateful. A couple of his stout friends made it easier, too.

In the end Joanna left the bed and dresser for Paul, but they moved the couch and leather chairs, which was no easy task. Once things were in her 'now' house it was switcheroo. The basement furniture made it to the Salvation Army and the family room furniture went to the basement. Her leather grouping remained in the garage while the new carpet was laid, a sand colored deep plush with cinnamon and chocolate specks.

Joanna couldn't bear to part with the hefty oak table. It was at home in the sunny kitchen. Her own little kitchen table was incorporated into a workstation in one of the bedrooms, where she used her computer.

Hurry, she thought. Staff meeting at 8:15. She picked up speed applying moisturizer, cover, and blush. Pearl and a touch of mauve on her eyelids, plus that new lash-curling mascara and she was ready. Barely glancing at her reflection, she finger-combed her golden strands. Each season, the cut had become shorter. She was satisfied with the saucy bob that dipped over her left eye and cupped just below her ears. It was an easy style and drew attention to the brilliance of her blue-green eyes.

Impulsively she dashed to the bedroom and opened the wooden box still on the dresser. She tried not to look at the doll. Her interest was the ring. Would it fit? It was perfect on the ring finger of her right hand. She wondered about the little grandma it once belonged to. She decided to put it on, then turning her thoughts to the morning meeting she dashed off.

Strategic planning was what her boss called. They had one every month. Toda's session involved training with newly installed technology.

The morning dragged. Joanna had used the new system and found the training unnecessary. She tapped her pen on her scratch pad. Now that her mind was made up, she was driven to pursue her search.

She couldn't let go of the dream. It had been puzzling and unnerving and had come and gone for a week now. In it, a figure, eerily hooded, slid out of control amid rocks and bushes down a steep mountain. The figure seemed to be desperately gripping something, but before it reached the bottom, that something, flat and flimsy, like Cara Dolly flew into the sky. It hovered and floated out of sight. The dream varied. Sometimes the hooded figure floated away while Joanna called out to save it. The vision ended only when Joanna awakened in a cobwebbed state.

The hooded figure had to represent her birthmother. Was she as blundering as Joanna pictured? Not knowing would eat away at her. She'd search her down; she'd show her how well her abandoned baby turned out. The time was now. She could do it alone, but...

The moment she could leave the meeting, Joanna dialed Janene's work number. Janene nearly dropped the phone when Joanna said, "Jan, I've decided. I need to find my birth mom."

Remembering Joanna's inflamed reaction concerning the subject a few months ago, Janene was speechless.

"Are you with me? You always pushed the idea. I thought you would approve." There was urgency in Joanna's voice.

Pushing her shock aside, Janene responded "Of course. I'd want to know as much as I could if I were you. Are you thinking of driving to Estes to search the hospital records?"

"I haven't really gotten that far with my thinking. Is that the place to start? What's your schedule like this afternoon" It's a beautiful day for a drive to the mountains. Don't you think?"

"Cripes, Jo. When something gets in your mind, you won't shelve it for a moment. Let me make a few phone calls and I'll get back to you. I may be able to get away right after lunch. If so, I'll drive. I want to try my new Honda on the mountain curves."

Janene's silver Honda gripped the canyon road as they swayed through the narrows. The Thompson Canyon became famous in 1976 when the horror of the Thompson flood hit the airways. Joanna and her parents had been in Estes Park the day prior for a mountain outing. She remembered poking around the little shops of the quaint tourist town. They had feasted on the traditional salt-water taffy and her parents bought her an Indian Tom-Tom. No one had the slightest suspicion that during the following night twelve inches of rain would funnel into the canyon carrying everything in its path, killing nearly 150 people.

Days later the mouth of the canyon lay gaping. The road was gone and in its place was an unbelievable tangle of rotting flesh, vehicles, appliances, snapped beams, and pulverized homes. Those who survived told unreal stories of heroism and tragedy. Many could never speak of what they saw or what they endured.

This August afternoon shadows stretched into the canyon. Shear walls rose from the highway and the Thompson River, snaking its way alongside. Rivulets and trickles that sneaked through crevices and around fauna, then collected in gorges making their way to the river were diminishing as the snow of the high country melted away, making ready for a new winter. Nevertheless, the narrowness of the canyon created a rushing force of tumbling foam. The power of nature's wonders awed Joanna. In the narrows trees were sparse, but as the canyon widened majestic pine climbed the steep hillsides, each striving to reach the highest. Splashed of Aspen stood their ground. In a month or so, they would enliven the autumn season with their golden brilliance.

Joanna vowed she would return to seek out the most magnificent patches when that time came. Most years she was too busy to take the time. This year she would make the time and celebrate her mother's love of nature. Yes, she would.

The Honda held the road well. Janene took the curves without braking and with seeming ease. Both were lulled into a calm quiet and enjoyed the relief from the Loveland traffic. Annoyingly, too often a string of vehicles crept up the curvy canyon delayed by an eighteen-wheeler tugging a heavy load. Thankfully, the traffic was light this afternoon and they made good time.

Janene's words were plaintive. "Can you believe we live only ten minutes from the mountains, and we rarely take the time to enjoy them?"

"I was thinking about the same thing. The last time I enjoyed the mountains was when I went camping, if you can call it camping, and relaxing with Mom and Steve in their motorhome in Poudre Canyon. That was over a year ago. It's a beautiful canyon too, perhaps a little more rustic."

Small talk and admiring the riverside cabins and elegant homes took up the conversation for the next fifteen minutes. Joanna's uncertainty crept into the conversation at last. "You know, here we are trekking to the place I was born without the tiniest idea of what we should do when we get to Estes. I don't even know where the hospital is."

Janene gave her good friend a cautionary glance. "Joanna…I hope you won't be angry with me when I tell you what I have to say."

"Tell me what?" A stupefied look filled her face.

"Well, years ago, in face the summer following high school graduation, I had a chance to learn your birthmother's name and I did."

"You what? You've known all these years? How did you find out and for heaven's sakes, *why* did you keep it a secret?"

"Let me tell you, keeping my mouth closed wasn't easy. But I knew how you felt. I would not betray that." An oncoming sports car veered into their lane. Janene jerked the wheel and the Honda swerved. "Cripes, that guy is going to kill somebody!"

Joanna seemed not to notice their close call. "So, you betrayed me by going behind my back and meddling in things that were none of your business!"

"I thought that if and when the time came, I could help you out. What are friends for anyway?"

"Yeah, friends can really fuck up, can't they?"

Shocked to hear the f-word come from Joanna's mouth Janene said, "Maybe if you hear the whole story you'll understand."

Joanna's eyes spit fire. "I'm listening."

"Way back when, Mom and I were talking about you. It was shortly after your dad left. I told her about the wooden box, the letter, and that you were born in Estes Park. I knew that Mom's Aunt Ruth was a nurse, and then it dawned on me, Aunt Ruth worked at the hospital where you were born. It's a small place and I figured she would know something. It took me a while, but I finally convinced Mom to ask her to do a little sleuthing. I was excited to think that I could be the one to let you know about her, your birth mom, I mean. That's how it happened."

Jo needed some time to think and let this news sink in. The silence passed.

"Then why are we going to Estes, if you already know my mother's name?"

"Well…there's more to the story."

"OK, what's the rest?"

"Your birth other was not originally from Estes. She was working at a summer resort when she got pregnant. She stayed with Ellie and Phil, the owners of the resort, all winter and into the spring until you were born. Ellie was also pregnant at the same time, so she took your mom under her wing. We are going to see Ellie. I called after we talked this morning and spoke with her husband Phil. She's eager to see you. It is a sad situation, however. She has terminal cancer and is not doing well. So, my dear Joanna, it may be a miracle that you decided to make your search now, before Ellie…you know. By the way, your mother's name was Dixie Donovan."

Joanna swallowed hard and tears took their turn dropping into her lap as Janene steered the silver car over the planks of a narrow bridge. Mountain fragrances invaded that new smell of the Honda and through the open window Jo caught the bubbling, babbling sounds of the pristine stream they were crossing. The sign ahead read *Welcome to Mountain Wonders Resort.*

What a beautiful place, Joanna thought. Shaded log cabins dotted the hillsides. Following the signs, they wound their way toward the office. To the right of the office stood a stately, sprawling lodge, framed with several stands of various pines. Nearby, hickory chip aromas wafted from a pit, the size of a gigantic hot tub. A slender young woman and a well-muscled man placed slabs of ribs on the blackened grate. The cheerfulness of red and white checkered cloths decorated the waiting picnic tables.

Off to the left Joanna could see the stables. A wrangler snugged the cinch of the saddle, then helped a girl, maybe twelve, swing up. Joanna smiled and remembered her own horse days as the horse and rider ambled up the trail and out of sight. Three youngsters splashed in a small pool as a mother sat alongside reading. The tennis court was empty.

"Phil's instructions were to pass the office and the lodge and take a right. Their house is along the stream." It wasn't far. "Wow, look at that place I can't think of a more charming house and more desirable setting." They eased into the driveway and Janene set the brake.

Joanna wondered what Ellie would say about Dixie Donovan.

CHAPTER 6

J oanna was unprepared for Ellie Springer. Regal, despite the soft fuzz sparsely framing her face, her cancer treatments had left their mark. She sat in a sturdy rocker, its wood betraying its age with its luster. Pillows threatened to swallow her diminishing frame but failed. A lap robe displayed a patchwork of color.

The expansive window through which she gazed bore not window coverings but framed nature's portrait. Rainbows of wildflowers making their final show before the season's end danced among clumps of the greenest grasses. The crooked stream wiggled itself to a place that spread into a lily pond, the yellow blossoms threatening to close before dark.

With such grace Ellie turned. Joanna was overcome by the tenderness of her eyes. She had been, still was, a beautiful woman. "Isn't it a lovely view? I can never get enough of the beauty around us. When we built this home five years back, we made sure that each room had its own special view, and you will notice that we have no curtains or drapes anywhere. No matter the season, God's glory reaches into our home and into our hearts."

Joanna imagined the rusts, oranges, and pale golds that soon would be autumn, the starkness of winter glistening with diamonds of snow in a winter's sun and the emerging mystery of spring uncoiling with rebirth. Yes, nature's live canvas.

"Please sit with me, Joanna, I am so happy you came. What excitement you bring to me this glorious afternoon." She indicated a chair just inches from her own where Joanna could feel the closeness of the beauty before her and beside her. "At last, you have embarked on the search for Dixie. I hope I can provide a link in that search and perhaps tell you of the Dixie I knew."

How sensitive, this woman. It was indeed more comfortable to think of her as Dixie than "your mother" which she was not ready for. "Thank you, Ellie, I do want to know all that you can tell me. But first, how are you feeling? Is there something I can get for you? Are you sure this is not too draining?"

Ellie's smile filled the room. "Today is one of my good days. This monster has been with me for four years. I thought we had it licked, but eight months ago it kicked in and I started treatments all over again. There is nothing more to do, except wait it out. I relish each day as a gift and have already enjoyed more days than the doctors believed I would have. No, Joanna, I am fine."

Joanna sat entranced as the tale of the beginning of her life unfolded. "Dixie Donovan grew up in Scottsbluff, Nebraska where everyone knew everyone's business. Her father was a very successful doctor with a general practice. Nevertheless, there was a lot of tension in her family, and it wasn't until later that I learned why. She ran away a few times to stay with friends, but each time she was talked into returning home. She bided her time until graduation. Then she took off, hitchhiking to Colorado.

"That was pretty risky, wasn't it? A young girl on the highway alone. How did she end up here?"

"It *was* risky. I certainly wouldn't want my kids hitchhiking. Anyway, she was lucky. A trucker picked her up. He grew up in Estes Park and told her it would be a nice place to work for the summer.

"So, you hired her?"

"It was one of those meant to be situations. We usually have all of our hiring done by the first part of April and this was the end of May, but that year one of the college students we hired failed to show and we were short-handed. When Dixie arrived, she spotted one of the posters Phil left in town. That spunky little gal walked the three miles from town, that poster in hand, and marched right into the office.

"There she stood in hip-hugger bell-bottom pants, an oversized t-shirt, braids, and a headband, holding the poster and saying, 'it must be your lucky day, because your new worker has just arrived and can begin immediately.' I was so amused, there was no way I could have disputed her."

Phil entered the room with cold drinks. Joanna wondered about Janene and learned that she volunteered to help prepare the evening cookout with Phil's and Ellie's on Rod. The muscled man at the barbeque pit and Sally, his wife. Rod and Sally were learning the business. The plan had been that Phil and Ellie would retire and do some travelling while the son and daughter-in-law took over the business. Life was not fair. Joanna feared that Ellie's travels would not be as a tourist.

The afternoon went much too quickly and thankfully Ellie seemed energized with her story telling. "Dixie was an excellent worker and was well-liked by the guests at the resort, no matter the age. Children particularly gravitated to her, but she sat for hours visiting with the older generation, too. She told me that she had a special relationship with her grandmother and hated the thought of disappointing her by leaving home."

Ellie's eyes fixed on Joanna's hand "My land. That's the ring, isn't it? Her grandmother's, the one Dixie left for you."

Surprised, Joanna nodded. "You knew about the ring then? Did you know about the letter and the doll?"

"She showed me the doll. I knew she wrote a letter, but I don't know what it said. Did she say anything about the man?"

"It was a beautiful letter, but the only thing she said about the man was that he was older and married and that he didn't know about me. From her brief description, apparel I got his coloring. Jo learned that Dixie did not tell Ellie about the man either. Ellie thought he was someone she met in town and was sure that he had not been a guest at the resort.

Ellie continued, "The pregnancy did not become evident until the end of the season in late August and only then because Dixie and I were both experiencing morning sickness. I was pregnant with Rod at the time and began to suspect that Dixie was also. I finally confronted her. She was brave and there were no tears, only concern that she had disappointed us. We invited her to stay for the winter. She was definite that she could not return home and we did not want to see her alone. We respected her wishes that her parents not be informed of the pregnancy, though I tried with all my might to change her mind."

"Dixie was very lucky to have you to help her through such a trying time."

"She was very appreciative and quite helpful, actually. We were a busy household. Tim, Rod's older brother, who was two when Dixie came, was quite a handful and she spent many hours with him while I worked in the office taking inquiries and booking reservations for the next season. Off-season is the time when we paint, make many repairs, sew new curtains, recover chairs or whatever. She was my right-hand gal until you were born. Looking back, I wish that we had more time for talking and sharing, but experience has taught me that when families are young, parents never have enough time to relish the moment. I wasn't sure what was going on inside of her."

"I'm sure you did the very best you could. Who knows what would have happened with you and Phil?" Joanna visualized a different young Dixie than the unnamed one she first envisioned—this one proud, burying hurt and pain, putting on a good front. But inside was she scared, lonely, uncertain? How could she not be? "You said that you didn't know until later what had caused the turmoil in Dixie's life at home. Can you tell me about that?"

"That came the night before she left. But I have to back up a little. Rod was born six days before you were. And when you arrived, Rod and I were busy learning all about each other, while little Tim, now three, wanted to help and hold the new brother. Phil was making sure everything was ready for the new season and the guests who would be arriving in a few weeks.

Dixie had a long labor. We took turns running to the hospital between all the other things going one. But you had your own mind and didn't take your first breath until about 2:00 in the morning. I finally got to the hospital at 10:00 and found Dixie holding you and talking to you. Perhaps she had shed all the tears she could, because she was dry-eyed and quite at peace. I was the one who kept flooding and having to leave the room. It was more than I could bear, especially with little Rod at home. She held you for four hours and that was the last time she saw you."

That image sent tingles to her toes and left Joanna numb. It was unreal. She had never pictured herself in a setting other than one that included Allison and Clay. Yet now she imagined herself in Dixie's arms. Her chest heaved as Ellie continued.

Dixie was restless after she was released from the hospital. The relinquishment papers had been signed, the letter, doll and ring delivered. Her sparkle and spunk were missing. We didn't know what to do. I didn't know if I should keep Rod away from her or if cuddling him was therapeutic. Then six days after you were born, she announced that she would be leaving in the morning. She had saved some money and planned to go to Aspen to live her dream of becoming a skier."

"We talked and sobbed into the night. To my horror she revealed that her father started touching her when she was about five years old. She was confused, but he convinced her that it was a special loving thing they were doing and a wonderful secret that they shared. By junior high age the touching involved sex acts that many married couples have never experienced. During high school she got up enough nerve to tell her mother, but her mother called her a liar.

"When her father was confronted, he said that she was a troublemaker, just trying to ruin the family. Her last two years of high school, she managed to stay away from him, but was too humiliated to tell anyone. She spent some time with her grandmother—her mother's mother—which saved her may times but was unable to confide even in her. Today, as I talk about it, it turns my stomach to think of that beast. It's beyond me that she was able to survive, finish high school with decent grades and have the personality that she showed to us."

"Couldn't you do something? She needed help."

Ellie shook her head and Joanna saw her dejection. "I begged her and begged her to get help. Stay with us and work this thing out. But she was determined to go, she was a survivor, she said. It was over thirty years ago, and I was young myself, and felt completely helpless. How could Dixie or I fight her father who seemed to have all the power?

Dixie was already filled with humiliation. It seemed like there was no answer. The next day we sent this young woman, who was older than her years into the world with all the love we could give and all the prayer? Is she still there?"

"She stayed in Aspen for a few years. We heard from her every three or four months. They weren't good years for Dixie, however."

Joanna signaled for Ellie to continue.

"We don't know the whole story, but she got involved with a fast crowd. Some were high paid models and a wild bunch out of Hollywood. She lived with some budding rock star for a couple of years who we suspected was abusive. We are sure that there was a lot of drugging and drinking and meaningless partying. We would have welcomed her back to help at the resort. We asked her many times. But I think she couldn't stop running and to come here she would have had to."

"What a waste of a good life. Is there a happy ending to this story?"

"Maybe. We've lost touch, but she did call us two years ago, when she was in Tucson to visit her mom. She'd been living in Mexico, and she'd become an artist. I've thought about trying to track her down myself, but with my situation…" Ellie's uplifted palm and outstretched fingers finished the thought.

"Is there anything else you can tell me? If you were me, what would you do next? Do you think she's still in Mexico?"

"Yes, my guess is that she's in Mexico. When we talked, she was heading out fast. Her father had died, but the visit with her mom had not gone well. I could tell that she was upset. Her dad's name was Melvin and her mom's name was Darlene. Maybe you could find something in the Tucson area. I know they retired there several years ago."

"Did Dixie ever tell her parents about me?"

"Oh, gosh, let me think." Ellie was beginning to tire. "You know, I think that was part of the problem when Dixie went to see her mom two years ago. She told her mom about you then. Yes, I remember, Dixie said her mom accused her of cheating her out of a granddaughter with her own selfishness, or something like that."

Joanna felt drained. Growing up she had never questioned who she was. Now, her life was a puzzle with so many pieces missing, and she was unable to tell what the picture was. Yet, the blood running in her veins could connect to someone out there. She would find all the pieces, no matter the outcome.

CHAPTER 7

Friday. Finishing up a few last-minute details and clearing her desk for Monday, Joanna dialed Amy's number. Jo worked two Saturdays a month and tomorrow wasn't one of them. The August heat was still on, and Amy's kids begged for a campout. Steve and Allison's motorhome had had two outings with Steve's daughter Corine, her husband and two kids. They all agreed to keep the motorhome in the family, and for housing it in the RV barn that her mother and Steve had built, she could use it whenever she wanted to. This was her first time. She'd been to the mountains many times with her mom and Steve, however. The water tank was full, the sewer tank was sanitized, propane checked, and her clothes were loaded. Amy insisted on bringing all the food for the weekend.

"Hello, this is the Ford residence. Can I help you?" Joanna could tell that the cheerful voice was Andrea, almost five. Everyone called her Andy. Yet for some reason Jonathon was always called by his full name. Perhaps it had something to do with personalities. Andy was a spunky spitfire, usually up to something dangerous or somewhat off-limits, while Jonathon was cautious, polite, and thoughtful.

"Hi Andy. This is Joanna. Are you ready for our campout at the lake?"

"Yup. Can I bring Patches?" Patches, the family dog, was cute as a button, but a yappy little thing.

"Not this time Andy. She'll be OK at your neighbor's. Could you give your mom a message sweetheart? I'm leaving the office early and

I'll bring the motorhome to your house so we can load up everything. Tell her I'll be there at 4:30."

Joanna eased the motorhome at a crawl, all thirty-some feet of her, until she was clear of the RV barn. She hoped she could maneuver the swing into the road from the pasture without side-sweeping the back of the rig. It steered like a car, but judging the length was the tricky part for this novice What a view. From her lofty perch with the expansive window, the little compact cars looked like jellybeans scooting along. At a stoplight, a graying man gave her a thumbs ups sign as he crossed in front of her. This was kind of cool. It would be a fun weekend. Dan, Amy's husband, had gone to the reservoir earlier in the day to reserve and pay for the campsite. The spots would be full before 3:00 on Friday. Dan wouldn't be coming until around six, so Jo and Amy had to get settled by themselves.

Miss organization, Amy and the kids waited on the front lawn with food, drinks, clothes, pillows, sleeping bags and fishing gear. "Look, I have worms." Andy held two wiggly things in her little palm. "We dug 'em in our garden last night."

Jonathon patiently held the worm container until Andy was ready to put them back, then instructed his sister to carry her sleeping bag into the motorhome. The loading process took only ten minutes, but an extra ten involved exploring and asking questions. Such excitement.

"Yes, the couch opens into a bed, and you'll sleep in your sleeping bags on it. I will sleep at the table. It comes apart to make a bed…Yes, the toilet flushes when you push hard on the foot-pedal. And you can brush your teeth in the bathroom. No, we won't be using the shower on this trip. We'll only be here two days…Well, the little TV beside the steering wheel shows everything behind the motorhome when we're traveling and it helps me when I back up…Yes, extra things are stored under the queen-size bed here in the back where your mom and dad will sleep. See the whole bed lifts up…Well, we call this the basement of the motorhome. That's where we keep the fishing poles, lawn chairs and wood for the campfire…Yes, you can take turns riding up front in the passenger chair, fifteen minutes for each of you, since it will take us only a half hour to get to the lake."

At the reservoir, the barricade marking their spot took a few minutes to remove. Dan made sure no one would park in their site. He got a good one. No more than twenty yards from the lake, it included a grassy area, a circular campfire pit, and a roomy picnic table.

Joanna was grateful that it was a drive-through. No backing this time. She set the brake and lowered the jacks. The rig was a little low at the front passenger side. A few presses of the buttons and the motorhome was as level as the lake. It took Jo and Amy a while to figure out the awning. Using a little muscle, they were able extend and secure the side arms. Amy set out the lawn chairs while the kids and Jo arranged the campfire wood at the pit.

"Hey, Joanna, can we have a *bomb* fire to roast our marshmallows?" asked Andy.

Joanna nodded and smiled. Somewhere Andy had heard about bonfires.

The women watched the kids make friends with the camper next door who had a dog. It was a friendly dog and the owners agreed that the kids could take it for a walk.

"Jo, I hope I don't have to wait too long to hear the whole story about the trip to Estes. All I know are bits and pieces from Janene."

"I'm eager to tell you and I hope you can give me your opinion. Oh, Dan's here. I guess it will have to wait. Let's get the patties on the grill."

As morning dawned, Joanna stretched her arms into an over-sized sweatshirt. It reached partway over her pajama bottoms. No one would notice. The motorhome swayed a bit as she stepped quietly on the dewy grass. She hoped she didn't disturb anyone. She found a flat rock and sat watching the sun rise above the hill and reflect on the lake. A few geese pecked at the grasses just out of her reach and made their satisfied sounds.

It was fun watching Amy and Dan parent. The kids certainly brought joy to camping. It was just simple stuff, cooking outside, watching the sky turn to crimson, seeing the moon sneak up, a campfire which brought squeals with its shooting sparks, gooey blackened marshmallows, silly songs, giggles, ghost stories. She made up a few herself. The children were well behaved. And trusting. But they had good parents.

Jo imagined Dixie at four, probably not unlike Andy. It made her stomach roll imaging what she had endured. It wouldn't leave her mind. Had anyone ever? Could anyone ever make it up to her? What about Dixie's mom? Darlene, that was her name. Was she as bad as Dixie's father? Joanna knew Amy would protect Andy. Why couldn't Darlene have protected Dixie?

The thought of contacting Darlene was scary, but it had to be the obvious next step. She had the phone number in her billfold of a Dr. Melvin Donovan in Green Valley, near Tucson. Darlene had not changed the listing. It had to be her.

The rest of the morning involved breakfast. Nothing like eggs and bacon sizzling in the open air. The children bantered about how many pieces of bacon they could have. Once the morning chores were complete, fishing came next.

Dan fixed the kids up with bobbers and worms and gave lessons about casting and patiently waiting. Dan tried one spinner and then another for himself.

The lake was part of a power plant belonging to the Bureau of Reclamation, which meant that the Bureau released water every few days which raised the water level onto the grass and around the bushy trees. Then the lake looked prettier and there was no mud to wade through. Perhaps the fish moved around more, as well, because as the level increased, the fish began to bite.

"I got one! I got one!" Andy yelled out. She tried to pull it in and caught the line on a bush. She tugged at her shoes and tossed them away, then waded in to 'fix it' she said. Up to her knees she couldn't move. "Dad, I'm stuck."

When Dan reached her, he found her tangled in a line left by an earlier fisherman. Joanna watched Andy grit her teeth as Dan scooped his daughter up and carried her to a grassy area, dragging the discarded line and sinkers. Only then did he realize that Andy was not only tangled, but she was also hooked by a barbed hook herself.

The brave little thing didn't say a word, but tears trickled down dirty cheeks as Dan worked and twisted the hook imbedded in her heel. It would not budge. What an ordeal. Soaking the area in antiseptic, the hook finally was extracted with the help of a pair of needle nose pliers.

Whimpering between quiet sobs, Andy asked, "Daddy, does it hurt the fish like the hook hurt me?"

Dan shrugged and grimaced.

"Well, I don't want to catch any more fish, just in case."

Amy and Jo completed the doctoring and urged Andy to keep her shoes on.

"Do I have too?"

"Absolutely!" And Amy meant it.

Soon, Andy went off to visit the neighbor's dog, as if nothing had happened.

At lunchtime, Jo called out to Andy. "Do you want to help set the table?"

"Yup," Often Jo asked her question just to hear the quipped 'yup.'

Jo and Andy set the table while Amy put the finishing touches on a chicken salad and a fruit plate.

"Hey Jo," Jonathon called out, "come watch me clean this fish. My dad showed me how." Such exuberance. Jonaton and Dan knelt at the edge of the lake with a plastic wash pan. "Dad said I can help cook them on the campfire tonight."

Jo glanced at Andy for a reaction and wondered if she would eat the fish that she didn't want to hurt. She didn't say anything.

After lunch Dan encouraged the kids to kick back for a half-hour—they did—and then they could hike around the lake and explore the inlet. Across the road, he scrounged up three walking sticks of appropriate sizes. Then the three of them were off.

Jo and Amy welcomed the time to relax under the awning and take in the beauty and freshness of this peaceful place away from the hub-bub of town. "Now can we talk?"

Jo leaned back in the lounge chair, fixated on a cloud hanging over the nearest peak and began her story. She sensed Amy's eyes bathing over her. The little cloud wafted to the south, expanded, and stretched until it became a series of puffs, much like the story Joanna conveyed. Amy listened.

"Wow. There are a couple of sad stories there aren't there" Do think Ellie has a chance?"

"It doesn't sound like it. All week I've been trying to put together a letter to her. I want her to know how much I appreciate her before it's too late. Would you mind listening to what I have so far? Maybe you can give me some ideas."

"Sure, Jo."

Jo returned from the motorhome with some folded sheets of paper and began to read.

Dear Ellie,

Thank you for so graciously sharing an afternoon with me. It was such a special time. I cannot tell you what a powerful impact visiting with you made on my life. Your strength, grace, and courage impressed and inspired me beyond my ability to describe. It is a privilege to have crossed your path and I carry a piece of your legacy with me.

I thank you for helping Dixie, my birth mom, in a very trying time of her life. Surely that support and caring made a healthy beginning for my life possible. I am grateful to know something about who she was and what happened to her. I am saddened, yet touched by her story, which impels me to continue this journey to locate her. In knowing her, I hope to find some pieces of myself that are missing. Thank you for your assistance in this search. I will keep in touch and let you know of my progress.

I congratulate you and Phil. You have raised fine sons and have built a beautiful resort nestled in the quiet of the Rockies. The love, vision and sweat that you and Phil put into it will be enjoyed season upon season.

I send my love and best wishes,
Joanna Johansen

"Hey, send it. It sounds good to me. In fact, it's great. By the way Janene said she received roses last week. Peace offering or something?"

"Not at all. We were never at ward, though I do remember being a little hard on her when she asked about finding my birth mom after

Mom died. I did and I do appreciate Janene. Her meddling in my life turned out to be a good thing and I wanted her to know it."

Amy smiled "You said you have a phone number that's probably Dixie's mom's, huh?"

Mimicking Andy, Jo said. "Yup."

"She knows about your?"

Jo nodded.

"If you call her, that part shouldn't be a surprise. But I can see how it would be difficult to…you know, like…what do you say?"

"Um. I could say, 'This is your long-lost granddaughter.'" Joanna spoke in a clipped tongue. "Or maybe…this is Joanna Johansen and I'm looking for information about my birthmother Dixie Donovan. Can you help me?"

"The second way. Yeah, That's it. Let's do it. Amy jumped up and headed for Dan's jeep.

Jo waved a hand toward the lake. "Let's. Oh, sure. Right here and now?"

Amy held Dan's cell phone out to her. "There's nothing keeping you from it. Now's as good a time as ever."

"She may not be home."

"Jo." Amy sent her 'the glare.' "Be gutsy."

It *was* easy. The call went through. Darlene was 'astonished' she said, but quite thrilled to speak with her granddaughter at last. She wished she knew where Dixie was, but she only had a few clues to her whereabouts. Joanna would be welcomed with open arms when she came to visit. She was coming to visit, wasn't she? Joanna would call again soon, and they could make plans.

"Mercy," spouted Joanna, "my knees shook the whole time." She had been standing near the front of the motorhome, because that was the best place for a good signal. "I need to sit."

"What's she like?" Amy looked wide-eyed most of the time, but more so now.

"I don't know. What can you tell by a voice? She didn't sound fat or ugly." Jo sent Amy her mischievous look and shrugged. "She was happy that I called. It looks like I have a trip to make soon, thanks to you."

"You would have called, but it's more interesting to share it with someone. After all, what are friends for? Besides the Quad Squad made a pact Remember? So far Janene and I are living up to that pact."

"Oh yes, the pact."

Joanna spoke into the straw-like mouthpiece of her headphone, "International Travel, this Joanna, may I help you?"

"Jo, it's Amy. I know Monday mornings must be hectic, but I wanted to tell you how much we all enjoyed the camping. It's just like playing house in your parent's rig. I told Dan we should start saving for some kind of RV. I wouldn't mind playing house more often."

Jo filed the papers in her hand and spun her chair back to her desk. "It was great for me, too. Thanks for bringing all that wonderful food. And Andy seemed Ok about eating the campfire fish that she didn't want to hurt." She snickered. "How's her foot.?"

"Fine. She's getting a tetanus shot today, though just to be safe."

"Before you have a chance to ask, I'm planning to visit Darlene. Looks like I can't get it into my schedule until late September. I think I told you I'm developing some new types of travel packages. One is for a two-week archeology dig and another, a one-week winter snowmobile trek in the backcountry. So, I'll be spending some time in Wyoming as well as trying to keep up at the office."

"Keep me posted. OK? I'm pretty busy the next several weeks too… Just a minute kids, I'm on the phone…Andy and Jonathon are making thank you cards for the camping trip. I need to help them find the stuff. Let's plan lunch or something soon."

Dixie

Stupid. Stupid. Stupid. I must be a sex maniac. Flight from my father and his pawing hands was not the finale I believed it would be. This is the fourth guy I've gone to bed with since I came to work at the resort. And I've only been here five weeks. There was a time when my life was innocent and unwounded. But it was such a short time, so long ago.

This is definitely different though. The first moment our eyes locked, there was instant electricity. Good looking, and personality all over the place. Hey, I've never felt so tingly before. He finds me sensuous and ravishing. He can't keep his hands off of me. It's the same for me. We just can't get enough of each other. Neither of us can concentrate on our daily responsibilities.

I know this will go nowhere. He'll leave next week when his training is over. He has a family somewhere. But I can always look back and remember being wanted and desired by my first love. I will remember his laughing blue eyes, the private jokes, the fun, and freedom we feel together. Nothing can blot this from my mind.

Tonight, he's rented a convertible and the moon is full. A romantic dinner, a drive in the great Rocky Mountains and lovemaking in the scent of the pines. I will remember it forever.

CHAPTER 8

The front door was open. That way she could glance down the hall and through the outer door into the dusky darkness as she pulled the last few things from the clothes dryer. The shuttle to Danver International Airport should arrive in fifteen minutes. She had an 8:00 a.m. flight and needed three hours lead time. Her flight would land in Phoenix and then there would be a short hop on a twelve-seater to Tucson.

Jo shook her head and smiled at herself. In this work she should know all the tricks about packing and traveling. Roll, instead of folding to avoid creases, include mix and match color coordinates, all wrinkle free and washable, take only a few basics. She could handle all but the 'few.' Inevitably she took too many clothes and ended up wearing one-fourth of what she packed. Did she need long skirts, short skirts, long pants, mid-calf, or regular shorts, dressy or ultra-casual? She wasn't sure, so she took them all.

This is Thursday. I'll need changes for Friday through Monday. Oh heck. She tucked in the extra white blouse in addition to the ones in vivid green, blue fuchsia and peach. She liked color, none of that basic black stuff. That was more Janene's style.

He's early. The headlights cast a cool, blue glow in the hallway. *The camera!* She was talking to herself more and more since she returned from Wyoming. *OK, tickets, keys, clutch purse, apple and cheese and juice for breakfast on the way.* All were stuffed into her shoulder bag. Grabbing her luggage, she lunged out the front door.

The shuttle nearly full, Jo found a seat beside a bobbing head with earphones. Good. There would be no need for conversation. October was promising a colorful fall. The nights were cooling fast, recent rains kept things from being tinder dry and the days displayed the typical Colorado sun against a brilliant blue sky.

Jo peeked around the bobbing head. Crimson, orange and pink striated with various tints of blue and turquoise stretched across the horizon. She watched the colors grow more intense, then fade to pastels, until the horizon glowed in dusty purple. A sliver of brilliant orange emerged and little by little, the sun lifted and bathed the morning.

It struck her that colors shifted gradually, yet so quickly, that she could see it happen, yet she couldn't. Orange became pink and turquoise became baby blue in mere seconds. Life. Just the same. It transformed before your eyes, and you didn't recognize it until it had happened.

She was thrilled that Lauren would meet her in Arizona. Lauren, the career girl too busy for a man, was hooked. Greg, a producer working his way up in the movie business, was now her center stage. His name peppered their conversation during their recent phone call. "This is Greg's fourth movie, and his name has become more prominent in the credits with each one. Lots more responsibility and a larger salary. He's good at what he does."

When Joanna mentioned her trip to Green Valley, Lauren was ecstatic. "You're going to Green Valley? That's near Tucson. Greg and I will be in Tucson next weekend to meet his parents."

"This sounds serious." They then solidified their plans.

Things transpired right before your eyes. It was settled. Yes, they would get together Saturday night. No, she didn't want a blind date. Jo was happy to meet and talk with Greg, but primarily it would be catch-up for Laruen and her. Darlene was scheduled for daytime Saturday, which would give them even more to talk about. She would be killing several birds with one stone on this trip. Monday was business. International Travel had a new branch there and Joanna was to assist with the training relating to the latest type of travel packages that she had been working on.

The apple and cheese hit the spot, but the juice left her thirsty for more. It would have to do until they arrived at DIA. She had been on the run the last several weeks and it felt good to relax and let her mind go. How would her meeting with Darlene be like? Her imagination gave her no clues.

She parked the red compact rental car in front of a white stucco. These computer-generated maps amazed her. She knew she was nearly there. Two more streets west and a fork to the right led to the red square making Darlene Donavan's home.

Two golf carts met her as she eased to the right. A gray-haired woman with a visor scurried around the golf cart driven by a shirtless, balding gentleman, nearly catching the rental car's bumper. Beneath the visor an arm waved apologetically, but the cart proceeded in hast. It was golf country, but most of the transplanted locals shuttled throughout the planned community with these motored gems to shop, visit neighbors or whatever, in addition to buzzing around the golf course.

Townhouses jutted toward the street, each with its own distinction, painted in white or shades of sand or salmon. All were tidy looking stucco with a tin patch of green in front of an iron-gated courtyard.

Treading on the pale salmon stones leading to Darlene's iron gate, she saw hanging baskets of color and pots lining the curved walkway of the courtyard. A gold braided cord dangled from a brass bell to the left of the gate. Tentatively Jo tugged until the tinkling sounds grew more clamorous. She was unable to see the door that opened from the townhouse into the courtyard but heard a low somewhat unsteady voice. "Just a minute, please. I'll be right with you."

Jo guessed that the doctor's wife had been, or was, a smoker. Her voice emanated that long-time smoker quality. The minute's wait felt like five. Jo held her pictorial life story. She cherished the album poetically designed by her mother as part of her college graduation gift. Balancing her camera and purse on the album in her left arm, she gave the silky blouse a last-minute shove into the waistband of her linen slacks. The emerald-green top, one of her favorites, showed off her little bit of tan and her saucy golden mane.

Jo wondered if she would like this woman. From what Ellie had said, Mrs. Donovan had betrayed her 'Dixie mother.' How could you respect someone like that? She breathed several deep breaths to quiet her nervousness. Her watch indicated 10:05. They would talk, go to 'the club' for lunch and return to the house for more visiting. Darlene had said, "Please spend the whole day. We have much to learn about each other. After all, you are my only granddaughter."

Once the iron gate clinked open, Darlene reached to grasp Joanna's free hand with both of hers. Several colored bracelets jangled as Jo felt her genuine squeeze. Yes, she was right. Jo detected the combination of tobacco and some flowery fragrance.

"Oh, my dear Joanna. What a special pleasure to welcome you to my home. Please do come in." Jo heard a throaty laugh. "Sometimes it gets a little quiet in my little house." And did she detect extra moisture in the redden dark eyes?

She was taller than Joanna imagined. Striking silver hair hung in straight bangs and a straight, shoulder length bob swished against her cheeks when she turned her head. She had a way of moving in little jerks, always with her chin jutting and nose tilted upward. Was it pride?

"Mrs. Donovan, I appreciate you taking the time to be with me. You certainly have a beautiful place."

"Now dear, remember I said on the phone to call me Darlene. I don't know if you will ever want to call me Grandma, but I am happy with Darlene. Thank you for the compliment. We, or I enjoy it here. We moved to Green Valley right after Melvin sold his medical practice in Scottsbluff and retired. At least he had five good years of retirement before the heart attack."

Jo felt the tenseness release as they toured the townhouse. It was larger than it appeared from the front. Everything was bright and airy. Lots of windows framed bits of greenery and numerous varieties of cacti.

An s-shaped patio snaked around the side of the house. They stepped onto a giant mosaic fashioned from rock of various salmon shades.

"What a beautiful design. It looks very Native American."

"Yes, it was designed by a well-known Native American who specializes in mosaic. I doubt if we could afford him now, he has become so famous."

Jo snapped several pictures. She wasn't sure what she would do with them, but it was nice to see where this grandmother lived. She took several of Darlene, but the setting that Joanna preferred was Darlene in her kitchen standing beside the tile island amongst hanging cookpots. The rings and bangles she wore at her wrists, neck and earlobes complemented her ankle length tunic. The color of her hair, the tunic sported side slits at the hem and roomy elbow length sleeves. Darlene had simple, but elegant taste.

Darlene poured two goblets of deep red wine. "I've been saving this for a special occasion. Melvin's hobby was wine making. This is one of his best ones. I only have two more bottles and then it will be gone. Let's celebrate. This toast is to you, my dear."

It was her first inclination to decline at this time of the day. She didn't. And the wine was a good one for sipping, not sweet, nor bitter. A fruity flavor with a hint of nut, she thought.

Darlene continued to light one cigarette after another. She carried a little pottery bowl designed to suck away the smoke. Jo was grateful to not have the smoke wafting around her.

With her second glass of wine, the words rolled off her tongue effortlessly. No more, she vowed, though Darlene offered her a third, which she declined.

Jo did most of the talking during the next two hours. Darlene appreciated and commended the work of her album and thought of one question after the other. Was she putting off any talk about Dixie? Jo wondered.

Lunch at 'the club' went well. There was not one particle of the chicken breast and pineapple nested on assorted greens left on Joanna's place. Darlene introduced several similarly aged women and men. Some had finished a round of golf, others a game tennis. A foursome in the corner played bridge.

Jo noticed Darlene avoided any explanation of the pair's relationship. Jo wondered how many times she practiced her words.

"I'd like you to know my young friend from Colorado. She's here on business as a travel agent."

Darlene knew almost everyone there and they continued to pass the table with friendly greetings or comments. Darlene remained the perfect and attentive hostess.

Returning to the townhouse Jo felt a little drowsy. There had been more wine during lunch. Any more sipping and she would fade away. Joanna decided that Darlene was about seventy-one. Yet, she didn't seem to be tired at all. Jo stifled one yawn and then another.

Darlene excused herself to freshen up in the powder room and returned with a flat, brown-wrapped package. "I have something I wish to give you." She brushed the dust away and tore off the brittle paper. Not too carefully, she placed two canvases on the expansive coffee table, lit a cigarette, and tossed her head as she blew out the gray cloud. "Well, what do you think?"

"They are exquisite. But I don't understand." Jo knelt to take in the careful strokes of color and shadow that nearly sprung from the two canvases. Each one must have been thirty by forty inches or so, Joanna thought.

The magnificence of the cathedral awed her. It stood with pride. Multitudes of spiraling steeples, ornately carved from stone, a delicate pink with a hint of salmon in color appeared to be cradling the wispy blue canopy of sky. At the third story a trio of bells with the appearance of pewter, grouped themselves in each of four narrow arched alcoves. The fourth story bore four more alcoves flanked by proud spires, and the highest section of the cathedral stretched into a mighty single steeple, graced with a cross at its apex. A luminescence danced in and out of the alcoves, windows and shadows insinuating a glowing sunset. Surely the cathedral had served a community for many years.

The other painting conveyed a starkly different mood. A young, underwear-clad girl, perhaps four years old, stood in a lake banked by sloping hills scattered with boulders of molten rock that had spewed from a volcano long ago. Her single black braid fell over her shoulder as she leaned toward a chunk of the molten rock that protruded from the water. It was her washing rock. She held a light-colored garment across a dished-out portion. Her other hand gripped an oversized gray bar of soap. Beside her floated a green plastic tub bearing other pieces of laundry. A determined pose revealed the seriousness of the task. The artist so captured the moment. Jo could imagine this young, dark-skinned laundress snapping her wrist as she dipped and slapped each item so expertly. Yet, there was more. A misty profile covered the whole canvas, deftly superimposed on the painting. The artist revealed the laundress in a gaze that belied a hint of smile. Looking to a brighter future perhaps? The artist left that for the viewer to decide. Jo had never seen anything quite like this.

"Dixie painted these, and I want you to have them."

Joanna's mind tumbled in a jumble of questions. When were they done? How did Darlene get them? Sure enough, there was the signature. Dixie Ann, but no last name in the right corner of each painting. Joanna hoped she would get some answers. Darlene intended to give her these paintings without questioning Joanna's connection to Dixie. After all, it could be a mistake. How was Darlene to know?

As if reading the perplexity in Joanna's face, Darlene's throaty voice filled the room. "My dear, the ring. I was assured that you are Dixie's child when I saw it. And yes, we have much to talk about so that you understand. I beg of you. Please find my daughter. My life is passing me by, and the hurts must be mended. Perhaps the paintings will help.

"I don't understand. If you don't know where she is, how did you get her paintings?" Then she remembered Ellie had mentioned Dixie's visit to her mother a couple of years ago.

"It's a long story. From the moment she was born, Dixie was a determined and precocious child. Melvin was finishing his last residency in Omaha, and I enjoyed the hustle and bustle of the city and my job as a dental hygienist. I was not ready to give it up to be a full-time mother, in the first place. So, I suppose there was a speck of regret and somehow

Dixie and I did not seem close. She was not a cuddler, whether it was her personality or my attitude, I don't know.

"Anyway, our relationship was never an easy one. Soon we moved to Scottsbluff where Melvin began his own practice, and it was a busy time for him. Nevertheless, Dixie and Melvin developed into good buddies. She was always on his lap, and he got the hugs. Looking back, I resented their closeness and felt left out. I busied myself with the hospital auxiliary and every committee and social activity I could in a small town."

Jo imagined the hostility that must have festered throughout the years. Is that why Darlene refused to listen to Dixie's story? He hoped she hoped she could ask this question gently. "I understand that an unnatural relationship developed between Dixie and her father, but you did not believe her when she told you. Was it because of the friction you two had?"

"How do you know about that? Accusations, that's all I've heard. Oh, I suppose it was *that* woman in Estes Park. She told you, didn't she? She had no right."

Jo heard the antagonism in Darlen's voice as her chin tilted upward. There was no need to defend Ellie, Joanna did not question that what Ellie said was true and the truth needed no justification. She wanted to say, "Listen lady, from what I hear, Ellie helped your daughter more than you ever did."

Darlene choked on her next puff and vigorously stamped the freshly lit cylinder to a shredded pile. Her tall frame slumped, and the confidence dissolved. A sob caught in her throat.

Oh dear, what should I do now? I didn't want to open a bag of garbage, just to understand and learn anything that could help find Dixie. Maybe this whole thing is a colossal blunder. Forget it.

Jo stood up. "Perhaps I should go. I…"

Sit right back down, young lady We are not finished."

"Then what happened?' Lauren leaned across the table of the plush corner booth.

The Latin quartet, engaged in a complicated rhythm, intensified Joanna's feeling of abandon. She was ready to talk. Greg sat at the bar with an old high school friend so that they could 'have their dialogue' he said, and Jo had been rattling non-stop.

Joanna saw that Greg and Lauren had a comfortable alliance. Their conversation was sprinkled with teasing, laughter, and compliments about each other's talents. Lauren's striking beauty might have dominated, however Greg, who would not be labeled as handsome, appeared quite so with his conquering personality. He was a kick but did not demand the limelight. He had character. Joanna approved.

"Darlene gained her composure and talked pretty straight out. What it all came down to is this...Darlene thought Dixie's and her father's relationship was unusual, but she looked the other way. Sex was overrated in her mind, and she seemed grateful that there wasn't much of it in her marriage. Dixie's sullenness in junior high was attributed to adolescence and by high school Dixie was a real pill to live with, for both mother her mother and her father. When Dixie raged at Darlene accusing her father of sexual molestation, Darlene didn't know that to do. She refused to believe it. Of course, Melvin denied it and made Dixie out to be a whore.

"Deep down Darlene knew there was probably some truth behind her daughter's accusations. A piece of her blamed Dixie herself for letting it happen, and if she let it happen, maybe she deserved it. When Dixie left after high school, she thought I was all over, and that Dixie would be fine. She was relieved to have Dixie out of the house. Then no one had to be blamed."

A shiver shook through Lauren. "Of course. She didn't have to feel guilty anymore. But can you imagine that she would actually think that Dixie would be OK and not carry awful scars?"

"You're right. Guilt is probably the biggest reason why Darlene didn't do more to find Dixie. She didn't admit it to me, but I think inside she knew that Dixie was hurting. I told you what Ellie told me. It wasn't some fondling here and there. It was bad."

"Do you think that Melvin and Darlene got along other than lacking in the lovemaking department? Did Darlene talk about that?"

"Mostly she talked around it. I got the feeling that Melvin looked down on Darlene and maybe all women and liked to be in control. Darlene said Melvin's father was a dictator and had been harsh with Melvin and his mom when he was young. Then she said something like, 'men try not to be like their fathers, but don't succeed.' My guess is that Darlene kept up appearances, but their relationship was pretty thin."

"I can't understand how she could allow her daughter to vanish. I would be frantic. What about her dad, didn't he wonder about Dixie?"

"Melvin told Darlene to let her go. If Dixie didn't care about them, why should they? Darlene was sure that Dixie would call or write sooner or later. As the years went by, Darlene had no idea where to begin.

Lauren sat shaking her head. "You said that she had two of Dixies' paintings. How did she get them?"

"Two years ago, Dixie's father died. Of course, they were living in Green Valley by that time and a couple of months later Dixie knocked on Darlene's door with two of her paintings in her arms."

"Boy, I bet that nearly put Darlene in the grave! Did she recognize her, after...how many years?"

"Twenty-four years since they saw each other. She didn't know her. It was her voice that she recognized."

"Why did Dixie seek out her mom after all that time?"

"Apparently, she called a cousin who was sworn to secrecy, every so often. When she knew her dad was gone, I suppose she hoped to mend fences."

Lauren sat in amazement. "That didn't happen if Darlene still doesn't know where Dixie is. What *does* Darlene know?"

"Darlene knows that she's been living and painting in Mexico since she left the states. I already knew about Mexico from Ellie, though Ellie wasn't sure if she was still there. When Dixie arrived, Darlene was dumbfounded, but thrilled to have another chance with her daughter and know that she was alive and well. Then the blame game started, and all the defensive walls were thrown up, blocking any reconciliation.

"Dixie blamed her mom for what she called an empty life and

Darlene told her that she made her own bed and ruined her own life, she'd always been a disrespectful brat, never thought of anyone but herself. And the shouting match escalated. Dixie walked out after she told Darlene about me. She was cruel about it. Something like, 'I had a kid when I was eighteen. I didn't want you to know about the baby. It's a good thing I gave her up. As a grandmother you would have made her life the same hell that you made mine. I'm glad I spared her that.' So, Darlene put the paintings away and tried to forget once more."

"She didn't know about you till then, huh? Another shocker. It's a miracle that the ole gal is still around. What do you think of her? And she had the gall to beg you to find Dixie for her. If you can make it better, it will relieve the guilt. Right?"

"I don't know. In some ways I pity her. I sense that much of her life has been empty. She has regrets, wants Dixie's forgiveness. She says she's willing to take any blame and wants to make up for some of the lost years. I think she means it."

"So, what's next Jo? How can you find your 'Dixie Mom' somewhere in Mexico?"

The quartet ended the set, and it was quiet. "I don't know."

CHAPTER 9

Jo hated herself. She intended to visit Ellie as soon as she returned from Arizona. She had talked to her on the phone before she left and Ellie was curious about the outcome of the trip. Instead, she buried herself at work and pushed aside thoughts of her newfound bloodline. In reality, all this new stuff about Dixie tugged at the edges of her consciousness and was not easy to ignore.

Rod's call really shook her. "Joanna, this is Rod, Ellies' son. Mom is losing ground and we're afraid she may not make it to Halloween. She wanted so much to have one more Christmas. And she wants to see you again. She is quite alert today. Can you come?"

Today? Good gosh, Halloween was only three days away. How could it be? She might not last that long. Jo expected to have other visits with Ellie. There was more about Dixie she yearned to hear. Yes, she'd come today.

Stepping from her trusty Taurus, the brisk mountain air tore into her lungs. She needed that. It was refreshing. Rod's sagging frame stepped from the shady porch into the sunlight. Ellie's illness had taken its toll on him as well. She quickened her step and their eyes met. His were golden, flecked with brown, surrounded with a soft fringe that captured her with melancholy vulnerability. Today, some of the sparkle was missing.

He indicated the porch swing. She sat and he joined her. Oh dear, is it too late? Has she gone already? Jo did not want to ask. Instead, she said, "It's been a very painful fall, hasn't it? I am so sorry for each of you. Too often keep going and don't have time to grieve or take care of ourselves. Is there anything I can do?" She grasped his near hand and saw those mysterious eyes lower.

"We have all held so much hope that Mom could beat this thing again, so much hope that we've been unable to face the possibility that she could go at any moment. So, when she said she wanted to see you again, I called. I'm so sorry."

"Sorry, why?"

"Dad's pretty upset. He thinks Mom's too frail to handle company. He's planning a Christmas celebration. He's decorating the tree now. Every ornament has a story, and this is the last time they will share those stories."

Jo's heart heaved. "He certainly doesn't need some near-stranger taking those special moments. I understand, Rod." Jo imagined the roughened hands of Ellie's heavyhearted husband gently unpacking each memory, and Ellie looking on from her hospital bed parked near the mountain-view window. Perhaps fond memories brightened her quiet eyes and tickled the corners of her mouth. Oh yes, these were important moments.

"Please, you need to be with your parents. I think I'll take a little walk before I head back."

"I'll check to see if Dad wants some help. But don't leave without saying good-bye. OK? You might run into Sally if you follow the road to the right. She's cleaning the Roadtrek. Dad wants to sell it."

Jo had no idea what a Roadtrek was, but it felt good to extend her legs and she would enjoy seeing Sally again. Her pace quickened as the tire grooves curved to the right. In front of a hovering log garage, she spotted the creamy colored RV, a miniature compared to the one her mother and step-father had used during their last years. All three doors gaped open. Inside, the motor of a vacuum whirred, yet not so loud as to drown out the familiar Enja CD that Jo played often at home. It had been her mother's.

The haunting mellow sounds wound round her and held her fast in their cocoon.

When there's a shadow you reach for the sun…
When there's a journey you follow a star…
And for tomorrow
If you really want to you can hear me say
Only if you want to, you can find the way
If you really want to, you can seize the day

She had never heard the words so clearly, not had they touched her so profoundly. Was this something her mother wanted her to hear? How could her heart feel so heavy, yet so comforted at the same time? She listened. *You can hear me say—you can find the way—you can seize the day.* Where? How?

How long time suspended and held her captive, she didn't know. The silky strands of another tune unraveled the trance and freed her body. She began to sway and turn as her moccasined feet moved with the rhythm and lifting message of the music.

Only night will ever know why the heavens never show
All the dreams there are to know, Paint the sky with stars
Who has placed the midnight sky So a spirit has to fly?
As the heavens seem so far And who has placed the midnight star?

Could her spirit fly? She longed to release the piercing loneliness entombed in its snare of denial. There was a rustle around her, and Joanna was overcome with the essence of long-ago maidens who shared this place, her aching and yearning.

The whirring vacuum had long since ceased. Mesmerized, Sally sat in the open doorway of the RV, her feet dangling to the ground. How she wished she might feel the cleansing and release she saw as Jo pranced and whirled with the mystical music of the Irish Enya. The long months of holding it together as her mother-in-law inched closer to death, seeing her own dreams evaporate, and watching her husband

and father-in-law curl deeper into their own shells, had left their mark. Sally's body had been whittled to a too-small size five and she carried her own burden of loneliness.

Unaware of the stinging teardrops that continued to plop as they dampened her lap, Sally pushed aside the heaviness and could have been a leaping deer as she found herself in unison with Joanna and her maiden dance. Their unabashed choreography shared nature's harmony on this site inhabited by eagles and pines.

Through misty eyes and grins, exhilaration liberated as instinctively their tempo varied with each new melody and rhythm. An observer would be roused in delight by the frenzied dance, their whoops, hollers, and yips.

With a joyous finale they caught each other in a wild embrace. There was silence. A bird called its mate and was answered. They were part of the unity of nature's symphony. Neither spoke. There was no need to talk of the primal expression they had embraced. Their stride had spring; their gaze held promise as they walked arms entwined toward the Roadtrek.

"Well, it looks like you have the RV all spiffed up." Jo broke the silence and stuck her head inside. "This is a nifty unit."

"Yeah, even though it's a mini motorhome, almost everything you'd need is packed in here, even a shower. It's only three years old. Phil bought it so Ellie could travel more comfortably. But no more travels." It was said with regret.

"I guess a lot has changed and you and Rod have had to take over the responsibilities concerning the resort operation."

"We agreed that the business would be ours someday. Rob's brother has his own career and has no interest in running a resort. But neither of us expected it to happen any time soon. And by that time, I hoped to be settled in a teaching job. I planned to go back to school to get my certificate. Working with children is my great love. Teaching would mean I could help out in the summer, but I did not expect to have any heavy responsibilities. And we want to start a family ourselves sometime.

"With everything in an upheaval, it sounds like you've had to jump right in. I can't imagine how tough things have been."

"Oh well, life is not always easy. You know what it's like to lose a mother too soon, yourself. And meeting your blood grandmother has to be a wild experience. How was the visit with Dixie's mother and what are your plans?"

Jo also wondered what was next. Each of her three friends had heard the story of the visit and when this question came up, the answer was the same, 'I don't know.' Should she trek off to Mexico and resume her search for her birthmother? They closed the Roadtrek and walked to Joanna's car. Sally wanted every detail and Jo complied. They poured over the pictures Joanna had taken of Darlene trying to see any family resemblance in Jo. As she finished, Jo's smile grew pensive. *Yes, I know the answer.*

"Hey, you two, what's going on? The sun will be setting soon." It was Rod.

Sally and Jo exchanged glances. "You'll never know."

"Dad and Mom have the tree beautifully decorated. Lets' go inside and have a little Christmas Eve toast."

"I'd better be heading back. It was an incredible afternoon, Sally. Seems like all of nature held us close." Jo took a deep breath. "It was quite healing."

"I know."

Rod was curious about this tender moment of understanding that passed between Jo and his wife. He was not one to butt in, however. "Change of plans, Joanna. Dad wants you to celebrate, too. He knows how much it will mean to Mom. She has always had a special feeling about your birth mom. Besides we're almost like siblings, being born only a few days apart." His smile was genuine.

"Please join us Joanna," Sally urged.

Multicolored miniatures twinkled on every brand of the long-needled pine, illuminating the beloved ornaments that Rod said held wonderful stories. Rod's brother and his wife had arrived and were arranging silver and gold packages around the tree. They were introduced to Jo and retreated to the kitchen where tinkly sounds could be heard.

The bronze glow of candles arranged around the room created an ambience of peace and calm and softened Ellie's emaciated cheeks.

Her downy gown, the color of a just-ripe peach, shrouded her tall, yet frangible frame tucked in a well-pillowed chair, not the hospital bed that Jo had imagined. Ellie held her hand out to Joanna. It was delicate and soft, and Joanna was struck by the prominence of each bone, usually cushioned with a fleshy palm.

Ellie's voice, sounding the whisper of a breeze, began, "I am so happy to see you Joanna, please join me." She motioned toward the chair on the right arranged as part of a conversational grouping. "And please tell me about your visit with Darlene. I've always wondered about her."

Jo glanced toward Phil. Would this be too tiring for Ellie, she wondered? His smile and nod were reassuring, and Jo began her story, encouraged by Ellie's smile and the intensifying brilliance in her deep, blue eyes.

When the story was completed, Ellie studied the pictures of Darlene. "She is an elegant woman, Joanna, but don't you think that her eyes have that clouded, hurt look?"

Jo exchanged the older woman's steady gaze. The sickness had not robbed the warm twinkle. "Yes, it's difficult to keep the eyes from telling the truth, isn't it?"

Phil pulled his chair beside Ellie's, politely putting an end to the 'Darlene story'. "Hey all, it's time for some refreshment."

Rod and Sally carried giant trays offering bubbly beverages served in tall stemware with a block of cheddar, crackers, and frosty grapes. Goblets lifted high, Jo was stirred, yet troubled about intruding in this pristine moment.

Phil spoke in a voice bell clear, unhurried with thoughtful pauses that allowed each idea to have full meaning. "Let us relish this precious evening with loving family and our family friend as we honor you Ellie, my loving and beautiful wife. Always my companion, lover, and workmate, you gave me wonderful sons. We share pride in them and the beloved wives they have chosen. Ellie, you have shared your love with us and all those who needed you, a young Dixie who created a new life and now that new life, her dear daughter, Joanna. One of the most glorious pieces of life is the wonder of memories. We will ever carry those memories and the presence of your spirit with us. Thank you, my love."

There was no mistaking the glistening in Phil's eyes, similar to those he had passed to his son. His smile, a fusion of love and compassion, expressed the feelings of each one in the room.

Despite its whisper, Ellie's voice remained unfaltering. "Cheers, to all my loves, as well."

It was a remarkable evening, evidently pulled together at the last minute. Ellie seemed to rise above her frailty and fatigue. Later, Jo would declare that it was indeed her last hurrah. Ellie opened package after package with resolve and piled the sparkly paper to her side. Each box held some special memory from the past. A nest of facial tissue held three ballpoint pens, a roll of adhesive tape and jar of petroleum jelly. It brought laughter and a smile to Ellie. How could she forget the first birthday present that Tim and Rob shopped for on their own. Tim, the oldest, knew that their mom was always looking for a pen and that Ellie used petroleum jelly on everything that ever became chapped—lips, cheeks, or hands—in the blustery winter. But it had been little Rob who remembered that adhesive tape was a real necessity in every home. The gifts had been so cherished it had taken months before Ellie decided to use them.

The well-worn decks of "Old Maid", "Crazy Eights" and two decks of regular cards—one of kitties and the other puppies—brought back memories of evenings playing card games beside a toasty fire. Jo learned that the kitties and puppies had been used as recently as last winter when Sally and Ellie skunked Rob and Phil in Canasta, a game she herself had learned from her own mother years ago.

Rob boxed and wrapped the rag that had been his soft, smooth 'blankie.' It gave him such comfort all those young years and Ellie remembered the day it was bravely put away—'cause he was a big boy now—the second day of first grade. They all laughed at the retelling of Rob stashing it in his drawer after he and Sally married and had to retrieve it from the trash. Sally couldn't believe that there was an old rag in Rob's underwear drawer, and she promptly threw it out.

One of Tim's recollections came in the form of a sling that he wore at the age of four because he slipped from a rafter in the barn and broke his arm. Naturally he was in forbidden territory at the time and tried to hide his swollen little arm until he could stand the pain no more and had to confess his disobedience.

Then there was Sally's package for Ellie to open, the elegant broach that had been in Ellie's family for four generations, the one Ellie had presented to Sally before she and Rod married. Each daughter-in-law had received a family heirloom. They enjoyed remembering the history of each piece and shared what it meant to them.

Phil's package to his precious wife held a hunter-green vest, well worn, yet still fluffed with its down filling. "Remember the year you made matching down vests for each one of us. We wore them sledding down Trixie's hill and later when the boys learned to ski."

Package after package brought meaningful memories, some crazy and fun and others touching and heartrending. Despite her feeling of being somewhat of an outsider, Jo sat entranced. She tried to push aside the envy that numbed her. There was no one who could share such experiences with her. Maybe a few with her father, but that would never happen. And as close as they were, Amy, Janene and Lauren could not take the place of day-to-day family antics, hurts, joys—those bygone days.

At last, when the final package had been reminisced, Ellie grasped a small box lying on the end table beside her. Her voice was of soft velvet when she said, "This is for you, Joanna."

Questioning, Jo took the unwrapped box. "But I..."

"It is a gift that your birthmother gave me before she left. She designed it and had it made by a Native American who had a little shop in Estes Park at the time. Somehow, I could never bear to wear it. This is its original box, and it has been in the back of my bureau drawer all these years."

Of pure silver, an inlay of mother of pearl, black onyx and coral swirled in a wide S design. In the open spaces of the S, pieces of turquoise were mounted. They were a delicate blue, not the blue-green that Jo had often seen. Each stone was accented by a spiraled strand of silver encircling it. Joanna fingered the stunning piece and turned it to see the artist's mark, an arrow attached to a T pressed into the silver.

Joanna's eyes misted. "How thoughtful and generous of you." She paused. "You said my mother designed this for you?"

All Ellie could do was nod. Joanna thought of refusing it. However, she knew that it held more meaning with her than it did for Rod or Tim. Another link to her Dixie Mom. She pressed it to her heart and knelt in front of Ellie who placed her hands on her shoulders and leaned to kiss her forehead. "I know you will meet her sometime, my dear."

CHAPTER 10

Finally, November was over. It must have been forty days long. Jo worked extra hours, shuffled a truckload of paper and stuck sticky-note lists on the mirror, the refrigerator and on her computers at home and at work. Spending long hours on the telephone irritated her, especially with unchosen music distracting her focus. Even so, her accomplishments while on hold, waiting to reach the proper department or person, were amazing.

Driving to Mexico would be quite different than taking a plane and required many preparations. How long would she be there? The plan at this point was three months. Her boss would keep her job open for that length of time. Of course, Jo planned to set up several Mexico travel packages that International would market locally, so she would not be entirely unemployed. Three months to find a needle in a haystack. That's what it felt like. Was it possible?

A neighbor had given her a lead on a house-sitter. Tonya, a grad student, seemed mature and trustworthy. Her Ph.D. would be in some bio-technical field that Jo couldn't even pronounce. With her research, coursework and teaching a freshman level class, she would be busy studying and not partying. Tonya was moving in tomorrow.

Jo found an insurance company that covered vehicles in Mexico, at least the medical and comprehensive part. For the liability and legal assistance, she needed Mexican insurance. *Vagabundos*, a travel club, offered the cheapest Mexican insurance and she was buying it by the year because it was more economical than by the day. The FAX machine grabbed the completed information sheet and did its usual hum and click. Jo's home office was nearly as well equipped as the downtown office, and she was gratified that much of her professional and private business could be completed at home.

One more down. Jo crossed out 'Mexican insurance'. What next? Making copies of her vehicle insurance policy, driver's license, vehicle registration and passport that she needed at the border crossing could wait until all of the insurance papers were returned.

The tourist tax needed to be paid at a bank once she was in Mexico. That was a while off. She learned that a debit card for her checking account could be used at ATM machines in Mexico and as a credit card which meant she didn't have to worry about carrying much cash, exchanging U.S. money, or having a credit card bill at home. The exchange rate for pesos at an ATM was the best rate one could get anywhere. Jo would cash one of her mother's Certificates of Deposit that was maturing in a few weeks. She should have plenty in her checking account to handle her expenses. 'Debit card' was already crossed off.

On another list was 'Card—Sally and Rod'. Actually, the card was finished, except for the verse and message. As a novice with watercolor, the best she could do at this time was practice making her own greeting cards. Sometimes they were flowers, birds, or fuzzy animals. This one, a profile of an angel-child kneeling and looking upward through eyes of innocence, came out all right she thought. It took her some time to compose the verse. Some of her verses rhymed. This one did not. It was a verse of friendship, appreciation, and hope. On separate paper she added an informal message updating Rod and Sally about her plans. She had hurriedly sent a card and flowers earlier, but this was a more personal message.

There had been no time for visiting at Ellie's funeral. Even if there had been, Jo would have been unable to loosen the lump in her throat without another fountain of tears. Ellie's death, only three days following the "Christmas Party", brought back the pain of losing her own mother.

Jo was particularly excited about purchasing the Roadtrek that Phil and Ellie had traveled in. It seemed as though part of Ellie would be journeying with her as she set out on this mission. She wanted Phil to know her feelings. His card was sent last week and bore a bluebird nestled in a pine bough.

She crossed off 'Card—Sally and Rod'. The next items were 'Mexican travel books and 'Maps'. Time was getting away. She must hurry if she hoped to beat the mail truck. Dashing though the garage rather than unlocking the front door, she stopped to grin at the mini motorhome parked beside her Taurus. That little jitney was going to be a kick to travel in. She was not the least bit worried, though several of her friends thought she was half crazy to head for Mexico alone.

The phone was ringing when she returned to the house. She picked it up in the kitchen before the answering machine kicked in. It was Amy. "It's good to hear your voice. I've been so busy since Ellie died. Sorry I haven't called."

"No problem, I've been on a tread mill, too. Say, Janene told me about your plans to live and travel in Mexico for a few months, searching for Dixie. I'm *proud* of you."

"Thanks Amy. I have most of the insurance stuff and job stuff organized. My list is getting shorter. It is exciting, too bad you can't go with me."

"Well, that's part of the reason I called. Dan's parents purchased a timeshare in a condo at Nuevo Vallarta and they're flying the whole family down for New Year's. Are you going to be near there?"

"I know I will be—sometime. I don't have my plans mapped out yet. That's next on my list. How long will you be there? It sure would be fun to meet up."

"We'll be there nearly two weeks, but Jo, I'm not just thinking about meeting up, uh... how would you like a traveling companion?"

"You mean you'd drive with me? All that way? Wow! I can't believe it. But what about the kids and Dan?"

"They're all for it. In fact, my protective Dan thinks that pint-sized me can really scare off all the banditos. At least he thinks the two of us could manage quite well. What do you think?"

"Amy…you're giving me chills just thinking about it. It would be a thrill having time together, plus I know you would be wonderful help."

"When are you planning to leave?"

"Probably the day after Christmas. Hey, I think that might work. Surely it we could make it to the Vallarta area in six or seven days. I'll pick up the maps and books at the bookstore today. Are you free tomorrow, say in the afternoon? My house-sitter will be here in the morning, and she should be settled in the basement by afternoon. We won't bother her, and she won't bother us."

"That should work. Usually Sundays are pretty free. What if I come by about 2:00?"

Jo cradled the hand-blown bowl her mother had called the Caribbean, because of its brilliant color. The sturdy dish piled with lacquered vegetables was a favorite of hers. She imagined her mother poking around a Mexican novelty shop choosing the brightest and most colorful chili peppers, tomato, corn, avocado, squash and more. She placed it on the oak buffet chest making room on the dining room table for the maps and Mexican travel books she had found.

Luckily, she remembered the stack of travel books the Quad Squad had boxed, then stored in the basement when they went through Steve's and her mother's things. The stack included *RV Travel in Mexico, Hidden Mexico-Beaches and Coasts, Traveler's Guide to Mexican Camping and the Mexico Atlas Turistico De Carreteras.*

Jo opened a chunky forest green spiral notebook, one of four, and recognized the quick penmanship that belonged to her mother. On the left, *Tues, Sept 22* and on the right, *day 42.* The heading at the top read, *Leaving Osprey Pt. Campground, Heading South toward Calif on Oregon coast.* Jo continued reading. *Off by 8:30--misty morning, Steve in shorts—confident of a warm day—As continue South on Oregon coast, winding through forest lands, but not so tall as those farther North. All morning foggy—missed the last 100 miles or so of the Oregon coast—Still misty and foggy as arrive in Calif. Passed several bulb farms and one sign—Easter lily capital of the world. Before arriving in Crescent City we begin to see Redwoods.* It continued on. She noticed the wide left margin held other tidbits of information. *Avg height, coast Redwood,*

300 ft (tallest 367) (oldest 2200 yr) bought fresh tuna—fisherman says marinate and grill is good

Yes, that was Mom, pages and pages of their experiences. Jo recalled their trip to the Northwest. At least they had wonderful travels and experiences together, the last years of their lives. Mom was one to live each day to the fullest. *If only she could do the same.*

Flipping pages, she came to *Mon, Jan 4, Mexico, leaving Loveland, day 1*, their last Mexico voyage. For sure there was a wealth of information here. Amy and Jo would have no trouble getting a tentative itinerary together.

Sure enough, at 5:00 the last copy of *Tentative Itinerary - Jo and Amy - The Magnificent Mexican Journey* was printed. It included daily mileage, camping information and everything they could think of to relieve any worries Amy's family might have about this trip. Maybe Jo would give one to her father, as well.

Her father was fifteen minutes late. At least she hoped he was late and had not forgotten their lunch date. She could not think of one more thing to add to the list she had been making during the wait, and had read *The Front Range Forum* a free paper stacked at the entrance of *Dino's Pizza*. Now Jo was completely bored and irritated.

"How's my gal? Sorry I'm late. I needed to finish an account before I left the office, since I won't be going in tomorrow." Her father slid into the seat across from her and placed a tall brown bag next to the window.

"Glad to see you, Dad. I was beginning to think you forgot. So, you usually work only mornings these days?" Jo thought he appeared more haggard, gray, and heavier than she had ever seen him.

"Yeah, but I'm taking tomorrow off to get the house ready for Cindy's family."

The waitress, approached and explained about the pizza buffet with pasta and salad and both decided to have the buffet.

Reseated with their plates filled, Jo began, "So who all are coming for Christmas?"

"There will be Cindy's mom flying from Texas and Cindy's youngest brother Roy, his wife and their three kids staying at the house. The other brother and family will be renting a motel, but no doubt they will be over for dinner most every night."

"That sounds like quite a house full."

"You can say that again. I figure we'll have sixteen, not counting the baby for Christmas dinner, with Cindy's kids and all. We really can't seat more than sixteen, Jo. We're opening presents on Christmas Eve and you're welcome to come, if you want."

Here it was, one week before Christmas and this was the first her dad had mentioned it. She was never included in Cindy's and her dad's Christmas anyway, though she hoped her father would realize that her first Christmas without her mother would be a rough one. But no. It was a good thing she had accepted the invitation to spend Christmas Eve with her aunts, uncles, and cousins on her dad's side of the family. They were thoughtful to include her.

"Actually, I'm spending Christmas Eve with Aunt Judy and the family. Janene and her family invited me for Christmas dinner, but Amy and I leave early the next morning and I need time for last minute preparations."

"You're still determined to take that trip, huh? Isn't it a little silly, spending all that money searching for some lost soul? Kind of like looking for a grain of salt on a sandy beach, don't you think?"

She was not about to launch a defense or reel out explanations that he wouldn't understand. "I'm sorry you can't be supportive about this..."

Clay cut in. "Double JJs"—he hadn't used that nickname since she was a child and she felt like one again as he cocked his head toward her— "we raised you as our own. It's a slap in your mother's face to deny that, by searching out someone who probably doesn't give one wit about you."

Her eyes locked with his and she chose her words carefully. Her voice was hushed. "You have no idea how Mom felt about this. You weren't there. She assured me over and over that she would support me if I decided to seek my birthmother, and said she was grateful that she must have loved me enough to allow me to grow up in a good home."

Clay's shoulders slackened. His annoyance was evident. "JJ, I guess I'm just worried. You have no idea what can happen to a young gal on the road..."

"Amy is driving down with me. I won't be alone..." She shouldn't be feeling defensive. She was a grown woman.

"Two young gals on the road just means juicier prey."

Juicier prey. That was it. This was nothing like Joanna had imagined. She was foolish to expect her father to pour over her maps and plans, ask interested questions and give pieces of advice that some fathers liked to give. She'd give it one more try. "You should see the little motorhome I bought. It handles well. Amy and I can cook, shower, sleep, listen to music, even watch videos if we want to."

"Well, if that's what you want. What do those things cost, anyway? It seems like you could spend thousands of nights in a motel for what you pay for those big campers. From what I can tell your mom and Steve sure wasted a lot of money traveling here and there, especially in the big bus thing they had."

She wasn't going to explain or argue. For Allison and Steve, it was their second home, like some people have cabins or summerhouses, only their second home was on wheels. And they slept in their own bed every night while seeing so much more of the world than her dad would ever see. Maybe he was jealous. Maybe it galled him that her mother had found adventure and happiness without him.

"Think so, huh? Well, mother lived a good life after you left, and she lived it in a way that suited her." She wondered if Clay felt the little jab. "And I intend to do the same, with or without your blessing."

Joanna refused to let the tug in her heart get to her. She would not feel sorry for herself. Her dad would never change and the sharing-visits she longed for would never be. Were all fathers like that? Amy and Lauren seemed to have fathers who could really listen and talk about hurts, growing, relationships, you name it. If she ever married, Joanna was determined to have a husband who would be a communicative father.

"In case I don't get to see you at Christmas, I want to give you your present now." She handed her father a package, wrapped and bowed in silver.

He stammered. "Uh, thanks Jo. Here's yours, too. He pulled the grocery sack to the tabletop, pushing aside the used plates.

"Well, shall we open them?"

Clay nodded and tore into his package. Jo had called Cindy for ideas and learned that her father's watch had given out. She chose a handsome gold one, a more expensive one than she would have bought for herself and had it engraved. *All my Admiration and Love, Joanna*

"Hey, this is just what I need Jo. Thanks." He would have missed the engraving if Joanna had not pointed it out. "Nice, thanks again." He put the watch back in its box. "Your turn."

Jo fished two items from the sack. The framed picture was not wrapped.

"I didn't wrap the picture. Cindy thought you would like a copy. We had family pictures taken for Christmas... uh, that is Cindy's family." He spoke the last part rapidly.

It was professionally done. Besides Cindy and her father, it included Cindy's son, two daughters, son-in-law and the granddaughter. "It's very nice, Dad. Please tell Cindy thank you for me. The background is beautiful. Where was it taken?"

"In the back yard at the photographer's home."

"Is Toni still planning on a summer wedding?'

"Oh, that is all off. You know how kids are. She's back home again. At least she can help her mother out with all that company coming."

Jo started on the wrapped package, which she was certain her father had done. She appreciated his effort. "Pretty package, Dad." She lifted the thick sweater from its box. Vivid purples, oranges, fuchsias, greens, and blues shaped the diamond design on a black background.

"I hope you like it. I know you always liked a lot of color."

"It certainly is colorful and should be pretty warm. It will be perfect with my black denims. Thanks Dad."

"Well, kid, I better run. Got to get to the grocery store. I have a list as long as your leg."

Jo laughed and shook her head. "Then you better get going." They both rose and before Clay could leave, Jo grabbed him in a bear hug. For several moments she held tight. "Have a good Christmas, Dad." Could she keep her eyes from misting? She tried.

"Yeah, Jo, Merry Christmas and have a safe trip." It was the last time they hugged.

Dixie

The summer crew left a month ago, each one back to some college campus where a future awaits. I wish I had a future.

Ben and I had a hard time saying goodbye when his training was over. Two weeks was all we had. In another life he would have stayed with me forever, he said. We promised to keep in touch and stay in each other's lives. He called me twice. I haven't heard from him in six weeks. There has been no one else since Ben. No more guys for me.

Three of us are still working at the resort. We're helping Ellie and Phil handle the last of the season, which definitely slows down in September. We close at the end of October.

Ellie confided in me last night that she is three months pregnant. She and Phil aren't announcing it to the family yet. I felt quite honored to be the first one to know. I wonder if she had an ulterior motive. I think she suspects. It's not fair. She's feeling great while I look ashen and can hardly keep anything down. We talked a long time. I told her a little more about my life. I think she knows why I ran away.

She wants me to write home. I said no, but I did promise to call my cousin Betsy. We've always been close. I shocked her good, but she swore to secrecy if I let her know where I am from time to time. My leaving caused a lot of family embarrassment.

I'm a forbidden topic. Well, whooptie-doo, too bad.

Ellie says I can stay through the winter. There is much to do—curtains to replace, the phones to man, painting to do, horses to tend. But what am I going to do with a kid? Can you run away from a kid?

CHAPTER 11

*B*risk, *overcast morning. All went well—off by 7:20. Mountains along the front range a peachy pink, where the sun reached over the clouds to wash the patches of snow. Through Monument and Colo. Springs snow on the ground, trees looked like a fairy land, but it made roads messy. Motorhome covered with frozen road gunk, a mess. Stopped for lunch at rest stop South of Walsenburg. Ate sandwich stuff we brought. Such fun and anticipation. Amy and I did not stop talking till reached the Pecos River Campground North of Santa Fe. Drove 415 miles today. Rolling, pine-filled hills around the area. No snow, but very chilly. Nuked pasta casserole Amy fixed ahead with greens and garlic bread. Pretty good dinner for campers. Used the heated campground showers. Won't fill own water tanks till out of danger of freezing.*

Jo smiled as she finished her journal entry. Sounded much like what her mother would have written. The day had gone quickly with Amy sharing the driving and all of their yacking. Both appreciated the time to catch up with each other's lives.

Amy had shared some of the difficulties of a family business. Joanna had assumed that everything was smooth with them. Not so. Amy told of feeling like an outsider sharing the office with her mother-in-law while Dan, his father and brother were on the job site. There were weeks when her mother-in-law refused to communicate with her except through notes. Dan was caught in the middle and the marital bond was strained.

"We were close to separation when Dan built the salon. I like having my own business and things have smoothed since. I help out in an emergency now that both of his parents are cutting back with the business."

"Will you return to work in the office when that happens? No. Dan and I are better partners at home than we are in the office. There I'm on edge with every move, afraid I will displease him."

"I can't imagine you being uptight around Dan. You seem so compatible. And you're always assertive and confident. You can handle everything."

Amy looked at her friend. "Things are not always as they seem. Every relationship is a mass of compromise."

"And so many women end up being the great compromisers, don't they?—adjusting their lives around men and excusing them for their behavior. I'm not saying that is the way it is with you." Joanna glanced at her friend to see her non-committal shrug, then continued.

"I saw it in my mother. I'm that way. It's a damn discredit to men, as well. How can we unlearn such detrimental submission?"

"Sometimes it's the lesser of two evils. We give in and fail to confront to keep things comfortable and smooth, rather than face the other inevitable."

Joanna shot back. "See, that's what I mean; we make the changes, the excuses. I did it with Paul. Deep down he has a heart of gold, but that did not make up for his irresponsible and unpredictable behavior. And how he could so easily allow me to pay the bills and bail him out of one mess then another, is beyond me. It's almost like he felt entitled."

"Join the human dilemma. For sure there is no perfection."

"You can say that again. I have this terrible flaw, myself. I'm afraid to let myself look at any man. I've come to the realization that I'm attracted to men I can fix, men that need someone to make them whole and that ends up being me."

On the road the next morning Amy took the wheel and Jo pulled out her *Learn Spanish - Quick and Easy* book and her Spanish dictionary. It was time to practice some phrases before they crossed the border. By noon they were getting the hang of pronunciation and had practiced the usual *Como esta? Muy bien, gracias. Y usted? Donde esta...? Quiero..* That one they knew from the Taco Bell Chihuahua who declared "Yo quiero Taco Bell." They might get laughed out of Mexico, but surely their efforts would be appreciated.

Deming, New Mexico was more spread out than they expected. They found campground row on the edge of town but were eager to get the gunk that had been riding with them the last two days off of the rig and chose to wash up the Roadtrek before registering.

The sun deceived them with its brightness. They were anxious for warmth, yet the breezy air was frigid, as it had been during most of the trip. The only car wash they found looked quite antiquated, but they were determined to get the crud washed off before they reached Nogales. What a fiasco. The first sprays of soapy water froze in chunks, pellets and sickles on the front window and hood.

"Keep spraying Amy, surely the water is warmer than the Roadtrek and eventually it will thaw the ice away."

"I don't know, if I remember my physics there is a point when water and ice can be the same temperature. It doesn't seem to be working. The ice is getting thicker."

"Let's try the back end. It's the worst."

In the end they wound up with sweat sodden clothes, steaming from the body heat they had created and a pile of mucky-looking towels. The effort was worth it and the rig looked better, they agreed.

Tomorrow would be a short day's drive. In Nogales they would fill the water tank, buy their last U. S. gas, and prepare for the crossover early the next morning.

At last, in Mexico. The roads seemed fine to Joanna, except for those places where there were no shoulders and the drop off could be several feet. With eighteen wheelers and wide buses whipping around them—and there were lots of these—she had to use an iron grip at the wheel to keep the rig from being blown over the side.

Maneuvering through each little village slowed their progress, particularly when one *Topes* after another loomed before them. These Mexican speed bumps could shake an engine loose faster than any jackhammer if a person failed to see them. Yet with eyes like little children taking in a Christmas tree laden with packages, they took in each new scene and sniffed each new smell.

Amy noticed the effort to keep each household tidy as they passed row after row. "Look at that woman sweeping her dirt front yard. Can you believe it?" The woman was dressed in a familiar 'Mother's uniform', a printed dress and coverall apron with pockets.

On her feet were plastic thongs. Her 'broom', which had long been a tangled ball, scooted bits of trash and leaves ahead of it.

Other women tossed scoops of water from a bucket into a dusty street from their doorsteps and a graying gentleman, slight in stature, proudly rode a bony burro packed with sticks tied in bundles.

Remnants of an early morning fire smoldered near bus stops where villagers visited during their wait. Signs warning *Pohibida Tirar Basura,* something about not throwing trash seemed not to prevent roadside garbage burning. These were scenes that would become quite familiar to Joanna as she explored this engaging land with its flavorful history and people.

They decided to take as many toll roads as possible to speed their trip, hoping to reach Nuevo Vallarta in time to be ready for the New Year's Eve celebration. Confusion with the arrows and *Libre* and *Cuota* signs led them to take the free road through Magdalena, a little town they expected to miss.

Amy rifled through the dictionary. "Jo Libre is free and Cuota means the one you pay for." They wouldn't make that mistake again.

Near Hermosillo they drove through their first *Caseta* and paid their first toll using the 'saved' pesos from Allison and Steve's zippered bag, labeled 'Mexico pesos, phone card, etc.'

"I'm impressed how organized your mother and Steve were. We would have had to stop for pesos somewhere before we hit these toll roads, though I know you wish they were spending these pesos instead of us." Jo heard the admiration in Amy's voice.

"Yeah. I hope Mom knows about this trip. Actually, part of her is with us you know."

Amy shot her a puzzled look.

"Her ashes. I brought them."

Not yet 2:30, the Roadtrek left the highway and turned onto the four-lane palm-lined thoroughfare leading to San Carlos. It was evident that this was not a traditional Mexican town. Signs everywhere related to the Gringo tourist. Her mother's notes indicated that it had not grown into the tourist mecca the developers had hoped.

Nevertheless, it housed numerous wealthy transplants, many who docked magnificent yachts in the several harbors nearby. Directly ahead loomed two jagged peaks, named by earlier Indians of the area *Teta Kawi* or goat's teats. Jo and Amy thought they looked like awfully lumpy teats, but neither knew much about goats.

There wasn't much of a downtown, mostly a strip of businesses along the road to the main harbor. On the way, Jo spotted a *Banamex* and steered into the gravel parking lot. There she and Amy paid the seventeen-dollar tourist fee for each of them and used the ATM machine to get pesos.

They couldn't decide whether to stay in the El Mirador campground on the other side of the peaks or boondock on the beach near the highway turnoff to San Carlos. They resolved to tour the area and check out the campground before making a decision.

El Mirador was a very modern and beautifully designed campground. Driving past the swimming pool, restaurant, laundry area and gift shop, Jo noticed that the campsites were good sized and able to handle the slide-outs and diesel buses. Their little Roadtrek was dwarfed in comparison. Making the loop they stopped behind an aging, yet well-kept white pickup, much better than some of the battered ones they had seen. Aluminum pole-work held the heavy tarp that tented the pickup bed. There were at least seven people peering into the back.

Jo leaned out of the window to inquire. "What's going on here?"

A Gringo, gripping the handles of a woven, bright plaid grocery bag, responded. "This must be your first time here. The produce man visits every day. He has good stuff. You'll have to take a look."

Jo and Amy joined the waiting group and watched the man, neatly dressed in white pants and shirt, work the crowd. Patrons left with homemade tamales or flat pies of *piña, platano or manzana*---pineapple, banana, apple. The produce man ripped away bag after bag from the plastic roll, weighed the potatoes, cabbages, strawberries, onions, carrots, oranges and completed each calculation mentally, identifying the amount in Spanish and English—*doce*, twelve pesos; *veinte cinco*, twenty-five peso—until it was Jo's and Amy's turn.

"*Hola señor, me llamo, Joanna. Soy de Colorado, estados, unidos. Como se llama?*" She was proud to try out her limited Spanish.

"*Mucho gusto, señorita. Me llamo Alejandro. Hable Espanol?*

"*Solemente un pocito. Pero quiero aprender mas.*"

Alejandro grinned widely and went into his sing-song English. "Ah...What you want to buy, my lovely señoritas? My orange juice, fresh squeezed thees morning. Heer..." Reaching into a cooler of crushed ice he raised a plastic liter as if to offer a toast, then stripped the plastic sealing ring and unscrewed the lid. "You taste. You weel like." He poured a few gulps into a plastic cup and offered it to Jo. "Your amiga taste too, no?" Her poured Amy the same.

"It's very good Alejandro." How could she not buy it after he had opened it? "OK, we'll take some orange juice."

"Take two, the other half price." He pulled a second liter into the air.

Amy and Jo laughed. "We'll be drinking OJ for a while, no? Amy glanced at Jo shaking her head.

"Fresh tamales? My wife make thees morning. Ah...I know what you like. I have a the shreemps, fresh thees morning. You like *grande o chico camarones?*"

Amy was intrigued to hear his voice raise at the end of each sentence. "You are quite the salesman, Alejandro."

"Like you say een America. I can sell refrigerators to Eskimos, no?"

"I am sure you can," both agreed.

They left when the paying and the handshaking was completed with tomatoes, jalapenos, avocados, OJ, onions, homemade salsa, and a half a kilo of large shrimp, beheaded, but dressed in their shells. The two would feast tonight.

"Come back soon." Alejandro waved, still grinning.

They decided to camp on the beach and headed that direction. "Jo let's check out the boats. We have plenty of time, don't we?" Away from the main street they found a place to park near the boat dock.

Sitting on the patio of a dockside restaurant sipping margaritas, they listened to the rhythms of Mexico and took in the action. A bronzed man dressed only in a swimsuit and white rubber boots, doused, mopped, and polished every corner of a glamorous boat, the size of a small house.

"Hey, that guy doesn't look too bad, Jo, pretty well muscled. And it doesn't look like he's the hired help. Surely that rig is his."

"Probably. Good as he looks, I think he's a little too old for me." There was a pause as each ordered another drink. After all it was their first afternoon in Mexico.

Smiling toward the bronzed man, Jo mused. "Do you suppose that's his daughter or his new plaything?" A stunning gal emerged from somewhere below. Equally coppered and scantily clad in a luminous orange bikini and matching fingernails, she looked the part of a well-pampered trophy.

Miss bikini handed bronze-man a tall frosty glass. His free arm wrapped her body and pulled her against his. She tossed her lengthy flaxen mane and laughed as his lips came down on hers. Hard. They certainly weren't inhibited. It was a long kiss.

Jo and Amy eyed each other. "She's definitely not his daughter."

Feeling the effects of the tequila, both giggled at the imaginary stories they were fabricating about the yacht couple and the paunchy tourist in shorts who flopped by. He wore sandals with colored socks that stretched above his calves. He was followed by a woman with a well-creased face, pitch-black hair, false eyelashes, and makeup to match.

Amy gave Jo a side glance and rolled her eyes. "Can you imagine?... Aren't we terrible? Just wait till we're that age. People will be joking about us. Heaven forbid."

"We'd better get out of here before we make a scene with our snickers. How about roaming the dock before we head to the beach?"

A fishing boat, nice sized but not the elegant yacht they had been eyeing, maneuvered into a nearby space. The attractive couple aboard waved them over. They wore wide-brimmed hats banded with bright San Carlos scarves. Billowy white shirts topped their swimsuits.

Introductions informed them that the retired couple was from

Washington and went by Joan and Peter. "Have you been in San Carlos long?" Joan asked.

Joanna gave them a brief account of their journey thus far but avoided the rest of the complicated story.

"How was your boat trip?" Amy wanted to know.

The ship's captain methodically looped and secured the docking ropes, while frying aromas curiously drifted from the cabin.

Joan did the talking and her husband stood by seemingly amused, but silent. "We are SCUBA divers and we've had twenty or so dives in Cozumel, a few in Florida, but never dived in this part of Mexico, so that was the plan today."

"How did it go?"

"We enjoyed it." Joan looked at her husband who nodded and smiled. "But we had to wear heavy wet suits rather than skins because of the cold water and we felt like those fat sumo wrestlers. Anyway, there's not much color on this coast. The Caribbean has iridescence and color you wouldn't believe. However, the starfish here are amazing. Aren't they hon? There must have been a dozen sizes and kinds. Some were spindly, others fat. And the fancy designs on their backs were something I'd never seen before. Then this afternoon..." She turned to her husband. "You tell them about the fishing, hon."

But Peter shook his head. "You're doing fine dear."

"Well, we decided to fish instead of doing another dive."

The fishing story was nearly finished when the steward stepped from the cabin with a steaming tray of corn tortillas and golden fried fish.

"This is as fresh as it gets. The catch of the day." Joan's pride was evident. "Please, you two, try some with us."

Their refusals were not accepted. Neither had tried fish tacos before. Following the steward's instructions each palmed a warm tortilla, slathered it with mayonnaise, topped it with chunks of crispy fish, squeezed the juice of fresh limes on top and squirted on a little hot sauce.

Jo noticed the tortillas were smaller, lighter and milder than the ones she bought at home as she bit into the folded concoction. All agreed that the tacos were truly mouthwatering.

Heading toward the Roadtrek, Amy said. "You're driving. I'm still a little dizzy."

It was no problem finding the open beach area where they knew they could camp for the night. *Condominos Pilar* was a couple of blocks down the beach, so there were people close by. The sandy knoll where they parked gave them a view of the ocean.

Nearing 5:00, there was plenty of daylight left and time to take a beach walk. Barefooted, they felt the packed sand with each long stride. They certainly weren't hungry, and both wanted some exercise, so this walk was to be a brisk one. Here and there they squealed at the frigid foam swishing over their feet. Beyond the condominiums, the beach curved toward an inlet to an estuary a half mile away. The tide was out, and they could walk out on sandbars imbedded with shells.

Jo picked up a long one, nearly an inch across the top that spiraled to a point three inches away. "Look Amy, it's an auger." Steve had filled the glass base of a lamp with various shells for her birthday last year and she liked the augers, but she hadn't seen one this large. In no time they each had a pocketful, the largest, they decided was six inches long.

The mouth of the estuary was a little rocky and hard on bare feet, so they turned back toward the beach, but not before they spotted several proud cranes and egrets reaching to stab their beaks into the shallow ponds. The tide was coming in and soon the water level would rise. Walking beyond the inlet to a rocky point, they sat to enjoy the rippling view.

"Look." Jo pointed to the left. "About thirty yards out." A pair of dolphins were enjoying their late afternoon swim. In unison black shiny fins rolled into view and disappeared. A few yards later the rhythmic pattern repeated. What a thrill for landlubber Coloradoans. They watched until their sea friends were out of sight.

Abruptly Amy leaped. "Jo, we'd better high tail it or we'll be up to our waist crossing the inlet with this incoming tide."

Later the pair sat in foldable chairs toeing the soft sand and watching the changing sky colors. The sun had dipped into the sea and left a turquoise skyline that blended into pinks and lavenders overhead where wisps of clouds hovered. Gentle swishes soothed them. They had feasted on garlic-buttered shrimp, guacamole, salsa, tortilla chips and orange juice over ice.

"Is this the life or is this the life?" Jo sighed. "Amy, it was so thoughtful of you to join me on this trip. You are indeed a wonderful and special friend. I love being with you."

Amy dabbed at the corner of her eye and nodded. "Me, too."

CHAPTER 12

B oth women awakened early following a restful night. The sun was lighting the east as they turned onto the road to Guaymas. They read from Allison's notes that taking the eight-mile trip through the city would allow them to miss one of the toll-booths for the Highway 15 *Cuota*. The traffic through Guaymas was busier than they imagined at such an early hour. Amy did excellent work navigating and they found the left turn that led to the highway with no problem. Today, they expected to make it to Culiacan, which meant traveling about 360 miles. The highway loosely followed the West Coast of mainland Mexico along the Gulf of California. They would pass Obregon, Navojoa, then leave the state of Sonora and enter Sinaloa.

This trip was not intended to be one for exploration. However, both wished that they had time to take little side trips to beach villages or Alamos, an historic mining town. Instead, changing terrain zoomed by as the Roadtrek rolled on. It took two hours to reach Obregon, an industrial city which sported a mammoth Super Walmart featuring Dominos Pizza and a very modern McDonalds.

"Can you believe it? I guess they like fast food in the big cities just like we do at home. Too bad it's too early for lunch or we might give one a try." Amy's finger traced the map looking for the next town. She had discovered that the only way to stay on Highway 15 when they came to a city was by spotting and following the signs and arrows naming the next town or city. She watched for Navojoa or Los Mochis. "There it is, Jo. At the next light we need to turn left."

Industries crowded the outskirts of Obregon. The flourmills, plus the seed, fertilizer, and pesticide factories, all involved the fertile agricultural area they were entering. Some industries could not be deciphered, but they had no trouble identifying the Corona Beer and Pepsi plants. Continuing south of the city, as far as the eye could see it was green. Irrigation canals patterned the area keeping beans, corn, and wheat well-watered.

Nearing the state border of Sinaloa, two young Mexicans with rifles slung over their shoulders waved them to the side of the road. The older of the two asked to come inside. He asked if they had any fruit and motioned for Amy to open the refrigerator. Yes, they had two oranges and one apple plus a couple avocados waiting to be made into more guacamole. They could keep the avocados, but he palmed the other fruit, bowed, and exited the rig, waving them on.

They continued to go in and out of desert and fertile land, enjoying the variety. Some villages were spotted off of the road a block or so, others flanked both sides of the road which required the typical *topes* maneuver. It was OK. It enabled them to observe the roadside business of the people.

This village bore a tire repair shop with a *Llantera* sign lettered in black paint on an unfinished wooden board. Four posts supported a canopy woven from aging palm branches, which shaded a trough of water used to detect tire leaks. A few tire irons, boxes and a blackened compressor attached to an orange air tube appeared to make up the shop. The shopkeeper's alternating stomps on an oversized tire and his levering efforts with the tire iron around its silver rim gave him the likeness of a giant chimpanzee jumping around. He paused, tipping the bill of his hat upward, making lively conversation with a strapping gent who leaned against one of the posts, bare arms crossed.

A few doors down three men and a well-rounded woman dallied in the entrance to *Ferreteria Don Juan*, a sort of hardware store. In the open doorway of *Supermercado Lucy,* several women picked around the vegetables while another waited for Lucy to weigh a plastic bag filled with fresh eggs.

A row of outdoor cafes, each with its own coil of smoke, reminded

Amy and Jo that it was lunch time and Jo steered toward one that looked the busiest. A leggy dog lazed near the walkway. Each nipple of her tummy was swollen. Somewhere she had nursing pups. Her eyes raised, then unconcerned seemed to signal 'it's OK to pass.'

They seated themselves in white plastic chairs stamped with Modelo at a wooden table topped with fading oilcloth.

A young girl, perhaps nine years old, brought a sectioned container filled with finely chopped cabbage, onion, cucumber, and tomato. She also left two bowls of hot sauce, indicating that one was very hot. Hungry, each ordered two of something that looked like open-faced tacos but were called by some unknown name. They decided on orange sodas and were surprised when they were served in tall icy bottles with straws that were too short for the bottles. No ice, but the soda was cold enough.

An adult version of the little girl slapped several thin beef strips on a thick grate. They sizzled when she randomly tossed them from side to side. From a cloth-lined blue enamel pot, she chose four tortillas and warmed them on the coolest side of the cooking grate. Once the meat pieces finished sizzling, they were flipped onto a chopping board which resembled a sawed-off tree stump. Using a cleaver-like tool, the cook chopped and chopped until they were the texture of crumbled ground beef. Then scooping the mixture onto the tortillas, she drizzled a white creamy substance on top.

Jo piled the vegetables and the hottest ground red chili juice over her meat filled tortilla and bit into the nearest corner. "Yum, this really hits the spot. Good seasoning. Can't decide what she used though." By the time she was chewing the second bite, her eyes and nose were watering.

Amy, a little more conservative with the hot stuff, chose the milder chili mixture. "I can't believe you would torture yourself with such burning fire, Jo. I bet your taste buds are so paralyzed, they can't enjoy the full flavor."

"What's this full flavor stuff? The hot is part of the flavor. I love it... though I'll be looking through blurry eyes for a while." Jo grabbed three of the undersized napkins and dabbed her nose and the dark mascara dripping onto her cheeks. "I know...I look like a wreck."

It was a filling meal and fairly reasonable in price. They figured that the two of them lunched on just over three dollars, including the giant sodas.

Amy's turn to drive. They bypassed Los Mochis and were surprised to see stuffed trash bags lining the highway. A group of people, some of whom were children, lugged bags being filled with roadside throw-aways. "It seems like this area is having a cleanup campaign. From what we've seen so far, they have a long way to go. Right Jo?"

Near Guasave, farmland again predominated. The identification of many crops escaped them. However, they could identify the sugar cane, beans, tomatoes—staked, and resembling cemeteries of poles—and corn, in every stage of growth. Neither had realized that one field of corn, three inches tall, another field knee-high, and another in the tasseling stage could grow side by side at the same time. At home there was only one corn season.

It took a while to make out the miles of orange flying by. At a gas stop, the mystery was solved. They learned that fields of marigolds were harvested for use in a food supplement fed to chickens.

Several small planes swooped low, trailing clouds of dust, in an attempt to free plants from bugs and they wondered how safe crop dusting was these days.

Goat farms and cattle farms began to take the place of the green fields. For cattle long horns seemed to be the choice, mostly a Brahma type with the fleshy hump. Young children waved sticks herding a group of these humped cattle along a winding roadside trail. What a country of contrasts, they commented as they reached Culiacan, a city of over 300,000 inhabitants.

Throughout their trip Amy and Jo had seen every type of Pemex station. Some villages had two pump set-ups on graveled corners that were potholed and awkward to get to. Other stations were modern and very busy centers. Regardless, everywhere attendants pumped the gas and made change at the pumps. So far, they had not found a Pemex that accepted credit cards. All gas was owned and distributed by the government and without competition, all gas was priced the same, a price that computed to two dollars or more a gallon.

By now Jo and Amy could spot the green and white Pemex signs a mile away and were on the lookout for a modern and spacious Pemex for overnight parking. Not ten minutes south of Culiacan, they found one. Eight to ten truckers were already parked in the graveled lot behind the station. A man tinkering with the engine of his eighteen-wheeler smiled and tipped his hat to the women as they drove by. Another, carrying a bag of chips from the snack bar waved and turned a toothy grin their way. Jo chose a site away from the trucks hoping to avoid the idling diesel engines.

Neither felt hungry, but both managed to wash down tuna sandwiches with some of Alejandro's remaining orange juice. Amy pulled the curtains tight, more to shut out the well-lit Pemex station, than for privacy, while Jo made the two couches facing each other at the back of the rig, into beds for the night.

Sleep did not come for Joanna. She couldn't find a comfortable position either, and the Roadtrek rocked with her flailing.

"Are you ever going to get settled, Jo?" Amy reached across the aisle and patted her friend's shoulder. Their eyes met in the dimness of the night.

"Sorry, Amy. I guess I just can't cozy-in tonight."

"Something on your mind? Want to talk?"

"Am I foolish to be down here chasing the moon? While you and your family are here, I plan to make it a bit of a vacation, but after you leave, what then? I have the name of a Dixie A. Donavon and two of her paintings. That's all? It would take forever to search out every gallery in Mexico, even if I knew I could find Dixie that way. I'm beginning to think my dad is right; this is a selfish, wasteful, and impossible venture."

Amy thought for a moment and started. "You may never find Dixie. But that doesn't mean that your search is a waste. You can have a wonderful adventure, continue healing from the loss of your mother. Maybe learn more about yourself."

"Yeah, maybe I can grow another right arm, too. Maybe I can..." She fumed, then started again. "I know myself. I know my faults and strengths. I just don't know what to do about them. Just like the one that I'm attracted to needy guys, when I want somebody whole." Joanna silently wondered if she was the one who was not whole.

"None of us knows what the future holds, Jo. Our lives can change in a day...or even a minute. Even if you don't find your birth mom, you may meet someone who holds the key to your future. Fate may have something in store that you have never imagined. You do believe in fate?"

"Absolutely not. We have to deal with whatever is thrown our way and make the best of what we have." Joanna paused. "What a romantic you are. You think there's someone out there waving a key saying, 'Joanna, I'm waiting for you'?" Her voice grew sassy.

"There you go, making fun of me. I'm trying say, you don't know what you'll find here, but you need to be open to the idea if it's not your Dixie mom, you don't need to go home empty."

Neither spoke again. Joanna smoothed the sheet over her ear, which she always liked covered when she slept and tucked a piece under her chin. Tomorrow Amy would fall easily back into being wife and mother. Children and a loving husband. Would they ever be a part of her life? She was not sure that she deserved them. She coiled at an image of herself as a lonely old woman pouring over travel brochures. What had happened to the confident, satisfied woman that she had thought she was?

Despite the tension the night before, excitement began to build when north of Mazatlán, the highway eased closer to the coast and for a short time they were able to look out over the Pacific Ocean. They wondered if those who lived close to this massive, powerful sea felt the same thrill. Neither had been to Mazatlán, and it seemed a shame to whiz right by. It would be fun to explore. Perhaps another time.

South of Mazatlán disappointment hit. Near Escuinapa the road was torn up and all traffic stopped. Ahead billows of dust looked like a bombing area, rather than road destruction as part of new construction. Finally, Amy gave up on the wait and turned off the engine. Several enterprising Mexicans, both youthful and elderly, made their way selling wares to truckers, busloads of travelers and the numerous other vehicles nose to tail along the halted traffic. Home-cooked shredded candied coconut, chunks of peeled sugar cane, warm flatbreads, and tamales, were pushed toward the window where Amy sat. Children, no taller than a yardstick, touted small boxes of Chicklet gum.

Amy hated to say "no, gracious" to everyone so she bought some of the candied coconut, which both found chewy and flavorful.

The delay was long and hot before they were flagged on by a roadworker waving a red bandanna fastened to a stick. Where a sign read *desvacion*, they detoured to the left, eating the dirt and rocks kicked up by the truck ahead. Everything in the motorhome rattled and shook. Jo jumped up to retrieve cups that hit the floor when a cupboard door bounced open.

"J J Jo, I'm so-o-r-r-y. I'm do-o-ing the b-e-s-t I c-a-a-n."

Jo laughed at Amy's stutter. Then the right tire pitched into a hole and threw Jo into the cabinet. One hand on the emerging lump on her forehead and the other clutching the back of her vacant captain's chair, she attempted to keep her balance. Jo could see that not only was the detour rougher than a riverbed, but the other problem was the dust that prevented Amy from seeing every boulder, hole or patch of washboard which might have otherwise been avoided. Jo hung on for dear life and tried to keep everything tight while Amy gripped the wheel with iron claws, staring through a thick sea of red powder.

The women had no idea how many miles of torture they endured, but they knew it was an hour before they steered onto a smooth new highway. They were tempted to stop to kiss the recently laid concrete and would have, if there were ample time.

When Joanna suggested a change of drivers, Amy was agreeable. "You know, I don't think my hands will ever be the same again." She lifted them to reveal the paralysis she felt and shook her head.

Leaving the main highway they drove through Villa Hidalgo, a busy and productive village sustained by the nearby agriculture and freshwater shrimp farms. Passing San Blas, they made their way south noting roadside stands selling *pan platano* (banana bread) of every shape and size. They were surrounded by banana country.

A roadside parking lot sparked their curiosity and they slowed to read the signs inviting visitors to take the tropical jungle boat tour.

Pictures of crocodiles, water birds, snakes, and turtles hinted of the animals to be viewed on the tour.

"I bet that would be a neat boat trip, particularly for the kids."

"Can't keep those kids out of your thought, huh? We'll put this on the list."

Beyond Aticoma, the steep climb and sharp curves continued until the Roadtrek reached the summit. Behind them, banana plants splotched the hillsides, and curls of smoke rose from the bottom of the canyon. Ahead, they beheld waves splaying foam and fog, as they crashed into the rugged, rocky coast below.

Jo pulled as close to the side as possible so others could pass, and they both stepped out of the rig. It was so far down, they barely heard the crashing sea. It seemed that they could almost feel the spraying mist however, and breathed in the earth's fresh, moist breath.

Winding down the mountain, the women were jolted by a sharp pop, then a woooosh. "*Wha*t was that?" Jo felt the Roadtrek pull to the side and slowed before the next curve. "I think we hit something."

Flop, flop, flop. The sound repeated itself until they stopped at a rutted drive flanked by several cement block dwellings. Jo saw two men and a boy peer from the back of the house on her left. Weariness shadowed her face as she watched them follow one another toward the wounded vehicle. Amy was out and bending over the mangled back left tire before Jo attempted to unhitch her seat belt and open the driver's door.

"Jo, I hope we have a spare, this tire has seen her days," Amy called.

The older gent dressed in dusty gray pants and a long-sleeved shirt limped toward them dragging his right leg. His toothy grin was missing its upper front teeth. "*Señoritas...*" Then he said something in Spanish that neither could decipher.

Joanna tried her Spanish. "*Buenas tardes, tienen una problema... la llanta.*" And she pointed to the problem.

"Hello." She looked up at the second guy, into a handsome face belonging to a brawny Mexican. She guessed he was in his late twenties. "My uncle, Ramon and I know all about tires. Miguel..." He rapid-fired some Spanish to the young boy who stood silently at his side. Miguel wasted no time shooting off on the dusty road.

"It seems you not only know about tires, but you know English, as well." Jo spoke as Amy continued to examine their problem.

"I work in the apples in Washington...eight years."

The women introduced themselves and learned that Ramon's nephew was named Francisco. Amy, always Johnny-on-the spot, produced the keys and unlocked the spare-tire carrier on the back of the Roadtrek. Jo thought the jack was somewhere in one of the storage units under the running board. Oh, why didn't she pay more attention when Phil went over the motorhome after she bought it.

Soon the young boy came into view. Miguel's half-run looked more like a wobble when he headed toward the tire crew hugging a hefty box in front of him. Ramon expressed much excitement and yelled something else in Spanish to Miguel as he dropped the dilapidated box in front of the old uncle. Ramon, still dragging his leg insisted on doing much of the work as he lifted a heavy-duty, shiny, jack, the hydraulic kind that rolls under the vehicle from the box. Jo was astounded that this little cluster of homes could produce such a fine piece of equipment.

Miguel retreated to the house, but soon returned with his mother, Rosa, who was able to make it understood that they were invited to come to the house. Amy and Jo followed Rosa around the small house to the back where several family members sat talking, laughing and drinking a brown liquid they learned was called *Tamarindo,* a sweetened drink made from the brown pods of some tree. Each tried a sip and found it tasty, though like nothing they had tried before.

In no time they were trading bits of information. Each knew a few words of English and with Jo's and Amy's diligent practice they were able to tell about Amy's six-year-old Jonathon and four-year-old Andrea, where they were from and where they were going. As neighbors from other houses began arriving with bowls of food and bottles of various drinks, the irregular-gaited Ramon joined the gathering. "*Salud, y feliz viaje.* Wheeskey?" Ramon said, elevating the shapely bottle in his right hand. Turning to Jo and Amy, he removed the lid and offered the bottle. He laughed and turned to Francisco as he joined his uncle.

Francisco rescued the moment. "The tire is fixed. Before you go, my uncle wants to have a toast and to wish you good health and happy travels. Also, we have much food. Please stay to eat?"

Jo and Amy did their best to explain their refusal. They did accept a good swig of Ramon's whisky, but the warmth of the brew going down could not match the warmth of fellowship they had experienced.

CHAPTER 13

I t was the last leg of their trip and nearing 4:00 p.m., already later than the expected time of arrival. Hopefully, Amy's husband and the rest of the Ford clan were not too worried about their delay. They licked their lips and rolled their tongues around trying out the name of each village they passed. Las Varas, La Peñita, Rincon de Guayabitos, Lo De Marcos, San Francisco, Sayulita. They laughed at their own attempts to get the emphasis on the correct syllable.

Near Sayulita their progress slowed. The area was a beautiful tangle of jungle, a haven for pink and purple morning glories vining over trees and bushes. Traffic became heavier and the hilly and curvy stretch made it impossible to pass. A truck, three spaces ahead, lumbered with effort, shifted down and spewed black smoke into the jungle overhang. It bore a precarious pyramid of bottled soda, so heavy that climbing the hills and rounding the turns slowed to a turtle pace. On its tail was a hefty farm truck harboring at least twenty Mexicans leaning on the tall sideboards, heading home from a day in the fields. In front of the Roadtrek the silver SUV reminded Jo of the one that slammed into her mother and Steve those many months ago.

She buried the memory, or tried to. Loneliness tugged at her, pushing aside the thrill she wanted to appreciate. Staring, oblivious of her own mechanical actions she directed the Roadtrek around each turn, then the next and the next.

Her trance was interrupted when the canyon opened and the traffic split into two lanes and those vehicles behind her zoomed by. Joanna stomped the gas pedal and the rig jerked.

"Thank heavens you're out of your stupor, Jo."

Joanna felt like she had been caught with her hand in the collection plate. "Was I that bad? I promise this is the end of my mood."

Joanna had five minutes to do some self-talk before they made the turn toward Nuevo Vallarta. They found a roundabout and the Mayan Palace placard. It was a maze of roadways passing colorful hotels, resorts, and condos before they located a parking lot outside of the registration building. Whew, 5:45. They made it and hoped that Dan and the kids weren't in a frenzy."

The plan was to leave the Roadtrek in the lot. The Fords had invited Joanna to stay at the family complex—two separate apartments with sleeping space for at least twelve people. She would play tourist while the Fords were here and help out with the children so Amy and Dan could have some special time alone and with Dan's parents, if they wished. After that? She would begin her search in earnest.

The resort was a hive of activity. Taxis brought travelers with their piles of luggage, and skiffed others away, most probably to various celebrations where they would watch the hours, then minutes, dissolve into a new century.

On the grounds, motorized carriages shuttled off with one group, then another, intent on reaching some particular spot traveling along a network of carriage roads webbing throughout the resort.

Jo and Amy grabbed the soft-sided bags that had been packed the night before, locked the Roadtrek, and hopped into the next carriage indicating their desire to find the building which housed the Fords' condo.

"I wish I could get my bearings. I have no idea which way we are going." Amy tried to make conversation. "Look at all the beautiful foliage. It always amazes me to see potted plants I grow at home reaching heights of four to six feet in the tropics."

Jo smiled and nodded. Around the bend and over a hump Amy glimpsed the brilliant melon, beginning to flatten as it edged toward sundown. Around the next bend it had disappeared. She flashed a questioning look toward Jo.

"Yes, I saw it. Looks like we'll have to spend our evenings near the beach so you can get your sunset fix." Jo was irritated with herself and this melancholy tugging her. It was not typical. She was usually thrilled by the evening sky-color and here she was making fun of Amy.

Miniature lights twisting and twirling around every bush and tree began to gain Jo's attention, glistening as dusk neared. Hidden spotlights enlivened the purples and pinks blossoming in gardens nestled around a waterfall and the winding stream.

"This certainly is a beautiful and romantic place." Could there be a romantic feeling if one didn't have a companion, lover or whatever? Jo wondered.

Both women were thrown forward but managed to brace themselves when the carriage jolted to a stop in front of one of several four-storied buildings. The youthful driver jumped out and grabbed their bags from the back storage compartment. Jo had one foot on the roadway when the carriage lurched forward. Jumping free, she watched in horror as Amy and the carriage sped off the roadway, down a grassy hill toward a lilied pond.

Paralyzed, the boy-driver was slow to gain his bearings. Tossing the bags aside he galloped toward the runaway. Jump, Jo thought, but Amy was determined to save herself *and* the carriage and had already hurdled the bar and back of the driver's seat. One foot landed square on the front cushion and the other hit the floorboard as she found the wheel and pulled herself into the driver's seat.

A crowd began to gather and cheered both the running driver and the petite, curly headed woman as she gained control of the escaping vehicle. Fingers pointed, hands clapped, and two young voices shouted when the craft came to a stop. Jo could hear Amy's howling laughter as she tried to communicate with the young driver who finally reached her side. She vehemently slapped the seat beside her. And nodding, the driver became a rider. Grinning, Amy throttled up the rig, left a little turf in her wake and began to climb the grassy incline.

Jo watched as Amy caught sight of her jumping youngsters, arms flagging the air. Behind them a sandy-haired man gave a thumbs up. Easily evident was the tenderness and pride in the smile directed toward the heroine and the jumping children. Jo pressed the back of her hand against her nose hoping to discourage the tears clouding her sight and took a deep breath.

Jo toweled the steamy mirror and was shocked to detect darkness underlining her eyes. It was going to take a lot to bring out any glamour tonight. Through the open slates above the door, she heard Andy's and Jonathon's retelling of their heroic mother.

Dan's parents, Clarence and Marilyn Ford listened to each detail, sorry to have missed the whole venture.

Their voices faded as Jo slid the on-button to her hair dryer. She twisted the round brush lifting and curling her blonde blob into a dip over-the-left-eye and behind-the-right-ear style, then spritzed the bob with hair spray. An extra dab of makeup hid the sunken eye sockets. She had read that wearing eye shadow the color of one's outfit was out of style, but she dusted shimmering emerald on her eyelids anyway and used the waterproof mascara, just in case she became emotional when the gong of midnight arrived.

Slipping her leg into the silky trousers a shiver tingled through her. Fastening the hook of the waistband, she turned sideways to view her figure in the mirror. A few pounds thinner than she had been before her mother died, not a pinch of flab inched over the band of her pants or under the cups of her lacy bra.

She pulled the matching emerald blouse over her head and fixed the linked gold belt, loopy earrings and jangley bracelets in place. Her mother's little talk about self-esteem rattled in her head. "It's important to like yourself. Be proud. When you pass a mirror it's OK to give a little, *hey, not bad.*" Her mom wasn't talking about outer beauty, but the inner type that gives a definite glow. She looked resolutely at her reflection and said aloud, "Yeah, Joanna Johansen. Not bad!"

Amy interrupted the moment. "Jo, we're meeting the family in the lobby. Are you ready?"

"I'm on my way." Jo fluffed her hair once more, pushed her feet into gold sandals and joined her friends in the living room.

Dan rumpled Jonathon's hair. "Son, can you believe how lucky we are this evening, escorting these three beautiful young gals, dining and dancing?"

Jonathon returned his dad's wink and waited politely for the girls to go ahead. It was Andy, dressed in a youthful version of her mother's vivid blue jump suit, who spoke. "Dad, can I dance too?"

"You sure can."

The evening held promise, Joanna thought. The promise would far exceed her expectations.

Near the Ford's condo, fresh fruits and colorfully arranged Mexican dishes were meant to entice anyone's hunger. A Mariachi band added to the spirited celebration. A second buffet including beef, pork, and seafood, with all the fixings, was set up at the other end of the resort. There a Latin musical group was featured. The Ford party decided on the Mexican event. Perhaps they would explore the Latin Quarter later.

Jo was impressed when she saw Dan's younger brother interact with Andy and Jonathon. John was playful and ingenious. He would be a wonderful father if Sherry ever came around to the idea of parenting. How he ended up with such a self-centered woman Jo could never figure. He was such a sweetheart. Perhaps once her claws dug in, he couldn't get away.

Assembled in the lobby, everyone waited for Sherry. Marilyn and Clarence introduced another couple, the Angelinos and their son Tony who was joining them for the evening.

Jo learned that the Angelinos were long-time friends of the senior Fords. Both families owned businesses in the construction field. The Angelinos had been vacationing in Puerto Vallarta for years and decided to get something more permanent. That something was a rundown beach-side bungalow in Bucerias, the last village Amy and Joanna had passed before arriving at Nuevo.

Antoinette Angelino, with her talent and perseverance had spent much of the last year spear-heading the bungalow remodeling project, while Mario flew in and out of Mexico, not yet ready to turn over the masonry business to his two sons-in-law. Interestingly Tony was not involved in the business but was an entrepreneur in Bucerias.

Sherry interrupted the cheerful gab, swishing breathlessly passed her in-laws toward John. Clutched between her fingertips, a double loop of black crystal beads caught the light with their iridescence. "Johnnie, luv, hook these for me please, my nails aren't dry yet." She held the candy-apple red nails toward him as if they were dripping.

John gently gathered her sleek black mane to the side and lifted the choker-style beads around her neck until the clasp met.

Sherry jerked and shot a look at her husband. "Ouch, damn, you pinched me."

"Sorry Sherry, I'll try again." The jerk had pulled the necklace from his left hand, and it dangled precariously in his right.

Sherry's lower lip protruded; she tossed her head, rolled her eyes, and placed a careful hand on a cocked left hip, waiting impatiently. In her black, strapless mini, every curve was evident. Jo decided that her studded stilt sandals fit the vamp she was playing tonight.

The children's eyes widened, and Jo felt embarrassed for John...for the whole group, in fact.

Dan and Amy headed their children toward the door. "I bet you two are famished." Dan looked at his wife. "Your kids haven't eaten since noon and here it is their bedtime."

"Dad." Jonathon gave his dad a look that defied the bedtime comment.

The walkway toward the lively sounds of trumpets and various stringed instruments was well lit and Jo was able to focus more on Tony's friendly face. He lost no time joining her side once the group's progression began.

It took Joanna a few minutes to tune into Tony's speech rhythm and style. His clipped and quick tongue, punctuated with animated gestures fascinated her and led her to the conclusion that this was a sharp man who could run circles around most people.

Dark wavy hair looked like it could be unruly and received a periodic swipe from his broad hand. Genuine interest shown on his face as he listened to Jo's "short version" of why she was in Mexico.

He paused, turned, and gently gripped her shoulders. "Joanna Johansen, when do I get to hear the "long version"? Soon, I hope."

She gave him an amused smile. She liked the way his prominent eyebrows, usually straight, arched up in the center toward his furrowed brow when he was serious or intense. "You aren't teasing me or tossing me a line, are you?"

"Never."

Moments rolled over each other. She hadn't had an evening such as this in a very long time. An excellent dancer, Tony made it easy to follow his innovative steps with the various tempos. They enjoyed sampling bites of every dish in the Mexican buffet. Most, Jo found quite tasty.

Even Andy was smitten. The dashing Tony had her trilling, yelping, and stomping with the spirited music. Sherry tried her claws on him, but his rebuff was so gentlemanly, it was a while before she realized what had happened and turned on the pout, whining to John about the "crummy evening".

Jo took her turn dancing with each of the Ford men and then it was Mario Angelino's turn. Tony's father was passionate about dancing. None of this standing in one spot and moving to the beat. They scooted to every corner of the dance floor shooing people out of their way, dipping and swooping and gliding. With Mario's oppressive embrace and body sopped in perspiration, Joanna felt like a squashed bug by the time Tony rescued her.

"Dad, may I kidnap this maiden. I think she needs a break."

"Hey, we were just getting started. Did you see us? I wouldn't let your mom know. But she just might out-dance her."

Lightheaded from all the twirling and swooping, Jo was glad for the liberation. "Does your dad ever stop? Too bad he doesn't like to dance."

"Oh, he likes to dance, especially with light-footed beautiful young women." Tony's voice was playful.

"Not me?" Joanna gestured coyly, her hand against her chest.

"It's you all right. You aren't one of those 'she doesn't know how lovely she is' ones, are you?"

Tony caught her hand in his and led her toward the carefully arranged lounge chairs beside a meandering swimming pool. A group of teenagers splashed in the jeweled light, the boys playing keep-away from the squealing girls.

Settling in the cushioned recliner, Jo wondered if others noticed the glow that she felt. Normally her manner was not flirtatious. Tonight, was different. Tony's pearled grin added to his aura of harmony and warmth.

"You certainly are easy to be around." She traced a finger down his arm, finally gripping a hairy muscular forearm.

Tony heard the teasing lilt of her voice and the way she hung on the word 'easy'. He flicked the bracelets decorating her slender wrist. Their tinkle accompanied the buoyant tone of the evening. "Here I was looking forward to a boring, entertain-the-elders-evening. And you spoiled the whole thing."

"I suppose you're waiting for an apology. I expected to end up being the caregiver for Andy and Jonathon while everyone welcomed the new year. What time is it anyway?"

Tony pressed the magic button that lit his watch dial. "Oh, the night is young. Not yet 11:00." Tony linked his fingers with hers and felt the smoothness of skin well- moisturized with the sea mist. His voice softened. "Joanna Johansen, JoJo—I like that, has a rhythm to it. I need to tell you that I am entirely overwhelmed by your charm and beauty. I'm amazed no one has snatched you up. My luck runneth over." His eyebrows made that center arch and his head tipped, questioning.

Joanna wasn't sure what to do with the jumble of amusement and embarrassment churning in her gut. "Golly, Tony, you really know how to blow a gal away. Thank you." She blew him a kiss that he 'caught' then pressed it to his cheek.

Both laughed.

Sherry's clattery heels approached. "We wondered where you two were hiding." Either Sherry was trying her breathy Marilyn Monroe, or she was feeling the affects of the alcohol.

John emerged beside his wife. "Honey, I'm sure that Jo and Tony are enjoying a good visit. We don't need to intrude."

"John--nie, don't be such a stick in the mud. Come on guys, let's try the other party."

John began to protest, but Joanna cut in. "I'd like to hear the other group, besides a nice stroll would feel good. Amy and I have been sitting all day for the last week. How about you?" The sparkle in her eyes caught Tony's.

Tony gripped both of her hands and helped her to her feet. His cheek paused against hers and he couldn't resist saying, "You have a heavenly fragrance, JoJo."

She tried to make light of the tender moment. "I'm sure glad I cleaned up for tonight. I had no idea I would be meeting Prince Charming."

Joanna found Sherry's babble during the leisurely walk to the Latin Quarter less irritating than earlier. Perhaps she had been overly critical, and Sherry wasn't so bad. Or the handsome Tony, cozying her with a firm arm at her waist, was a distinct distraction.

John and Sherry were well matched on the dance floor. It wasn't long until most eyes were on the sensuous couple. Jo had no idea where John learned all these steps. Not in Loveland, Colorado, she was sure. Joanna saw little similarity between Dan's assertiveness and his brother's demeanor. In fact, her image of John had been as the shy backward member of the family. Maybe not. He did not seem self-conscious, not even about his wife's suggestive movements in her sensual dress. Jo was fascinated.

"Shall we give it a try? I'm no expert like Amy's brother-in-law, but I have a little natural rhythm and...some imagination." Tony's boyish expression stirred and confused her.

"So, I've noticed." Jo licked her lips, tossed her head and twirled into his arms. Their eyes locked as he lunged her into a deep dip before they found their feet and bodies instinctually gyrating to the Salsa rhythms. Feeling sexy on the dance floor was new to Joanna. At home she would have been completely mortified for anyone to see her dancing and eyeing her partner with such impetuosity. She savored the sensation of daring and power flowing through her veins. She believed it was the same with Tony. Energized by exhilaration, they stopped only to welcome the New Year when the band slowed and softened to the familiar Auld Lang Syne melody.

Holding Joanna gently, yet securely, Tony's hypnotic baritone sent tingles through a body melded as one with his. "May auld acquaintance be forgot and never brought to mind...We drink a cup o kindness yet and days of Auld Lang Syne." Why were tears stinging her eyes while the sweetest smile graced her lips? "What do you say, M' Lady? I'd say may this acquaintance ne'r be forgot."

I ran. I ran from that rosebud mouth and those squinty eyes searching mine. I dare not remember my little Cara. I ran from Ellie and her friendship. At first, I let her know where I was. No more.

High in the Rockies I found escape and excitement in the jolting clatter of cymbals, drums and whining strings, blasting rhythms that masked my pain. I was captured by fascination; Buddy and his guitar won me. I followed into a life of bottles, reefers, and experimentation.

When the snow flew, we were invincible on the slopes by day and by night we were a fog of melody and beat and thrill flaming our senses. We had it—this musical crew and its band of followers—our own wild, hippie world.

Buddy wanted more and the group split, four of us searching action and fame in California. We climbed aboard a new roller coaster of highs and lows. Buddy's knack for finding the best talent, his innovative writing and tenacious rehearsal schedule could not guarantee work. Even when the gigs came, the crowds were fickle, and survival became primary.

In the clutches of our men, three of us slaved in kitchens and eating rooms, supporting us all, never sure the dollars earned would stretch. Confident the big break would come, no one was willing to change direction. I don't remember who mentioned it first. The hashing and rehashing. Yet soon it was scheduled—A hit on a liquor store, just to tide us over. Gnawing feelings longed to end this reckless spiral. Yet powerlessness allowed only feeble pleading, the snare was so seizing.

Gripping the wheel for the get-away, I trembled that first time, then the second, but nothing like that last hit when crouching the counter, bravery kept the cashier from yielding to the demands for the contents of the register. To this day I hear the piercing crack, crack...crack, crack in my memory. Shoving Nicki, who had been on watch, Pike exploded through the doorway. Like frightened deer, she followed. My panic was nearing hysteria. Pike commanded. I obeyed and drove.

At our pad, robotic motion took over as I stashed a bag with money, clothes, and what food was in the fridge. At the last moment we stripped the bedclothes from the bed. It took no more than five minutes. Crammed in Pike's truck, we headed toward the border.

Fleeing the city I heard a siren here, over there. Eyes clamped closed, I waited for bullets to pierce my flesh. They didn't come. The world held me paralyzed.

Yet, Mexico and morning arrived, and I understood the voiceless command. *You have not escaped! Run and carry your wounded heart!*

CHAPTER 14

He was looking at her with that center arched eyebrow look which she found so appealing. Reaching across the table he caressed each hand in his own and thumbed the bracelet on her left wrist. "This is the bracelet you told me about last night, isn't it? The one your birthmother designed for Ellie."

She had done most of the talking, well into the early morning hours and had not revealed so much of her inner self to any man before, not even Paul. Tony had a way of drawing people out and listened as intently as a Daddy Robin, head cocked waiting for a worm to move in the ground beneath him.

Tony heard the uncertainty she felt and the fear of possible rejection, not only in her words, but also in their tone. His nature was to protect, to prevent her from hurt. Yet, meddling in her doubt would solve nothing. He would not presume to know the answers to her own questions. For now, he wanted to spend every possible moment with this women he found so enticing. He wanted to share his world with her.

Jo nodded. "Yes, it was Ellie's. I treasure it. It connects me to Ellie *and* Dixie. I wear it often."

"Even as a young girl, Dixie must have had an artistic eye. Her design is quite delicate Jo, yet it expresses a kind of earth-bound power in the mother of pearl, turquoise, onyx and coral. Don't you think?... I believe it was made for your wrist, M' Lady."

His words and smile moved her, and her own smile greeted the waitress who approached their table. "Are you *y tu amiga* ready to order, Tony?"

The restaurant, owned by Suzanna a transplanted American, featured breakfasts and lunches particularly familiar to Gringos, who filled all but one of the eight tables crowding the interior of the colorful and spotless eatery. Suzanna hired local women who looked festive in white peasant blouses and billowing multicolored skirts.

"Yolanda, this is Joanna. She's visiting the area for a while, staying at the Mayan Palace, but maybe we can get her to stay here in Bucerias when she gets tired of resort living."

"*Mucho gusto, Yolanda.*" Jo tried out her limited Spanish.

"*Egualmente.*" Yolanda answered.

They ordered omelets, which came with the usual refried beans, plus pancakes, a specialty of the restaurant. Yolanda left to fill cups with steaming coffee.

"Do you know everyone in Bucerias?"

"Well...I get around. Besides as a businessman, it pays to know your constituency. Don't you think?"

"I'm sure. You know... I'm afraid I monopolized the conversation last night, I mean this morning. Or you pried every little piece of my life from my lips." She eyed him with mischief. "Today it's your turn."

Tony's arms nearly winged a passing customer as he spread them, eagle-style. "My life's an open book. What do you want to know? Tell you what, after breakfast, how 'bout a stroll on the beach and you can pick my bones clean?"

"I'm up for it. If you can keep going on three hours of sleep, I'm determined to manage with four. I still can't believe you drove home after four and were back at the Mayan by eight, camping near my doorstep till I awoke."

"Can't miss a moment with the new girl in town, don't you know?"

Following the hearty breakfast, Joanna was relieved to stretch her legs as they plodded through the soft sand near the swishing waters. Shaking granules from her sandals for the third time, she gave up and removed them. Barefooted was the only way to walk the beach anyway. There was something mystical about marking the wet sand with each foot and toe print, only to watch it be washed away as a wave, propelled by unseen forces swirled over it and retreated to the sea. From time to time a shell that had been the home of one of nature's fascinating creatures tumbled in the fleeing foam and came to rest.

Jo approached a pile of quarter and dime sized rocks thrown from the sea and toed them in search of a few shells for her pocket. The first one she spotted was a glistening olive, so called because that was what the shape resembled, she supposed. It was larger than most and fit in the palm of her hand like some worry-rocks she had seen. The pointy and spiraled end was etched in the color of nutmeg. Replicated etchings covered the smooth shell surface as if daintily penned, yet in jagged peaks stretching its length and breadth. No one could create such perfection and exquisiteness, Jo decided.

To the left, another wonder of nature stopped her. Cradled in the pebbles was a nest of four shells. The larger, iridescent in pinks, purples, and greens, held a smaller one, nearly black. Then came a purplish one and nestling in it a bitsy pink, half the size of Joanna's smallest fingernail. With the rolling and pounding of the sea, how could such beauty arrange itself so randomly? Or was it random?

Tony had removed his sneakers, tied the strings together and slung them over his shoulder. He did not want to intrude on Jo's discoveries and the awe that shone in her face, so he waited to be invited back into her world.

"I suppose you stopped shelling long ago." She held her treasurers toward him.

Stepping to her side he marveled at her wonders. "Actually, unless I'm jogging, it is almost impossible for me *not* to stop to examine those beckoning treasures. However, I rarely pocket them anymore, but allow them to be returned to the sea."

Not without guilt, Jo slipped the pieces that would find their place on her dresser tonight into her pocket and reached out for Tony's hand. The couple detoured around a rock-pile and continued along the beach.

Jo had been unaware of the passing scenes as they walked. Then her eyes latched on to a building with a sloping floor upheld by weathered poles at least twelve feet long which dug themselves into the beach-sand. "Wow, it looks like those tables, chairs and customers might be dumped any minute with their food and margaritas."

"Oh, yeah, that's the Dugaral. And you're right, every year it seems to lean further and further toward the ocean. When the tide is high the waves surge around the poles. They must be buried pretty deep. Despite being like the leaning tower of Pisa it's still a good place to eat. We'll eat there sometime." Tony squeezed her hand and gave her a look-you-over glance. "Good seafood, but not as cheap as it used to be. Bucerias is becoming more and more touristy."

"If I'm going to pick your bones, you better start talking. And you might as well start at the beginning. Right?"

Joanna heard a sigh. "You probably noticed that my dad has an Italian accent. Even after all these years, it's not something easily left behind."

"So that means that he was born in Italy?"

"He lived there until he was twelve. His parents both died of some illness—Dad never knew what exactly—when he was ten and his sister was eight. They were farmed out from one uncle or aunt to the other. The whole family had always been quite poor, and no one really wanted them. Then luck struck when some neighbors had family visitors from the U.S. The Varas and their two younger kids took to my dad and his sister, Tonya. After a few months it was arranged that they would go to live with them in Colorado."

"That must have been a scary thing. I suppose they spoke no English."

"Right. To hear Dad tell it neither wanted to go live with the Vara family in that foreign land, but Dad was told that he was the man of the family now and should take care of his sister. He was to be strong and do nothing to disgrace the family. If they were sent back, surely they would be left to the streets."

"Apparently the Varas didn't adopt them, since your dad has the name Angelino."

"No, Dominick and Annie were their guardians. Anyway, even at twelve Dad was tough and strong and right away he began helping on the small farm that the Varas owned. Dominick worked on the side, laying brick and cinder block, and needed Dad's help. Dad also worked hard in the two-room country school to learn English, which was the key to doing well in the other subjects. Aunt Tonya was very shy, so, late into the night he would tutor her and make her practice speaking English. The first years were really hard. The Varas were good people, but they were strict, and Dad and Aunt Tonya ended up working twice as hard as their own children."

"Do you think your dad resented that?"

"No, it was just the way things were, besides Dad was taught to be respectful of his elders and I think as time went on, he was grateful to have a better life than he would have had with his poor relatives in Italy."

"Do the Varas still live in Colorado? Do you have contact with them?"

"Well, after Dad graduated from high school, he went to work with Dominick for three years. Then Dominick was injured on the job and never worked after that and seemed to go downhill. I guess he had some type of workman's compensation. Dad stayed with the Varas until Aunt Tonya got married. She was a year out of high school by then. And Dad moved out on his own and saved up enough money to start his own business. For several years he sent the Varas a check every month, but there were some hard feelings, so they didn't talk much. When Dominick died, Dad was twenty-eight. He had met Mom and they were engaged. After the funeral Annie returned Dad's last monthly check and said that his debt was paid. Whatever differences there were seemed to get patched up. We see Annie once and awhile. She lives near her son, Duane in Fort Collins and must be in her mid-eighties. She's right on target mentally, but frail physically."

"You must be proud of your dad, how he faced adversity. He's a real American success story don't you think?"

Tony chuckled. "Don't get me wrong. I love my father, but we're like oil and water when it comes to getting along. Imagine this scenario. "Mr. Italian slash American-success-story has daughter one to dote on and take care of—remember the admonishment to care for his sister, a female. Then daughter two, a spirited, Miss Independent that Dad could not help spoiling. Finally, three years later the long-awaited son who is destined to follow in his father's footsteps. NOT...Well actually I made attempts at every age to please my father and make him proud."

"I can envision the picture." Jo shook her head.

"Sports, good grades, student body president, college scholarship. Then I tried the business for two years. When I walked out, Dad brought in both my sister's husbands. We weren't speaking and it was meant to be a slap in the face. But I was relieved, particularly since they have worked out perfectly, which helped get me off the hook.

"Are things OK with you now?"

"It depends, on what you mean by OK. We talk and do things together, but there is an underlying tension that never goes away. My dad thinks I always go off halfcocked. He refuses to listen to my ideas. When I *was* in the business, I made several proposals; they were good ones, I'm not stupid, you know. He shot every one of them down and he did so with great vehemence."

Tony's voice held fury and frustration. "Three of my proposals were implemented later and he gave the credit to one of the associates. He acted like they were some fantastic innovations that he never heard before."

"I can't believe you're talking about the Mario I met last night. He didn't seem hard core. Are you sure he doesn't have memory lapses?"

Tony's laugh was full of sarcasm. "Are you kidding? He likes to make me squirm and cut me down. He thinks that's the way to build toughness. He grew up tough and by gosh, his son is going to do the same."

"What brought you to Bucerias? Was it a lark or a way to run away?"

"The folks bought a time share in Puerto Vallarta when I was in high school, and they usually let me bring a friend when we came during spring break. We had great times, mostly around the pools, parasailing, doing the usual tourist stuff. So, I got to know the area. By the time I was eighteen we were dancing all night at Christies, a disco and getting to know some of the Mexican Yuppies from PV. There are some, you know."

"I imagine. Then what?"

"When we wanted to get away from the hubbub of PV, we came

to Bucerias. It was two years ago that my folks bought the fixer-upper and began working on it. I was at loose ends at the time, having spent three years working in the computer market, traveling, and developing web sites for businesses. Of course, I'd also just been dumped."

"You dumped? That's hard to believe." The couple paused in their walk. Jo turned to face Tony. His eyes searched the ground.

"I suppose I was intrigued by her past. She had gone with one of the Bronco football players, not a starter, but a Bronco, nevertheless. I ended up being a diversion while they patched everything up. The big hurt was that I had to learn about it from someone else when she just...stopped being available. I suppose you've never been dumped." He looked up for her answer.

Joanna scrunched her face, thinking. "No, not really. The last relationship I had, we ended it pretty much by mutual agreement. We weren't going anywhere." Jo threaded her fingers through her hair. "Come to think of it, I haven't had too many serious relationships. Those that I had, were with men that were more helpless than whole. I'm trying to understand my attraction to that type. Perhaps I've turned over a new leaf, though." She looked sharply at Tony.

"Really?" His dark eyes that had intrigued her from the very first moment, softened and searched hers. "Sometimes you go on letting life happen and don't think about it much. And then something makes you want to slow down and try to figure things out. Like now. What's the real stuff?" Tony motioned to a palm log poking through the sand. "Want to sit?"

Joanna wondered where this conversation was going. They sat, knees touching, fingers entwined, neither looking at the other. "What do you mean by real stuff?"

"When you feel attraction, electricity, immediate connection, that love at first sight stuff. You know what I mean?"

"Well, yeah."

"Is that real? Can you really count on first impressions? Is that a good basis for building a relationship? Or should a couple spend months and months being friends, learning all you can about each other and let the love grow and flourish." Purposely he was being dramatic. "Is that the way it should be done?"

"You're talking about us." It was both a statement and a question.

"Yes. From the moment I saw you last night, it was like...fireworks, tingles, I can't keep my hands off of you. This woman is...wow. Now tell me you didn't have some of the same feelings." He shook a pointing finger toward her.

Jo coyly tried to keep things light. "Because I called you prince charming you think you are the love of my life?" She glanced his way. "Because I looked at you with come-hither eyes on the dance floor? Because I couldn't get enough of your kisses when we said Happy New Year or goodnight? I don't know if you know how to read a gal." There was a perfunctory pause. Her voice softened. "Yup, it's the same for me. Now what are we going to do about it? Is it real or some latent hormones out of control?" There she said it.

Tony leaned back laughing at the sky. "JoJo, wherever this goes, it ought to be fun. Can I kiss you right now?"

"If you can catch me." Leaving her sandals parked by the log, she raced toward the sea, where waves were gaining strength. She turned to face Tony who appeared ready to pounce, and scooped splashes of seawater dousing him pretty good. "Ha. You'll find out I'm pretty quick on my feet." Spinning, she took a few steps deeper, ducking Tony's pursuit and feeling smug, but only for a moment. Facing her was a lone maverick wave that began its curl over her head, before she could even think to dive beneath it. She was tossed and slammed to the ocean floor twice. Gulping sand and seawater the force pulled her upsidedown toward the sea. Then it was over. On all fours she struggled to stand as the wave retreated.

Tony was there to pull her to him, and they stood in knee deep foam as Jo coughed, spit and sputtered. He didn't want to laugh, but the whole scene had been rather comic. Later they could laugh, but now he soothed her and led her toward the beach.

They had moved two steps when Joanna howled. "No! No! No!"

Tony was baffled. "What is it? Are you OK?"

"My bracelet, my bracelet, it's gone." She held up a bare wrist, then dropped to her knees groping in the swirling waters.

Tony's shoulders slumped helplessly. He would help her look, but knew it was hopeless.

Waves continued their repetitious cycle. No giant mavericks again, but the sandy waters prevented seeing the beach floor and spotting the brightly colored bracelet. By this time, the salt she tasted no longer was from the sea, but the tears that spilled and spilled. An older woman jogging with her black lab stopped to inquire about the loss. Tony explained about the irreplaceable bracelet. She registered her concern and stood for several minutes observing Jo who continued to grope in the waters and periodically was slapped in the face with a forceful wave.

Tony waded toward Joanna, hoping to bring whatever— encouragement, comfort. He didn't know. Something bumped his foot. He reached down and retrieved it. The bracelet! His whoop most probably was heard a mile away.

Dazed, Jo was motionless, then jumped to her feet and continued jumping. "You found it, you found it." She was a sight—sopping with tangles of hair drooping across one eye and hiding her nose. The woman with the dog grinned widely.

When Joanna reached her, the woman spoke. There was a gentleness to her voice. "I am delighted that this experience has a happy ending. I prayed that God would help in the search." She tipped her head. "I think it helped."

Stunned, Jo was speechless, but continued to nod in the affirmative while the tears again flowed.

CHAPTER 15

Her feet tucked under her, Jo smoothed the T-shirt over her knees. She wished she could find another like it. Hand painted, it reached to her ankles and had been used as a cover-up for swimwear, a throw-on robe, to sleep in and for lounging. Freshly showered and with towel-dried hair, Joanna's telling painted mental pictures for Amy.

Her friend mused, "If Tony hadn't already captured your heart, you'd be indebted for life after he found your bracelet. Amazing."

"If he hadn't stepped to that certain spot...If the lady with dog hadn't sent up prayers...Oh I don't know about all these ifs. Anyway, I'm certainly grateful."

"And you still don't believe in fate, huh?"

Joanna's hand dismissed the question.

Amy walked to the wide window in the living room and opened the wooden slats to allow for more light. "I hadn't met Tony before. But he seems like a great man. Fun. Not afraid to speak his heart. I'm really glad you two hit it off. How old to you think he is anyway?"

"I haven't asked him. But if he graduated from college at twenty-two, spent two years in his father's business and three years with the computer business and he's been here, maybe two years...he might be twenty-nine, maybe thirty. Do you suppose he'll dump me if he knows I am 31?"

"I doubt it. By the way, what are your plans for tonight?"

"He's taking me someplace special in PV. He's picking me up at five. Say, Amy, I'm sorry to abandon you and the kids. I expected to

"

hang out with your little rascals so you and Dan could have some romantic time."

"No problem. This is good for you. It's your turn for some fun and romance. The kids had a great time today, mostly in the pool or on the beach. Besides Marilyn and Clarence are good with the kids and when they aren't playing bridge with the Angelinos, they are definitely available."

"Tony said that there's a New Year's party at his parent's house today and that your in-laws are invited. He wants me stop by with him, and see the house. No way, I'm still a mess from the bracelet incident."

"Does Tony live with his folks?"

"Yeah, he's the gardener, the pool cleaner, the handyman, the night watchman. I guess it helps since the Angelinos are in and out a lot and only spend three or so months at the cottage. He would like to have his own place, but for now the arrangement is good for both sides. What's going on for you guys tonight?"

"A little fiesta with some Folklorico dancers that I always enjoy. I'd better scout out my family and get them cleaned up. The kids need a little relaxing time before dinner. I may have trouble convincing them though."

The drive through PV was wild. Traffic was crazy and the New Year celebrations seemed to be continuing. Weaving the winding highway south of Puerto Vallarta, Tony made a sharp left, bouncing onto a dirt road that seemed like straight up through the jungle.

Tony's Jeep lunged over another hump along the steep climb. "How do people get to this place if they don't have a Jeep?"

"You think this is bad? This is nothing like many roads in Mexico. This is such a popular place people would crawl to get here."

"Ohhh! Look." A ring-tailed creature, not unlike a raccoon, only stretched out an extra foot in length sprouting a pointy snout, scurried ahead. "*What* is that?"

"A coatimundi. We see them every once and a while. Some people even capture them for pets, but they can be a little vicious."

"Probably about like the baby raccoon we caught when I was growing up. Say, how far up this mountain do we have to climb, anyway?"

"Your twenty questions are almost up." His sparkling eyes again. She sighed and felt a shiver that ended its voyage at the top of her head. "Thar she is."

It was the thatched cottage in her childhood Hansel and Gretel book. Well almost, a little more rustic. Flagstone paths curved to the main door and around the side toward a cozy patio, also protected by a thatched roof, where waiting waiters in black pants and starched white shirts stood. Miniature lights twinkled everywhere in the approaching dusk.

Tony escorted Jo toward the patio, which appeared to be fully occupied with customers inclined in their private conversations. Tony said something in Spanish to the waiter who led them to a lone table in the front corner. It was raised a few feet and the surrounding rails gave the feeling that they were in their own private gazebo. Seated, her 'ahs and oohs' displayed her wonder. From their perch high on the mountainside, the ocean seemed to stretch forever. Then it met a changing sky, setting the stage for the sinking of the dazzling sun, still too bright to look at with the naked eye, but promising a spectacular finale as she eased into the sea.

Tony pointed to his right. "It looks a little misty at the edge of the bay, but over there beyond the strip of hotels is Bucerias. It's just before the land juts into the sea." Directing her eyes across the horizon, he continued. "Those peaks in the distance are Marietas Islands. That's where most of the SCUBA diving takes place. And that mountainous ridge to our left is the south bank of *Bahia de Banderas*. This whole area is called the Bay of Flags. Today is a good day to see it since it's not too cloudy or humid."

As the evening progressed, it seemed to Jo that she and Tony must have known each other more than twenty-four hours. They had packed so much into that timespan, yet there continued to be new topics to explore. Both admitted their ages. Jo learned that Tony had turned thirty the day before Christmas, which she thought must have been a bummer, but Tony insisted that he liked having a Christmas time birthday.

Jo tried her first bowl of *mariscos sopa,* a wonderful thick broth hiding tasty chunks of shrimp, lobster, octopus, scallops, and white fish. "I don't know if I can eat the main course, I am so full." However, when the stuffed red snapper and crisply prepared vegetables arrived, it was so delicious she took her time and devoured every bite.

Watching the return voyage of the Matterhorn, a tourist Viking ship, as its shadow slid across the glistening ocean, Jo and Tony made imaginary stories about its patrons, unseen behind lit globes reaching their tentacles into the darkness.

He sounded like an announcer for the super bowl doing a play by play. "That couple looks like honeymooners. He's massaging her neck. She likes it. Oops, his hands are wandering to other places. I wonder what's next. Right in front of everyone who's moon watching on the deck."

"Tony, I think you're a voyeur." Joanna started her own lingo. *"I've* been noticing that elderly couple on the benches in front. They must be over seventy-five and still holding hands and snuggling together." She propped an elbow on the table and leaned her chin into her palm. "Do you think that people can stay in love that long?"

"Oh maybe, if they find someone as fascinating, stunning, self-reliant and crazy as you. It might be possible."

"Stunning? Fascinating? Crazy, maybe. I think you are reeling in your line." And he's pulling me in—hook, line and sinker, Joanna thought.

Tony stood, then leaned to nuzzle a kiss in her hair. "Joanna, I love the little bit of lavender in your fragrance. Umm. Are you ready to leave this view and this cozy place?"

"If we have too...As long as you're coming, too." She turned mischievous eyes toward his. The usual sparkle and flicker had been replaced with tenderness. "Thank you for bringing me to this awesome place. Everything has been perfect," she said.

Both seemed introspective on the drive back to the Mayan and there was little talk. When Tony turned to the right instead of circling the roundabout leading to the hotel, Jo raised an eyebrow to herself. Either Tony was getting them lost or he had something else in mind. For sure, as he changed directions numerous times, she was lost. At the end of a cul-de-sac yet to be developed, Tony cut the engine and hopped out. "Want to join me?" It was another romantic setting. The moon, though not quite full, threw its reflection across the rippling ocean and relieved the darkness. Gentle waves, unseen, could be heard playfully making their own music.

The two strolled over a hill onto the beach. Shoes tossed aside, they sat together, toes digging into the soft sand. Intensely aware of the deep breathing of the other, neither moved.

Tony's arm drew her near to him. She turned her lips to his and felt those tingles again. He smelled and tasted of spice, adding enticement to the fiery passion burning in the kisses she returned. When Tony's hands wandered, her eyes flashed amusement. She nibbled at his nose. "You got that idea from the honeymooners, right?"

"You think I don't have any ideas of my own?" Tony lay back on the sand with Jo snuggled to his side, cradled in his muscled arm.

She slid an exploring hand under his knit shirt over a taut abdomen. She felt a moist steaminess. "I'm sure you have many ideas of your own." She couldn't stop grinning.

CHAPTER 16

At precisely 10:30 a.m., the phone rang. It would not stop. Dragging herself from the bed, Jo found the noisy beast. " Aaa...Ford residence. This is a...Joanna." She had trouble leaving the web of tangled dreams that had taken over her morning sleep.

"It's me. Did you have sweet dreams?"

"You said you'd let me sleep until at least 10:00."

"Well, Hon, it's well past that. I've been at work for an hour and a half."

They had agreed that Tony needed to keep his shop open today. He had been closed over the Christmas and New Year holidays. No doubt both Gringos and locals would be lined up to get on-line. He had expanded his cyber cafe to include three computer lines. Many of the locals were able to call relatives in the states for a few pesos with his system. Snowbirds from the states used the cyber cafe to exchange e-mails with friends and family. A good many U.S. and Canadian visitors did their on-line trading in the stock market.

He shared the office with a local realtor, which meant that despite folding screens dividing the cramped area, too often the atmosphere was zoo-like. The business was a one-man operation, but Tony was trying to change that. A well-trained person needed to be there to help the computer novices when they got into a pickle and answer the numerous questions that inevitably came up.

A young Mexican was in training to handle the business. Jesus had been tramping the beaches, selling carved ironwood pieces when Tony found him. He lived with his mother and three younger siblings and had been helping support his family from the time he was six. Jesus began as a child selling *Chicklet Gum*, then graduated to miniature carvings. Commonly, a couple of children roamed through restaurants unrolling a length of fabric to display *una familia* of turtles, dolphins, dogs, cats. The animal groupings were carved from black, green, blue, or white stones and always included a family of four or more, from baby to adult.

In his younger years, Jesus hurried to hit the beaches after school. When he finished his eighth year of school, he quit to take up beach-vending full-time. Because of his persuasive salesmanship each member of Tony's family received sizable ironwood carvings last Christmas. It was time for this bright young man, now eighteen, to take a new life path.

Jesus learned quickly. His English was improving and soon he could take over more responsibilities in the business. Tony hoped to open another office as well. The need for more on-line services was growing up and down the coast. Jesus and his family had gone to visit relatives in a distant mountain village for New Year's and the return bus would not arrive until noon, so Tony was manning the shop alone.

"How's business, today? As wild as you thought it would be?" Joanna was now fully awake.

"They are lined up out the door. I'm trying to limit each person to half an hour. Otherwise, most won't be able to get online. Jo, I know we agreed not to see each other today, that you wanted to spend time with the Fords, but why can't we at least do dinner tonight? My treat, bring Amy and her family. The kids will probably get a kick out of the leaning Dugaral. Besides, I'm itchin' to see you."

"You can't possibly afford all of us on a struggling businessman's salary. But maybe we could work out something. I'll have to talk to Amy and Dan."

"Great. Well, I'll get back to my patrons. The woman in the corner is motioning in frustration. Call me back as soon as you can. OK?" He had given her his cell so she could call without having to use the phones at the resort.

Jo pulled on a T-shirt and shorts, scrunched a little mousse in her hair and embarked on her search for Amy, Dan, and the kids. Stretched out by the pool Dan flagged her down. "Hey Jo, it's good to see you among the waking. Decided to relax, myself. The kids nearly wore me out yesterday."

"Where are those angels anyway?"

"See that little open-air building with painted flowers on the wall? That's the craft place and today it's decorating pottery or something."

"That ought to be fun. By the way Tony has invited us to join him at a little restaurant in Bucerias this evening. Are you up for it?"

"Sounds good to me. See what Amy says."

A good dozen or so multi-aged tourists engrossed in creating their own designs were seated at round tables. Jo found Amy, her mother-in-law Marilyn, Jonathon, and Andy at the back table. They dipped brushes into colored pots, concentrating on their own pieces. Andy saw Joanna first and waved a dripping yellow brush at her. "Come on over, Jo. Look. See what I'm making."

She was dabbing a cheerful sun on her brick-red pottery piece, a saucer-sized plate that could be hung on the wall or propped in a plate holder. When finished, it would have a cloud and a blob, not unlike a dolphin flipping above a wavy sea. Jo was excited about trying her own pottery and picked a fat squatty vase from the choosing table and sat to admire each creation in progress at Amy's table.

A quick call to Tony. Yes, they would join him at the Dugarel around six. All were looking forward to it. But she was going to have to hurry to finish the vase she decided to paint and couldn't talk long.

Joanna chose earthy tones in various shades of cream, beige and brown. She would accent her design in shiny black, similar to a piece she had admired in the resort lobby. Making a light pencil sketch, her design took shape and when she began to fill the spaces with the muted shades, Jonathon called attention to her work. "Grandma Marilyn, Mom, look at Jo's design. Doesn't it look professional?"

Jo leaned sideways to reach him and gave him a hug. "Thanks for the compliment." She was tickled by his "professional."

"Mom says your first mom is a painter too." Amy grimaced at her son, wishing he had not brought up the subject of Jo's birthmother. Perhaps it was something she didn't want to think about right now.

"I guess so. I have two of her paintings. I'll show them to you sometime." Joanna explained to Marilyn about the paintings. "I'm hoping that they will help find Dixie. Particularly the church. Perhaps someone will know where that church is."

Marilyn brightened. "My friend's hobby is churches, and she must have three hundred photos of churches, mostly from Europe, but I think she has a bunch from Mexico, too. Maybe I can take a snapshot of the painting and when I get home, see if she has an idea where the church is."

"That would be great, Marilyn. I can use all the help I can get."

Andy joined the questioning. "What does she look like? Is her hair like yours?"

"I really don't know, Andy. I saw a picture of her when she was young. But people change as they get older. She has dark eyes and hair...is about all I know."

"Then how will you know it's her if you see her?" Little miss inquisitive.

Jo shook her head. "I don't know that either. I'm hoping that someone at some art gallery will know her and tell me where she lives."

It seemed to satisfy Andy's puzzlement. "I hope so too."

Marilyn changed the subject. "Have you been to the Angelino's place, Joanna?"

"Not yet. I understand that Antionette has done a lovely job refurbishing it. Do you like it?"

"Oh yes. You'll see the difference when you see the before pictures. I'm not sure I would have seen the promise in the place. It is lovely. However, its character was maintained, which I think is important."

Jonathon and Andy each chose a "family" at the tilting Dugaral when two young boys, surely no older than Jonathon spread their wares across the table. Dan let them pick out a family to take home. Andy liked the black seals and Jonathon the green iguanas.

Another remarkable sunset tinted the airy clouds with brilliant cerise. Intrigued by the incoming tide swishing below the stilted and leaning restaurant, Andy and Jonathon peered over the rails. Jonathon was the first one to notice the extraordinary display making its way toward them. All were amazed and enchanted by manta rays doing their best performance taking flight from the rocking sea as they worked their way north.

"Look at that one. Ooeee, he's re-e-ealy sailing. And there's another one." Andy's squeals heightened the excitement and when the food arrived it was fortunate that the manta rays had moved on.

Toward the end of the evening, Andy wound up on Tony's lap giving blow-by-blow accounts of her last two days. Tony listened carefully, then spoke. "Andy, Jonathon, how would you two like to go on a jungle tour in a boat?"

"Can we, can we, Mom, Dad?" Jonathon's eyes lit up. "What do they have there?"

"It's pretty neat. Jungle birds, crocodiles. Only thing it's a pretty good ride to get there, maybe an hour and a half."

"Can we go in your Jeep?"

Tony knew that kids were intrigued by his Jeep. "What do you think Joanna? Can we put up with these youngsters tomorrow?"

"Amy and I passed a place on the way, not too far from San Blas. Is that the place?" Tony nodded in agreement. "If you can get away from work, let's go."

It was decided. Amy and Dan could have a free day to explore on their own. They wanted to drive north to Saulita and watch the surfers there. They would take the Roadtrek. Dan wanted to see how it handled. Tony volunteered to pack a lunch and everyone was instructed to bring swimsuits and towels.

CHAPTER 17

It was nearing 10:00 when she and the Fords returned to the Mayan Palace, not too late to call her father and assure him of her safe arrival. At home in Colorado, she didn't speak to her dad for weeks and often months at a time. She couldn't remember calling to wish him happy New Year's before. But this was different, she had much to tell, and she couldn't release the thought that by coming to Mexico, she had abandoned her father. He had not needed her before, but *if* he ever did, she was no more than twenty minutes away, ever.

The phone was ringing. The same tightness she always felt at this end of her father's line crept into her throat. *Come on Dad, answer the phone. You never go to bed before all the news and sports are over and Cindy always goes to bed early.*

"Hel-lo. Hel-lo." Cindy's hello stretched like taffy and her voice sounded like the spooky goblins on the ancient record Jo and her three friends listened to over and over in the Johansen basement those years ago.

She sounded weird, drunk, or dazed, Joanna thought. "Cindy, this is Joanna. May I speak with my dad." Jo was in no mood to try to make conversation with her father's wife.

"Where are you?" More shaky goblin groans.

"I'm still in Mexico, Cindy. I wanted to wish you all a happy New Year." She tried again. "Is Dad there?"

There were muffled sounds, then a wail. "Oh......my water, my water..., my robe... it's soaked." Jo pictured her sprawled in bed half propped by billowy pillows, hair dangling over one eye, balancing the phone in one hand, waving an empty water glass with the other. "Clay, damn him he's so...slow. He went to the store...I need medicine."

"I'm sorry you're not feeling well, Cindy. Maybe I can call back later."

Silence. Jo waited for a response, trying to decide whether to hang up without one. Then she heard the click of another phone. "This is Clay Johansen. Can I help you?"

"Dad, it's Jo. It's...it's...good to hear your voice. You've been on a medicine run, I hear. Is Cindy having one of her migraines?"

"Yeah, something like that. Give me half an hour. Then can you call me back?"

The half an hour seemed like a long one. Joanna thought about her dad, dealing with Cindy's health issues. He had never been one to coddle anyone. In fact, when Jo or her mom had the flu, a cut or any type of injury, Clay was less than sympathetic and his attitude was 'good God, let's get on with life, no one is dying here'. He certainly waited on Cindy hand and foot. What did she have that sucked him in so solidly? It was beyond her. Yet Joanna usually walked around on eggshells in Cindy's presence, as well.

Jo knew that things had always been less than hunky-dory. Several years ago, she stopped by to see her dad without being invited and found trash bags of his clothes on the front porch. It looked like she was throwing him out. Awkwardly, Clay met her at the door and said that it was not a good time to come in. Jo promptly left and never again visited uninvited. And the invitations since that time, she could count on one hand.

Her father answered promptly when the thirty minutes were over. Joanna knew that her father would never understand this search for Dixie, but he did not press it and seemed genuinely happy to talk with her and interested in the trip with Amy and the events that had occurred since their arrival at Nuevo Vallarta. Tony's name was sprinkled generously into the conversation, but he either ignored or did not pick up on the idea of a budding romance, and asked no questions nor made any comments. He wished her well on the jungle adventure with Amy's children, said work was fine, Christmas had been a zoo, but they had gotten through it.

There was a weariness in his voice that disturbed her. Like he was trudging through quicksand, wearing lead boots. She had been as upbeat as possible, but her mood had no impact on her father. *Shake it off Joanna. He made his own choices. You have your own life and must not allow his to dampen yours. Better get some rest and be up for the trip tomorrow. January 3*

What a day! Joanna wrote in her journal. *Tony drove the kids and me to the jungle tour near San Blas. Lucky we were one of the first. When we returned, the parking lot was getting full. Rode in a flat bottom panga. Boat motor a little loud and fumes strong when putzing slowly. Guide spoke little English, but he did a good job pointing out high points. About 2 1/2 hours till returned to boat dock. Kids thrilled with every sight.*

Neat area. Parts overgrown. Cut roots and vines made a jutting canopy as we wound through a tunnel of mangroves, its maze of trees sending roots from tall branches into the water. If we stood, we would scrape our heads. Once out of the tunnel we saw slender statuesque white egrets, multitudes of turtles from 6" to perhaps 18" across—always heads up searching out the sunrays. When we came too close, we heard plop, plop, plop as they escaped into the flowing spring. A huge termite mound wrapped around a tree trunk.

Many birds hiding, camouflaged in the trees—gray bird, gray tree; green tree, green bird. Crocodiles basking proudly. All shades of green lush plants. Then again in a tangled mass of roots and wandering ropy branches that curled into knots and statues looking like contemporary art. The ferns! Wow! 6 feet or more in height, unfolding from their coil, beautiful, healthy—accented with spires of wide heavy grasses jutting maybe 10 feet skyward. Iguanas glaring as we pass. Ended at the mouth of the mountain spring. Swam with what looked like catfish in the clear fresh pond formed by the gushing spring as it left the mountain. Jonathon cautious at first. Interesting. Andy is the brave one, paddled everywhere, trying to catch the fish.

Tony's lunch hit the spot. He really outdid himself. (Should I hold tight to this one?) Chunks of cheese, he says, Tipo Chihuahau (a nearly white cheese similar to Jack) fresh pineapple slices, bananas, mangos, pieces of those boat-shaped rolls (bolillos) slices of avocado, cucumber and jicama squirted with fresh lime, crisp tortilla chips sold here in Mexico (4" round stacked 15 - 20 in a package) Everything, yum!! Tony brought peanut butter and jam sandwiches—just in case for the kids. Sandwiches went wanting. Kids devoured everything. Good eaters. Good kids. Wonder if mine will be as good. Will I ever have any?

Drove on north to San Blas before heading back. Found the Mercado Centro. Bought veggies, fruits and two long slender Sierra—fish with yellow spots and a two forked tail. Fascinating watching the fish-lady fillet the fish with those machete-type knives. She included the bones, head attached. He says he is cooking for us tomorrow. (What kind of man is this that I'm hanging out with?) Looking forward to seeing the house his parents refurbished.

Tony was thoughtful about loaning Jo the Jeep so she and Amy could drive to PV. He explained that steering the Roadtrek through the narrow, cobbled streets and parking it would be tricky. Dan and the kids had hooked up with a boat and its captain and hoped to do some whale watching.

Crossing the *Rio Cuale*, they maneuvered a couple more blocks and made a left turn onto one of the narrow streets where a single parking spot lay vacant. "It looks pretty tight Jo, but I know you can make it." Amy continued to be a careful navigator.

Once parked, they felt like two giggling schoolgirls bravely exploring unknown territory. They walked through the flea market where cubby-hole after cubby-hole sported t-shirts, blankets, shoes, multicolored pottery or wooden carvings, and busy shopkeepers shined piece after piece of silver designed for every part of the body.

"Señoritas, you like? Almost free today." Grinning, Jo mocked the man who had spread tablecloths before them, hoping to make a sale. They both preferred the individual shops and pouring over the work of talented artisans and quickly found the exit.

A tiled walkway umbrellaed by what Jo called giant rubber plant trees wound its way along the *Rio*. Up-stream some Mexicans continued to wash their laundry in the lazy river, but here its banks had been transformed into an inviting paradise bedecked with exclusive open-air shops.

"Joanna, look at that blue two-piece." A dusky blue ankle length outfit caught Amy's eye. They spent the next half an hour examining one outfit then another. Each article was a one-of-a-kind original. Though subtle, the Mexican touch was unmistakable and designed for simple elegance. They learned that the up-and-coming designer lived in Puerto Vallarta and each year her creations were becoming more expensive.

Neither, planned to make any purchases, this was just a gal's out-on-the-town day. However, Amy could not resist an ankle length slim shift in a creamy soft yellow, trimmed in corresponding polished embroidery at the neckline, the hem, and on each side of the generous slit. She also bought a sand-colored print bearing muted swirls of peach giving the illusion of pearled shells. This sleeveless two-piece sported an unusually wide and deeply squared neckline then draped to the fingertips over a soft flowing skirt. Ironically Jo walked out with the dusky blue that Amy originally spotted.

Both decided that they had blown their wad and needed to keep their hands out of their purses and continued their out-on-the-town day, chatting and perusing.

"You know, it would be fun to have a room at home completely done in Mexican decor. Furniture, pottery, wall hangings, tile. Hum." Joanna examined a handsome platter at the tile shop and thought of her house sitting vacant except for the college girl who was house-sitting. Home seemed so far away.

"Sure, if one had the money *and* the room." Amy's eyes raised to detect her friend's reaction.

"I suppose you think I have the money *and* that big old house sitting nearly alone."

"You've never had to share with anyone, being an only child, and now you are pretty free to do what you want and *maybe* you'll get around to looking for your lost mother." Was that resentment Jo heard in Amy's voice? It was not like her.

Joanna responded with added sarcasm. "Dixie's not lost. I'm sure she knows where she is." Maybe I'm the one who's lost, she thought and put the platter down, not too gently. "You don't have it so bad. Your folks are still alive. Dan is a wonderful husband and father, and his folks are fine grandparents. You have great children. I'd give anything to have my mom back. You have no idea what it's like to be alone." Jo glared at Amy then looked the other way.

The festive mood was broken. Neither spoke as they squeezed by other shoppers browsing through *Mundo de Azulejos,* (world of tiles) the tile and pottery factory she had been eager to visit, the place where her mother had purchased the tile that decorated the condo she still owned.

On the second and third floors, workers sat painting each stroke on tiles, sinks, signs reading *'Mi Casa Es Su Casa'*, pots of every size and shape, and various pieces of dishware. Others fired them in hot ovens. She suddenly felt claustrophobic and couldn't stay there one more minute. She didn't like this roller coaster of moods.

They walked on to *Mundo de Cristal* and watched men in casual concentration working the lengthy steel poles, dipping them in the fiery furnace, pulling out taffy-like strands of glowing molten silicon, slapping and rolling them on steel tables, swinging the poles, then blowing and blowing until a bowl, tumbler or vase emerged. The fascination in the process did not lift Joanna's mood.

At lunch they ordered Piña Coladas and sat sipping, avoiding each other's eyes until Amy broke the silence. "Jo, I was really out of line earlier. I don't know why I let some resentment creep into our relationship. You know how much I love you and want your happiness." There was a pause. "I didn't think I had a jealous bone in my body, but..."

Joanna did not blink away the tears. Unashamed she let them spill. "I've always thought of myself as tough and in full control. Now every time I turn around, I'm on this great high or fighting tears. I don't even know what the tears are for anymore. What is wrong with me?" She leaned her elbows on the table and cradled her jaw while trickles found their way to puddle on the shiny oilcloth.

Amy did not know what to say to console her. "These last months have been awful for you. I can't even imagine...losing your mom and Steve, sorting through your mom's whole life. Breaking with Paul, moving into your parent's old home, finding out about Dixie, Ellie's death, meeting Darlene, coming to Mexico. All bottled together with the contrast of this new relationship with Tony. Golly neds, come to think of it...it's enough to drive anyone wacky..." Amy gave her friend a lopsided smile. "It will all pass."

Jo waved a hand to the air. "No, you're right, I'm probably going bonkers and hopefully it's temporary."

"Mommie, Mommie, we saw em, we saw em." It was Andy loping toward Amy and Joanna as they stepped from the motorized cart with their purchases.

"I get to tell. Andy, you promised this time I could tell." Jonathon was a few steps behind his sister looking disappointed. Dan pried himself from the sun-chair and stood with a noble stance grinning but made no attempt to quash the squabble.

"Let me guess, you saw some iguanas, right?" Amy was good at diffusing trouble.

Both children shook their heads furiously in a no.

"Maybe crocodiles?"

Disgustedly Jonathon again shook his head. "*Mom,* that was yesterday on the jungle tour. Crocodiles and iguanas aren't out in the ocean."

"OK, you can tell her." Andy's eyes sparked like fireflies, and she waited.

All sat on the grassy mound and heard of the whale watching trip. Yes, they had seen two pairs of humpback whales sounding and spouting. One had come close enough to see its eye as it breached the water then made its dive, its tail rolling into the easy foam. Jo left the family in their exuberance as details were retold. How could Amy have the least bit of envy? To Jo, she had it all, family unity, roots, and stability.

Joanna took the wrong turn only once searching the network of roads leading to the Angelino's remodeled beachside home. She knew she had arrived when she saw the gate, wide enough for any sized car. Carved and grooved it held a shine that must have taken a dozen coats to produce. A matching people-sized door to the left was ajar and Jo peered inside. A tiled driveway held a bug of a car, in red. There was space enough to park the Jeep, but Jo left it out front. This part was one of the few sections of Bucerias that was neither cobblestone nor dusty dirt.

In the courtyard, grew the creeping, wide-bladed grass of this part of the country. Flowerbeds of color flanked the curved walkway toward the entrance. On the right hibiscus and roses intermingled while at the opposite side variations of green and yellow plants provided contrasting textures of spikes, creeping groundcover, squatty bunches, and palm-like branches. Painted walls rose twelve feet on either side and gave the courtyard privacy.

"Yoo Hoo! I'm here." She stood at the wide entrance, tiled in glistening blue with white speckles and peered through the open doorway.

"Hey, hey, it's JoJo." Tony approached her, drying his hands on a hand towel, then tossed it over one shoulder. "Look at you. Do I detect a shopping spree today?"

She wore the new purchase. Like Amy's cream outfit, the skirt fell softly toward the floor and the slit approached her thigh on the left front. The separate top was seamed at the left shoulder then dipped below the right armpit leaving her shoulder bare. Shiny embroidery embellished the hems, diagonal neckline and slit. The top barely reached her waist, so that any movement revealed the skin of Jo's lean body. She felt feminine, yet sexy. For jewelry she wore only the ring of Dixie's grandmother, the nearly lost bracelet and jingly silver earrings.

Her playful mood had returned, and she gave him a come-hither smile. He pulled her to him. He smelled of smoke and shaving cream. She felt the warmth of his kiss and the low cry of a kitten escaped her. Pulling away, he twirled her around, patted her firm bottom, saying, "Later. Come on in. Mom and Dad are on the verandah."

The heels of the silver sandals she had spotted just before the shopping trip ended, clicked on the red brick tiles, laid throughout the house. From the hall she entered a roomy kitchen that looked out over the ocean. White tiled counters trimmed in blue and yellow held wooden bowls, spoons, and boards ready for use. Yellow walls reminded her of a sunny morning. Antoinette had chosen brick red, gold and brown to decorate the adjoining sitting room. Joanna admired the Indigenous flavor of the fabrics on the couches and in the wall hangings.

Stepping down onto the verandah, Tony cupped a hand at the back of her waist directing her toward the vast wooden table filling a good portion of the outdoor room. Two of the leather barrel chairs were occupied by Antoinette and Mario, who sipped drinks from squatty handblown glasses. "Dad, mom, you remember Joanna?"

Mario rose and grabbed Jo in a bear hug. "Of course, my dancing partner." Jo could not help but remember the sweaty feel of that night. It brought a crooked grin to her lips.

"It's so nice to be here and see your home. Tony says he's cooking for us tonight. I imagine it's to your credit, Mrs. Angelino, that Tony knows his way around the kitchen so well."

"Joanna, please call me Antoinette. I feel like an old lady being called Mrs. so and so. Actually, Tony was a Godsend when the girls were so busy in their activities. Even as a little guy he helped out in the kitchen, at least until he got so involved himself that he was gone more than he was home."

Tony left to tend to the heating embers in the cooker, while Mario stirred a drink for Joanna. "Remember I'm Mario to you my little lady." Jo wondered if all of the Angelino men devised pet names for their women. "By the way, that's a fine outfit you're wearing."

"Thank you, for the drink and the compliment."

Swirling the liquid in her glass Jo followed the curving walk toward the patio overlooking the *playa*. Two kidney-shaped pools tiled in deep blue, the right one more of a wading pool, were connected by a waterway, which she crossed on a cobblestone, arched bridge. At Tony's side, she turned to get a full view of the back of the house. Dark wood framing each window was a nice contrast to the honey-beige stucco. Above the red tile of the verandah roof, second floor windows created a lazy-eyed look. What a pleasant, peaceful place. She turned toward the ocean leaning on the wrought-iron railing and stared at the sandy beach fifteen or twenty feet below.

"The fish are on the grill. Won't be too long now." Tony brushed a buttery sauce the full length of each fillet and turned to lean an arm on her shoulder. Pointing to his left, he said. "Remember the Dugarel?" Not waiting for an answer, he went on. "It's less than two blocks in that direction. Just trying to help you get a perspective of the place."

"Uh huh. So how do you get to the playa?" He thumbed to the right. "Ah, I see." She moved to the stairway and peered down a spiral that went around twice. "Neat."

Mario stepped inside and Joanna joined Antoinette who was putting the finishing touches on the table set with broad plates, each painted in a different design—sunflowers, lilies, leaves and vines, all in the vibrant blues, greens, yellows, and oranges that are so common with Mexican pottery. "The table looks lovely Antoinette. Is there anything I can do?"

"No, my dear, Tony has planned the meal, I've set the table and Mario is filling the water goblets with ice and water."

"Is Mario the gardener as well? The yard is beautiful and well planned." Bougainvillea in vigorous bloom spread against the right wall. A stately palm gently waved its welcome, surrounded by an array of flora. Most were plants she could not name. Lavender, purple, and pink flowers, foliage varying from the yellows of a ripe banana to yellow green, deep green, magenta and variegated rose. In the back corner herbs and lettuce greens in sculptured rows made their own splendor. Contoured patches of grass completed the back yard.

"Are you kidding? No, I'm the gardener. Tony lends a hand on occasion. I had help from some of the locals in planning and buying." Jo nodded in interest. "We do have a man who comes in once a week and does the heavy trimming and cleaning. Things grow quickly in this climate, you know. Of course, the palms need to be tended to and watched. When the old palm branches dry up, a falling one can do a lot of damage in the crash. And we never let the coconuts on this one become very large. Our man climbs up and cuts them out before they become dangerous."

At dinner, Tony indifferently accepted the acclaim from Joanna and Antoinette for the delicious food. She was certainly impressed. Shrimp cocktail in flared dishes began the meal. The Sierra was seasoned with a buttery garlic and pepper sauce. Carrots had been sweetened with honey and ginger and virtually melted in her mouth. Fresh garlic crusted the grilled bread. Lettuce greens, tomatoes, and onions, drizzled with a light vinaigrette completed the meal.

Mario, in his jolly voice roared. "Can you believe that Tony's mother has nearly robbed my son of his manliness teaching him the way in the kitchen? But I cannot win. This boy, he does not listen to his father."

Everyone laughed as if it were a joke. But Joanna wondered if the comment was meant to cut. As the evening continued, she found the light banter between Tony's parents amusing. "Mamacita thinks she wears the pants in the family." Mario's booming voice broke into laughter. "But I only let her believe it."

Joanna believed it was the other way around. Antoinette's strength and resolve was evident. Most certainly in her quiet way she was the major decision-maker in the household. Her grandparents had immigrated from Italy when her mother was a child, and she wore her Italian heritage proudly.

When Joanna asked Mario about life in the old country, he gave her a troubled look. The flat of his hand slapped the table and he spit out a succession of Italian words, harshly and gravelly. Then his waving hand dismissed the question. "Sorry Joanna. The old country did nothing for me. It is something I cannot speak about."

Antoinette rose, smiling. "Joanna, would you like to see the house?"

Joanna declined touring the bedrooms upstairs. Somehow seeing Tony's room seemed like an invasion of his privacy. Usually, she didn't want people in her bedroom, especially when she was a little lax and left a few things lying around.

Antionette explained about getting the crumbling walls redone, expanding the kitchen, creating the verandah, having the roof tiled, the wiring completed, the floors torn out, plus all the shopping for fixtures and fabrics. Joanna's admiration for this woman soared.

Later, when the lamp glowed in the upstairs window and the evening cooled, Tony wrapped Jo in a soft, fringed shawl and they curled together in a giant basket chair pillowed by downy cushions. They searched for shooting stars. They saw only one. It seemed to last forever. Could this be forever? Then she dozed in his arms.

Dixie

Have you ever watched someone die? Even when his body held no warmth, we tried to get Pike to breathe. Reckless and even evil, he had such control over Nicki and me. In California he betrayed all of us, even Buddy, who was left bleeding on the floor of the liquor store during the heist. He promised no guns. Here in Mexico, he's squandered what money we had on drugs. Even so, I would not have wished death on him. Such a useless way to go, overdosed on bad stuff. Nicki and I quit long ago.

We've landed in Mazatlán. We needed the tourist scene to make a living. The big resorts like to hire English-speaking workers, so finding a job was no problem. This last month we've had a big art conference with several workshops going on in the resort where I work. Several well-known painters have given classes. We had artists from France, Italy, the States, all over.

An artist from New York has taken a shine to me. This time, no romance, no partying, nothing illicit. When I'm off work and when he's not in a workshop, he is teaching me to paint. Others are paying thousands of dollars for a week of lessons, and he charges me nothing. We both were surprised to find that I have talent. Norm calls my stuff raw and gritty with a kaleidoscopic of color. He says I will find a milder tone as my heart heals. How does he know about healing?

He is gentle and asks nothing of me. I wonder. What if he had been my father? At the end of the month, I learn that I remind him of his daughter. Two years ago, she took her own life.

Before he leaves Mazatlán, he surprises me with a small showing of my eight paintings, the ones I completed under his caring eye. I can't believe it. Three of them sell. I see the pride in his eyes. At our good-byes, through watery eyes he said, "I wonder had you been my daughter."

CHAPTER 18

Fifth, sixth, seventh, eighth, ninth. *Wow, I'm sure behind with my journaling*, Jo said out loud stretched in the lounge chair hugging the tiled pool. The tap of her pen left peppery specks on the page. She treasured the journal Amy had chosen for her Christmas gift. Appropriately, the cover bore a clever collage of travel maps printed on durable fabric. Inside, the pages were delicately lined in blue, which Jo was glad for. Otherwise, she usually wrote uphill. Lately it was downhill, however. A miniature, thumbnail in size, and in the same blue of a flower or animal introduced the first line of each page. This page sported a turtle.

Amy scrunched her nose at it. That's how her mind felt. Slow as a turtle. She couldn't remember what had happened each day. They all seemed to fuse. There had been daily walks on the beach, mostly with Amy and the children; she finished two books, both quick reads, light romances, and mastered the boogie board, riding the ocean waves with Dan and the kids. She shook her head thinking about Dan shooting in toward the shore with Andy on his back, a chokehold around his neck, her head held like a proud ostrich, keeping the foam from hitting her face. Andy was so successful that Jonathon also got the courage and the memory of their delighted squeals sent prickles along her skin.

One afternoon there was a water volleyball game. Even the elder Fords, Marilyn and Clarence joined in. They, with Amy and Dan, John and Jo made up one team against several other tourists. Sherry was pouting that day and refused to participate. Jo had learned that Sherry was hot and cold. One day she was as pleasant as could be and displayed clever quips right and left. Another day, she was a tigress and treated everyone, particularly John sharply. When one observed Sherry's eyes flashing, watch out! Joanna felt sorry for John and was glad to see him have some fun.

Jo found she could still spike the ball and she and John were particularly good in setting shots for each other. Her competitive nature got the best of her however, and she spit mouthful after mouthful of pool water with her amazon efforts. Following the wins, two for three, they all became a little giddy at the after-game celebration while Sherry continued her sulk from a far, glaring at John the whole time.

Two more creations from craft time graced her dresser at the resort. One was a tree like affair that could hold earrings, rings, and other jewelry, and the other a painted fish with its mouth gaping open. For the moment it held her various shades of lipsticks and glosses.

A brilliant tan was not a number one priority, but here with all the outdoor living a coppery glow was virtually involuntary—especially with skin like hers, apparently inherited from the unknown father. Would either of her birth parents ever be known to her? Today neither seemed important. Maybe she was not here to find Dixie, but perhaps for a far different purpose.

Was it only ten days ago that she and Tony met? She chewed on her bottom lip thinking of the many hours talking, teasing, exploring or just sitting side by side. They usually saw each other in the evening since his business was open every day. Except for yesterday. They had the whole Saturday to themselves with Jesus left in charge of the internet cafe.

They explored Mismaloya where much of *The Night of Iguana* was filmed in the sixties. Richard Burton's and Liz Tayor's presence really put Puerto Vallarta on the map back then. Now, the beach was greatly commercialized and only a building or two remained from the original film set. They sojourned to *Eden* and found the restaurant prices out of line, but enjoyed roaming around and spotted the helicopter from Arnold Schwarzenegger's film *The Predator.*

Most enjoyable, however, was the winding excursion on dusty

routes cut out of the overgrown jungle. They motored through lazy pueblos steering around brown dogs sprawling, refusing to move for the approaching Jeep. Children skipped alongside waving with great exuberance. Elderly men, hatted in straw and sitting on stumps, spat in the dirt, then tipped their heads back in laughter. Aproned women glanced warily and continued their sweeping, building little piles of dead plant life and plastic castaways. Smoke coiled from iron boxes on stilts as young men or women flipped pieces of *pollo asado* or *carne asada,* chicken or other meat roasted on blackened grids.

It was well past lunchtime and Jo begged Tony for food and a leg stretch. This little pueblo was particularly lush, fed by a meandering stream, no doubt spring-fed. It seemed undusted. A well-tended banana crop, trimmed of old dying and drooping leaves, climbed the rocky hillside. They stopped to admire the flowering buds hanging pendulum style from the stalk where bananas clustered above. Majestic, and magenta in color, the shape of a giant teardrop, one could fill the palm of a large man's hand. Joanna noticed that as the bananas grew, the distance between the flower and the ripening fruit diminished and that petals from the astounding bud one by one curled up, dried, and dropped to the ground. How had such a marvelous scheme transpired? Both were entranced.

Hens, clucking with seeming nonchalance, scratched, and pecked near their broods who ventured no more than a few yards. Two cocks strutted their feathers, iridescent in orange, brown, and black. Their crimson combs, gold beaks and flashing eyes fixed hypnotically, then the birds flared and spared, talons spiking. After three or four tries the pair sauntered off, each giving the impression that he had been the victor.

The front yard of one of the cinderblock houses, this one freshly painted white, also served as an outdoor restaurant. There sat four square plastic tables covered with real fabric, no oil cloth, each in a different plaid color-scheme. An elderly Mexican couple, he in his straw hat and she still in her apron were finishing their meal and used tortillas to sop the red sauce from the Mexican brown-ware pottery. No plastic, red plates here.

Four whole chickens split through the breast lay spread-eagle over the smoldering coals. They were orange in color, most likely brushed with red chili seasonings, Joanna supposed.

Tony inhaled long and hard. "This is one of my favorite Mexican dishes, *pollo asado.* In this part of Mexico, roadside stands are busy all day long cooking up these birds."

"I've noticed them. Well, I finally get to try one."

A young woman came around a bamboo curtain partitioning the restaurant from the rest of the yard. "Please take a seat." She gestured. "I am surprised to see travelers so far off the main roads." She spoke excellent English, though with a definite Spanish accent.

Jo decided that the woman didn't quite fit the image of the pueblo, dressed in a three-tiered gathered skirt, nearly brushing the bricked floor, and a deep red peasant blouse, neatly embroidered in black. Wide beaded bracelets were fitted at her wrists and beaded necklaces looped over her chest.

"Your restaurant is a godsend. We've been wandering these hills for a while now and I think we both need a relaxing meal." Jo addressed the pretty woman and noted a gentle smile and exceptionally white teeth when she opened her mouth to speak.

"No one's in a hurry here. We have an ea--sy way of moving," She said, emphasizing the character of the place. "The chickens will be finished cooking in *mas or menos--diez minutos.* I also have *sopa.* Would you like some before I serve *pollo, ensalada y salsa?*"

Tony and Joanna turned toward each other and nodded. "That sounds wonderful. My name is Joanna, and this is Tony."

"*Mucho gusto.* I am Mariana. I have *Jamaica por bebida* today or would you like a soda?"

They both decided on the blood-red drink made from the blossoms of the Jamaica plant, which reminded Joanna of cranberry juice. Then Mariana again slipped behind the bamboo.

"Don't you love the way that names sound in Spanish? Mariana sounds much softer, yet romantic than our harsh sounding English." Joanna crossed her arms and leaned them on the table and lowered her eyes.

"Maybe I should call you...Joana." Tony softened the J and made the ana with an ah sound.

With an exasperated shake of her head, she rolled her eyes at Tony, just in time to see Mariana come into view with a tray holding two bowls, two filled glasses and a flat basket covered with a cloth, the weave and color of one of the nearby tablecloths.

Piping hot, the soup, heavy on broth, included slices of a pale green squash, carrots, green chilis, bits of onion, garlic, tomato, bacon, and a few red beans with thin round noodles. Floating on top were several thin slices of avocado. "If you like *la sopa* with more fire, you may add *salsa*. She indicated the red sauce in the black three-legged pottery bowl.

"Thank you, thank you. It looks delicious." Adding the red sauce Jo blew on each bite before savoring the spoonful. "Boy, these people really know how to make a tasty soup. In hot climates one might think that cold food would be more palatable. Yet I love it...both kinds of hot. Makes my nose run though." Jo searched for a tissue and dabbed vigorously.

"Well, you're in for some education, JoJo. Hotter climates often grow hot, spicy foods and seeds. People in hot climates eat more hot foods in temperature *and* in spiciness, something to do with increasing perspiration, which offers a built-in air-conditioning system. And people in the northern cooler climates have more bland foods, tasty, but bland. Think of the Irish stews and English meat pies."

"You're kidding. Where did you learn that?"

"You must have missed the Multicultural foods class in high school. You'd be surprised how much we learned. Kind of a sneaky way to learn about other cultures. But it *was* one my favorite classes, made an A too. Course I liked the teacher."

"We sure didn't have that class in my high school. Sounds like you had a crush on the teacher. No wonder she gave you an A. I bet you had everyone snowed back then."

"Back *then*? What about now? By the way, I *earned* that A. Nobody gave *me* anything." He leaned back in his chair and gave her a haughty glare.

"Why you pompous brute!" Did he sound a little like his father, coming from a hard life in Italy to make it proudly on his own?

"Who uses the word pompous anymore?"

"I do." Jo flipped her hair and jerked so that her nose tilted.

So, the meal went. When the chicken was cooked, Mariana cleavered the joints to separate the parts, brought yellowed rice and a cabbage salad tasting of lime and a bit of mayonnaise. They ate from the brown pottery, adding dashes of the three salsas, chopped from fresh fruits and vegetables.

A few neighbors came to buy. A boy looking to be about ten rolled a handful of pesos in his hand as Mariana cleavered another chicken, placed a stack of tortillas in a thin plastic sack, salad in another, the red sauce in one and the rice in yet another. When each was knotted, she clamped her tongs on the dissected chicken and placed it into a heavier plastic bag, added the smaller bags and knotted the whole thing handing it to her customer.

"*Gracias.*" The boy looked at his bare toes holding the pesos out to her.

"*De nada, mi amigo, Manuel.*"

Mahn-wel, the accent on the last syllable. How much more beautiful the little boy's name sounded, unlike the shy boy in her sixth grade who spoke little English and had been there only one semester. They had called him Man-u-el with the accent on the first syllable. She wished she had known how to say it correctly back then. Maybe he would have felt more accepted.

When all the grilled chickens had been purchased, Mariana sat to the back of the yard and lifted the lid from a bushel-sized basket, woven in grasses, the color of wheat. She fished out a pile of plaid napkins and fringed a set of four quickly, yet with swan-like grace.

Tony continued to pick around the last pieces of the chicken. It was a small one, but too much for Joanna and her stomach could hold no more. Joanna stretched her legs and back, rising from the rigidity of the Mexican chair. She was sure they were easy to make in that design, but they usually left her feeling a little stiff. She chose a plastic scooped out chair and carried it to Mariana's side.

Mariana finished another plaid set, then began fringing the solid colors, bright orange, hot pint, brilliant blue. Joanna supposed that these came from some factory and that Mariana's job was to fringe and finish the pieces before they were shipped off to tourist areas to be sold.

But she was wrong. Mariana wove them herself. She had two looms in the back, on which she wove table linens of every size, shape, color, and design. She completed each item from start to finish. Then they headed off to market. Sometimes she fashioned personal orders featuring specific color combinations. Usually, she created what she felt sold the best. Mariana cut the large pieces into napkin-size, fringed them and stitched them on her sewing machine to keep them from fraying. She was designing some yard goods to be used for clothing, but needed to finish the table linens and rugs she was working on first.

"Jo, I think I'll hike around the area. Do you want to join me?" Tony extended his five-foot-ten-inch frame and twisted his torso from side to side.

"Thanks Tony, but I think I'll visit with Mariana. She's going to show me her weaving studio."

He dug some folded peso bills out of his pocket and laid them on the table. "Sounds good. Then you won't feel abandoned." It was a statement, rather than a question.

"Not at all. Don't get lost."

He shot her a look, but didn't say anything, just gave her a salute.

"Your Tony, he seems like a good man. Let me clear the table and then I'll show you the studio."

"Yes, he's a good man."

Behind the barren home was a bricked path to another similar sized building. On either side various plants, some flowering, some potted, filled the narrow backyard. No grass. Joanna found that it was hard to guess what was beyond the front door. Often massive and ornate courtyards seemed to be out of sync with first impressions—a broken sidewalk and a sewer smell.

The windows were barred with wrought iron, but no glass, unlike Mariana's home in front, that included bars and the typical heavy frosted glass. Inside the studio were two looms, the smaller used only for table runners or placemats. Several shelves displayed stacks of colorful plaids similar to the ones on the restaurant tables. Other companion pieces in solids lay nearby. Spools of yarns in polyester, wool and cotton blends stood like soldiers waiting to be chosen. Two worktables held fabrics in the process of having the edges finished. Some would end up fringed and others would be hemmed by machine.

Jo admired the rich yellow on the larger loom. The slubbed yarn gave it an interesting texture. The woolen runner in process on the other loom was the color of raw cranberries with blue, turquoise, green and touches of yellow woven in Indigenous designs. Joanna loved the colors of Mexico.

Mesmerized, Joanna watched as Mariana demonstrated the weaving process, using hands, legs, knees, and feet to lift and lower, throw the shuttle, and push the yarns tightly against each other.

"What a workout you get hand looming each article. Bet you're in good shape." Joanna was impressed. "Doesn't your back take a beating... hunched over all that time?"

A thoughtful smile emerged before she spoke. "No. When I am creating something new, it is like nurturing a new life, and what discomfort there is I do not notice."

Joanna nodded thoughtfully. "Have you lived in the pueblo long? Surely you did not grow up here. And who taught you this wonderful art?"

Joanna learned that they were nearly the same age, that Mariana was raised in Guadalajara and received her college education in business. She worked for a large company for several years and made decent money, but spent little, since her parents wanted her to live at home. Her father, a busy and well-known doctor, was not always available when her mother entertained or attended the opera and other festive events. It was left for Mariana to be her mother's companion.

She and a man named Miguel had been in love for several years. He too was a fine man, like Joanna's Tony, she said, but something kept them from committing to marriage. He grew more distant with her and eventually they drifted apart.

As Mariana placed her hand over her heart, Joanna detected a flicker in her eyes. "In Mexico," she said, "there is this thing, *la espina,* like a spine or a thorn in the heart. I know that I have it, so I decide I need to get it out. That is why I am here, two years now." Then she caressed the smoothness of her loom. "These are the looms of my grandmother, gone now three years. I wish she could see me using them."

"Perhaps she can, Mariana." *A thorn in the heart.* Joanna was silent for a moment and thought about herself before she went on. "But why *this* place? It's so far away. How did you know about it?"

Wisps of dark hair escaped the long braid down her back and scrolled at her temples adding to her gentle countenance. "I came here because my aunt and uncle moved to Guadalajara and left this house empty. They wanted to be closer to my mother. This seemed like a good place for me to be."

"What about *la espina?* Is it gone?" Joanna looked toward hooded eyes and saw the gentle nod and the peaceful curve of her lips.

"It is coming."

CHAPTER 19

"You're not moving out already?" Sherry seemed to be pleading. "What will I do the last two days without you around?"

Jo wanted to get her little Roadtrek settled in the Bucerias campground before the Ford's two-week stint with their time-share was over. Organizing and packing the things she had brought from home, plus the extra items she somehow acquired since her arrival, absorbed her mind until Sherry spoke. Like the tentacles of a creeping vine robbing the nourishment of its host, *guilt* squeezed round her. How could she lose that feeling? Joanna was determined *not* to take responsibly for everyone's happiness, yet she felt guilty when she didn't.

Yesterday's beachside visit began with Sherry and Joanna relaxing and chatting together. Joanna had hoped to counter the loneliness she had sensed in Sherry with her friendly interest. However, hearing about Mariana, the weaver, and *la espina,* Sherry buried her head in her hands, weeping. How could this tender story move her so? As Sherry's story unfolded, she understood Sherry more fully and John's commitment to her.

Joanna learned that Sherry's earliest years seemed to be fairly normal and happy. Her father, a high school Social Studies teacher, head football coach and assistant baseball coach took his work very seriously. He developed close relationships with his students, and it was not unusual for them to call him at home about schoolwork, sports, or personal issues. When some of his poorer athletes couldn't afford new football or baseball shoes, Pete found odd jobs, such as lawn-mowing or leaf-raking to help the kids out.

Beth, the stay-at-home Mom, read every book about childrearing and carried each new idea she read to an extreme. Most of Pete's and Beth's arguments centered around Sherry. Pete thought his wife was too rigid and needed to be more flexible and use more common sense. But Sherry's mother was determined to produce a well-disciplined child and by the time she was four Sherry was spending several times a day in "time out."

Trance-like Sherry remembered. "I found it nearly impossible to please my mother. Each toy had a particular spot on a certain shelf or in a specific box. If my mother found one out of place I spent "time out" standing and looking at the wall. If I complained or got tired of standing and wanted to sit on the floor, Mother added five minutes to the twenty she had already set on the timer. To this day if I hear a ding from a timer, I feel nauseous and sick to my stomach."

Joanna pictured an innocent child with sad, wide eyes, being punished unjustly for a toy out of place. What a contrast to the teamwork her own mother promoted for many of the household chores—setting or clearing the table, picking up toys, folding clothes. "Sounds unfair, Sherry. Just for toys being put in another spot? At least they were put away."

"Oh, it wasn't just for toys. I did "time out" for not eating all of my meal, for running outside without a coat, for failing to close the bathroom door, for having to be reminded to brush my teeth at a certain time." She clipped off misdeeds, one after the other. "When I was frustrated trying to tie my shoes, when I spilled *anything* or tipped something. Accidents were not forgiven."

"Didn't your dad ever take your side?"

"He didn't see it most of the time. He came home late after practice, and I was expected to be ready for bed by then. I didn't say anything to Dad. I was just trying to be a good little girl."

There was a pause. "Did things get better as you got older, Sherry?"

"Nah...her behavior became more bizarre and by the time I was in school, I don't think she wanted me around. Sometimes she put me in the shower and turned on the cold water, yelling at me about my evil ways. Mostly I ended up locked in the dark closet, forced to squat on the floor. If she opened the door and I was sitting on the floor or lying down, the time was doubled."

"That must have been horrible in that darkness."

"At times I hated her and wished her dead, but then I pushed those ideas from my mind. Mother said, 'Wipe those evil thoughts from your mind. You'll have one of your nosebleeds and it won't stop. You'll bleed forever.' I had quite a few nosebleeds as a child. They scared me to death, and I was afraid that she could be right. Maybe my bad thoughts made my nose bleed. Eventually, I think I just learned to blank everything... and later it was almost a peaceful time...in the closet. I leaned against the wall, and I could sit like that for hours. At least she wasn't bothering me or threatening me."

"How terrible...terrible. I am so sorry. She must have been...so troubled."

There was irony in her voice. "Oh, there were times of great fun and laughter. She did wonderful crafts with me and taught me songs, rhymes, and games. She made darling clothes for me and spent time doing my hair with cute clips and various hair bands. We'd play dress up and she'd let me try her makeup. During those times my life was nearly that of a fairy princess. Then in a flash, something would set her off and off I'd go to the 'black hole.' I mocked her once about living in the 'black hole' and she backhanded me, landing me across the room in a heap."

"She sounds manic to me."

"Yes." Sherry nodded. "Back then we didn't know so much about bi-polar and manic-depressive behavior and it wasn't until early high school age that I put a name to it...when I studied psychology and talked to my teacher."

"By then your dad must have had some clue. Didn't he get her some medical help?"

"Actually, Dad had her in and out of doctor's offices from the time I was ten or so. But she did a good con job for a while and the doctors didn't spot anything. They recommended counseling, but to hear my dad tell it, no good came after a few sessions and he refused to go back.

"As time went on, she and Dad grew farther apart, and Dad spent even less time at home. Her erratic behavior crept into their relationship and Dad couldn't handle it. We finally got her on some meds. They helped a little and I learned to cope with her outbursts. One minute she would yell and carry on. Then she'd be sorry and generally she'd get into a paranoid state, wailing and wailing, thinking everyone was talking about her or spying on her."

"That's when you were in high school? How did you live through it?"

"I *had* to be strong. I protected her. I took care of her. I talked the knife away from her when she held it to her stomach...more than once." Tears began again. "We finally locked the knives away. I had very few friends. My schoolwork could have been better. I *thought* I was strong." She was sobbing uncontrollably, and everything came, child-like and in spasms. "But now. Everyday, I wonder. I am her daughter. Am I becoming her? Would I hurt a child as she hurt me? I don't want John to leave me."

Joanna listened, comforted, encouraged. "Sherry, of course you are strong. Look what you did. But anyone who lived through such horrendous times needs help with counseling and therapy. You can't do it alone and should not expect John to be your, your..." She searched for a word. "Well strength and the one to give your life meaning. You need to find that on your own, but with John beside you." She was way over her head.

Joanna was worried for Sherry and for John. Apparently, so far, he had tried to manage her ups downs, which seemed more quirky than serious, with love and understanding. How long until it would be too much for him? With the right help, Joanna thought that she could be as OK as most people are.

Joanna continued her gentle persuasion and Sherry finally promised that she would take control of her life the best that she could when they returned to Colorado. She would seek some therapy before she drove her own self loony with uncertainty and worry. "I need to get *la espina* from my heart, don't you think?"

Joanna grinned, then sobered. "So, what has happened with your mom?"

According to Sherry, her mother seems to be tolerating her medications, but is virtually a recluse. She lives with a kindly Aunt, never married, who provides a good home. Beth's main interest involves coloring with crayons and colored pencils. Sometimes she creates things on her own, but usually she fills in the pictures of coloring books—animals, cartoons, pretty ladies, story-books—which Sherry takes when she visits, and her mother proudly displays when she is finished.

Her father remarried, a teacher also, and they now have two sons. Sherry sees them on occasion and is glad to know that her father is happy. Their times together are pleasant, but the talk usually centers around her half-brothers and her dad's coaching and both of their teaching careers. Sherry said that she and her dad seldom talk about her mother. "It's like it all never happened."

Joanna was surprised at their commonalities of distant fathers, of divorce. Yet, until her mother's death she had a wonderful connection. Sherry never had that.

Today, however, Joanna had her own concerns and was annoyed to think that Sherry expected to continue the closeness they felt yesterday. Oh heck, she didn't need to be so selfish. "I could use some help getting settled in the campground. I'm still a novice at getting everything hooked up in the motorhome. I may have to read the manual, while you follow. What do you think?"

Sherry's eyes glistened. "You want me to come with you? I'd love it, the two of us setting out on this little adventure. I'm ignorant about RV's, but a willing learner."

"Yoo-hoo." Marilyn Ford's voice found its way toward the bedroom. "Joanna, are you here? I need to take a photo of your picture before I forget."

"Oh yes, thanks." Joanna loosened the twine holding the wrapping around the church painting. They had all admired it the other night when she displayed it to the Fords. Their favorite however, was the one Jo called *The Laundress.* Nevertheless, the church or cathedral, was the most promising clue to her birthmother's whereabouts. Could knowing its location lead her to Dixie? Sometimes it all seemed so impossible.

Tonight, Jo planned to treat the Fords and the Angelinos to dinner near the Bucerias campground. She wanted to do something to repay the thoughtfulness and generosity of both families. Several evenings Antoinette had prepared supper for her and Tony with Mario tending the grill or the drinks. Joanna found the pair animated and fascinating to listen to, even in their combative banter, which seemed more game-like than contemptuous. Mario was definitely rougher around the edges, but she saw his charm emulated in Tony.

"Bring your clothes for tonight," she said to Sherry. "We can get beautiful together and meet everyone at the restaurant. I think I'll wear my emerald green outfit, the one I wore the night I met Tony. You'll probably want something that covers. Tony says the garden restaurant might be cool in the evening." Sherry's clothes usually didn't cover much of her body and probably she needed to wear something warmer for dinner.

It was three when they pulled out of the parking lot. The rig was sparkling clean. Juan, the barefooted thirteen-year-old who hung around the resort doing odd jobs for the guests, had scrubbed and polished it the whole afternoon the day before, while Jo and Sherry had their visit. Juan asked for an equivalent of five dollars. Joanna saw his silent eyes dance when she doubled that.

Sherry's voice echoed the verve of a child at play. "Hey, this is fun." They pulled onto the busy highway connecting Puerto Vallarta and Bucerias. The CD played a tune that seemed to say, travel on, push on, with its beat and intensity. "I admire your independence and guts. I can't imagine you and Amy heading out on your own like you did. There is this feeling of freedom, of adventure…just heading down the road, isn't there?"

No answer was needed. Some of the simplest things, like drinking in the passing landscape brought the greatest pleasures. And friends. Another friend was never a bad thing, Joanna decided.

Each RV pad included a roomy cement patio with colorful greenery and hibiscus, blooming in yellows, pinks, and oranges. When she registered two days ago, she reserved a spot on the south side, halfway between the oceanside and the roadside. Pulling into her place, Sherry and Jo heard the waves in the distance. Three men, none wearing a shirt, seemed to be the welcoming committee, and arrived at the Roadtrek all at once. Well-tanned, it was evident that they had been here a few months. How different each was, one with a round belly above his drooping trunks, another tall and lean with a few hanging flabs of skin, the last, short, and stoutly built, still sporting the muscles of his past. They looked to be in their sixties and seventies. Jo and Sherry eyed each other as Stout spoke.

"Howdy gals, we've been waiting for some lovely women to bring some color to our campground. Haven't we guys?"

Lean chimed in. "Don't listen to Barney, here. If there is anything we can do, just call on us. I'm Tom and this here's Toad." A tanned woman, just a mite of a thing, dressed in a one-piece swimsuit and a fringed wrap that hung around her waist, joined the threesome. "Now Vera don't you horn in on this welcome party."

Vera's speech had a hint of Irish in it. "Don't let these old fogies intimidate you. They're mostly full of hot air. I'm Vera, Toad's wife. Tom and his wife Linda and Toad and I are Canadians. Barney and Barb are from the U.S."

Sherry and Joanna introduced themselves, and following a bit of explanation, Barney said, "So, Joanna is the only one who is going to stick around?" He seemed a little disappointed. "You're going to like it here. It's a little tropical paradise with the breezes and the mist of the ocean keeping a just right temperature."

Sherry gazed around at the clump of bamboo, the variety of palms and the lush foliage splayed in the campground. She eyed a red tile building, built in the round, with a wide stairway leading to a landing and the second floor. "That's quite an interesting building. Don't see round ones too often."

It was Barney's turn to talk. "That's the office and the owner's home. The upstairs has several apartments for people who don't have RV's. Used to have a nice restaurant in the back that opened onto the patio. They closed that a few years ago. Story goes, that Elizabeth

Taylor bought this spot and started to build a house for herself. Back then there were no houses between here and the highway way up the hill. The top floor wasn't finished and one day a tour bus went along the highway, and she heard the loudspeaker blast out that this was Liz Taylor's new house and all about her."

Tom finished the story. "Yup, story goes, she upped and left, never finished the place. Couldn't even have privacy here."

"So, Liz Taylor walked these grounds? Hmm." Jo brought a halt to the cheerful chat. "We need to get hooked up. I'm a little green, so it's going to take a little while."

Barney stuck his muscled chest out a little. "Gals, us guys hooked up enough of these rigs to do it in our sleep. Right?" Casting a look at his partners, he added, "At your service."

In no time the sewer hose was secure in the sewer hole, the water hose was linked to the Roadtrek and provided water to the sink, the toilet and the shower, and the electricity was plugged in. Lights worked, the stereo and the refrigerator. What a good feeling. After checking the campground shower and toilet rooms, Jo decided that most of the time she would use them rather than her own little cramped shower and bathroom. They were conveniently close by.

Now time for a little rest. They were meeting everyone at seven for the evening meal and had at least an hour and a half before time to clean up and dress for dinner. They decided to take Joanna's lounge chairs to the beach where they lazed side by side in the half-shade of swaying palms. "Thanks for inviting me to come along, Jo. I can't tell you how special this is for me."

Dinner at *La Lomita* was delightful. First there was the enchantment of the garden lit with candles, pottery globes revealing cutouts of every jungle design, and strings of glistening lights. A meandering tree lifted itself from the center of the garden floor and spread its umbrella leaves into a canopy. Stones of varying shapes and colors mingled with tiles in curves, zigs and lines to create a mosaic terrace where guests grouped around colorfully spread tables. Two cats lazily explored, then found cozy spots on the half-wall to the side of the terrace and lay gazing into the night.

Then there was the food, carefully prepared by the couple who lived in the house adjoining the terrace garden. Each evening three entrees, which varied from night to night, were featured. Tonight's selections included a tender white fish, lightly seasoned and served with a dill sauce; a chicken breast topped with a thin slice of Manchego cheese plus a lime sauce delicately flavored and sweetened; and a beef fillet served with a mushroom sauce and crumbled bacon. Each came with whole baby potatoes, thickly sliced vegetables, and toasty chunks of bread. For the first course they enjoyed thin crackers and pâté which Joanna found mild and flavorful, though she had no idea of its origin. The second course was a salad of greens, cucumbers, tomatoes, and avocados coated with a light vinaigrette. Following the main course, one could choose the flan, or a regular custard topped with pineapple. Beverage choices included iced tea, coffee, and limeade. Alcoholic drinks were separate. Tony insisted on choosing three special wines. After all, this was a kind of good-bye party as well.

That was the other extraordinary part of the evening. Her wonderful friends. The Fords were leaving the day after tomorrow and the elder Angelinos were heading home the following day. Mario wanted to check on the business and they would return toward the end of February. Joanna was not looking forward to her good-bye to Amy. How she would miss their talks and her chippery personality. She'd said good-bye to Jonathon and Andy, who stayed with the next door neighbors at the condo. She loved the way they invigorated her life. No doubt the next time she saw them they would be taller and more worldly. And easy-going Dan, what a peach. No Sherry and John around, either. She thought of them with tenderness.

Joanna had secretly observed Sherry tonight. The harshness was gone and in its place a contentment that left her even more beautiful. Her outfit, a finger-tip length tunic over trousers, was of linen in a soft melon shade. More important than how she looked, however, was her loving attention to John, rather than her usual antics, which involved drawing herself to the notice of others. If Sherry searched out some therapy, surely this peace and satisfaction would not be fleeting.

When the laughter and discussion grew raucous and the jokes

somewhat tainted, Jo wondered at the reaction of others. Yet, groups of diners huddled in their own worlds and seemed not to notice.

One toast followed another, each wanting to recognize a special memory or experience from the past few weeks, too quickly coming to a close. No good-byes for Joanna and Tony, though. She was settled for the time being in her campground and Tony had his business to run.

"Here's to Tony and Jo." John raised his glass to theirs. "May the road rise to greet you, may the wind be always at your back, may the sunshine warm upon your face, may the rains fall soft upon your fields, until we dance together again."

Marilyn shook her head at her son. "My son the master of improv. Would you believe it from the kid who played bashful most of his life?"

Inevitably they trooped out of the lovely garden which would always be connected in their minds to a special time and place with exceptional people. Everyone wanted to see where Joanna had settled, so on the way to the Taxi stop, they toured the campground. Tom, Barney, Toad, and their wives were playing cards in the dim light of the RV spot next to hers. Strings of chili peppers in green, red, and yellow looped from the awning. Wind chimes gently tinkled the air.

This time Linda rose to greet them, and the card game was delayed while both groups mingled and made neighborly conversation. "You take care of our Joanna, guys." Admiration glowed from Sherry's face. "Independent and capable as she is, she'll need a little watching over once and a while."

When they finished hiking the three blocks to the Taxi stand, the hugs and good-byes seemed all too quick. Jo watched the red of the taillights as they climbed toward the highway and heard the rumble of tires blubbing on the cobblestones, then both escaped her senses. Tony pulled her close and murmured in her hair. "Need some company tonight?"

"For a while." They turned and walked the cobblestone street, ignoring the narrow sidewalk, toward her campground.

CHAPTER 20

Dad you gotta be there. Joanna stabbed at the last digit of the PIN on her phone calling card and waited for it to ring. She felt some urgency to let her dad know where she could be reached. Why, she didn't know.

The pay phone was a shady spot half a block from the campground so standing here was not a big deal, except the street could be noisy at times. *Come on, somebody answer.*

She wanted to avoid the possibility of getting Cindy and decided to call her dad's office. Shirley, the office manager answered, and Jo was glad to catch up with her news before she buzzed her father. Shirley had replaced Cindy when the affair was going on and Cindy had taken another job, so Shirley had been there a long time and knew Clay Johansen as well as anyone. Cindy was not one of Shirley's favorites and Jo was not surprised at her comment.

"That wife of your dad's sure keeps him hopping. I don't know how he puts up with all that he does. He doesn't say much, but I can read between the lines with the little remarks he makes."

"I keep hoping that things will get better. But you don't think they are?"

"No, and he's back smoking again after what? twelve years. He seems agitated and jumpy."

"Oh no, and I'm way down here. I don't know what I'd do if I was there, cause Dad never is easy to talk to, but at least..."

"Well, maybe I'm reading more into things than I need to, but I'd like to see your dad really happy. He used to be clever and funny."

"Shirley, I want Dad to know how to reach me, but I'll tell you, too. You can contact me if there is something I need to know. I expect to be here at least two weeks. I'll be doing some research, contacting galleries and places that may give me a lead for this search for my birthmother."

"I have it all down. Glad to know where you are. I don't want to use too many of your nickels, so I'll buzz your dad. You take care and have a good time. Hope something turns up with your birthmother. Bye, now."

"Clayton Johansen. How can I help you?" His voice sounded hearty, not at all what she expected because of Shirley's attitude.

"It's me, Dad."

"Well, Joanna. Still playing tourist in the sunshine? You must be missing our crisp weather. Actually, the winter decided to skip us this year. Not bad here."

"Glad you're not fighting snow and ice. I'm not really missing home yet. Amy and her family leave today. We already said our good-byes and that was hard. How is the new year going for you?"

"Nothing different. It's beginning to pick up at work. Been slow. Course I only put in a few hours a day. No traveling to speak of. Everyone else does that. And Cindy has me doing some projects on the house, converting the storeroom into a guestroom. Lot to do there."

"You'll enjoy that. You and Mom were always handy at remodeling projects."

Clay let that topic pass, changing the subject. "Oh, have you checked your e-mail today?"

"No, did you send me a message?" Jo was stunned to think that her dad had taken the initiative. Always it was Joanna who made the contacts.

"Not me, but Janene Santini called and said that she wanted to reach you immediately. Wanted to know how to get a hold of you. She sent an e-mail to you, but didn't know how often you got on your computer."

"Is everything OK? What'd she say?"

"Didn't say much, something about coming down to see ya."

"Are you kidding?" Jo's mind whirled. Janene coming to Mexico? Maybe she should persuade her dad to come too and get away from the pressures he must be feeling at home. "Hey dad. What about you? Why don't you come down for a week? It's relaxing and you would enjoy scouting the beach and we could catch up. Give you a little change."

"Aw JJ, like I said, it's picking up here, and I have that room to do. You know I'm not much for relaxing or talking anyway. It wouldn't be fair to Cindy, you know." His voice had lost the spark that she heard earlier.

"She's gone to visit relatives and you stayed home. What's the difference?"

"Just can't do it. Talk to me about what's going on with you."

She told him more detail about the campground and her new neighbors than he probably wanted to hear. It was no coincidence that she was in Bucerias where Tony had his business. But fortunately, it was a good place to work out of. She could look into travel packages for travelers who didn't want the big, tourist-hotel thing and do some on-line research that she hoped could give her clues about her birthmother.

"Are you sure this isn't some wild goose chase, Jo?" The sigh that followed seemed heavy.

They had gone over this before. "Yes, Dad, it *is* a wild goose chase. Of course, the main clue that I have is the church painting and if Amy's mom doesn't learn anything from her friend, I'll ask people everywhere I go. I haven't read through all of Mom's Mexico books, yet I want to find out all I can about places where gringos might settle to do their art. At least that's my idea."

"How long you gonna keep looking? This not working might become a habit. Surely your mom's money will run out sometime."

Jo chortled to herself and shook her head. It was useless. "So, you're worried I'm going to become a no good beach bum? You know I've always made my own way and paid my own way." She tried not to let resentment color her words. He hadn't even paid a dollar of child support. Her mother had not asked for it and he had been in his own world with the prospect of supporting Cindy's three children, and he had not offered. The college fund that her parents had established when she was young paid for most of her education. Her part time work paid for the rest. He had no right to question her decisions. She certainly had not berated him for his. And look where he was now.

"I've always been proud of you Jo. You've done well. It's just that..."

"You think it's ridiculous for me to search for my birthmother."

"No, if she was here in the states, it would be different."

At least he had conceded that it was OK for her to look. Exasperated, she let out a whoosh of air. "I'm down here, right or wrong. I'm going to enjoy myself, the people I meet and the new experiences I'm having. And I'll do some work. Besides, I'm not only searching for Dixie." She couldn't tell him about *la espina*. "I need to do some of my own soul searching and find my own self."

"Don't go all weird on me Jo. We raised you to know who you are. We were always honest with you."

"Yes, you were Dad. Thank you very much. I had a good childhood." This conversation was going nowhere. She felt like a disobedient child when she talked with her father. "Hey, I want you to have the phone number of the campground and all that stuff. You have my e-mail address and I'll check it every few days. I'll call you next week and let you know if I've had any luck."

"You better call Janine. Take care. Bye."

Joanna pressed the palms of her hands on the rim of the pool and lifted herself to the edge where she sat watching the surface dance, reflecting the waving palms and cerulean sky. Exhaling and inhaling, she hoped to bring oxygen to her tight limbs. The twenty laps weren't difficult for her lungs, but her arms and legs were limp. It was her mother who said, "When the brain is taxed and your nerves are on edge, work the brawn." Joanna recalled the seriousness of her mother's eyes when she talked about balancing the mental, emotional, and physical stuff. Joanna had not always appreciated her wisdom and wished she had listened more intently. Many of the words endured in her head, but her mother's voice was vaporizing. She longed to hear it again. Jo knew her mother would be with her one hundred percent on this journey, cheering and encouraging. "You can make it. You can do it. You will find what you long for."

Kicking at the water and rolling her shoulders the limpness began to vacate her body. Tomorrow. Janene would be here tomorrow. Of course, she was thrilled to have her dear friend, the one who had known where she was born and helped her find Ellie, spend the week with her. On the phone Janene had been breathless with excitement explaining her spontaneous decision to fly down for a visit. If Joanna had not called, Janene planned to fly in, get a taxi at the airport and arrive on her doorstep unannounced. She knew the name of her campground from the last e-mail Joanna had sent.

That would have been all right, but anticipating her arrival, doing a little planning and picking her up at the airport was what Jo preferred. Things had a way of working out. Fortunately, unhooking the sewer, water and electricity, so that she could take the Roadtrek to the Airport was not difficult.

Joanna snatched her towel and watch. There was plenty of afternoon left. At her motorhome, she toweled and fluffed her hair, slid her painted toes into leather sandals, knotted her fringed Mexican serape around her hips and hooked her sunglasses over her ears. The hike to the square and Tony's internet place was less than a mile. After the swim her body was revitalized and her pace quickened to a clop, clop, clop steady rhythm that only varied when she made her way around some unattended repair-work with mounds of dirt and rocks encircling a gaping cavity.

At the cyber cafe, the aging man Tony stooped over, seemed all naked arms protruding from a white tank top and wispy fluffs of snowy hair. The image of a young bird breaking from its shell flashed through Joanna's mind. What a glorious paradox. This man who most likely thought that traveling in a model-T as a young boy was a miracle, now clicking and smiling, made his way through cyberspace.

Seeing her approach, Tony touched the man's shoulder and wound his way around two small tables. He held her to him for a good minute, the flats of his hands firm against her back, exposed and steamy. "Hum… Seeing me gets you all worked up, I see!"

She pulled back, doubled her fists, dodging and ducking, boxing toward his chin. "No, just my usual physical workout. Fifty laps in the pool and a three-mile jog."

"In those clothes and shoes?" He eyed her slim body, yet curvy enough. The lines of her one-piece black suit were simple. Halter style, scooping low in the back, a plunging front, teasing the eye with ever so little of her soft roundness escaping.

She thought she was proper enough, serape and all. She certainly had seen plenty of people bulging from skimpy thongs and strapless thin bands. Jo bit into her lower lip. This was not the beach, this was a business. Oh gosh. In another place she would have had fun with Tony's wandering, lustful eyes. Jo retreated behind the folding screen where the real-estate office was. It was empty. Tony followed her.

"Looking for a little privacy, huh?" Stepping forward to kiss her, he was startled when Jo grimaced and put both hands up in a halt position. "What's the deal here?"

"I guess…I'm under-dressed. I feel exposed. Do you have a shirt I can borrow?"

"Jo, you look great. Can't a man ogle a little? Don't be embarrassed. People come here in less than that all the time."

She looked like she was cornered and didn't know how to escape and continued to chew on that lip, her eyes darting.

"Jo, it's not that bad. I said you look terrific. But if you'll feel better…"

He returned from the back storage room with a white long-sleeved dress-shirt. "Here, I keep this around in case I need to dress up a little and can't get back home to change."

She put it on and rolled up the sleeves. "Thanks, that feels better." *Then* they kissed.

The rest of the afternoon was spent on-line chasing one site and then another searching for churches of Mexico. Why didn't she start this earlier? She tried Mexico churches and came up with lists of various denominations—Presbyterian, Baptist, Lutheran, Seventh Day Adventist. That was no help.

Then she keyed the words famous churches of Mexico. This led to 2,482 entries with a short blurb following each heading. She tried the heading, Colonial Cities and found information about Dolores Hidalgo, Zacatecas, Guadalajara, Patzcuaro, San Miguel de Allende, Guanajuato. She scrolled through the information looking for descriptions of church buildings similar to Dixie's painting. Churches were named, but no description and no pictures.

In the San Miguel section, a paragraph caught her eye: *Artists have long been attracted by San Miguel's timeless beauty and the city has become quite an artist colony, with a fairly large community of North American writers and painters who live here year-round.* The article went on to list the most fascinating attractions: *Jardin Principal (Main Garden) is San Miguel's popular meeting place surrounded by beautiful buildings such as La Parrroquia (Parish Church), originally built in 1683, the outstanding landmark in San Miguel.*

This entry led her to search the other colonial towns. Several seemed good places for artists—Patzcuaro, Guanajuato, Guadalajara. This needed more research. She clicked through twenty of the two thousand plus entries, and nothing produced what she needed. She jotted notations concerning some possibilities for follow-up, but this seemed fruitless. Perhaps later.

She and Tony had not seen each other since the night at the restaurant. It seemed a whole lot longer than a day and a half. Yesterday was Joanna's day to settle in and do some washing.

Tony heard about the calls to her father and Janene. He had all kinds of ideas for when Janene came. What infectious enthusiasm. Tony insisted she take his Jeep to the airport. No use disconnecting everything. She'd just have to hook it all up again.

"Up to cooking tonight?" Tony asked. "Give me forty minutes and we're outta here."

"Sure, but your folks may have a lot of packing and last-minute stuff before they leave tomorrow. I don't want to intrude."

"Jo, you're behind the times. They left today. We'll have the place all to ourselves."

"I can't stay too late. I need to pick up Janene tomorrow, you know."

"You said she comes in at 11:30. It's not even twenty minutes away." His eyes did that sparkle thing, then locked with hers. He licked his lips, grinned, and nudged her.

"I know what you're thinking. No way." Pressing her own lips inside each other, she shook her head side to side. "I don't even have a toothbrush."

"I have gobs of toothpaste. Didn't you ever have to use your finger at camp when you forgot your toothbrush?"

"Me, forget my toothbrush? Never."

That night being in his bedroom did not seem intrusive.

The morning mist drifted in through the open window as she padded around on the cool tile of Tony's second floor bedroom. In his white shirt she looked respectable, though she wore nothing else. She leaned on the windowsill watching the swooping, graceful flight of the terns, their long pointed wings and deeply forked tails. One dived near the surface of the rolling sea, then took to the air gripping a silvery fish.

Pelicans, in their gray, brown and black, spread their powerful wide wings, gliding, and soaring, only to smash into the sea with their bomb-dives. Bobbing awkwardly, they extended their bills and gulped their prey through large distensible pouches. To the right a rank of six pelicans soared toward their friends, barely grazing the building waves. Oh, the world was alive and awakened. A new day.

"Hey sleepy head. Your breakfast is ready." Downstairs she heard the clink and clank of pans.

Tony had laid out his mother's brown, Mexican pottery on woven green and blue placemats. Steaming mugs brimmed with coffee, bacon drained on a paper towel and, pancakes, ready to be flipped, made giant polka dots on the griddle.

"Boy you sure know the way to a woman's heart, don't you." Joanna tugged at the ties to his apron as he made the last flip. He turned and kissed the tip of her upturned nose. It tickled. She sniffed and swiped her palm against the kissed spot. "Sure, smells good in here and I'm famished."

"I imagine so. It *was* a good night, wasn't it? Hey, you look nifty in my shirt. Why don't you keep it?"

She nestled her nose into the sleeve. It smelled like Tony. A whiff of his cologne and perhaps the soap that was used in his wash. "That's sweet of you, but I'll return it... one of these days."

They were in no hurry. Each tasty bite was savored. Their eyes danced and glistened in tantalizing dialogue. A vibrance hung in the air that neither wanted to disturb.

"Tony Angelino, it's really comfortable being with you. I hate to leave, but I don't want to be late to the airport."

The naughtiness flashing from his dark eyes foretold his words. "Come here my tasty JoJo."

Joanna straddled his lap and looped her arms around him. Tony's hands made their way under the man's shirt caressing the softness of her belly and the roundness of her breasts. He kissed her neck, and his fingers lightly pressed the taut nipples. Shivers quivered over every inch of her body.

"Like I said, I like you in this shirt." He gave her a taunting smile. "How much time do we have?"

"None," she said.

"Too bad."

Minutes later Tony opened the magnificent gate, so that Joanna could back out of the courtyard of the beachside home. "We'll come by about six. Will that be early enough to get to that barbecue place you've been talking about?"

"Sure. Can't wait to see you do that karaoke thing."

"Well, we'll see. Janene will get a kick out of it, I know. You're a sweetheart to lend me your Jeep. I could have driven the Roadtrek, you know."

He waved her on. "Get outta here." Then blew her a kiss.

It had been less than four weeks since she had seen Janene, yet it seemed like eons. Back home was another life. Jo paced on the coolness of the marble. She knew that the plane had landed, but no one had entered the baggage drop or customs checkpoint. Young Mexicans, dressed in white polo shirts held signs for various resorts. Krystal, Playa de Oro, Royal. Groups congregated around the roped section hoping to spot a passenger. Once people began sauntering in, Joanna joined others at the rope.

She checked her watch. Fifteen minutes at the rope. Then she glimpsed her friend's dark tousled head, cocked with a hint of arrogance eyeing her fellow travelers. Catching sight of Joanna, Janene tossed a brown leather jacket over her shoulder and waved. Luckily, going through the checkpoint, she was not one of those who had to open and display her travel goods and quickly made it through.

Janene dropped her bags and coat and the two embraced and eyed each other at arm's length. "You look great." Joanna was the first to speak. Janene looked sensuous in her well-fitting jeans, sleeveless white shell and western boots.

"I was about to say the same. Wow it is warm and humid. I sure need to abandon these clothes. It decided to be winter for a day and I left Denver in ice and snow. It's been really mild you know, until last night."

"That's what Dad said. I have Tony's Jeep. I told you a little about him. And the top's off, so we'll let the travel breezes cool you down."

"You must have him hog-tied, for him to loan out his wheels so generously. Tell me, is it really serious? He must be something to catch *your* eye, Miss picky."

"Talk about picky, near as I can tell, you won't even look anymore."

"Too often their mentality doesn't get off the ground."

"I don't think Tony fits that stereotype. He's bright, a bundle of fun and energy, a bit of a tease and his allure..." She liked that word. "You'll just have to wait and judge for yourself. He's taking us to La Cruz tonight. It's a village kitty corner across the bay from Bucerias. They have karaoke I guess, and good ribs, according to Tony."

It was one-sided chatter from the airport. Janene was usually the race-driver type and Jo couldn't help showing off a little, cutting in and out of the traffic, taking the topes too fast, bringing a squeal from Janene as she caught the air. Pointing out every spot she knew to the novice Mexico traveler, Jo barely kept one hand on the wheel. A red Jeep loaded with what looked like college boys honked and waved.

They followed for a few miles but were cut off by a mammoth diesel Mercedes bus, which Jo managed to stay ahead of.

Arriving at the campground, Jo prepared a fruit and cheese plate, which they ate on the beach, since Janene was anxious to get close to the ocean. Joanna borrowed some boogie boards, and they spent an hour fighting crashing waves and gulping seawater. Finally, they learned how to catch the curl just right and had many good rides jetting through the spewing foam.

For a while they paddled out beyond the waves and floated. Janene's genuine excitement and enthusiasm about being with her in Mexico surprised Joanna. Janene was always a ball of fun, but her attitude generally oozed of cynicism, and she held everything in check maintaining an inner cool, never really letting go.

They were about chest deep as they dismounted the boogie boards and made their way toward shore. Janene's voice was alive. "I really needed a break, Jo and this was a good time for me, since I wound up another big sale. All work and no play, makes Jan a dull girl, don't they say?"

"I'm thrilled you came, but really surprised. The Janene I know has refused vacation after vacation when I found a good deal. Remember?"

"When I read your e-mail, I decided. No more missing all the fun. Besides, we made a pact and I'm here to be a part of your search. In fact, I've been saving some info about this adventure you're on. Ooooooeeee." Janene hopped back on the boogie board. "What was that?"

"What happened? Are you OK?"

"I don't know. Something zapped me." She twisted around to look at her ankle and saw blood trickling.

Joanna stood fixed, wondering if something would zap her. Feeling foolish at her lack of bravery, she waded to Janene, trying to examine her foot when a wave rushed in pushing her off balance. "Let's get you to the shore and check this thing out."

It had been a stingray, to be sure. Janene felt something touch her foot on that last step, then instantaneously it whipped around her ankle and jabbed. Now she stretched in a lounge chair in the shade while Clara and Norine dashed to their RV for medical supplies. The two traveled together in a Class-C RV, the type that has a sleeper over the cab. Norine, who had been a nurse, seemed to be the strong and capable one who did the driving and most of the talking. Clara, more petite and pretty, appeared shy and sweet. Today, they both jumped right into the care-giving role.

Norine produced an antiseptic to drench the puncture and an antihistamine to fight the reaction of the toxins in the sting. Clara fashioned a bandage with gauze patches and medical tape. The area was already puffy and beginning to darken like a bruise.

Norine asked the questions. "Are you dizzy or feeling sick?"

"No, just some throbbing around the ankle."

"Are you allergic to antihistamine?"

She was not. Clara rolled a soft towel and propped her foot. "You relax and keep that foot up for a while and if you begin to feel sick or dizzy, we'll get you off to the Medical Clinic."

Janene resisted all the pampering she was getting. Being tough was part of her demeanor and it took all she could to keep still and follow the directions of these two elderly companions. "Really, I feel fine." In full control, her voice dismissed concern. "It's a good thing this happened today. It's probably a once in a lifetime experience and now I can go back in for a swim or boogie board ride knowing that I've had my mishap." She wagged a finger at Jo. "And JJ "Don't be thinking that I'm going to miss our night at La Cruz. I'll be good, laying out here for an hour, then I'm back in action in paradise."

Joanna grinned at Janene and her ever unyielding veneer.

CHAPTER 21

I t was Janene's night. The view was spectacular from the second-floor restaurant. Sleek sail boats colored the eye in clever designs with varieties of *rojo, azul, verde* until they became silhouettes against ripples reflecting the *rosado* sky, first brilliant and then with the softness of the pink cheeks of a newborn.

Endless chips, salsa and gigantic stemware brimming with margaritas accompanied the retold story of *the sting.* Patrons from surrounding tables came to inspect the now-bare ankle, its purplish bruise and puncture where the barb did its work. Someone produced a thick black marker. "You have to write something!" Several agreed.

"Over here, Nene." Tony insisted that the shortened version of her name fit her. She was direct, straight-forward, no frilly dilly, not that her name wasn't beautiful, he had said. She had given him a sharp look. The accompanying shrug seemed to indicate acceptance. Now he led her to an open section of the well-inscribed wall. Sailors and other visitors had left their mark: *The Carpenters, Peter, Janie, Tim and Scott; The Happy Wanderer Feb.25; The Sea Dolphin, Bill and Patty, March, 23.* Spots had been chosen as high as could be reached standing on a chair.

Tony did not release her hand until they reached the wall. Then he gingerly lifted onto the tallest stool he could find.

"What shall I write?" She searched his laughter-filled eyes. Not typical for Janene. She always knew what to do, write or say. No one ever told *her.*

"Nene, this is your first day in Mexico. You had a momentous experience. Record it for posterity."

She thought. Taking the thick marker in her left hand, she scrawled her message.

> *This Warrioress tasted*
> *The power and salt of the sea*
> *Endured the sting of a ray*
> *Was stirred by kindness*
> *In this great land*
> *(Nene)*
> *Jan. 15*

Jo remembered Janene's haughty declaration during one of the sleepovers with the Quad Squad "I believe in a past life I was a warrior, strong and powerful."

Warrioress seemed to fit. Mystified, Joanna read the 'was stirred by kindness' and the 'Nene' parts of the inscription. Janene was not likely to publicly admit any stirring and she had never been called Nene until Tony came up with the idea. Was she referring to Clara and Norine, the nursemaids of the afternoon? Jo had not done anything in particular to 'stir' her. Was it Tony who 'stirred' her? Perplexity. That's what she felt.

She thrust the thoughts aside and cheered along with the others who whooped and laughed. "Our warrioress." This was Janene's night.

Platters of ribs with all the trimmings kept everyone gooey fingered and lip smacking. Jo offered her leftovers to Tony. Not one more bite could be swallowed. The mood was jubilant when Joanna, Tony and Janene plus a dozen or so, retreated to the bar on the first floor where the karaoke was to begin.

Another evening Jo might have felt quite gutsy and belted out with best of them. Tony gave up on his encouragement and she watched while one after another bravely stumbled over the words and failed to keep on tune yet doing so with such enthusiasm. One couple, apparently regular participants, chose a Country Western ballad originally by Dolly Parton and Kenny Rogers. They did great harmony, and both had nice voices.

It mattered little whether people were good or not, the cheering was equally raucous. Country Western seemed to be the theme of choice, and many worked to get the right slur and twang.

Someone started the rhythmic chant. "Warrior-ess, Warrior-ess, Warrior-ess."

Tony helped Janene to the raised platform. A dynamite package in her jeans and tonight a bright yellow sleeveless shell, her whole body pulsed with the beat. Tossing her head and brushing her fingers through her hair left it in disarray. Widening her stance, she felt the rhythm and launched into song. By the end of the first line, she had the key right and her confidence was unstoppable. A rich guzzling voice came from down deep. The subtlety of her moves heightened the sensorial tension in the room. The following ovation encouraged her to try another, equally sensational.

Tony had his turn. He gave swiveling-his-hips his best with an Elvis Presley number. When he returned to his place beside her, Jo gripped his knee. "I suppose you will want me to call you Elvis, from now on."

He put his arm around her shoulders and gave her a squeeze. "Was I that good?"

"Are you game to try one together?" Janene stood by the table drumming her fingers, waiting for a reply. "Come on. Or is JoJo determined to play the wallflower tonight?"

Everyone was having a good time. Why couldn't she join in? Outside, looking in was how she felt. Tony and Janene really put themselves into their rendition and much whooping and hollering followed. This was Janene's night, afterall. Let her have it. Joanna convinced herself she was being generous, remaining on the sidelines.

It was 1:30 before Tony jolted to a stop in front of the campground. "Whoa baby."

Janene slapped the seat in front of her. "Thanks for getting us back happily unencumbered and well exhilarated. Wahoo, what a night."

"Yeah, and guess who had the biggest cheering section. Nene, you won by a mile. Isn't that right, Jo?"

Joanna wanted to yell out. *Hey I didn't know this was a contest. I thought it was a night of friendly fun.* "Shhhhhh. Can't you two keep your voices down? Most of our neighbors probably hit the sack hours ago." She had to say it. All the way back Janene and Tony yelled back and forth reliving each song. It irked her.

Tony hopped out and bounded to Jo's side. "May I help M'Lady? Oh, that's right we need to keep it quiet." He shushed himself, made a swooping bow and took Jo's hand kissing it before she stepped out. "And Warrioress, do you accept chivalry?"

Janene tripped getting out from the back seat. She teetered toward Tony who caught her and whirled her onto the cobblestone street. Clamping her hand over her laughing mouth, Janene said, "Sorry, I'm usually not such a klutz. Hey Jo, are there any more Tony's hanging around that you could introduce me to?" Then she addressed Tony. "Hey, pal, it was a great evening."

"It was my pleasure to have the company of two extraordinary women." Quietly he opened the gate. An arm around each woman, he escorted them to the Roadtrek whispering, "We'll have to do it again sometime."

Joanna pulled away. "I'm bushed guys. Time to get some shuteye. No doubt you're exhausted too, Janene." Fuming, she rushed into the Roadtrek, leaving the door wide open for Janene. It was several giggles later before she came inside and by that time Joanna was already under the sheet.

She didn't feel like talking and played too tired while Janene tried to make small talk and get herself organized in the small quarters. She didn't want this tension with Janene. Tomorrow they would really talk.

By morning Jo had forgotten whether she was ticked at Janene or Tony, maybe both, but the animosity had dimmed. She decided some things were better left unsaid. Her original plan before she knew Janene was coming was to check out some small-town resorts for International Travel today. She decided not to change her plans. Together they could have their own exploration.

The digital clock blinked to 9:30. It felt good to sleep late and awake refreshed, but there was still plenty of time to get organized for the road trip. With her unhurried stretch, a low moan escaped her lips. Janene's outburst jarred her senses.

"That's it. I forgot to tell you. I've been struggling all night in my dreams. You know those dreams that you need to be at a meeting, or the airport and you can't find it and you're panicked you'll be late?"

Jo had had many of those restless times. "Don't you hate those nights? You wake up more tired than when you went to sleep. What did you forget to tell me anyway?"

"I was waiting for the right time to tell you after I arrived yesterday. And on the way in from boogie boarding, I said I had some news. But the stingray hit me. And I completely forgot. Remember?"

"Vaguely. What is it?"

"The church. It's probably on your e-mail now."

"What are you talking about?"

"I talked to Amy Friday. The day after they got home. Anyway, Marilyn went to the one-hour developing place and straight over to her friend's house and in no time, they found a match for Dixie's church."

"Already? Where is it? I suppose it's two thousand miles away."

Janene jumped up and pillaged through her carryon case. "I wrote it all down. However, she was going to try to get the info e-mailed yesterday."

Jo rushed for her Mom's Mexico map. In her hurry, a stash of books tumbled on her head. "Darn." She let them lay and sat on the edge of her bed waiting.

Janene's voice rushed. "OK, OK. Here it is. *La Parroquia, which means parish church, a famous landmark in San Miguel de Allende.* Does it sound familiar?"

"Does it? I can't believe it. The day before you got here, I was surfing the net and that name came up on the screen, but I didn't have enough information to make a solid connection. San Miguel..." It took several minutes to spot it on the map. "Here it is. Not too far from Guadalajara. I think Guadalajara is maybe three hours from here by car. I bet I we could make it in a day."

"There's more about the church and the town. Apparently, Marilyn's friend keeps good information about each church in her collection. Wanta hear it?"

"Sure."

"First built as a colonial church in 1683- In 1880 Zeferino Gutierrez," Janene stumbled over the name and continued. *"an uneducated mason was inspired by postcards of European Gothic cathedrals and started the present facade. He sketched designs in the sand with a stick. He maintained the original interior, which is based on a Latin cross. St. Michael, the Archangel and namesake of the town occupies the main altar. The three bells start ringing early in the morning. Located on the SW corner of the main square, Jardin Principal. San Miguel has a higher concentration of artistically active Americans than any other Mexican City. Named after the patron Saint, Michael, thus San Miguel. Later de Allende was added after Ignacio Allende, a captain in the Spanish colonial army, a leader in Mexico's early struggle for independence.*

I think there is more on the e-mail. But I tried to get most of it down."

"The piece I read said something about a large population of artists in San Miguel also." Joanna hoped that meant Dixie was one of them. She lifted her bed and brought out the painting of *La Parroquia*. Now it had a name. And the two stared at the majesty of this neo-Gothic parish church and its ethereal spires and bells.

Jo lay back on her rumpled bed. Salty droplets clouded her view of the ceiling, collected, then squeezed from her blue green eyes. Jumping up she grabbed Janene, dancing her around the small space. "Thank you, thank you. You seem to end up being my messenger, don't you?"

The rest of the morning was a blur. Dressing and nibbling on fresh bread, jam, juice and coffee, then hastily making certain everything was put away, they made ready for the trip. The trip to San Miguel would have to wait until Janene left. Joanna didn't want her to feel unappreciated or spoil her week of vacation.

Today, they were off to Saulita. Jo ran to the corner phone booth to call Tony. He had stepped out. She gave Jesus the message and hoped he understood. They were off to new adventures and did not know when they would return. They would talk to him tomorrow.

The Roadtrek was disconnected from its necessities, and they headed north. Ten miles of winding mountain roads later they turned toward the busy village, dodging a burro, three jumping children and umpteen potholes. Edging closer to the hub of the village, Jo turned onto an angled dirt road squeezing into an empty spot. "I think it's better if we walk. I dare say this village was not designed for motorized traffic with its narrow ups and downs and arounds."

They passed typical *tiendas* displaying fruits, vegetables, shelves of cereals, boxed juices, pasta, sauces, plastic bags of various colored dried beans and square towers of eggs separated by gray cardboard partitions, each layer holding thirty eggs. Moseying in and out of each shop or emporium, the women were surprised at the variety and high quality in the glassware, furniture, fashions, and household appointments. They were particularly taken with the freestanding Indonesian drums carved from dark woods, the color of ebony. They ranged from ankle high to waist high. An unusual resonance emanated when the stretched skins were gently tapped.

Jo jotted notes on her palm-sized pad. When pursuing a booking package, she needed to get a real feel for the area and what it offered. Around the corner, they saw the blue of the sea and walked toward the beach. Amy and Dan had been here to watch the surfers, but other than being a good place for surfing, Joanna knew little about Saulita.

They found a taco stand and sat watching splashes of color bobbing, waiting for the right wave. Janene nodded to a gal who arrived at her side. Her flimsy fitting dress with thin straps draped over a lean frame, exaggerating her youthful pointy breasts. The weight of her backpack pulled her shoulders back giving her arms the look of wishbones. Tawny, wooly dreadlocks hung over her brow and were clamped together at the back of her head.

Janene took the plunge. "Hi, I'm Janene and this is Joanna. Do you live here?"

Miss dreadlocks awoke from another world. "Ah, oh…hi. I'm Star. For the time being, I'm staying here. A bunch of us camp on the beach at night down by the RV park."

Janene continued. "How about a taco? While we're eating you can tell us about the little town. What do you say?"

She did it again. Joanna watched as Janene took over. It was always a subtle one-upmanship, 'I know better than you do, just watch'. Someone who lived here yet wasn't indigenous to the area was bound to add to the information Jo was searching. Yet it irritated her, especially when it turned out Janene was right.

"Sure, whataya wanta know?"

They learned that the village was an interesting mix of Americans and Canadians, some here for the winter, others were year-rounders, some rich, others not so rich, some who had set up businesses. Added to that was the surfing hippie-type crowd. Hardworking locals ran the little shops and *tiendas*. It seemed an interesting mix, not a magnet for all tourists. Despite the trashy feel of the town, it was a busy place with elegant and elaborate mansions dotting the hillsides. A few artists had fancy houses overlooking the sea. Star's friend in the RV park was an artist and took her to one, one time. She could show them if they wanted.

Jo had this urge to look for artists. Maybe one of them knew Dixie. They decided to go. They walked past the square where music boomed, the base vibrating Jo's chest. "Just like at home," she said."

Ten minutes later, they reached a fork in the steep road. Star asked. "Do you know about the miracle in the village? It's been written up in the Bucerias paper for Gringos. You said that's where you're staying, right?"

Jo shook her head. "Haven't heard about it."

"It's only a block out of our way. I'll show you. They stopped in front of a hut, roofed by palm branches. Skinny sticks formed the walls. A few stones served as steps down into a dark opening.

Star advised, "You have to stand on the second step and look through the doorway to see it."

They learned that the peasant woman who lived in the primitive home, a devout Catholic, was frying pancakes on her griddle, a thin cookie-sheet-like pan when an image of the Virgin Guadalupe appeared. Moved by such a miracle she placed this shrine so all might see and be blessed. Once the priest came and took the griddle to the church, but the vision disappeared. It was returned immediately, and the vision reappeared.

"Look!" Star motioned them to follow. "It's all right. She is very proud of her miracle and wants to share it with others."

Jo steadied herself onto the second step and looked in at the pan propped against the wall. The image filled most of the sheet and looked ever so much like the Mexican Virgin Guadalupe in the framed picture at its side. She wore a flowing gown and a long scarf draped over her head, slightly bowed in reverence. Two planks formed shelves in front of the "miracle" and bore candles—some flickered in the dimness, flowers—both fresh and plastic, and doilies—colorfully crocheted.

"Many villagers stop to honor the Virgin and the peasant, leaving flowers and lighting candles. Do you see her?"

Janene took her turn. They both saw.

No one spoke as they continued the walk toward the artist's home. The climb was steep, then leveled at the top. Beautiful homes bedecked with trumpet and bougainvillea vines seemed planted at the end of red bricked driveways. What a contrast to the little "miracle hut" just down the hill along the dusty, dirt of the road.

Star led them through a massive archway into a courtyard, immaculate in its grooming, bearing tropical flowers, variegated green plants and a small pool reflecting the blueness of the sky. Canopied by the gentle palms, the effect was one of solitude. Another massive archway framed the entrance to the splendid mansion where a sign stood. *Artist studio and gallery upstairs.*

Star explained that two days a week, Roselyn opened her studio to the public. Star chose to wait outside, since she had been there before and did not want to feel the awkward stares today as she had the time she visited with her friend.

Climbing the spiral stairway built of heavy stone and tile, Jo and Janene looked down into the mammoth living and dining rooms. Everything was grand scale, the couches strewn with dozens of pillows, the coffee tables, end tables, lamps, oriental style rugs on the tiled floor, and the dark carved dining table with its eight heavy chairs. Before they rounded the corner, they glimpsed stuccoed walls, a deep rubbed-on golden shade, where humongous paintings were hung.

The final step opened onto a terrace, which looked over more gardens and the hypnotic sea, its motion, color, and spray. Roselyn welcomed them and offered refreshments spread at the far end. They refused the refreshment, introduced themselves, and entered the spacious studio through glass sliding doors.

The room was huge. Color everywhere. One wall, a vibrant green and another a deep purple, created a sense of drama. Dozens of paintings, both watercolor and oil, looked down upon them. Smaller ones lay on the several worktables, amid hundreds of pyramids of paint tubes and cans of brushes, impersonating floral arrangements. This was a working artist's loft, busy and productive, yet organized and neat.

Fascinated by the tall, regal artist, all in white with a lacy caftan layered over a slender skirt, slit on one side, Jo wondered about her Dixie mother. Might she be something like this woman with merriment in her eyes and the golden glow of her skin, masking the crinkles peeking around the corners in her face? Had she been blonde at one time? Her hair, a soft brown was pulled straight back, first braided with colored yarns and then coiled into a sizable bun above the nape of her neck. A bright, orange-red mouth spoke in an easy and friendly manner. Yet Jo sensed that this woman was all strength and business.

Equally talented in oils and watercolor, she used pigment, shadow and light expertly in floral displays, still life and landscapes. On the couch below the vibrant green wall, pillows formed their own artwork in stitchery scenes. Jo learned that Roselyn was the designer, but the stitching belonged to a group of Huichol Indian women.

Joanna examined the glossy edition Roselyn had authored. Page after page of instructions and examples filled the book. They heard others talking about prices. The unframed miniatures started in the hundreds and the hanging framed masterpieces were upwards of $10,000.

She was reluctant to ask about her birthmother. Was she afraid Dixie wouldn't measure up to this woman who apparently enjoyed much fame? When she did ask and explained that Dixie A. Donavan had done some work around San Miguel de Allende, Roselyn said she had not heard of her; it had been twenty-five years since had been to San Miguel.

The walk back to the center of the village was brisk. Janene and Star kept a steady conversation. In her own world, Joanna heard little of it. Good-byes and good wishes, then Star trekked down the beach toward her group's camping spot.

Joanna stopped at several hotels, filling her notebook with information, while Janene waited, watching the surfers who picked the precise moment to rise on their slender boards. When she was finished, the two decided there was enough time to drive on to the next village.

San Francisco, affectionately referred to as San Pancho was a quieter spot, fewer hotels, not so much action. One held some promise, but Jo had difficulty communicating with the personnel who spoke not a word of English, so they followed the signs toward another hotel away from the village. Jo and Janene wove through groves of mangos and citrus. Dust kicked up behind them and swirled. Joanna shut the window.

"Have we missed it? Do you suppose we should have turned off back there where the road split?" The road was becoming narrower. "I'd hate to end up at a dead end where we couldn't turn around."

They both searched for signs, any clues. Over a small precipice, the road widened, and cobblestones reappeared. White painted walls, tall and thick hid all but short glimpses of fine villas climbing the steep hillside facing the ocean. A capital E with an arrow indicated parking space across the street.

"I guess we found it, Jo. Take a sharp right. I know you can make it."

The hotel was a sprawling complex in white stucco. The restaurant seemed to be a hub of activity. Posters of tours and trips—horseback, kayak and canoe—were plastered on a bulletin board. The packed schedule included fiesta night, game night, a night with a Spanish guitarist and a beachside cookout. There would be a presentation concerning the turtle conservation project, tonight.

A few guests were vacating the lounge chairs on the beach; others sipped beverages on the terrace; young kids splashed and squealed in the pool. Janene ordered a drink on the terrace while Jo asked for the manager and obtained what information she could about the resort. A polite and handsome Mexican insisted on giving her the grand tour and loaded her down with flyers and information. Sometime later, Jo sheepishly found her friend's table.

"Sorry Janene. I didn't expect to be so long. It looks like you found some friends. Good deal."

"Hey, Jo, I'm on vacation. Not watching the clock or working, like you are. Meet the Block's. Jennifer and Alan. Newlyweds."

"We've been hearing about you and your last couple of days. What a kick." Jennifer reached out for a handshake. "Nene says you might be able to join us for dinner and stay for the turtle presentation. Afterwards we'll be releasing turtles to the sea."

Jo was interested in the "Nene" part. Maybe it fit her. Janene seemed to like it. She'd be damned if she would use it, though. "Sounds good to me."

Jo and Janene enjoyed the newlyweds, their wit and snide humor. Alan played the "thorn among the violets" for all it was worth. His wife didn't seem to mind the mild flirtation. By the time the meal was finished, and two more rounds of drinks were downed, Jo was feeling a little swirly.

She was relieved when an elderly man opened his case and set up the slide projector and screen. Talking through a bushy mustache, the man explained that he was part of a group that was organized several years ago to protect the sea turtles or *las tortugas.*

"For eons, the turtles have been coming to the nearby beaches to lay their eggs. They use the pull of the poles to navigate when they return to their nesting grounds, the place they were hatched. They often lay twice a year and then perhaps for two or three years a turtle remains out in the seas without nesting.

"The local beaches supported up to 5000 turtles for years, but poachers have been stealing the eggs and killing the turtles for meat and turtle oil for decades, reducing the numbers dangerously, to 300. There is some excitement about reports from fishermen who are seeing more young turtles this year. Hopefully the project is having success, but it will be twelve or more years until the little ones that have been released are mature enough to mate and lay eggs.

"Today we are up against poachers who dig freshly laid eggs to sell in bars to men hoping to improve their virility. These poachers can earn $300 in a few nights, a month's wages for many. The story goes that early Spaniards making their voyages to the new country observed turtles mating for up to twenty-four hours at a time. They admired such virility and began eating the eggs in hopes of gaining the turtle's sexual prowess.

"Mating occurs in the open sea, and about 29 days later the mommies are ready for laying. They come ashore at night and choose the middle third of the beach between the water and the land. Apparently, this is the safest spot for the eggs and the hatchlings. She digs a deep trench with her back flippers, then hovers over the spot, laying between seventy to one-hundred and twenty eggs. She covers the nest with sand and flops around the whole area to pack it.

"When we dig up the eggs, we store them in Styrofoam boxes between layers of sand. A little larger than ping-pong balls, they are soft and somewhat leathery. Incubation time varies and is partially controlled by temperature of the sand. Sex determination is also controlled by temperature. Once they begin hatching, they wriggle themselves to the top of the boxes. Tonight, we have a group of newly hatched turtles waiting to be released."

Once the slides and questions were completed, Jo, Janene, Alan and Jennifer took their turn to pick a turtle for release. Jo cupped her hand over the nearly black hatchling. It prodded her fingers with its pointed nose and pushed against her palm with persistent flippers. "My little guy is ready to be on his own. I can't let him have one little peep hole or he'd be out of my hand." *Hold on little guy.* She needed that same tenacity. She needed to be on with the search for Dixie. Now.

Step by step Joanna drew closer to the sea. All the way the little guy wriggled and twisted looking for a way out. Joanna had been concentrating on the hatchling and failed to see the sliver of a moon. It was a smiling moon, and nearby a star hovered, startlingly bright. *Just follow that star little one.* She wanted to follow the star that she now had, a clue about Dixie.

Joanna knelt, uncupping her hands, releasing the little guy and watched with pride as he waddled toward the foam, leaving miniature tire tracks in his wake. She looked at the smiling moon with its side-kick star. *Go baby, you can make it. They could both make it.*

I *think* I'm all grown up. But…If I missed so much of my childhood, is it possible? I'm feeling that spine again. Buried in my chest, festering. Yet there is no reason for it. My days are peaceful. Mary, next door, and I have an easy relationship. Such a zesty person, she brings flavor to our time together. I paint and she weaves wonderful cloth. Oscar comes in nodding and smiling in his polite way.

Nicki went back to California before I moved here. I thought San Miguel would be the perfect place for me. It is an artisan's mecca. Well, it has been, but there's this tug in my chest. Yet I can't leave. Don't know where I'd go anyway. I can't help but wonder about little Cara— correction—grown up Cara. I have to bury the wondering about that life that grew inside me. I wouldn't choose myself for a mother or my own mother Darlene, for that matter.

Buddy's been here for six months, trying to get his life together. When he was all patched up, he had to do his jail time. That's where Nicki found him. She did some time herself. Jail was really rough on Buddy. He tried music again when he got out, but nothing worked. I'm happy to be here for him and I surely owe him. He did the time. He's less broken as a man than he was when he arrived, but there is no going back when it comes to our relationship. We both know it. And though there's not much here for me anymore, I can't leave him stranded.

CHAPTER 22

"Didn't you get my message? I told Jesus we would be late." Joanna stood on the corner once again, the phone to her ear.

"Tony's voice was brittle. "I didn't think late meant the next morning. I was worried sick when I found your campsite vacant last night."

It irked her to think he had been checking up on her. Or was it he was eager to see Janene again. "I'm sorry you worried, but I'm a big girl and have been taking care of myself a long time, you know."

"Do you think it's safe for two good looking gals to camp just anywhere?"

Her voice was curt. "We didn't camp just anywhere. I wasn't willing to drive that curvy road in the dark. We were fine at the square in San Francisco. There's a light pole there and other than the barking dogs, we had a good peaceful sleep.

"OK, OK. So, how's Nene doing? Enjoying her introduction to Mexico?"

"Yes, Janene is fine and enjoying Mexico. In fact, we're planning to see more of it. We're heading to San Miguel de Allende in the morning." There was a curtness in her voice.

"You're what? That's a pretty good trip from here."

"I know. Hey, my phone card is almost used up. Can you get away for lunch? We can talk more then."

Once the *bolillos,* (those boat shaped Mexican rolls) egg salad with slices of tomato, avocado and fresh pineapple were devoured and Tony was updated about yesterday's adventures plus *La Parroquia of San*

Miguel, Jo spread her mom's maps and travel books on the fold-up table. Tony had not been that far inland, but he had driven to Guadalajara several times and figured it would take three-and-half hours in the Roadtrek.

If they used the tolls most of the way, they could make it to San Miguel in eight or nine hours he thought. There would be a whole day of tromping the town inquiring about Dixie and a return trip the next day. They would have two days after their return to see PV or whatever, since Janene's flight did not leave until 10:00 at night.

"Janene are you sure you want to spend your vacation this way? We're going to be two days on the road."

"Why do you think I came down here? To laze around the beach the whole time? Besides I'm just as excited as you are about finding Dixie."

"Wouldn't it be great if you were with me when I found her, especially since you helped me start this whole thing taking me to see Ellie?"

Tony looked from one animated face to the other. "I can see that I'm not needed. Besides I have work to do at the shop. We're putting in a coffee bar and the new coffee machines just came in."

Janene gripped Tony's arm. "Hey, we didn't mean to ignore you. No use running off. We're almost finished with our plans, don't you think? Jo."

"I think so, just need to replenish the fridge, so we can save time and money, eating on the way."

Tony stood, jangling the keys in his pocket. "How about dinner out tonight. I'll treat my two beauties."

"Thanks Tony, I think we'll relax on the beach. Let Janene get off that ankle with the sting, though the swelling has gone down. Right?"

"I'm fine. Hardly know it happened. But we'll need a good night's sleep before our early departure. Jo is right about skipping a night out."

"Well, OK. We'll celebrate when you get back. Tony pulled Jo toward him. He rocked her with his hug and buried his cheek in her hair. The little bit of irritation Jo held onto since the karaoke, melted. She felt secure in his arms, had been missing this and held tight.

His words were for her only. "You take care and be safe M'Lady. I'll miss you...so much. I know this is important. I hope you find her."

Their tender kiss lingered on her lips, even as he waved bounding through the gate. He revved the Jeep motor and was gone.

Everything was set. Toad and Barney had all kinds of advice. "Get off the *cuota* at Magdalena. The *libre* road through Magdalena and Tequila is good. You'll save a hefty toll. Besides you may want to stop at some of the tequila distilleries. They have nice tours. Going through Guadalajara watch for the sign that says Mexico, which means to Mexico City. A good piece outside the city it splits and you head toward Leon, go around Guanajuato, through Dolores Hidalgo and finally you'll find San Miguel. It'll take ten hours or more, probably."

Stretched out near the beach, the hours crept for both of the women. "What time is it Jo?"

"It's only three. Just thirty minutes since the last time you asked."

She let out a long sigh. "I feel prickly all over. Surely in a few days I'll know more about her. What if she doesn't like me, says go away, leave me alone? I'm afraid to find her and afraid not to find her."

"I can't imagine what you're feeling. My heart is in my throat thinking about it and she's not even my mother. If we find her, I can get a bus back, you know."

"*If* this turns out well and we find her, don't worry. We'll stick to our plans, return the next day. I'll definitely be here to see you off at the airport. No matter what, I have to come back. Tony's here and I've paid for two weeks. Might as well get my money's worth."

Jo slept fitfully. Immersed in an entangled dream she climbed a slippery mountain, gripping jagged stones which left her hands bloody, achieving a few feet, only to slip back one. Desperation drove her on and on until, with a final grasp at the pinnacle, she pulled herself to look over it. A filmy apparition floated before her, faceless except for grinning teeth. Its arm waved her back. The pointed rock broke in her hand and she slid down, down, down until she awoke, sweaty and jittery. It was a variation of the recurring dreams she had earlier.

The clock stared at her. A quarter till five. The alarm would go off in an hour. Janene's breathing was soundless. "Are you awake Janene?" It was a whisper.

"I've been watching the clock for the last hour. I can't go back to sleep. Shall we get up and get an early start?"

"Might as well."

When they pulled from the campground a hazy light was creeping over the horizon and the winding trip north of Bucerias was void of heavy traffic. Thankfully, it was too early for the tractor-trailers that often pulled two or three units, grinding over the mountain road. Janene was as good a navigator as Amy had been.

The conversation was non-stop. Janene heard about Amy's and Jo's trip, the experiences she and Amy shared during her stay, about Sherry, Amy's sister-in-law, Mariana, the weaver and *La espina.* Janene told of her latest real estate deals. The only subject that seemed off limits was Tony.

They made the right exits and left the *cuota* at Magdalena, stopped to stretch their legs at Tequila and bought a couple of cute barrels of the Mexican juice at one of the roadside stands. It would have been fun to take a tour. Another time maybe.

The traffic was heavy going through Guadalajara, but following the *Mexico* signs got them through without a hitch. Still brown, the rolling hills bore little but miles of chicken farms with long white roofs covering open-air buildings sided with canvas, so that the chickens were out of sight. The chicken smell prevailed long after they left the area.

They found the *Autopista,* a long section of toll road, quite expensive, but they made good time and were glad to pay the fees. Before turning toward Leon, they pulled off at a *caseta* to eat and buy gas. Neither was tired after five-and-a-half hours on the road.

Near Leon, they commented about the pollution hovering above and passed a huge GM plant with rows and rows of cars and trucks of all colors and styles awaiting shipment. No more *cuota,* but they found the *libre* quite good and enjoyed driving through some of the villages. On the outskirts of Dolores Hidalgo, simple white buildings displayed colorful ceramic pots, jugs, pitchers, plates, statues.

"Look at those pots! Some look large enough to hide in. Do you think we have time to stop?" It was a good time to take a break.

Jo remembered some of the dishware her mother had purchased, not too different from these. She could not resist a platter painted with the white Mexican lily that would match those that her mother had bought. Janene chose a pot, small enough to stash in the Roadtrek and for the trip home.

"Would you trust me at the wheel? I'd be happy to drive, you know."

"Hey Nene." She said it. "I'd trust you with my life."

Janene smiled. "You know, I've never had a nickname. The closest thing was Janny which I hate. I kind of like it."

"Me too. Perhaps Janene is a little fancy and soft for you. Don't get me wrong. I don't mean you're hard or harsh. But Nene does seem to fit."

Janene gave her one of those looks. "Hardnosed, determined. I admit it."

"Then it's Nene from now on? I don't know if I can change."

"Whatever. But Nene does feel comfortable."

Janene enjoyed driving the Roadtrek and handled it well, twisting over, around and through the rolling terrain. Jo relaxed, watching the countryside slide by. "Well, what do you think of him?" It was time to clear the air.

"Who?"

"Come on don't play games with me?"

"Oh...He's witty, interesting, good-looking. I can see why you like him. You two really hit it off, didn't you? Janene glanced and caught her nod. "I'm darned happy for you. Being Italian, myself, I can read those snapping eyes."

"You can? What do they say?"

"Hum...'I'm passionate, fun-loving, love life, determined'. He's no simple man."

"I'm sure about that."

Jo thumbed through the Mexico travel book and found San Miguel de Allende. "It says that this is one of the most beautiful mountain cities of Mexico, a busy trading center for jewelry, tin work, wooden furniture, pottery, textiles and filled with many art galleries."

"I'd say it sounds encouraging, Jo."

"Hope so. The piece about *La Parroquia* has about the same info that Marilyn's friend sent. There's a little map here which should help us find the square."

They had been on the road over ten hours when the *Bienvendidos* sign for San Miguel greeted them. It felt good to be nearing their destination with plenty of daylight. Jo eyed the map and looked for street signs. She finally discovered that the names of the streets could be found on the sides of the buildings at the end of each block. They passed a resort/hotel on the left with plenty of parking, thinking it might be a possible stopping place for the night.

The road narrowed, which meant pulling over when they met another vehicle, then jogged to the right. They felt closed in by the buildings rising on each side of them until they came to a crossroad. Eyeing the map, Jo said, "Turn here. I think this must be Allende street, where the church is."

They wheeled along a couple of blocks, then the street widened. To the left was the main square, shaded by trimmed laurel trees. To the right, there it was, *La Parroquia.* The spires glowed, bathed in the rays of the sun, not yet set, while deep shadows crept around each nook and cranny as dusk advanced. The whole effect gave the feeling of powerful, yet frangible. They stopped and stood before it.

"My Dixie mother was here. To be sure."

The square seemed to beckon humanity. Circling in the Roadtrek they saw numerous people in lively conversation, perched on wrought iron benches, painted green. Others played music in their small corner. Venders with pushcarts displayed colorful and tasty wares.

"Jardin Principal, San Miguel's popular meeting place." Joanna inhaled deeply, then continued, "Let's go back to that resort and see if they will let us park in their lot without renting a room. I don't think there is a place for our little rig down here with all the narrow streets."

At the desk, they finally made their questions understood. Yes, they could park in the lot for the equivalent of two dollars. Their auxiliary battery would hold up for a while and everything they needed was in the Roadtrek. They decided to find a restaurant for supper. No cooking tonight.

As the morning light filtered around the drawn curtains, Jo moved soundlessly from her bed, hoping not to awaken her friend. Writing in her journal she ended the segment with—*Will I look into the face of my Dixie mother today?*

Nene opened the curtain above her bed and addressed Jo and the morning sun together. "Good morning sunshine. I had the best sleep."

"Me too." Not wanting to rush the day, Joanna suggested a hearty breakfast. She started the coffee and rattled the pans digging for a small skillet. "I'm pretty mean with omelets. How about ham, green pepper, onion, and cheese?"

There they sat, pajama clad, cradling mugs of unfinished coffee, filled with the delicious breakfast. Nene started, "I have no regrets about my past and no desire to relive it, but once and a while I ache for those carefree feelings of childhood."

Jo smiled. "I know what you mean. Right now, it's a tad like the old days after a sleepover. Lounging in our PJ's, but with mugs of hot chocolate in those days."

"And remember those dares." Nene's eyes danced.

"You always won didn't you. You were the nervy one, not afraid to dial a boy one of us had a crush on. When his mom answered, you'd ask for him then we'd hang up when you handed us the phone. I was so embarrassed. But not you."

They remembered....and laughed while cleaning up from breakfast, making up the beds, dressing, brushing teeth. "Nene, it must be a real bummer for people who have no one to remember the past with."

"I never thought about it. You're so right."

Now it was time to hurry the day. Jo and Nene gathered the book with the map, Dixie's two paintings—protected by pillowcases—and headed toward the center of town. All morning they trekked up and down streets, in and out of shops. They would have admired the textiles, tinwork, furniture, and jewelry, if finding galleries displaying paintings was not the top priority.

They trudged on. San Miguel indeed was a place where many Gringos had settled. But no one knew a Dixie Donovan.

Propping the paintings, Jo and Nene collapsed on a green painted bench. They had come full circle, back to the square, where artists displayed their watercolors of local scenes, a youthful couple played wooden flutes and others made selections from the novelty and food carts.

Jo stretched her arms and rolled her shoulders. "This place is a lot bigger than I thought. I'm afraid this is going to be a dead end."

"We haven't walked that section behind us. Let's grab something from the food cart and head on that way for the afternoon."

Joanna said, "You keep the bench. I'll go buy the food. What do you want? That cart over there has flat tacos and the other looks like hot dogs."

"How 'bout hot dogs today?"

When Jo returned, she carried hot dogs in one hand and gripped two long necked bottles of pop with the other. No Janene and no paintings. Where was she? Joanna sat to wait, irritated with her friend.

The hotdog was half gone before Janene appeared with the paintings under her arm, virtually dragging an elderly man toward her.

"Jo, this is Oscar."

Joanna looked into a dark, well-worn face with watery eyes, soft in their gaze. His trembling hand tipped a sweat-stained hat exposing a full head of silver, cut short in its tight curled frizz. His other hand stomped a wooden cane on the stone surface.

"Happy to make your acquaintance, ma'am. Your friend tells me yore looking for a woman by the name a Dixie. I tell you, a pretty, young woman by that name lived next door to me and Mary for a while. She moved on, but I did see her do some painting. Fred, he has a gallery back that away, sold some of her stuff. He jus' might know where to find her."

Joanna could hardly swallow the bite in her mouth and it had to be washed down with the pop. He told her all he knew. Oscar and Mary came to live in San Miguel thirty years ago. Mary was a weaver. Oscar designed jewelry back in those days.

"Growed up in Loosiana, a piece from New Or'lns. My father was a whittler. Boy he could do jus' about anathing with wood. Guess I favored 'im. Gave up the jewelry making ten years ago. Mary, now, she kep up the weavin' til the last day. Gone three years now. It's kinda lonely. Many friends from that time back, gone, you know. Mary and Dixie used to talk, so she coulda told ya more 'n me. Those two could talk, you know, but I always kept my peace, working over those gems and stones."

Jo and Nene listened, taking in the gentleness of the old man.

"I know you want t' hear what I know about Dixie and not me life story, so I'll get on. Le's see now it was two years she lived next door. Before that somewhere else in the town, so's I can't tell about then. There was a man who was there for a while, then he moved off and not long after, she left too, about six months before me Mary passed on. She was, that's Dixie I mean, an easy-going gal, no fancy stuff for her, just simple, but those big brown eyes could read you like a cat."

Jo pulled the paintings from the pillowcases. "Does this look like anything you saw of hers?"

His poky drawl continued. "Well, yeah, I saw that church-one before and she liked to do those indigenous ones, of the Indians, you know. I'd say I knew your gal."

Jo pumped his hand thanking him over and over for the information. Oscar with his kindly nod wished her well and Nene snapped a couple shots of the two.

It was almost a run on the way to Fred's gallery. It wasn't far. Inside, four or five rooms ambled one to another, each adorned with wonderful oils. Many were signed with Fred's mark, but there were works by other artists as well. One room was filled with landscapes of Mexico. Another with still life of fruit, juicy enough to eat, flowers, dewy with dawn. Beautiful Mexican women looked down, dressed in velvets, satins, and native shawls. There were old men and women, each stroke of the brush revealing their charm and character.

Making their way full circle they stopped at the room facing the street. Its open window welcomed the sun's luminescence and a soft breeze. Perched on a stool sat a bearded beefy man wearing paint-blotched bib overalls, no shirt. His graying hair, tied with a blue cloth reached halfway to his waist. A giant easel and a six-foot wide painting dwarfed the man. Every detail of this very ambitious work had been sketched and nearly half of the canvas glistened with the painter's oils.

From a hilly vantage point, the whole city, houses and balconies, spires and steeples, gardens and trees, shadows and sunlight would delight the viewer's eye.

"What do you think?" His voice was as booming as he looked.

Jo was awed. "I think this will be an amazing work. I can't imagine tackling something so ominous."

"Ominous, you think? I've been a while sketching and setting this baby up. But she's beginning to take shape. Look around all you want. We have some good works here. People like to look. Sometimes they buy."

Nene took control. She reached her hand toward the man. "You must be Fred. I'm Nene and this is Jo. Actually, we're looking for some information about a woman who lived here a few years ago. Oscar says you know her. Dixie Donovan. Jo, show him Dixie's paintings."

Joanna propped the works for him to see. "She signed them Dixie A."

"I sure do know her work. Some of her Indigenous paintings were my favorite. She did several of that type with the opaque silhouettes like that little girl at the washing rock. Not too many people can accomplish that look. You say you're looking for her?"

Joanna told Fred more of her story than usual. Perhaps because he radiated such tranquility, despite the enormity of everything about him.

"She sold, perhaps twenty paintings here during the three years I knew her. She never mentioned a daughter. One time I asked her if she ever had kids. No, is what she said. I'll be darned. I sure wish that I could help you. In fact, I didn't know she had gone for several months. Still had one of her paintings in the gallery. Sold it last year and she can collect the five-hundred dollars whenever she wants. Never know, she might wander in one of these days. Tell you what. You have e-mail, I suppose?"

Jo nodded.

"Much of my business is on the Internet these days, so I'm well equipped. If she ever comes by, I'll let you know."

Jo felt deflated. "We're going to check with the people who live in her old place, but if that's a dead end, I guess this is the best I can do." She handed him her card. "Thanks so much, Fred. Your work is impressive. Hope things continue to go well for you."

"I'm more into creating than making money. Just so I have enough to do what I like, more painting. If you come back this way stop in, won't you?"

CHAPTER 23

J oanna tightened her grip on the wheel and glared at the road in front of her, while Nene watched the vegetation in its winter brown being left behind.

"Don't be too disappointed, we know she's real, we found some people who knew her, we know where she lived for a while."

"I can't believe you walked the whole square asking everyone if they had heard of the artist named Dixie Donovan."

"If it was a popular hang out, it seemed logical that someone should know her. And I found Oscar, didn't I?"

Why didn't she do that herself? Joanna didn't know.

Janene continued, "And there was a man in her life. Too bad Oscar didn't know more about him, his name or something. Did Dixie tell her mom anything about a man?"

Joanna shook her head. "When Dixie went to Arizona, she mentioned having lived in Aspen, then California, but Darlene didn't know why or how she ended up in Mexico."

"Cripes Jo, I can't believe that Dixie told her mom so little about her life here. Oscar said she left San Miguel two years ago. Do you suppose that's when she went to Arizona to see Darlene?"

"I'd say the timing fits. Evidently, she decided to leave Mexico to mend things with her mother or even stay there, once she knew her dad was dead. I guess all hell broke loose when Darlene was confronted about the sexual abuse. All talking stopped. And Dixie took off again."

"Maybe she didn't return to Mexico. Do you suppose she's somewhere in the states, after all?"

"I don't think so Nene. Darlene told me about a cousin that Dixie kept in touch with throughout the years. It was something Dixie threw in her face before she left. Something like—'Even Betsy knows more about me than you do *and* she's more important to me than you are.'"

"Darlene called the cousin after Dixie high tailed it and begged her to level with her. Betsy admitted that they kept in touch, but Dixie had always been careful to keep her whereabouts hazy, so that she couldn't be pressured to tell. A few months later the cousin did call Darlene with the news that Dixie had returned to Mexico and not to worry, she was OK."

Nene tapped a rhythm on the door-jam, then blurted, "Surely, she'll call again and if the cousin tells her about your search and how to reach you, Dixie can contact you. Call the cousin, Jo."

"Dixie may not want to talk to me. And it might be another year before Betsy hears from Dixie."

Janene threw her arms up in disbelief. "You're chasing all over this country to find Dixie and then you are afraid to leave her a message? You sound like some wimpy child who makes excuses for not playing with the next-door neighbor. Call the cousin, Jo."

Joanna turned up the music. Was she resisting because it was Janene's idea and not hers? Numbed, her mind flashed from one thought to another, like a slide projector on automatic. She was suspended, not going forward and not going backward. She *wanted* to move forward and thought of Tony who would comfort her in her discouragement. Was this relationship moving forward or was it stuck? Nene was right about her Dixie mother, though. She was not an apparition, she was real, others had known her. She would move forward *and* call the cousin.

Once the Roadtrek was back in its place beneath the waving palms and snugged against the patio slab, Jo reached to rest her hand on Janene's shoulder. "Life has an interesting way of unfolding. Only one week ago I talked to Dad, and he said that you had called. I didn't know then that you'd bring news about the painting and that we'd journey hundreds of miles together following that clue. You step in at the right time, don't you? If it wasn't for your pushiness, talking to every Tom, Dick and Oscar, I might not have found Fred. He is a definite link. Eventually it may pay off."

Janene turned to her friend and said, "Too bad Lauren can't be here. She'll feel left out when she realizes both Amy and I have been a part of the pact and she hasn't."

"Well, don't you even hint such a thing to her. She has her job to do…without being put on some guilt trip." There was a bite to her tone, but it softened as Joanna added, "Friend I need a hug."

Both pushed themselves from their captain chairs and stood in the little kitchen embracing. Nene avoided Joanna's eyes. "I know I sometimes come off a little bossy. You're important to me and I want you to have all the happiness you deserve. This has been a tough year for you, losing your mom and Steve and now the uncertainty about your birth mom. Whatever the future holds, you'll find the right way." Nene loosened her squeeze and the softness in her voice brightened. "Of course, you can't rule out Dixie's cousin. Right? There's still light at the end of the tunnel."

Joanna nodded.

A tap at the door caused a blank stare between the two. Jo's voice was hushed. "Good gosh, we're not yet parked and the welcoming crew is here."

It was little Vera, Toad's wife. Joanna opened the door and stepped out.

"Joanna, I'm so glad that you made it back. I wanted to be sure you got the message right away. So, I've been watching for you."

Joanna sighed. "Is Tony checking up on us again? Did he think we should have been back earlier? Barney was right. It's a little longer trip than Tony thought it would be."

"No, dear. It was a long-distance phone call from the states. Mrs. M. called you from the office on that bullhorn of hers. Late this morning. Seeing how you weren't here Toad went right on up. It was someone by the name of Shirley. You should call her at the office or if it is late, at her house. Here are the numbers." Vera handed her a yellow slip of paper heavily scrawled with numbers.

Five-fifteen. Surely everyone would be out of the office. What in God's name was Shirley calling about? The last time Joanna had talked to the office manager in her dad's office, she had been worried about Clay. It had to be about her dad. Joanna's heart pounded. Grabbing her purse, she bee-lined it for the gate, rounded the corner heading for the payphone half a block away.

Digging for her phone card, her fingers lost their feeling and didn't want to cooperate. Punching the numbers was no better and she tried three times before she got them right with no mess-ups. Shirley's line was busy. She tried the office and got the night machine message, hung up and tried Shirley's home again. Shifting one foot to the other, Jo looked behind her and saw Nene outside the gate watching. She tossed her hands up in a shrug and yelled, "Line's busy."

Nene stayed her distance, letting Joanna have her own space and time. But she was there if she was needed.

This time the number went through. Shirley picked it up on the second ring. Jo wished to slow her racing heart and tried to sound casual. "Hi Shirley. I got the message that you called. How's everything?"

There was a pause, then a rush of words. "It's a big mystery. Your dad is missing."

"Missing! How can he be missing? What do you mean?"

"He didn't come in to work yesterday. Didn't call in, just didn't show."

"That's not like Dad. He'd call or come in even from his deathbed. Did you check his house?"

"No one answered and we figured there was some mix-up. Surely, he forgot to tell us he was taking a day off. Then last night Cindy called, asking what happened at work and said that he hadn't come home and that his car was gone. He still hasn't shown up. It's just all too weird and so unlike your father."

"I don't know what to think or say. Unbelievable."

"I knew you would want to know. The police are in on it today. We are really puzzled. If he had an accident on the way to work, someone would have seen. You know how it is, about a mile and a half of country road, and then you're on the highway. So, they seem to be ruling out an accident on the way to work. You know the police, they think he left to cool off from some spat. Cindy insists that everything is hunky dory."

"I'm coming home. I've had a wrenching gut about dad for a while, particularly since last week when we talked."

"Hon, I hate for you to make that long drive. I'm not sure what you can do."

"No, I mean I'll fly out as soon as I can get a seat. Maybe he took a mountain drive before work and he's lying in some ravine. I need to be there when they find him."

Her feet slapped the sidewalk back to the campground. Numbness invaded her whole body. She might have been sleepwalking. Janene's questioning eyes met her at the gate, but she couldn't speak. Instinct led her to the Roadtrek where she collapsed in the lawn-chair, burying her face in her hands. Her friends gathered around, not pushing, wondering.

It was a full two minutes, then Joanna spoke. "My dad. My dad is missing. I need to get a flight home."

"Maybe you can take my seat Saturday night." Janene would give her friend anything if she could.

"It's not likely that the airlines would make an exception about using other people's tickets. And I want to get out earlier if at all possible. That's two days away." Upside down again. That's what her world was becoming.

Everyone rallied. Toad got the airport on the phone. Luck had it that there was one seat on the 10:00 p.m. charter. To Denver, no less. No layovers or plane changes. Tony and Nene could take her to the airport. He was coming right over. Nene would stay in the Roadtrek until she left and get it parked in the overflow space that had no hook-ups. That was cheaper than leaving it where it was. Besides a couple had reserved her site for a month and would move in the day her two weeks were up. Jo left extra money with Toad and Vera. She had no idea how long her 'jitney' would need to be parked in the overflow. Of course, Tony would make sure that Nene made it to her flight on Saturday.

When Tony arrived, Joanna was shoving things into a duffel bag. She had no reason to bring any serious luggage in the Roadtrek, so she had none. But the duffel and shoulder bag where she stashed her cosmetics, were all she needed. She wouldn't need to check her bags and getting out of the airport would be quicker.

The door opened and Tony caught her from behind, spinning her to him. He held her dishrag of a body close. His voice was low and comforting. "I'm so sorry. Surely when you get home, the mystery will be solved. I guess we'll have to postpone our celebration. But you need to eat. You have plenty of time for a bite before we head to the airport."

She shook her head while tears plopped on his shoulder. He pulled back holding her in front of him, then tipped her chin to look into somber eyes. "JoJo you *need* to eat something."

More shaking of the head. He led her to the bed and sat holding and rocking her, not knowing what to say or what else to do.

Janene came in looking for a sweater. "Hey guys, that cool breeze is making me chilly. I need a wrap."

Joanna's voice buried in Tony's shirt came out muffled. "Nene, it's cozy in here. You don't have to stay outside."

"I didn't want to intrude on you two."

Joanna's voice gained a bit of strength as she unwrapped herself from Tony's arms. "You ninny. You're not intruding. How about putting a sandwich or two together? I'm not hungry, but I bet you two are." Here she was organizing things, thinking of others, probably a needed distraction. "We need to use up that ham and cheese before you park this thing. I don't want mold in the refrigerator when I return. And get out those *Sabritos*."

For an hour and a half, they ate and talked. Nibbling on the potato chips encouraged Joanna's appetite and she ended up eating a sandwich after all. Ordinarily Jo didn't talk much about her father. Now it felt good remembering puttering in the garage with him, grease up to her elbows. Clay knew his way around engines, though he seemed helpless with most everything else around the home. One of the most memorable times was a few months before he left her mother, when she and her dad worked all afternoon on her very first car, a classy Mustang.

"He'd been moody for a long time. But that day we had the best time. He and his humor were in top form. Boy did we kid and laugh, but I learned a lot, too." Sitting cross-legged on the bed, she patted the pillow and arranged it behind her back. "What makes men mess up with that forties and fifties mid-life crisis thing?"

Tony threw a potato chip at her. "You don't think women have their own mid-life thing? It's not only men you know." He did that arched eyebrow thing and continued. "When did the thing hit him?"

"About forty-seven, I guess. But he had been a boob for a couple of years before that. When Cindy came along, he was ripe for someone to make him feel young and desired. How about Mario? Did your dad go through that time when he seemed to see his life passing before his eyes—on the downward slide?"

"I'm not sure I was aware of what was going on with Dad during that time. I don't think he ever cheated on Mom, though he can really lay it on thick when a desirable woman comes around. And you know how Italians are. They think they are virile and God's gift to women no matter their age. But I was too caught up in my own life to know if he had some inner struggles. Besides we had this silent war going on between us."

Nene cut in. "What did I tell you? These Italian men are multifaceted."

Tony howled. "What's this multifaceted bit? I guess it takes one to know one."

It was three a.m. when she let herself into the dark house. Lucky to catch the last shuttle out of Denver to Loveland, she was ready for sleep. She had dozed much more than she expected on the plane, but she didn't know what she faced at daybreak and wanted to be as rested as possible.

The grad student house-sitting. Oh dear, she'd probably scare her out of her wits. Tonya had been using the basement when she left, but Jo told her she could move to the extra bedroom upstairs if she wanted.

Tip-toeing, she made it to the kitchen, turned on the stove hood light, jotted a sticky pad note, pressing it to the cupboard door and made her way to her bedroom, being certain to miss the spot on the stairs that always creaked. In her own room, she closed the door and crashed on the bed. It was cool and felt good to snuggle under her fluffy quilt. *Dad, where are you?*

Coma-like she slept, not stirring. Rousing fully for the morning came gradually. Usually, she could jump right up, rearing to go. Not this morning. She should do something. Where should she begin?

She grabbed the phone and dialed her dad's office. "Shirley, it's Joanna. Is there any news?"

"None. It's hit the papers. There's a picture and a 'please report any information about this missing man' article on the front page. You aren't home, are you?"

Joanna said that she was. She was going to call Cindy, and then she planned to drive to some mountain picnic spots that she and her parents had enjoyed when she was young. She'd keep in touch.

Almost sick to her stomach, she hoped some food would settle it. The refrigerator was nearly as bare as she left it. Juice, milk, eggs, cheese, butter and a bin of salad-makings were all that she saw. A loaf of bread sat near the toaster. Books, notebooks and a computer rested upon the table of the adjoining dining room. In place of the sticky note she left, was one from Tonya.

So sorry about the horrible trick that life is playing on you. Glad you made it back OK. I will be on campus until 6:00 p,m. or so. If I can do anything please let me know. Tonya

P.S. All has been fine here. No problems. I'm still holed up downstairs, but I have been doing my schoolwork up here where there is more light. I hope I'm not in your way.

Toast with butter melted into it and juice sounded good. She was sure that Tonya would not mind. She was hungrier than she thought and toasted her third piece of bread and poured another glass of orange juice before dialing her dad's home. She had no idea what to say to Cindy. Cindy's daughter answered. Jo explained that she was home and wanted to know if there was any news. Before Diane replied Jo heard a child babbling in the background, then there was a crash and the child wailed.

"Just a minute, Jo, Cody just knocked over the lamp."

There were muffled sounds, then Jo heard Cindy's voice come on the line. The pitch was shrill and her words staccato. "Joanna you need to come. Now! You need to be here!"

"Have you heard anything? Has Dad called?"

"He's just gone. He's just go-o-o-ne." Her voice trailed off.

Joanna backed her Taurus from the garage. A skiff of snow lay on the north side untouched by the sun. The morning was crisp and bright, despite the dullness of the brown lawn and naked trees. Her dad came to mind as she passed the pole fence that both of her parents labored over before Joanna could have her horse. Clay's hand was evident here and there. Joanna thought about the various ways people leave their marks in the world. Mom's marks were scattered all over the house and in the landscaping. But mostly she left them in Joanna's heart. She placed a hand over that spot. *What about Dad? What did he leave in my heart?*

There were times when she had to grit her teeth over her dad. Now she'd give anything to say those words his own mother, her grandmother, had said so many times. "Now Clayton, you sit right down here. I'll pinch your head off if you don't mind me. You don't need to be leaving so soon." *What happened to you Dad?*

When Joanna arrived, Cindy's youngest, Piper, was portioning pills to her mother. "Mom, now remember, you can't have another one of these for three hours. I know you're upset, but pills are not going to help you think." Cindy gulped them in one swig and faced Joanna.

Wild-eyed, her piercing voice cut the air. "Joanna, I'm so glad you're here. He was high-jacked. I just know it. No one will believe me. They should be setting up road-blocks everywhere."

Diane sat to rock Cody, who watched the whole scene warily, clinging to her mother. "Mother, the police are doing all that they can. The description of the Explorer and license has been released. It's on the front page of the local paper. They are sending it out on the Denver TV stations today."

Piper handed the newspaper to Joanna so that she could read the article. The picture was a little fuzzy, but it was a good one. Joanna decided that it had been cropped from the family pictures that had been taken before Christmas, her present from Cindy. The article was not long and said all that anyone knew. He had been missing for two days.

"Did you see him the morning he disappeared?" Jo wanted to know all she could.

"Of course. We leave for work around the same time. He doesn't have to be there until nine, but he likes to go early. He kissed me when I left and told me to have a good day. I went out ahead of him that day."

"Does he always kiss you when he leaves?"

"Not always. Usually there's too much of a rush, but he did that morning. What are you implying?"

"I don't know. Just wondering about his state of mind. Was he down or discouraged, moody, depressed? Did he pack any clothes?"

"Not as far as I can tell. All his clothes are here, I think."

"Shirley said he was smoking again. I know he quit some time ago."

"That was his business. He knew I didn't like it, but I never bugged him about it as long as he didn't smoke in the house. I tell you there is some crime here and no one will listen to me."

"In Loveland, Colorado? I don't know. I suppose it's possible. I don't know what to hope for. That he's inconsiderately and selfishly taken a vacation, bound and gagged in some hotel room, sitting at the bottom of a ravine, trapped, waiting for rescue, or..." Joanna couldn't finish the sentence.

Cindy stretched out on the couch. Apparently, the pills were taking effect.

Joanna stepped toward the front door. "If there's anything I can do, let me know. I need to be doing something. Perhaps I'll take my car up in the hills. To some of our old picnicking spots. Is there a place you think he might drive to, that I can check? Piper, Diane, what do you think?"

No one came up with anything. Jo let herself out and stopped to look in the detached garage where he kept the Explorer. It was neat and tidy. The cords to his saws and drills were unplugged and wound securely. The hand mower and riding lawn mowers stood in the far corner. The floor was swept clean. A pack of cigarettes and a lighter sat on the work counter. A few tools hung on pegs. Joanna opened two tool chests, shiny and new, and found them full of well-ordered tools. If he was on the run, he left everything behind.

Three hours of driving. It was futile. In the hills a few inches of melting snow hugged the roadsides. No recent blizzards, apparently. Some of the old picnic spots had sprouted cabins; others were empty. She could drive for a month of Sundays and know nothing more than she knew now. It was more likely that she would find Dixie than find her father. *We need a clue, Dad.*

Heading home, she stopped at the Police Department, introduced herself, gave them phone numbers and learned what she could. The major TV stations had run a segment at noon and would repeat it at five and ten. The highway patrol and city police in Colorado and the adjoining states had the license and description of the dark green Explorer with the beige stripe.

Nothing to do but go home. She stopped for gas and some groceries, thankful not to see someone she knew. Before parking the car, she stopped at the old-fashioned, black mailbox, almost afraid to open it, wondering if her dad had mailed her something. Nothing but junk, which she tossed in the trash before going inside.

The afternoon was uneventful. She sorted the mail that Tonya had been collecting, checked the bank statement, posted the automatic-pay electric, phone and gas bills, then balanced her checkbook the best that she could, unsure about the exchange rate for the ATM withdrawals she made in Mexico. The dinger was set for forty-five minutes. No real cooking tonight. The lasagna she bought, and a tossed salad would have to do. Too bad she didn't have a *bolillo* to toast along with it. She fell asleep waiting for the ding.

The shrill ring of the phone jolted her, and she dashed to answer it before the answering machine kicked in. She made it.

"Jo, its Nene. Tony thought I should wait until after supper, but I just couldn't. Has there been any news?"

"Nothing. A missing person's piece was in the paper today and it's supposed to be on the TV also. I couldn't bear to hear it, so I didn't turn on the five o'clock news."

Joanna told her about the visit to her dad's house, the haunting feeling she felt poking around his garage, the fruitless drive to kingdom come and back.

"So, you're at Tony's house and he's fixing supper for you? Well, celebrate for me, won't you?" That green-eyed monster crept over her. She should be there with Tony, *not* Janene. She heard the dinger making its signal.

"Tony wants to talk. I'm going out to watch the grill. You two have a good visit."

"Janene, my lasagna is done, and I need to go to the kitchen. I'll pick up the phone there."

"Bye mi amiga. Love you. I'll put him on."

She took her time turning off the dinger, the oven, checking the lasagna, setting out the tableware, her salad, the dressing, and Parmesan cheese before picking up the kitchen phone.

"I'm back. Looks like my dinner's ready. I'm alone, you know."

"I was afraid we'd lost connection. Good to hear your voice. I'd give anything to be dining with you. Sounds like there's no word. Maybe no word is good word. Sure hope so. It must be tough. I miss you. I'm thinking of you."

She knew this whole thing was not his fault, but there was no way she could respond to the caring in his voice and hers remained icy.

"Yeah, well I think no news is God awful. You have no idea what it's like! Waiting for who knows what? Till heaven knows when?"

"No, I don't. Nene and I both feel completely helpless. We hurt for you." Jo remained silent. He went on. "Apparently your flight was fine. At least that worked out well and you got home as soon as possible."

"Yes. A flight I wish I never had to take." Her pause lingered awkwardly. "My TV dinner is getting cold, and *Nene* probably needs you at the grill. I'll let you know if there's any news. Thanks for calling."

CHAPTER 24

Saturday. Janene would be back in Colorado late tonight. *Wonder what she and Tony are doing today? Walking the beach, learning each other's life story?* Joanna thought of the walk she and Tony had the day she took the dunk in the ocean and lost her bracelet. She looked at the rescued stone-studded silver encircling her wrist and Dixie's grandmother's ring on the same hand. She wore them both everyday, just *not* when she was near the ocean. No ocean here.

Clicking through her e-mail, she read and deleted each one. Nothing important, except for a message from Lauren. She would finish her design work with the latest movie in a week or so. It would be a month or two until her next job got rolling. This time it would *not* be as a costume designer. She had been asked to test for a part in a movie. It was a minor role in a film depicting the difficulties during World War II. This one would be on the big screen. Low and behold she was offered one of the lead roles.

Can you believe little ole Laurie Mac from 'Small Town' Colorado projected on screens across the country? I came out here to design, but I really can't pass this opportunity. Am I crazy to try it? Is this the mistake of my life? Do I want to be discovered?

Pride and stirring filled Joanna as she learned of her friend's new direction. It was indeed a giant leap from the ungraceful Laurie Mac of sixth grade to the unpretentious, yet breathtaking Lauren McBride who would bring fresh enchantment to the screen.

Greg was still in the picture. He was encouraging her all the way and continued to be the jewel in her life. Nothing about her dad. Sent two days ago. Lauren probably didn't know about the "missing father." She was so upbeat and happy, Joanna hated to toss her some turmoil.

Maybe she should call her. It was always heartening to hear her voice with that country girl quality entangling a touch of raspy, making it sensuous and fascinating to listen too. If she could act, they'd love her in the movies. No. E-mail was better. A typed message was rather impersonal, but she didn't feel like explaining the last two weeks of her life right now.

The doorbell rang. An image of a police officer, with serious face, standing tall, flashed through her mind. Bare feet, no makeup, hair barely combed, she took the stairs in double time, pausing before the locked door. She couldn't open it. The bell rang again, and she flipped the locks.

Amy stood propping a large Tupperware bowl on her hip. With her other hand she pulled open the screen door, bumping Jo with her entrance. To a surprised Joanna she blurted, "Oh my dear friend. Another lemon thrown your way and I'm so sad." She set the bowl on the floor. They hugged, each breathing deeply.

"It seems like forever since we saw each other, but it was less than two weeks. Come in. You're a blessing. I was going to call, but..."

"Me too. Then I decided to take my chances and stomp on your doorstep." Amy brushed by and headed for the kitchen.

Somehow with Amy around, the tempo picked up. "I was just reading Lauren's e-mail. Have you heard?"

Amy virtually jumped up and down. "Yes, I can't wait to hear more."

Once Amy was updated on the latest happenings she said, "Jo, I need to tell you how much the time you spend with Sherry in Mexico meant to her. None of us can believe the change. She started counseling and found a support group, which she says she owes to you. And her self-confidence and attitude has done an about face. We are hoping it continues."

Stunned and feeling touched, Joanna remembered how she resented Amy's sister-in-law, her selfishness, and the way she treated John, until the two shared that afternoon on the beach. Tears threatened and she pressed her hand against her nose fighting them off. "Wow, that's some good news."

"Most of her harshness is gone and John is ecstatic."

"Amy, I'm glad to hear about it, but I really didn't do anything, except listen, and try to be her friend."

"Whatever you did, it was the right thing at the right time. So, pat yourself on the back and accept the praise."

Something she had done had turned out right. Too often lately, other people had to point her in the right direction.

Toward noon, Amy took over the kitchen, pulling things from the cupboard and snatching the bowl that had been placed in the refrigerator. The conversation grew somber as Joanna talked about her father and what she knew. It was easier for both of them if Amy busied herself with the salad. The worry and tears were put on hold.

The salad took shape on the two stoneware plates Amy had selected. She started with three types of greens, then arranged a sunburst of carrot strips, cucumber spears, green pepper, and red onion rings, thin as paper. Amy listened. She sliced the well-seasoned and grilled chicken breast, positioning it in the center, sprinkled fresh blueberries—definitely out of season—and slivered almonds generously about, then doused the whole thing with a light lemon-honey and mint dressing.

Joanna finished. "I feel so helpless."

"The waiting, the not knowing. It's unbearable, isn't it?" Seeing that she was all talked out about her dad, Amy asked, "What's new with Dixie?"

Amy heard about the trip to San Miguel. "If Fred sees her, he'll let me know."

"Will he tell Dixie that her daughter is looking for her?"

"I'm not sure. We didn't exactly talk about that point. I didn't ask him not to. Janene thinks I should call Dixie's cousin. I would have if things hadn't been so crazy after I heard about Dad."

"Let's do it."

"Now?"

"Why not? Beats sitting around twiddling our thumbs."

"You're right. Darlene will want to have an update anyway. The last time we talked, she begged me to find her daughter for her."

Finishing the hearty salad, they huddled around the phone.

Darlene was thrilled to hear from her "granddaughter" and remained hopeful, she said. Naturally she could have Betsy's phone number. It was worth a try. Darlene believed that Dixie was more likely to honor the request of the daughter she didn't know than her very own mother, whom she evidently hated.

Jo said more than she intended, particularly about her father, and they talked a good forty minutes. Darlene thanked her for confiding in her and was genuinely concerned and sympathetic.

Betsy had a similar twang in her voice. If Jo had not known, she would have thought she was still talking to Darlene. Dixie's cousin maintained she did not know where Dixie was, but poor girl, she always had a good heart and deserved to know about this daughter, out looking for her. Yes, she would write it all down. Jo repeated the information twice before Betsy had it right. "Oh, this is so exciting. I sure hope she calls soon. But you never can tell."

Joanna wanted to know more. Surely if Dixie had kept in touch all these years, there was something deep in their relationship. "Betsy, what can you tell me about my birthmother? You must have been pretty close when you were growing up since you're the only one she didn't break the ties with."

"We were close. Oh dear, how do I begin? Well, you know that Darlene and my mom are sisters."

"Yes, so that means you had the same grandmother. Did you know that Dixie left

your grandmother's ring in my birth box? And I wear it now?"

"Oh, the ring. Yeah, when Grandma Lucille remarried, Dixie got the ring, and I got Grandpa's gold pocket watch. I always wondered what happened to the ring, if Dixie still had it. But you know our visits when she calls are always much too short. Not enough time to talk about everything."

"But you knew about me, though?"

Betsy rushed on. "Not at first. But what can I tell you about Dixie?

Growing up she came to visit Grandma Lucille and Grandpa George for a couple weeks each summer. They were still on the farm near Kearney, and we lived in the little farmhouse next door. So, Dixie and I spent many hours together. She loved helping with the chickens, feeding, watering, and gathering the eggs. I remember thinking we'd really be in Dutch if my parents found us making mud pies with eggs instead of water. And one time we dissected a dead baby chicken which I thought was gross, but she said she was just curious and wanted to know more about the world."

Joanna caught herself smiling and trying to imagine the child that Dixie had been. "Go on, I really want to hear more." She gave Amy a hand signal that indicated 'this may take a while' and Amy nodded and signaled back 'not a problem.'

"Dixie was the levelheaded, methodical one and I was the scatterbrain. Still am, I guess. I must have been about eight and she was ten, when she started her sketchbook. One section was birds, another flowers, animals, all labeled with a little information about each one. Then one year Grandma Lucille bought her a camera and she started an album of her photography. Same organization, plus all the lighting information, time of day for each picture and I don't know what all. What discipline. She'd work for hours.

"Sometimes I'd get bored with her projects, and she'd consent to head out to the straw pile, and we'd lay for hours searching the clouds for lifelike forms, pretending to be famous people, and just talking. She usually imagined she was some famous photojournalist for National Geographic on some safari, far from civilization and I was going to save the world by being a heart surgeon which Dixie disputed since I couldn't even dissect a dead chicken." Betsy giggled.

"Did she talk about her father and mom back then?"

"Not much. Sometimes she said things like, she'd like to come live with us, hated to go home. I hardly saw her once she got to high school. Her dad wouldn't let her visit Grandma anymore. Course Grandma had remarried and moved away by then. One excuse or another about being needed at home, needing to have a summer job. Our family visited them a few times, but just for Christmas or Thanksgiving dinner. Anyway, all that didn't click in for me until much later." Betsy's lively voice grew cautious. "Um. I don't know if you know about the thing with her dad."

"If you mean about the sexual molestation. I know." Joanna explained about Ellie.

Betsy's voice caught when she responded. "It's such a crime. Poor gal. Sounds like you know more about that than I do, though. When she told me, she swore me to secrecy.

"We hadn't been in touch at all. It was the year after you were born—I was a senior in high school—and she called from Aspen. It really got me. She sounded pretty out of it, swearing, carrying on, not the self-control that I always saw in my cousin those summers together. She told me what a beast her father had been and that she wished she could put a spell on him, hoped he would burn in hell.

"By the time she got to the part about *you* she was sobbing. I can remember, like it was yesterday. Sounded like everything about her was becoming contorted, twisting into a gnarled grotesque form. That's what it sounded like. I begged her to come see us. To tell somebody about her dad. That she couldn't let him get away with it. I couldn't get through to her.

"Toward the end it sounded like all the life had been sucked out of her, the voice of a whipped child and she was begging—*You can't tell anyone. Promise. Not about my father, my baby, where I am, what I am doing. Promise.* I made the promise that I wouldn't tell. But she had to keep in touch. And for the most part she did, yet there was always a bit of mystery. She didn't let me know much. After Aspen I never knew exactly where she was."

"Do you think things got better for her? Did she find happiness? Did she marry?"

Betsy seemed to think for a minute. "She told about painting, meeting people, but was careful to leave out the details. As far as I know there were no important men in her life. When I told her about her father's death she really freaked. I thought she might be relieved, but she kept yelling that he couldn't die on her. The last time we talked, she said she was fine. Never wants to see her mom again, though."

"When did she call?"

"Gosh it's been, I suppose eight months since we talked. It was like usual. She sounded pleasant enough. But you know, I never hear any spark in her voice. It always seems a little flat, a little distant."

Joanna felt both drained and invigorated when she hung the phone in its place and turned to face her dear friend. "It seems Amy, you've done it again, encouraged me to take the bull by the horns. Somehow both of those phone calls gave me hope. I know a little more about Dixie. I may have to be patient and wait for another clue."

The two finished their visit while Amy gathered her things and piled them to take to the car. On the front step Joanna waved generously, grateful for their friendship and their time together. She caught the faint tinkling of the phone. A dream-like fog surrounded her as she entered the house, taking her time answering it.

Surprisingly it was still warm from her grip, and it took a moment to register the woman's voice. She introduced herself as Detective Sorenson from the police department and verified that she was speaking with Joanna Johansen. She sounded all business and anxious to get this call behind her.

"Miss Johansen, there's a piece that has been picked up and will air this evening. We need to inform you before you hear it elsewhere. A cashier at Jones Hardware sold some type of hose and duct tape to a man matching your father's description on the morning he disappeared. It may or may not be connected. However, the airways are writing it as if there's a connection. Just wanted you to know. Sorry about all this. We're calling Mrs. Johansen with the same information."

If Joanna felt her life was in limbo when she left San Miguel, this was a gazillion times worse. She was profoundly sorry for her father's wife as well. When they talked last night Cindy was well sedated and scarcely coherent, so neither gained much comfort from the other.

She had to get out of the house. Dropping off a few rolls of film for processing, she paced the isles of Kmart, thumbed through a few paperbacks, replacing them on the shelf. Ending up at her office, there was little she could do aside from answer the phone and field a few questions. She had been out of the loop and was not sure how long she would be in town. It was Sunday and the reduced staff was busy. No time for talking. She tried writing up the information she had from her trip to Sayulita and San Francisco, but the words were all jumbled, and she gave up and went home.

There was a message from Janene on the answering machine. Unwillingly she returned the call, but kept the exchange brief, concentrating on the 'missing father.' She was not about to hear *Tony did this, he was such a dear getting her to the airport, he was so gracious with that, he sure is a peach.*

Reading the latest Good Housekeeping from her mother's subscription, not yet expired, was unsuccessful. The words passing before her eyes meant nothing. Most of her watercolors were in the Roadtrek, so she dawdled with a puny set hoping to lose herself designing something interesting but was discouraged with her efforts. Scanning the TV listing channel, a movie title caught her eye, a comedy she had missed with Walter Matthau. Even Walter, who never failed to make her smile, could not hold her attention.

Thankfully, Tonya was mostly out. She was a good person, but Jo hardly knew her and was glad not to have to make the effort.

So, it went and the next day she resolved to do some early spring cleaning and lit into moving furniture, scrubbing floors, reorganizing the closets, some filled with linens, sheets, and towels from her mother's life. She packed unneeded items for give-away and the third day dug into window washing.

This was a monumental task. The windows were the pop-out type, but needed a good deal of muscle, old as they were. Once she lifted them out and cleaned them, they were a bear to reassemble. She did a quick mental computation. All the upstairs windows were double hung and included storm windows. Ninety-six sides of glass to clean in the upstairs alone. Her mom used vinegar water and newspaper which she said left no streaks, so that is what she did.

By early afternoon, she changed the murky water for the last time, only two more windows to pry from their casings. She looked at her hands, black from the ink in the newsprint and wiped brow-sweat with the sleeve of her sweatshirt. She remembered her mom's words about using the muscles. She was right. Physical stuff was just what she needed.

The radio boomed another tune and she hummed along. This window was a bugger. Giving it one more push, it loosened and she pulled it out of the frame, grunting. There was a far-off tinkling sound. Cutting the radio, she realized it was the phone in her office down the hall. When she grabbed it from its cradle, the answering machine began its routine, and she helloed over her own voice with the cheery greeting.

It was Cindy's daughter, Diane. Her father had been found. Hikers spotted his car off a deserted road near Packer's Valley. The body would be at the hospital where the coroner would complete the death certificate in a couple of hours. Her mother wanted Jo to come over. Would she come?

She knew the officer was on his way and met him at the door, leading him to the living room. They sat across from each other, he with a clipboard on his lap.

Joanna made a brave attempt to keep her shoulders upright. "Please tell me all that you can. It's better to know, I think."

"Ma'am, as you know a couple of hikers found your dad's Explorer." *Damn why did he have to be so polite?* "He had driven off of a logging road back in some trees near Packer's Valley. A hose was attached to the exhaust. He left a note..." *She needed to know that.* "and apparently turned on the radio and lay down in the back. Of course, when he was found the battery was dead and the gas tank empty."

"He's been dead since last Wednesday, then?"

"Yes, Ma'am. It looks like things were quick. Probably sometime before noon. We have too many of these in our county and for reasons we've yet to determine, Colorado has one of the highest suicide rates. Somehow, in these situations, sadly, this is the only way they think they can escape their pain, hurt, or whatever is making life unbearable."

"I knew that my dad wasn't happy, but nothing like this entered my mind. When we talked, I couldn't reach him. If only..."

"Ma'am you can't blame yourself. Even if you knew his true state of mind, it's not likely that you could have changed things. One of the most difficult parts of situations like this one is guilt. Don't let it get a hold of you."

They talked on, he maintaining his politeness, she holding her composure. Then he rose to leave. "Ma'am are you alone?"

"My house-sitter will be home in a few hours."

"Can I call someone to be with you until then, or can I take you some place?"

"No, I think I need to be alone for a while. I'll be going to my stepmother's house later. By the way, do you know if he was wearing a watch? I gave him one that I had inscribed for Christmas. I'd like to have it if I may."

"Don't know about that Ma'am, but I'll check on it." He handed her a copy of her dad's note." "I thought you would want a copy." She read it. "Are you alright? Do you want me to stay a bit longer?"

"No. Thank you for coming."

A puppet on a string. Dance puppet, wave, bow, jump, turn around! No, the other way, run now, face the world, hold your head high!

Joanna threw her clenched fists overhead and cried out, "Cut the strings, let me go. I want to run my own race, dance my own dance."

She thought about *la espina*. What makes it go away, come out? She sat silently for a long while, then opened her journal and penned her thoughts.

Oh Dad, how could you not know how much grief you would leave? I may marry someday. How could you not want to walk me down the aisle? Not want to know or hold your grandchildren? How could you cheat me so? You picked me for your daughter, then decided you didn't want the job. How could you? Mother had no choice. She loved every breath, every second in this world and her life was snuffed as suddenly as a candle in the wind. You thumbed your nose at God and said, "Life is no gift to me. What you gave me wasn't good enough. I don't want it. I'm bailing out." If things were not right, you could have changed them. You did not have to be a helpless coward!!!

Joanna examined the copy of her dad's message—firm, weighty writing in an emphatic right slant—and read it once more.

Cindy

I can't face another day. Life is empty. I am empty. There is <u>nothing</u>

inside. I'm of no use to anyone anymore. I was a dud at being a father and a grandfather. You'll have to be there for the kids.

There were some good times, but not anymore. I can't take it.

Your uncle knows about the investments. The insurance policy is in the file. You're young and you'll find someone else.

Have my body cremated and take my ashes to the mountains.

Clay

The tears spilled as she gripped her pen, oblivious of the splotched script.

I cannot fathom the depth of your pain. Oh, Daddy how did you come to have such an emptiness? Oh, Daddy.

Where did that daddy go? The one who bounced her on his lap as she giggled, holding on for dear life, his shirt in a child's grasp, until buttons flew, rolling across the floor. Afterwards, when achievements came, with a broadened chest he declared "My JoJo, the only one who can pop the buttons right off my shirt."

He tricked her by raising the training wheels of her bike, all shiny in purple and white. She peddled the whole block before she knew he had let go. On the return trip he beamed—his stance wide, hands on hips—commandeering the middle of the road. That daddy, gone long ago, but not like this…

When she arrived, things at her dad's and Cindy's house were melancholy, yet all were making an effort to be controlled. Diane tried to keep Cody's attention with a book. Joanna had only seen Diane's husband at their wedding and wondered where he was. Piper had called her brother in California and her grandmother in Texas. Both would arrive tomorrow, she said. The uncle who handled her dad's investments had arrived from Boulder and was pouring through papers spread on the dining room table. Cindy was in the bedroom.

Some of her father's family were there and Joanna welcomed their warm greetings, then her aunts led her to the kitchen. Running a pot of water, Judy signaled Lana to search for the coffee. She found enough to brew maybe two pots and said, "Can't imagine who will do all the shopping, now that good ole Clay's not here to be the errand boy."

Judy wagged a finger. "Now Lana, you promised you'd be a good girl. We better stick to safe topics. Jo we'd like to hear about your trip, right, Lana?"

There was so much to tell, even in the condensed version. She began. Judy's husband leaned through the doorway. "Honey I'm going for subs, chips, and pop for everyone. It's getting past suppertime. Lana, I'm taking your husband with me."

"Thank you dear. That's a good idea." Smiling with a shake of her head, she added, "Always the practical one."

The condensed version of Joanna's voyage was nearing its end when Piper stepped into the kitchen. "Jo, Mom wants you in the bedroom. Can you go now?" She nodded.

Cindy sprawled on the wide bed, a soft blanket tucked under her chin. A small globe in a corner lamp did its best to replace the sunlight, now retreating toward the other side of the world. The grieving woman did not attempt to rise, but waved an arm, more frail than it should have been, toward an arm chair.

Her words were barely intelligible, like a tape recorder, its battery dying. "I don't know why we didn't make you part of the family. It's just...I don't know. We were his new life. I needed him. Oh Clay how could you do this to me? To all of us?"

So now she tries to kiss up to me. Must be some guilt there. Woman you drove him to it as sure as I'm sitting here. Joanna Johansen, get a grip. "I miss him, too. We will all miss him." She breathed two breaths, long and slow. "And there's no way to understand it."

"You know how he loved you. You were very special to him. I'll need you at the funeral home tomorrow."

Yes, she would be there.

At the funeral home, there was a long discussion about the service. Should it be immediate family, only? How do you celebrate the life of a person who commits suicide? Pastor Bill had called Joanna and offered to help in any way that he could. Cindy was leaning toward a family only memorial but was definite about *not* having Pastor Bill do the service.

Aunt Judy, who represented her father's side of the family, held out for an open service. "You can't exclude all his fellow workers. They were like family. And his old golfing and tennis buddies?" She won, but it was to be simple. Someone from the mortuary would read the two scriptures they chose from a list of suggestions that dealt with life and death. Joanna wanted the verses in Ecclesiastics about everything having a season. They would end with this, rather than a prayer. Did anyone else want to speak? Joanna had tried to write something like she did for her mother's memorial and couldn't find the right words, much less the right thoughts. No, no one wanted to speak.

Someone told Cindy it was best not to keep anything of Clay's around and get it out of sight immediately. Today was that day. She had been told that her help was needed and reluctantly she would do her duty. They must have begun early, because four ballooning trash bags greeted her on the porch, waiting for the Goodwill truck.

"I guess we don't need you after all, Joanna." Cindy's words were crisp and military-like this morning. She handed Jo a brown envelope. "Here are some pictures you will probably want."

Four filled trashbags and an aging envelope. What a zenith to a man's life. Joanna opened the envelope and saw her dad's eight by ten high school graduation picture, once paired with her mother's. The rest were those of Clay's side of the family, snapshots of her grandparents, cousins, aunts and uncles at various family functions, pictures given to Clay after his father's recent death.

Piper called to her mother. "That realtor you wanted is on the phone. Can you talk?"

While Cindy took the call, Jo ambled to the garage. Her father's golf clubs, not there the other day, stood shined and erect in their bag. Expectant. She stood for only a few minutes when a voice interrupted her thoughts.

"Joanna." The same military voice. "I need to meet with the realtor.

Do not touch anything here. The appraiser needs to see everything that I will be selling." Then as an afterthought she said, "Please!"

After the memorial she would put in her appearance at Cindy's house for the sake of her dad's side of the family. But after that she was *outa here.*

Tonight, Amy and Janene were bringing in pizza and margaritas. No Lauren, this time. Joanna hoped that the gnawing tension she felt would not be evident to Janene. Whether it was justified or not, she was jealous of the time Tony and Janene had spent together.

Things went smoother than she expected. Amy already knew about Tony, and Janene hardly mentioned his name, except to announce, "I have a new nickname. Did Jo tell you? It was Tony's idea and I like it."

Pouring over the newly developed photos of Amy and her family and a few from Janene's visit, directed much of the conversation. But the main focus was Cindy, the woman who had the gall to order her to help sort through her dad's things, then to dismiss her saying they didn't need her after all *and* not to touch anything in the garage, treating her like some naughty child. They spoke of her unpleasantly, spewing their words like hissing snakes. Joanna was not at all penitent.

The day of the memorial, Joanna floated, feeling disjointed. Cramped in the family section at the funeral home, she saw that the benches were nearly full, and the memorial was ten minutes away. Watching Cindy, stiff in her pose, all in black— dress, shoes, purse, even dark sunglasses—Joanna realized that her own attitude had relaxed.

The future was predictable however, and she was glad to be leaving tomorrow. Cindy would cut his memory from her life as easily as cutting out a paper doll, burning it, leaving only the gaping hole. Anything he stood for would be gone. His golf clubs, rackets, saws, drills, tools, clothes. There would be nothing for Joanna. She didn't need anything. The pictures she had were enough. And the watch. Just this morning the polite officer stopped by and handed her a small bag. "I believe this is the watch you asked about," he said. He *had* been wearing it when he died. She hoped he appreciated the inscription. "Please don't mention it to his wife. She might not approve."

Joanna was surprised when the music began. The first reading was a blurr. Then came the piece about Clay's life. The man spoke with feeling, but it was evident he had not known Clay. It was a nice service, but it could have been about anyone, so bland and impersonal it was. Perhaps she should have spoken. What did it matter? They weren't putting on a show. The final reading came.

There is a time for everything, and a season for every activity under heaven: a time to be born and a time to die, a time to plant and a time to uproot, a time to kill and a time to heal, a time to tear down and a time to build, a time to weep and a time to laugh, a time to mourn and a time to dance, a time to scatter stones and a time to gather them, a time to embrace and a time to refrain, a time to search and a time to give up, a time to keep and a time to throw away, a time to tear and a time to mend, a time to be silent and a time to speak, a time to love and a time to hate, a time for war and a time for peace.

Each word settled deeply in her heart. They definitely hit the mark. *A time to weep and a time to laugh.* She could do neither. *A time to search and a time to give up.* She would search but knew she might have to give up. Now she wondered about what was ahead. And her dad. *A time and a season. Dad's season past. A time to be born and a time to die.*

The phone barely hit the cradle when the sick feeling hit. My insides wretched from me as I spewed and coughed into the pan at the sink. My cousin Betsy gave me *the news*. **My father is dead**.

How many times have I wished him dead? Yet on the phone I yelled, "How can you do this to me? How can you die? You've not yet been punished."

The afternoon found me balled on my bed lying in a litter of bedclothes, steamy with dampness. A vision of his approaching face, hands and body smothering me, taking the breath from me, left me in anguish.

I was barely five when the bedtime touching became 'our' secret. I *let* him touch me. I stayed quiet as if I were dead. There were times that I felt dead. I didn't stop him.

At twelve when it hurt, I didn't stop him. But in high school I made him crazy. I stayed away. I was wild. I ran away, time and again. I'd end up with a friend. Her parents would give me a lecture and in a few days I'd go home.

I taunted my father. You can't have me anymore. I'm doing it with the whole football team. It drove him mad.

Oh mother, where were you? Hiding your head in a hole. Being Mrs. Socialite and Savior of the community. *What about your daughter?* I tried to tell you. You called me a liar, a trollop. You believed the denials of my predator. Would you have listened when I was younger, before my sophomore year, when I was so ashamed, so embarrassed?

I paid with my life. Neither of you paid a penny.

CHAPTER 25

The last leg of her journey. Being a travel agent, one would think she might appreciate airports. Not so. Inevitably, the flight transfer meant running to make it from one concourse to the other before the next plane took off. Today was no different. During the first leg of the early flight her mind was a muddle of reflection.

She fingered the watch her dad had been wearing when he died and read the inscription, *All my Admiration and Love, Joanna*. Would Tony be offended if she offered it to him? She admired Tony, who was much like the father she recalled as a young child, humorous and often full of fun. In fact, she was growing to love this man. Perhaps seeing him wear the watch would help her feel that connection to her father. *Oh, it was probably a dumb and stupid idea.*

Positioning her headrest and closing her eyes she willed her thoughts away, imagining Tony's surprise when she would walk into his shop this afternoon. They had not talked since her morning drive to Cindy's to help pack her father's things. It was *before* she was rudely dismissed by her stepmother, *before* the memorial and *before* she decided to get out of Dodge ASAP. He was expecting her to call him tomorrow. Instead, she would greet him in person.

Shoving her bags on the seat of the Taxi, she climbed in, wanted to leave the hubbub of the Puerto Vallarta airport. On the way she rummaged through her bag, replaced the U.S. money with pesos, filed her nails, anything to pass the twenty minutes to Bucerias. She filled her lungs with the humid air. Even her hands felt the contrast to the Colorado dryness.

Anticipation made her jittery. *Let him be there.*

Not yet noon as the Taxi made its momentary stop in front of the cybercafé. She saw Jesus and a tall, graying man in conversation. The tall man gesticulated in the air, then they both laughed. *Where was Tony?* Jesus stood stunned as Jo stepped into the open-air room.

"Buenos dias Jesus. Esta Tony aqui?"

Jesus appeared confused. *"No. Tony esta en Colorado. No conosces?*

Joanna did not understand. Didn't he say that Tony was in Colorado? Didn't she know? Impossible. Why? She talked to him two days ago and he was sorry he wasn't with her. Surely, he wouldn't fly to Colorado when he knew she was returning soon. He wasn't there for the memorial.

With his best English and her meager Spanish, eventually she understood. Mario had a severe stroke and Tony caught a plane home late last night. She collapsed on the tiled step into the cyber cafe, leaning on the bag in her lap. Deflated, she looked up at the imaginary puppet strings that seemed to be controlling her life. Again. And shook her head.

Trudging the mile or so to the campground, bags drooping over her back, one would have thought she was on a thousand-mile trek through the wilderness. Maybe she was.

She stopped at a pay phone, tediously entering the numbers of her calling card and heard the perp, perp, perp as her fingers touched the buttons. She did not have the number of the Angelino's and it took time to reach the operator with the needed information. No one answered. Joanna left the most concise message she could on the answering machine, reflecting the irony of their situation. She would call in two hours.

The perp, perp, perp continued to play in her head until she entered the gateway to the campground.

Clunk....Clunk....Clunk, followed by cheers, whoops and piercing whistles came from the far corner of the campground. The Saturday afternoon washer-board contest was going strong. She dragged herself to the space where the Roadtrek was parked and went inside. It smelled close and stuffy, and she mechanically opened the curtains and windows, then lay down to think.

Ker-pow. She had not allowed herself to feel that last stab, sinking, the thorn could stab no deeper. This had to be the bottom. Cast away by a mother supposedly anguished about giving her up, losing a portion of her father when he split from the family, then the great pain of losing the one who always stood nearby. *Oh Mother. Mother, how I miss you. Always will.*

Now no more father. Not even a piece. *Oh Dad, when you were alive I had hope for the two of us.* Not even Tony was here for comfort. Agony twisted, gripped, pulsated until finally sleep interrupted the depth of her pain.

She awakened before the whole afternoon was spent and lifted herself from the bed, its spread drenched in sweat from the restless slumber. *Go on, go on. You have to go on.*

A cool shower refreshed her body. Bit by bit her mind trailed after. Before the sun had set, she made three more attempts to reach Tony. Nothing. She could not remain here. She was still parked in the overflow and there were no sites available. She wanted a quiet place to relax and sort out her life, ease the spine, the thorn in her heart. She would not leave Mexico until it was done, whether or not she found her Dixie mother.

Hearing of her plight, Barney and Barb had an idea. There was a quiet village about twenty miles away. They had stayed in Lo de Marcos for a week before heading home last year and would have gone back but couldn't leave the friends they met each year in Bucerias. A wonderful couple, Leticia and Basilio owned the campground.

It took some rummaging, but Barb came up with the card and they all traipsed to the corner pay phone to make the call. Leticia was most gracious and there was a site that could hold a small rig. It was decided. She would be there early tomorrow.

Her last evening in Bucerias was spent on the beach around a glowing campfire with the friends who had taken her under their wing. They were like parents away-from-home. That's all she had now and thought about her mom and Steve making friends like these on their travels. Joanna was grateful they had been so happy and vibrant, enjoying wonderful experiences together till the very end. Not so with her father.

Joanna had settled in for the night when a rap sounded on her door and Linda, Tom's wife, called out. "Joanna, Joanna. You have a phone call."

She threw a T-shirt over her skimpy pajamas and opened the door. Linda continued. "Tom was afraid you wouldn't hear it over here and sent me to get you. He's up at the office now keeping the line, so Mrs. M. won't hang up." No one called the owner by her full name. It was always Mrs. M. She usually made a few attempts with the bullhorn when a phone call came in for the travelers, but never sent anyone to the RV with a message. Fellow-campers helped each other by signaling and carrying messages.

Jo read the glow of her watch. Nine-thirty. Dashing over the cobblestones in the driveway, her shoeless feet barely touched them. Tom held the phone out to her. Mrs. M. had closed the windows and the cord dangled through a crack between them. Breathless, she stood on the verandah in front of the office making her thanks known to Tom.

It was a relief to hear Tony's voice. "Finally, we've made a connection. I didn't have time to call you the night of Dad's stroke. I just high-tailed it home."

"Here I thought I would surprise you with my early arrival. What a dirty trick for both of us. Tell me about your dad. Is it bad?"

It was. He was in a coma, and it was uncertain if he would ever come out of it. The whole family maintained a constant vigil. They wanted to be there for his last breath, if it came to that. They talked to him. remembering every anecdote possible, hoping to bring him out of the coma.

She told him about her move to Lo de Marcos and asked about a time to call, once she was settled. He had no idea. His sister and he were going back to the hospital in the morning. So far, his mother had stayed all night, every night at Mario's side. She could try the hospital if there was no answer at the house. Feeling intrusive about that, she said she would try the house the next night but understood that it might be empty.

In the Roadtrek, once again hoping for sleep, her mind pictured Mario wiping his dripping brow, declaring that Tony should not let on to his mom about what an expert dancer Jo was. He was such a spirited man, hurling laughter, and joyance about. Lifeless in a sterile bed was not him at all.

Glad for morning Joanna filled a mug with steaming brew and positioned it in the cup-holder, then drove one last loop around the campground, waving farewell to her friends. The winding road north held some familiarity, and it was a nice feeling being on the road again. No Amy or Nene, but today she needed to be alone.

She thought about Mariana, the weaver who told her the story of *la espina*. Mariana said the thorn in her was not gone, but it was coming. How do you rid yourself of that thorn? Joanna hadn't asked Mariana that question. This was the first day of the rest of her life. She believed that. As a start she vowed to live day by day, hour by hour, appreciating what she did have, not feeling sorry for what she didn't have. Could she do that much?

The crunch of tires as Joanna steered into the campground echoed the easygoing feeling of the little village she would come to know. Parking in front of the office she decided to pay for only one week. There was some drama about living week to week, not knowing what adventure lingered around the corner. Survival was about anticipation, expectation, looking forward. *No more weeks like the last few, please.* On the other hand, some stability would do just fine.

Leticia spoke excellent English and invited her into the office where they did their business. It was tidy and spotless. Several shelves of books and videos waited to be borrowed by the residents. Joanna completed the registration form while Leticia called for Manuel, who arrived shortly and stood patiently in the doorway.

"This is my son, Manuel. He will show you to your site, number sixteen."

She held her hand out to greet him. "Buenos dias, Mahn-wel," careful to avoid the gringo pronunciation of Man-u-el. "I'm Joanna." She looked into warm eyes that flashed in unison with his shy smile, then disappeared behind the brim of his hat when his head bowed toward his feet.

"Good to know you, Joanna." Her name rolled across his tongue like music. As they walked together to her site, each caught the other in a once-over look, sharing their mutual amusement with a grin. She wore well-fitting shorts in white, and a trim, melon colored top.

He flapped along in dark thongs that had seen many miles, wearing only his shorts, striped in black, brown and tan and that military-green hat with the floppy brim that proved to be his hiding place from time to time. Beautiful skin, she thought, flawless in its toasty brown, head to foot. Ebony down was scattered across his chest and peeked above his waistband toward his belly button. Perhaps three inches taller than she, there was nothing bulky about this man. Yet there was no doubt about his strength and agility.

He motioned toward her site and said he would be happy to show her around once she was situated. He was going to clean the small pool, designed with children in mind and then tend to the newly hatched turtles waiting for tomorrow's release into the sea. More turtles to be released. She was interested to hear that this little village had its own turtle rescue program and Manuel had a little nursery where the eggs were being hatched.

It was a quiet spot, more so than Bucerias, and held many fewer rigs, but had many more bungalows, all white in fresh paint. Potted plants, many flowering, reminded Joanna of a tropical garden, not a campground. Giant greenery provided privacy between each RV site, magnifying the garden feel. Joanna suspected Manuel was linked to much of this beauty.

Two residents paused on their walk through the campground to welcome her, learn her name, where she was from and how long she was staying. Soon she would know the routine. They seemed to be surprised to find a single young woman traveling alone in a rig. The campground held couples in their fifties, sixties and seventies, some who came to this village year after year. At times there were families in the bungalows and things became livelier, but not today. By the way, they said, there would be a gathering at the terrace tonight for snacks and drinks about five. She was invited. Hazel and Harry from Alberta hoped that she would like it here. She was sure that it was just what she needed.

This time she connected all of the hook-ups on her own. She put out the awning and placed her two lawn chairs and fold up table beneath it. Her space seemed a little naked as she noticed the rugs, mobiles, colorful furniture, and Mexican prints that gave each home away-from-home, individuality. Perhaps she'd find something to spruce it up if she stayed that long.

What to do first? Dig out her watercolors, explore the beach, hit Manuel up for the look around, record her delinquent journal entries? She slipped into her swimsuit. It was going to be the beach. If she could borrow some of Nene's daring, she might even look for a bikini, something she had never worn, She tucked some pesos in her fanny pack snapping it in place around her waist, just in case.

An expansive terrace held a dozen square tables neatly covered with blue and white oilcloth. A couple sat talking across one table sheltered by spreading umbrellas. Several reclined in sprawling chaise lounges, reading or sunning. Two men shared a pair of binoculars and noted the action and coloration of the several birds flitting from palm to palm or bush to bush.

She dropped her sandals on the spacious platform leading from the terrace and stepped into the soft sand. Shading palms, in their stateliness welcomed her. To her left, Manuel leaned over a small, dark rubber boat near the fence. Vigorous little swimmers, charcoal in color, fought over bits of fish that Manuel had distributed.

His stance reflected his pride and his voice registered seriousness as he explained that these were the sea turtles that had recently hatched. He wanted to be certain that they were hardy and strong before they were released. Tomorrow afternoon was the time. All residents in the campground were invited.

"You're going for a walk on the beach?" She saw that flash of his eyes again and that quiet, faintly amused smile. "Enjoy." He nodded.

She guessed that the beach was a good mile in length from rocky point to rocky point where the mountains jutted into the sea. This morning was a flat sea, the gentlest of waves. A sudden frenzy interrupted the serenity. Fascinated, Joanna paused to watch nature in progress. Broiling schools of fish created a foamy brine as birds of every size blackened the sky, using their cunning to capture their prey. Shrill squacks, cries, and whistles blended in piercing fusion, heightening the chaos before her. Such determination and singleness of purpose these amazing creatures. What could we humans learn from them?

Beyond the rocky point to her left she counted seven slivers of light dancing on the faraway ripples. Fishermen, manning their flat bottom *pangas* hoping for a good day's catch. A wonderful day for a walk, she aimed for the jutting rocks at the far end toward her right. Her feet splatted in the gentle swish. So healing. Her stride grew brisk. She felt a growing confidence. Out loud she murmured to the world, flinging her arms skyward. *I hope for peace, joy, healing of pain and hurt, the heart to right wrong. For me and for all mankind. May my wishes be transcended and in the mysteries of the world, touch some needy place. I'm thankful for this day, for each breath, for growing strength.*

What a glorious walk. She explored the estuary she discovered along the way. Egrets, snakebirds, ducks, and other water birds unfamiliar to her, enlivened the meandering waterway. Reflections of greenery at the shoreline and the hills beyond, compounded the beauty.

Reaching jagged peaks that had tumbled from some ancient volcano, she picked her way along the sanded spots, gazing into pools remaining from the night's tide. Sea urchins extended their prickly spines. Tiny fish that found temporary protection from preying scavengers dashed into hiding at her reflection then timidly returned when no danger was apparent. Crabs in their dark camouflage scooted sideways out of sight when she stepped near, then also returned cautiously, feeling comfortable with her presence. More lessons from nature.

The waves gained momentum and her roosting place became riskier. She felt the spewing mist waft over her and without warning the sea sent a crashing breaker, knocking her backward. She spit salty foam, wiping madly at her eyes. She was learning to respect the sea, *so like life that sent no warning but crashed around you and demanded a response.*

On the return trip, she stepped into an open-aired restaurant where a vendor was hanging beachwear. Browsing through airy shifts, fringed at the bottom, she spotted the swimwear. There was *her* bikini, just the right amount of skimpy in a sunny yellow. No good at bargaining, she paid the full price in soggy pesos, then swinging the plastic bag and humming, she returned to the campground.

Manuel walked with a couple toward one of the bungalows. The man carried a baby. The woman led a small boy, looking every bit a little man, as she and her husband kept up a lively interchange with Manuel in Spanish. His hat had been abandoned and Joanna found his unruly thatch ruffled by the breeze quite appealing.

Several of her neighbors were gathered around a young boy and a white plastic bucket. *"Camarones?"* he asked as she approached. Shrimp sounded tasty and Joanna decided to buy some. They were as they came from the sea, beady black eyes, long orange feelers. She had no idea if it was a good buy. Liz and Al said they seemed within reason and the kid was probably trying to help feed a large family. A rusty can was the dipping and measuring container. Pushing the ice aside and draining the extra liquid, he indicated that one full can was a *medio kilo*. That is what she bought. One half of a kilo. In her Roadtrek, she rinsed them in purified water to which she added a capful of chlorine bleach to insure their cleanliness. She would behead and shell later.

Her cupboard was bare, so she walked toward the village where she had seen various *tiendas* or little stores on the drive in. The sun was high as she made her way alongside a marshy area populated with more water birds. She saw several iguanas basking beside the road. The big ones, some as long as her arm did not budge as she passed by, while the smaller ones scurried away. *Don't run little guys. I'm not your enemy.*

Once on the main *calle* she was surprised to see an Internet sign and paused in an empty doorway that led to the living quarters in the back.

"Hola, hola." It was a few minutes before she could rouse someone above the spirited music.

A short young woman with a wide smile looked expectantly.

"Tiene Internet?" Joanna hoped she said it correctly.

The woman's lower lip protruded slightly as she nodded. *"Si, si,"* in a voice that said *of course.* Then she raised a roll-up metal door revealing a small room holding a computer and printer. Joanna spent some time reading her mail and sending messages. There was something from her quad squad friends. All sent words of encouragement and admiration. Nothing from Tony. Completing the latest update, she clicked on send. What would she say to Tony? She hated to think of the anguish he must be feeling. She anticipated reaching him tonight, but keyed a long message, just in case she didn't reach him again.

Wandering in and out of one store and another she made her way along the main street. She found that the grocery stores had just about anything she would want. Some were dusty and disorganized, especially the coolers holding the milk, chunks of white cheese, yogurt, hot dogs and butter. None of the fruits and vegetables were refrigerated, but there seemed to be a fairly good selection.

The corner market was such a contrast. The white tiled floor gleamed. Shelves of carefully arranged cans, bottles and boxes brought to mind an artist's pallet. The selection of vegetables and fruit was sparse, but the cooler held of all things, Philadelphia cream cheese. Shrimp and her own cocktail sauce of horseradish and ketchup over cream cheese, served with crackers was the appetizer she would take for tonight's gathering.

As heavy as her packages were, her step remained lively on her return trip. She was pleased with her purchases--*crema acidificada,* which she learned was sour cream, a liter of milk in the *ultrapasteurizada* package that required no refrigeration until it was opened, boxes of orange and grapefruit juice, plenty of produce and of course the cream cheese. She was proud of her success at the *carniceria* where she was able to buy a pork loin and a *medio kilo* of ground beef.

Evening on the terrace was lively. Meeting each couple, she mused at the variety of personalities, some subdued, others boisterous, all quite friendly and welcoming. She visited with Leticia and Basilio, the owners of the campground. Her first impression of Basilio was that he was most outgoing and something of a jokester, very unlike his son.

Liz was a water colorist, still learning she said, but she had had a lesson or two and Joanna was invited to paint with her. Joanna suspected otherwise about her expertise and was hoping to learn and not just piddle with experimentation.

Manuel came late, just as things were breaking up. His hair had been wetted and combed back and he looked handsome in his polo shirt and shorts. He was nonchalant about the jibes labeling him a workaholic who labored dawn to midnight. He grazed through the appetizers, eating as he went ignoring the stack of paper plates and declined a beer or glass of wine.

Shaking his head, in all seriousness he said. "No more drinking for me. Too much when I was young. Now I don't like it. It gives me a headache." He tapped at the side of his head.

Joanna found his clipped English and Spanish accent enticing. It kept rolling around in her head. They didn't speak. He nodded his greeting as he moved through the group and took a seat near Al who had asked him something about the turtles. Joanna said her goodnights, explaining that she needed to walk to the village to make a phone call. Hazel and Harry assured her that she would be safe on the dark little road.

There was no answer. She had waited and tried again, twice. No luck. Far off, music played, a dog barked, a donkey brayed. She was alone.

CHAPTER 26

Painting with Liz was proving to be most rewarding. She helped with laying in the lights and leaving the whites and working in the deep shadows. Joanna had chosen to paint Liz's photo of a fisherman returning with his catch, nets slung over his back. He was close to losing his britches, which gave the picture much character and a definite flavor of Mexico. Liz had done this one herself, so Jo could be guided by the artist's interpretation. She had a good start when it was time to put everything away. This afternoon belonged to the turtle hatchlings.

On-lookers were captivated by the afternoon turtle release. Campers in bright beach clothes urged their charges to the foamy waves. Squeals and cheers echoed as the shelled animals were washed away. Unlucky ones were carried back, flipped upside down to spots they had struggled to cross earlier. Gently righting the creatures, the liberators were cautioned. "Don't step back. There's a little guy behind you." Dozens of little ones found their way while twenty or so could not be coaxed to move one little flipper.

Joanna helped to gather these immobile creatures and Manuel and she returned them to the makeshift pool where he provided clean seawater and fish for food. They immediately took off swimming. They seemed healthy enough.

"Another day I will take them out and release them directly into the sea." His eyes flashed toward hers. "You will go with me?"

She returned the sparkle in his eyes and nodded.

A new day. Joanna put on her sneakers and jogged into the village.

Walking the beach had been her only exercise. It felt good to run and she kept the pace until the last block. Drina, the grinning e-mail gal had to be summoned from the loud music again. But in no time, everything was booted, and Joanna was reading Tony's words. They were dated yesterday.

There was no change with his father, but things were no worse. His mom was holding up. She was a tough lady and rarely left her husband's side. He had spent the day with the business. Even with his brothers-in-law, they were shorthanded without his dad since they had several new projects in the works. So far, he didn't mind. Perhaps he was feeling guilty about being such a butthead when he refused to be a part of the business those few years back. If only he could make it up to his father. They continued to hope for the best. It ended with. *Nene wants you to call her about seven on Thurs. night if you read this in time. Love Tony*

Today was Thursday. Twenty minutes before seven. It wouldn't take her that long to walk to the phone booth, but she wanted to give herself plenty of time. If the closest phone was being used, she'd walk a few more blocks to another one. The evening was cool, and she searched for something to cover her bare arms. Shrunched in her small closet –there it was—Tony's long white shirt. That would be perfect. Burying her face into it, a trace of his scent remained, and she tried to picture his face.

Nene answered on the first ring. "Wow, it's good to hear your voice. Tell me everything that's happening."

"Not much. But I'm enjoying the quiet after that awful time when I was home." Joanna told her about the turtle project and her painting, the campground, and the little village.

Nene sounded pleased with herself. "We have a surprise. And some encouraging news. I'll let our mutual friend tell you." Joanna waited, wondering who she meant by we.

"Hi. I'm the surprise. It was Nene's idea." Tony's voice rang in her ears. "She has been a real trouper, bringing Mom and me sandwiches and tonight she's fixing dinner."

Probably everything from the deli. Janene was definitely <u>not</u> handy in *the kitchen. How could she? How could he? Absence makes the heart grow fonder. Wasn't that it? Looked more like outa sight, outa mind.*

The cheerfulness was forced. "She's all heart, isn't she? I'm happy that Nene's been there for you."

"Let me tell you the rest of the story. Nene took a stint this afternoon so Mom could get some rest. As I said in my e-mail, I've been working in the business during the day. Anyway, while Nene was there, Dad began to come around. She had the nurses and doctors come right away, got a hold of Mom, did all the right things."

"Sounds encouraging."

"There's a long way to go. Can't understand his mutterings yet, but we all know he said Antoinette when mom tried to get him to swallow some liquids. At least he recognizes us."

They made a few more attempts at small talk, but there didn't seem to be much more to say. They were worlds apart. Following another lull, Joanna ended it. "It is so good to hear the good news and it's great that Nene has been such wonderful support. I'm not sure when we will be able to connect again with your schedule so up in the air but keep me posted on e-mail when you can."

It was another beautiful morning as Joanna lounged on the patio engrossed in Villasenor's <u>Rain of Gold</u>, a multigenerational saga of both sides of his family tree as each struggled through the hardships during the Mexican Revolution and after. Liz and Al thought she would enjoy it. She spent most of the day with her nose in the book and was touched by the grit of the people she read about. Daringly, she wore *the yellow bikini* bearing her flat tummy which she decided needed a little color to match the rest of her body. A shadow crossed her book, and she looked up into dancing eyes.

"I am taking the turtles to the sea now. Do you want to go?"

She dashed to the Roadtrek and pulled on shorts and a T-shirt. When she returned, Manuel had carried a yellow canoe to the water's edge, where two lifejackets and a pan of turtles waited. As she neared, he pushed it into the shallow water, placed the turtles and a lifejacket in the bottom, then handed her the other jacket and gave instructions about getting in without rocking the boat. Holding firmly to the canoe he walked out, controlling it so the surf would not upset them. At once he lunged, pulling himself aboard and they slid over a wave before it broke.

Paddling with a steady rhythm, they passed the rocky point to the left of the campground and floated for a few minutes while Manuel peered below.

"This is a good place to release our friends. There are some ledges where they can seek shelter and find food until they are sure of themselves."

One by one they slipped the wiggley fellows into the water and watched them disappear, seemingly at one with the sea.

Joanna called out, "Be happy little guys. Have a good life."

"You want a longer ride?" Manuel held the paddle poised in the air.

"Sure." She would not miss this opportunity.

He paddled tirelessly passing one beach then another. She told about herself and asked about him. He was eight months her senior, grew up in the village and in Guadalajara where he spent his school years. The campground had always been his second home. He spent three years studying agriculture and botany, worked several years for a fertilizer company and had begun to work at the campground toward the end of last season.

Leticia and Basilio were expecting to retire when this season ended. It would be up to Manuel to run the business. There was a sister and brother-in-law who lived in Guadalajara, but they had their own careers. His plan was to hire someone to run the office.

He was happy here working among the plants and keeping the bungalows in good repair and had several ideas about the landscape that he wanted to implement. The lily pads had already been completed in front near the entrance. Had she seen them? No, she guessed she hadn't.

Manuel steered them to a quiet cove protected from crashing breakers and pulled them ashore. He guided her to a lazy pool encircled by rocks and dove in. Floating on his back, toes breaching the surface, he enticed her to join him. "This is the best swimming pool that I know. Come in. I am not a shark. At least not often. I think you look very brave and can fight off a shark if you see one." He swam in circles, hands together in a pretend shark fin.

"Men should protect their women from sharks, not be one." Tossing her shorts and shirt in a heap she challenged his taunting, diving directly at him. When she surfaced, he was nowhere in sight. "You bugger, where are you?"

Powerful hands gripped her from behind and lifted, propelling her cannon-like above the water. After a deep plunge, she came up spitting. "I guess you *are* a shark." The subdued man had some fun in him after all.

They felt like children in their playful banter, chasing and showing off their tricks. They tossed a dried coconut about, then Manuel dived for treasures to present to her. He teased her about her yellow bikini and called her a *mariposa amarilla* which he explained was a yellow butterfly.

"So you think I am a *mariposa amarilla*, no? Like this?" Laughing she waded to the shallows imitating the flutters of a butterfly.

He followed with cunning in his eyes. "I think you are a most—how do you say?—sexy yellow butterfly."

"And I can't decide if you are a fox or a shark. How do you say fox in Spanish?"

"Zorro." He trilled the rr's with special significance.

Joanna attempted an imitation. "Yes, *zorro* is what you are. Mr. Fox, you just don't want anyone to know."

Finally, they left the secluded lagoon and sat side by side, digging their feet in the soft sand and squinted toward the horizon shunning the brilliance of the sinking sun. The last little glimmer of dazzling orange slipped from view and in its place a vista of mauve blending into rose and a delicate pink stretched where the sky met the sea. Joanna felt a shiver crawl over her. Manuel rose, retrieved her shirt, gathered it around her shoulders, placed his arm around her and drew her against his warm skin. She shivered again. He looked into uncertain eyes with his gentle smile.

With someone else she might have worried about the return trip in an inky sea, lighted only by the half-moon. But Manuel had her confidence and she felt completely safe.

Propped in her bed, she balanced her journal on her knees and began the day's entry.

Feb 1. A new month. Hard to think back to December when Amy and I took off for Mexico. Now here I am in this quiet little spot, feeling suspended again. Could have walked to the village to call Tony. Only 9:30, but just don't have the inclination tonight. I have no idea how things are going for Mario. I'll check the e-mail tomorrow, maybe some word from Tony.

Today was quite a day....

Finishing her writing, she heard some clinks and clanks, then the steady zzee, zzaw, zzee, zzaw of someone cutting through wood. Parting the front curtain she peered toward the open doorway of the campground shop. Shadows played on the wall. Manuel. Indeed, he did work into the night.

The campground was waking up when she footed it to the terrace carrying a steaming cup. She sat alone, sipping, enjoying the peace, listening to the surf sneak in and out and then with a boom, catch her full attention. Manuel stepped from the beach onto the patio, shovel in hand. He had been burying some six pounders already dead when they were beached during the night. Now the shovel held an empty plastic bottle, a plastic sandal and a crunched potato chip bag. He deposited them near the stairs in the covered barrel labeled *inorganica*. Beside it stood one for *aluminio* and one for *organica*. In this campground everything was separated and recycled. "It's the locals who mess up the beach, not these people." He motioned toward the campground.

Manuel was down on those who did not take care of the environment. He rarely ate shrimp because of the harm shrimpers did to other sea life. He told her about his compost pile and the amount of recycling he did, then directed her to the lily ponds.

How could she have missed them, only a short distance beyond the campground entrance? Here his ingenuity was at work. Three over-sized discarded satellite dishes formed perfect ponds for an array of bright water lilies in various shades of purple, pink and blue. They required little care because of the perfect balance of little animals and plants living in symbiosis in each pond.

Alternating plots of grass and sculptured sand led one's eye gracefully one to the other. Several floras of greenery, each in its own distinctive shade and variation, some rigid and others delicately fluttering seemed perfectly placed. Magnificent tree trunks reached toward bright green foliage shaped in mammoth fans. A few cacti hoisted themselves from the sand. One, taller than any man, stood proudly. Manuel pointed to a hidden crevice. There it was, the tree frog that had taken residence, nearly invisible in a matching color. He said that it rests in the day and is busy at night.

Afternoon found Joanna alone. The curtains pulled to shut out the light, she sprawled on her bed staring through the haze. Tony's e-mail had been a blow that she didn't see coming. It didn't sound like the Tony she knew at all, the one with all the life and laughter, the one who knew where he was going and how to get there, the one who oozed confidence and charm. It was like he wrote it through gritted teeth. She fingered the copy she had printed before she had blipped it from the screen, then crunched it in her fist and continued to stare.

It said:

My Dear Joanna

I wish we could be together. This long-distance relationship is rough, especially with all that is going on with me, my family and the business, not to mention all that has happened with you. You know how much I care about you and how important you are to me. Because of that I don't want to jeopardize any future we might have. We had such a whirlwind beginning, but with 2,000 miles separating us, I don't think our relationship can grow as it should. Please understand. I'm asking that we put our relationship on hold.

Quite honestly, I'm feeling a great deal of pressure here to prove myself with my dad. He is still an invalid and is not able to communicate, but he is alive and I need to take this opportunity to make everything right for us now. I do not want to live with regrets.

I want us to keep in touch, but at this time I cannot handle the responsibility of a relationship. Even if you were here, I would need to put some space between us in order to take care of present priorities. I do not expect things to be this way forever. In the meantime I don't want to be a ball and chain around your neck and though I would like to say wait for me forever, until I work all this out, I want you to know that I hold no claim on you. That would be unfair.

I wish you well in your search for your birthmother. May you stay safe in your travels. Please keep in touch.

Love, Tony

The next few days took their time. Joanna settled into a pattern of beach walking, painting, and reading. She couldn't make sense of Tony's message. She tried to read between the lines. What was he really trying to say? Was it Nene and a way to let her down easily without blaming one of her best friends who moved in on her relationship? Did being apart bring him to the realization that what they had was like one of those summer flings that were very romantic and fun, but never went anywhere, once summer was over? Or were inner struggles occupying his very soul and denying him the right to the path he had been taking?

She had swallowed hard when she returned his e-mail. Should she be mad or should she be sad? She had said simply. She understood and wished him well. She did not say she would stay in touch.

She and Manuel spoke occasionally. He admired her paintings of the lilies in the pond and the poinsettia plant that was larger than any she had ever seen.

Sometimes as he worked in his shop, she'd take him a hamburger or sandwich. She learned about the little snakes found in the area, the size of earthworms, sightless as they burrowed in the earth and that the shrimp plants with their gold spired blossoms attracted hummingbirds. So much better than hanging colored sugar solutions as was so popular in the Rockies near her home.

One evening she sat watching him work into the night, a single light bulb tossed over a branch, filling pots with his fertile compost and creating carefully thought-out plant compositions. No, he didn't need help, but they could talk a little. She wanted to know his thoughts about marriage. He told her marriage was fine, that he had considered it. Angelica and he had been part of each other's lives for four years, until she left last summer to study music in Salzburg. Their relationship was up and down, and she needed to experience more of the world, he said.

"What happens when Angelica returns?"

He shrugged and continued his planting.

"Do you keep in touch?"

It was a moment before he answered. He was talking toward his feet again. "No. She sent a letter once. I didn't write. But I think everything is good for her there. She doesn't need to hear from me."

Each day when she thought of Tony, a melancholy overcame her, but he came to her mind less often now. Sometimes it was difficult to bring his face into focus.

She and Manuel had fallen into the pattern of an after-dark walk on the beach each evening. Away from the campground he often held her hand. Their awkwardness dissolved and the easy playfulness they felt at the lagoon continued to grow.

The only thing that threw a wrench in the routine was the anticipated arrival of Lauren. Actually, Joanna was thrilled. If she *had* to pick, Joanna would say Lauren was her favorite. Arriving early Friday afternoon, they'd have ten days together before Lauren headed to Colorado for ten more days with her family. Then back to California where the movie thing would begin.

Joanna had heard from Tony. He said little, except that his father had been moved to a nursing care facility and had taken a few steps with a walker. Unintelligible, his speech persisted as the most frustrating to Mario and his repeated efforts to talk ended up in noisy tirades. No mention of Janene. Joanna believed that Nene was the real message between the lines.

She had decided to respond if he contacted her, but she would not initiate contact. Her message was brief—words of encouragement and the bit about Lauren, nothing about her life and daily routine.

Manuel offered to take time from his work and drive her to the airport in his little truck so she would not need to disconnect everything from the Roadtrek. She refused his gracious offer needing alone time with Lauren and feeling awkward about the tight squeeze three in the truck would make.

It was the right decision. Things were backed up at the airport and it took an hour and a half for Lauren to finally get her luggage and find Joanna. They had not seen each other since Arizona when Joanna told her about meeting Darlene. Each had heard bits from the other, but there were a lot of details to fill in. Joanna thought she looked even more beautiful than ever, yet with that countrygirl wholesomeness.

They stopped at *Famars* a favorite family restaurant along the highway at Bucerias for a late lunch Taking plenty of time to enjoy the plentiful food, they felt no pressure to hurry, and visited on into the afternoon.

Lauren listened as Joanna described the events involving her mom, dad, Tony, Janene, everything at the new campground.

"I hate this crummy feeling I have about Janene. Of course, since Tony, she wants to be called Nene. How could a best friend move in on a man I was just beginning with?"

"Geez Jo, Janene has always been a little forceful, but I can't believe it either. Maybe it's just two friends hanging out and you have the wrong idea."

As usual Lauren couldn't think wrong of anyone. "I don't know. Perhaps we were slipping away from each other, even before Janene arrived. It's probably for the best. I think there's too much going on in my life—me and my punctured heart—for me to be able to make a relationship work, anyway."

"I noticed 'Manuel this' and Manuel that' sprinkled in your conversation. What
about him? Do you want two men on a string?"

Joanna flushed and turned away. "I don't want *any* man on a string, Lauren! Manuel is...interesting to say the least. Just hanging out with him is... well it feels really comfortable."

"How about him? Is he smitten? There was a twinkle in Lauren's eye.

"No! He's not smitten! I think he likes being with me though. He's one of those actions-speak-louder-than-words men, polite, thoughtful, almost chivalrous. He's forever looking me up to show me some butterfly, bird, or new blossom. He's so patient with my ignorant questions. He's handy, always inventing or recycling something. And he has a cute way with humor."

Joanna grew more animated as she talked about Manuel. "I love to hear him talk. He has this low, mellow voice, a little business-like and with a little bit of broken English. I have to admit it tugs at the heart strings."

Lauren laughed. "I think I know who's smitten."

Not a strong swimmer, Jo had no desire to swim laps in the ocean, but was not about to let Lauren bob around out there without someone watching. Lauren had agreed to stay out of the sea until Joanna was showered and was ready.

Manuel looked up from his beach raking which he did every morning, removing debris and smoothing the area beyond the terrace, and greeted Joanna as she stepped from the terrace.

"Good morning, Joanna." There was that flash in his eyes. Joanna returned the greeting before Manuel continued. "Your friend likes an early swim, no? It is good that you are here to watch, since this beach is unfamiliar. Sometimes the under tow is strong. I told her I think this morning is safe."

"Thanks Manuel. I'm sure it is, but I'll keep an eye on her. You are right about being cautious." She told him about the maverick wave that filled her with liters of seawater and about losing, then finding the bracelet that she wore.

"It is very beautiful. I see it is very important to you."

Lauren tromped toward them, untied the sweatshirt draped at her hips.

"Can't wait for that swim. Manuel gave me all kinds of advice."

Joanna watched Lauren meet the waves and paddle beyond them.

She admired the firmness of her strokes as her long, strong body slid easily and confidently.

Manuel leaned on his rake. "You and Lauren, you'll be here tonight? Tomorrow?"

The question surprised her. "Sure. No plans tonight and the only plans for tomorrow are Sunday breakfast in the village and enjoying the beach. Lauren and I aren't talked out yet."

He nodded. "Good."

She continued. "We're driving to PV sometime this week. Can we pick up anything for you when we go?"

He couldn't think of anything right now.

Nearing bedtime, Joanna and Lauren giggled over some childhood memory. No pajamas tonight, just oversized T-shirts. The workshop was silent. Manuel was probably at the terrace doing a little night watering.

There was a commotion outside the rig—feet shuffling and whispers. Then they heard the twang and plink of some instrument.

"Somebody must have company." Joanna turned off the light hoping not to appear nosy and parted the curtain to peer out on her side." Her voice was hushed. "Nothing here."

Then the sound blasted them full force. They had to see what was going on. When they stepped from the motorhome, they stared into the faces of three men singing with great gusto to the strumming of a guitar, plunking of a stringed bass and the sustained sounds of an accordion.

Manuel motioned toward the two chairs sitting in the beam of the yardlight. Joanna and Lauren obediently sat tucking their shirts under them. Manuel bowed, pulling something from behind and presented each woman with a bird of paradise. One by one, campers gathered around, listening to the serenade. Many cheered and clapped to the rousing music. They announced each piece. *De Colores, La Bamba, Si Yo Quisiera, Cielito Lindo, Guadalajara.*

All the while, Manuel stood proudly by and then announced the last song, a solo in a deep baritone.

Motivos

Una Rosa pintado de Azul,
es un motivo.
Escribir un poema es facil,
si existe un motivo.
Unos labios queriendo besar
son un motivo.
Y me quedo mirandote aqui,
encontrando que me motivo mejor
eres tu.

The final *aplauso* completed, the crowd dispersed, murmuring along the way. Joanna strolled toward Manuel. She saw flashing eyes, a satisfied smile. He cocked his head as if to say, 'did you like it?'

"So, this was what all the mysterious questioning was about. It was wonderful. I've never been serenaded before. What a treat. You're a treat." Gripping both of his hands in hers she felt their warmth. "What was that last song about?"

"Motivos?....Hm...Something about a rose, colored blue is possible, writing a poem is easy if there is a reason, sweet lips kiss if there is a reason and quietly I look at you here, and find that my best reason for being *eres tu*. It is you." He pulled from her grip and wound his arms around her, holding her close for just a minute, kissed her soundly, then released her. She searched his eyes, he hers. Each saw the faintest of smiles on the other's lips.

CHAPTER 27

Full speed ahead. Just when things were relaxed and peaceful, some news changed the pace. This was good news though. She had very little time to try to make sense of the serenade, which certainly swept her off her feet. And now all her feelings about that had to be swept aside.

It had been midafternoon when she left Lauren to herself on the beach, feeling an obligation to check her e-mail. Her mailbox was empty except for one single entry, titled 'I have news.' *Who has news?*

She waited for the message to fill the screen. *Fred.* Envisioning giant Fred in roomy bib-overalls, exposing his massive arms and hands, she thought of his genius that created amazing works with strokes of color and making it seem as easy as stirring gelatin into boiling water.

There it was.

Dear Joanna,

I hope this message finds you well. I don't know if you have had any success with the hunt for birthmother Dixie, but here is what I know. I was not here when she came to the gallery last week. My wife and I were in Mexico City making some deliveries. I have a woman, Carolina, watch the business when I am gone. I didn't think to tell Carolina about your search. However, while we were gone, Dixie picked up her money and said she was returning to Guanajuato where she is living.

I am sorry that I don't have an address or know more. I hope this little bit helps.

Painter Fred

She was at Fred's gallery last week and now she is living in Guanajuato. Amazing. She and Janine had gone by Guanajuato on their way to San Miguel. Her heart pounded as her fingers danced on the keys. She sent a million thanks and hoped that this would lead her to her Dixie mom.

She dashed off to find Lauren with the news. Joanna fell in a heap beside Lauren's lounge chair panting and gasping between words of excitement. Lauren finally understood and jumped up ready to take off this very minute.

Hazel and Harry looked up from an afternoon card game, curious about the commotion. When they heard the news, Harry, always on the run, hurried off to collect maps, paper and pen. Hazel followed in her own time. She knew she had flyers from last year's visit.

When the couple returned Joanna and Lauren got the scoop on Guanajuato. This trip would be a bit shorter than the one to San Miguel. Their "advisors" explained that the campground near Guanajuato was pretty poor and driving into town with the Roadtrek could be a nightmare. They decided to do as Hazel and Harry suggested--use *Hotel Hacienda de Cobos.* The rooms were inexpensive, they said, and there was a roomy courtyard with ample parking. Everything they needed would be close-by in the motorhome. Besides, all of downtown was accessible by foot from that spot.

Joanna settled her bill with Leticia and said she hated to leave the beautiful campground and hoped that she would be back. Leticia was certain she could find a place for the little rig when they returned from Guanajuato and wished her well in her search.

"Thank you for your hospitality and kindness. Please give my best wishes to Basilio. I hope your house is coming along well. It must be difficult to have him gone so much." She knew that Manuel's father would be away at least a month. He was building a retirement home near Guadalajara and Manuel had taken on extra duties in his father's absence.

Leticia continued writing on the information card. "Over the years, often one of us stayed here, while the other took care of things in Guadalajara. We are quite used to it."

"I guess Manuel is your right-hand man. He keeps everything so beautiful and in such good repair. And he's quite ingenious."

Leticia looked up from her notations. "Perhaps it will not be easy... saying good-bye."

Joanna tried to read her look. Was it approval or disapproval?

Awed by this new experience, RV-ing in Mexico Lauren's head seemed to be on ball bearings taking in each new thing. They saw fields of pineapple, tobacco, bananas, papaya, mangos, things Joanna was growing accustomed to, but she let Lauren make her own discoveries, not wanting to be the know-it-all.

Stretching her lean arms, Lauren sighed, enjoying the magic she felt. "Geez. Joanna, this is the best trip I've had in my whole life. Just the two of us on this great mission. Being in California has sure cut into our time together."

"I've missed you too. So far away. But I'm thrilled things are going so well for you. You've earned it, with all your talent and hard work."

"Thanks...So what happened last night?"

"Last night?" Jo feigned ignorance.

"When you went to find Manuel to say good-bye, dodo bird."

"Nothing...I did all the talking. He kept working, watering everything around the terrace. Refused to look me in the eye."

"A hard guy to read, isn't he?" She hesitated. "What did you say to *him*?"

"I made a damn fool of myself. Gushed all over, thanking him for the canoe trip, the sunsets, the serenade, all the time he made me feel at home there, for being so patient with my hanging around and all the questions. Said that I hated to say good-bye, that I wanted to come back if I could."

"He didn't say anything?"

"Just acted kind of mopey. Nodded a few times and said he hoped I found my mother."

"Huh! Well, he kept his distance this morning, but there he was waving us off as we left."

Joanna sighed. "I bet you think I'm back in the teen years, a love starved goon or some kind of nut. Just when Tony evaporates from my life, I get loony over this brooding Mexican."

Lauren's head shook from side to side. "Every oak tree started out as a nut who decided to stand his ground."

Joanna shot her 'the look' and Lauren continued. "Naw. I found him fascinating too. If I wasn't entangled, I would have given him a second or third look. There certainly is some mysterious energy between you two, though. I could see that."

Jo smiled toward her friend thinking that Lauren would probably be too tall for Manuel anyway. Then she admonished herself for her old-fashioned attitude.

Lauren went on. "If a romance continued and you found your birthmother, would you consider staying in Mexico?"

"I don't know. His old girlfriend should be coming back before too long. They broke up when she left for Europe to do her own thing. He doesn't think they have a future, but I think he still cares. She may return all psyched and renewed, ready to pick up where they left off. As a foreigner I don't know if I could compete with that."

Joanna floored the Roadtrek and skirted around a chugging truck with its double trailer. "Let's get off me. We haven't really talked about *your* movie. Talk to me girl."

It took most of the next hour before they hit Guadalarjara. Lauren told her about reading for the movie part, which was much more informal than she expected. She had not been overly nervous, partly because she had not gone to California to be an actor. In fact, from what she saw on the other side of the camera, she was hesitant about acting. And she was doing fine as a costume designer. So, the whole thing started as more of a lark and out of curiosity than anything else. Once she knew they were offering her one of the lead roles, she arranged for some private lessons which she found a lot of work but a real kick in the pants. She definitely wanted to give it her best shot, the best performance she could.

Set in the early forties, the movie was about farm life during the war when resources were in short supply. The brother, an enlisted US Marine ends up missing in action, the daughter's boyfriend leaves for the Navy and the father dies leaving the mother and daughter to run the farm. The focus was on the grit and strength of mother and daughter and the bonding that occurs between the two women who had never been close. A seasoned and well-known actress had the role of the mother and Lauren was to play the daughter.

It all sounded so out of Joanna's realm. She tried to imagine Lauren before the camera, being someone else. "How do you get into the role Lauren, become the character from the script? And in another time period?"

Lauren answered her in a spinning-a-yarn tone of voice. "I have a lot to learn and no doubt I'll be taking one day at a time. However, I think my character, her name is Sharon, is a lot like me. Easy going, a slow simmer until things get too hot, a bit of a daydreamer, smarter than she looks, a lot like the father she has lost. While the mother is a spitfire, always steaming, can't stand anything that is *not* a hundred miles an hour. Of course, that's part of the turmoil the two women face."

Jo mused at the 'smarter than she looks' part. Lauren wasn't one of those dumb beauty types. It wasn't that. But her laid back, easy going image didn't seem to fit what it took to compete in the Hollywood scene, making business deals, conjuring up designs and meeting deadlines. Yes, she had a good head on her shoulders.

"I just hope all that Hollywood hype doesn't get to you. That you stay the same 'smarter than she looks gal'."

They both laughed and Jo zipped around another slow-moving truck as they hushed the talk to concentrate on making it through busy Guadalajara.

As the scenery on the other side of the city grew less interesting, Lauren concentrated on the travel books that had been Steve's and Allison's. "Jo, it says that *Guanajuato State is near the heartland of Mexico and the soil is volcanic ash mixed with rich nutrients washed from the mountains.*"

She read on about the Spaniards arriving in the area in 1526, about

Cortez being responsible for introducing oranges, peaches, and other fruits. Then she read about the city of Guanajuato.

They learned that it lies in a narrow canyon, over a riverbed that serves as the underground transportation route, was designated as a National Historic Monument and played an important role during the revolution.

"Listen to this part Jo." *When Father Miguel Hidalgo and his followers came to Guanajuato and stormed the granary where the Royalists and Spanish were barricaded, they were turned back with artillery, hot oil and molten lead. A hero, Jose Barajus, nick-named Pipila which means scrawny necked baby turkey, out smarted them by putting a slab of rock on his back which protected him while he carried straw and started the fire to burn down the door. They killed many Spaniards, but this first revolutionary movement was crushed and four of the leaders, including Father Hidalgo were beheaded and their heads were placed in cages and hung at the corners of the granary.*

"Sounds like the place is full of history and there will be a lot to see. I hope we can enjoy some of it. If we end up traipsing all over Guanajuato like Nene and I did in San Miguel, we'll see a lot."

Even with the map, entering Guanajuato had them confused. The road twisted this way and that. Despite the Roadtrek compass, they were all turned around.

Lauren positioned the map every which way trying to figure if they were still on the right road. She looked up just in time to see an arrow and the words *Hacienda de Cobos*. "Here! Jo! Turn right! Now!"

It was just as Harry and Hazel had described. They moved the bare necessities into their room knowing they could prepare a few meals and change clothes in the rig whenever they wished. They found the back alley that descended to the main street. That was slick.

The *Comercial Mexicana*, a super grocery, dry goods and appliance store was only a couple of blocks away. Buying gas and paying for three days in the hotel meant that their pockets were nearly bare. They were in luck. They found three different ATM machines at *Comercial* to choose from.

Lauren sounded amazed. "Hey, getting along in a foreign country is not that difficult, is it?"

Jo was amused by Lauren's lack of sophistication, especially living in California all this time. *Don't lose this innocence and simple awe of the world Lauren. I love you the way you are.* "Let's spend what is left of today getting the lay of the city. Tomorrow morning, we begin our search in earnest."

They kept to the main street crooking through the town flanked by terraces of buildings, colorfully decking the hillsides. Single file was the only way to walk, so that oncoming walkers, also single file could slide by. The street made a jog, then another as they passed several government buildings, a basilica and well-tended gardens.

Toward the end of the main street, they stopped at *Jardin de Union* or Union Garden where the red terrazzo of the square was occupied by hordes of people, either on the move or seated on iron benches. Surrounding the popular gathering place were restaurants, an ice-cream shop and numerous novelty shops.

A church, medieval in its attitude and much less elegant than its next-door neighbor, the *Teatro Juarez*, rose up across from the square. The pair chose the theater that was open for tours and ventured in.

The grand chandelier from Paris and the enormous bar bearing massive carved woods, burnished in character, reflected the wealth of the city in the late 1800's. Though the theater continued to be the site of the annual Cervantes Festival and many other fine events, much of the interior had lost its elegance as it aged. Nevertheless, they detected the panoramic view of the Golden Horn of Constantinople, which had been painted in France so many years ago on the drop curtain of the opera house. And they sensed the spirits of the centuries as they explored the seats in their cubicles stacked one above the other, surrounding the lofty performance hall.

Returning to *Jardin de Union*, they chose an outdoor table in front of the raised gazebo at the square's core and ordered their meal. Musicians with their various guitars and accordions, wove between the patrons in each restaurant looking for paying customers. Joanna and Lauren declined their offers, visited, and watched the passersby then studied the menu, trying to make a decision.

Individuals carrying various sized cases and wearing black pants with black jackets over white shirts milled about, then situated themselves on folding chairs in the oversized gazebo. There were toots, bongs and tinkles for some time. Then the director's baton signaled for the tuning notes.

Joanna and Lauren decided that this must be the local community concert band. The members seemed to be very diversified and included quite a wide range of age groups, some silver-haired and others perhaps college-age. The friends munched leisurely on the grilled fish they had chosen and enjoyed the fine music group, who played a nice variety of familiar show tunes and classical works. The square was crowded with locals attired in professional dress, university students overburdened with backpacks, young parents pushing their offspring in wheeled carriages and school-age children making their rounds time after time.

Lauren sopped up the juices on her plate with a tortilla and pushed it aside. "Jo, I was just thinking about the time you showed us that antique box with the letter, the doll and the ring." Lauren glanced toward her friend's hand.

"Yes, I've been wearing it since I left Colorado."

Lauren continued. "You were *so* indignant when Janene asked about searching for your birth mom. In my wildest dreams I would never have imagined being here with you and doing just that. And fulfilling that pact we made."

"That crazy pact. I'm glad you're here, Lauren. If Dixie doesn't like me, you can scrape me off of the payment."

Lauren smiled. "She would have to be a jerk to not like you, Joanna. But can you handle it if she chooses not to have you in her life?"

"You don't think I can?" Joanna waited for an answer.

"My grandmother mended many skinned elbows and knees with her magic ointment and a bandage. She said you can't leave the bandage on forever. It has to be removed so that the scab can form properly and do its work. When it naturally falls off, you know it's all healed. She said that it's the same thing with other hurts in life. I hope you're not hiding under a bandage. You need to let that ugly scab form so that inside you can heal."

Joanna reached across the table and squeezed her friend's hand. "Thank you for the advice, Lauren. I know that denial can follow a person for a long, long time. I *am* trying to work through my sadness. I don't want to ignore or bury the pain only to have it fester and erupt later."

"I didn't mean to sound preachy. I have always admired your strength and determination, but…"

Joanna waved away her concern. "Yes, I know. And if my birthmother turns out to be a jerk, I'll confront her and tell her so."

Lauren chuckled and replied, "I doubt it. Suppose we should head back? We need to be ready for our big day tomorrow."

"Sure. Do you think we'll get lost if we take the back streets to the hotel?"

"Probably. But if we get lost, we'll get lost together."

Veering away from the main street, they left the *calle* where taxis, buses and cars trafficked and wound through back-street walkways cloaked in velvet. They sauntered beneath the balconies of which they had read, some adorned with garlands of vines and flowers, and discovered a quaint plaza where children played and graying men in their straw hats gossiped while women in withering skin, wrapped shawls about themselves.

"Do you see what I see?"

Both had spotted the gallery at the same time.

"Let's go Laurie Mac."

The first room swallowed the meager light with its size, and they found themselves squinting as they wound their way between massive chests, beds and tables. A wide door opened to another, equally dim. Lauren stepped inside and motioned Jo to follow. "Come on. Looks like this one has all the paintings, urns and stuff."

Joanna remained hesitant. No one seemed to be in charge. In fact, there was no one in sight. "Hola. Hello." No answer. Well, they would have to hunt on their own.

Lauren stood in the middle of the room, searching the wall, side to side. "There must be a hundred paintings in here. But they all seem old and dark don't you think?"

"They don't look anything like the two I have, but I'm not sure what we are looking for. See if you can read the names on them. Look for Dixie A."

As hard as they looked, not one of them had Dixie's mark.

Even at my age I want to feel the giddiness of this adventure, my first plane trip since I was thirteen. That trip is a happy memory. I was angry with my grandmother's new husband for taking her so far away from us but getting away from home and going off to Arkansas all by myself felt perfect. They showed me the best time. I will never forget the hours shopping, talking and the long walks in the rolling woods. I almost told Grandma. What if I had?

One evening Grandma gave me her ruby ring. Did Cara's mother give it to her with the letter and doll? I wonder.

Though you're gone from this world, dear Grandmother, sometimes I feel you near me. I'll be landing in less than an hour. I'm confronting your daughter about my past. Do you think she'll keel over from the shock of seeing me? Will she know me? I have some of your guts dear little Grandma. I know I can do it.

You would be proud of my painting, though I haven't painted much in the last month. Somehow the inspiration is gone. I have two of them with me to show Darlene. Sorry Grandma, it's hard to call her Mom.

I'm determined to get some answers, some apologies, some explanation, some healing. If she could be sorry, if she could take some of the blame, then could this festering be gone? The soft part of me imagines her arms cradling me, as one cradles a child, our tears mingling, thankful for each other, thankful we are not alone. In this fantasy, her sorrow and self-blame are intense and she wonders how she can ever make it up to me. The hard part of me would never allow her to hold me.

CHAPTER 28

The shower was hot and had good pressure and Joanna let the spray run over her body longer than usual. Sleep had been intermittent. All night her mind played scene after scene. Childhood pictures and one snapshot of Dixie, shooting an angry stare in a graduation gown were the only ones she had seen of her birthmother. Why hadn't she at least copied the graduation one? Now it was hazy in her mind. Dixie would be thirty-two years older than the picture anyway, somewhere around fifty. Joanna knew that her eyes and hair were dark brown, or had been.

She imagined her. A product of the sixties, long graying hair in a center part, dressed in a gauzy blouse and ankle length skirt, decked in combat boots and beads looped over drooping breasts that had never regretted the absence of a bra. Then her mind caught a flash of a petite slender woman, jet-black hair, dyed to fit her Mexican home, drawn back into a twisted bun. Or perhaps she was the type to wear jeans and an oversized blue work shirt. That image caught her barefoot, brush in hand, poised before a masterpiece in progress.

Joanna emerged from the bathroom in her own jeans and oversized blue work shirt, cuffs rolled twice. Towel dried and spritzed, her hair looked more golden than usual from the Mexico sun. She lightly touched her lips with color and brushed mascara on her lashes.

Lauren, stretched out with her face in her pillow, raised a sleepy eye. Her early morning voice had a soft croak to it. "What time is it? Geez, you're up and dressed already?"

"It's seven. I don't want to hurry you. This is your vacation. Enjoy the rest."

"Boy I slept like a rock." Her good friend turned to her back, stretching and wiggling to loosen the kinks. "I'll hurry and we can head off."

Jo gave her friend a pat. "Take your time Laurie Mac. I need to limber-up my legs. I noticed a *panaduria* about a block down the street. I'll check it out and bring us something for breakfast. We'll brew some coffee in the Roadtrek."

"What's a *panaduria?*"

"It's a bakery. *Pan* is the word for bread. Do you have any requests? The donuts and sweet rolls are a little disappointing for those of us used to the sugary stuff at home, but the breads are delicious."

Lauren wasn't picky, she said, whatever Joanna chose would be fine. Threading through the back alley, she traversed the sidewalk of the main street, already busy with shoppers carrying their woven plastic shopping bags, and other pedestrians talking on cell phones, some carrying briefcases. The *panaduria* was closer than she remembered. Waiting for a break in the traffic, she took time to focus on her surroundings. Above the bakery across the street, shouts in unison countered the droning sounds of cars and buses. The windows were flung open, and she saw the quick jabbing and kicking moves of both males and females, dressed in loose-fitting belted white shirts over pants.

At that moment, there was a break in traffic, and she dashed across and into the *panaduria*. A long table showcasing open shelves of various shaped loaves divided the room. In similar cases around the room, donuts, rolls, cookies, and pieces of cakes cut in square and diamond shapes were neatly displayed. Twenty or so patrons mingled among the racks grasping individual selections with long tongs, placing them on aluminum trays large enough to hold several loaves of bread. Joanna chose her own tray and tongs from the dwindling stack and wandered between racks, having difficulty with her choices. There was no real hurry. The wait in the checkout line would take a little time. The

French style loaves looked inviting. Some appeared to be nearly two feet long, too long to store in the Roadtrek. The smaller ones would work. *Blanco or integral?* She decided on the whole wheat instead of the white, thinking that the extra fiber would be good for digestion. The crescents were not the best nutritional choice but looked especially enticing. That was all for now and she took the last place in the snaking line.

Two women in white smocks deftly wrapped and bagged each customer's choices, stacked the trays, removing the tongs, then took turns at the cash register. One woman worked silently while the other expressed some greeting to each patron. Those she knew were called by name and she seemed to know when to speak in Spanish and when to use what seemed to be her native tongue, English. When Joanna's turn came, the rush of customers had declined and the quiet one loaded the stack of trays, carrying them to the tray table and departed to the back room, no doubt seeking more baked goods to replace the empty spaces on the shelves.

Joanna glanced toward the friendly clerk, noting the name Ana on her badge and returned the smile she received before Ana spoke. "Hello, I don't remember seeing your face before. Visiting our city?" Using the tongs she placed a crescent on a large square of tissue paper, folded one half over the other, pinched the two corners and tossed the roll over and over until it had made a half a dozen rotations, leaving it encased in its own little package.

How to answer these simple questions. Joanna made a stab. "Yes, my friend and I hope to find an artist that I believe is living here. Maybe you can give me an idea about galleries to visit and where they are located."

Ana momentarily paused the rhythmic folding and tossing to look directly into Joanna's eyes. "What kind of artist are you looking for?"

Joanna found herself staring into coffee-colored eyes, more shadowed than she expected from such a pleasant face

"I believe she is an oil painter."

Using the tongs Ana scooted the whole-wheat loaf into a brown bag and deposited the crescents on top, closing with three expert folds. Ana continued, "There are little shops all over. I do know about a few places."

She pulled a rather crudely designed map from below the counter and the pair bent over the map while Ana circled eight locations.

The bakery attendant looked up at Joanna. "These may give you a start." There was an awkward hesitation as Ana lowered her gaze then she continued, "How long do you expect to be here? A.... What is your name?"

"Oh...I'm Joanna. I suppose four or five days."

Ana rung-up the purchases while Joanna dug for pesos in her fanny pack. Ana handed Jo a flyer titled *Yoga with Ana* and explained. "I teach yoga three days a week." She pointed overhead. "Upstairs. We share with the martial arts program. Perhaps you and your friend would like to relax your bodies after tromping around the city. I assume you have a place to stay?"

"Oh yes. We are at the *Hacienda de Cobos*." Joanna reached to take her package. "Thank you for the map and the gallery ideas. We may take you up on the yoga thing. Who knows?"

They both smiled and Ana moved to assist the next customer in the chain of patrons forming behind her. "I'm glad to meet you, Joanna. I hope you have a good day. Perhaps I will see you again."

Returning to the parking courtyard of the hotel, Jo found Lauren in the Roadtrek brewing a steaming pot of coffee on the gas burners. The two breakfasted on the flaky crescents, smathered with homemade apricot jam that Jo had brought from her mother's cupboard. Already a year and a half old, it needed to be eaten. Little by little many things of her mother's hand were disappearing. Somehow her mother's jam gave her sustenance, something she needed on this hunt for Dixie.

It was an interesting but grueling walk, one that took them on the steep climb behind the *Jardin de Union*, where they had eaten the night before and to the great statue of *Pipila,* the hero who had carried the slabs on his back. They couldn't believe the massiveness of the landmark yet did not take time to explore it fully and continued along the ridge where a host of artists of all types displayed their work in very fine shops.

Joanna decided that Guanajuato was much larger than San Miguel where Janene and she had tromped, and the galleries were not easy to find among the tunnel-like walkways. Two storied buildings hugged each side, one attached to the other in an endless serpentine. Wrought iron balconies ornamented with plants, meandering vines, statues, and pottery, jutted out overhead. Again, they wished they had time to appreciate the architectural beauty.

The pair found themselves going in circles and retraced their steps, yet pursuing, they crossed off one spot then the other. No luck so far. The women had not spotted one painting with Dixie's mark and no one knew of such an artist.

The downhill hike toward the main street was certainly more agreeable and quicker than the rigorous climb that led them to the ridge. It was well past lunchtime when the pair completed the loop, having tromped through six of the galleries circled on the map Ana had given Joanna and many more they found along the way.

They were famished when they wandered into the market, a large gymnasium type of building where Tarascan Indians and Mexicans spread their goods for sale. Cheeses, meats, vegetables, fruits, fish, and poultry covered tables, booth after booth. Whiffs of simmering sausages, meats and spices led them to a center section where hungry patrons roosted on stools scooping thick steaming soups and mixtures with generous spoons.

They saw the barren skull of a goat, its flesh floating deliciously in a spicy, thick broth, chili-red in color. Bravely they each ordered a bowl and were served a basket of corn tortillas, still hot from the griddle. Despite their knowledge of its origin, they liked the food. Rising to leave they again wished there was time to enjoy their surroundings, to ogle the market and the skillfully arranged foods that rivaled the palette of any artist.

Searching, the final two galleries took them beyond the hotel. They found the first one in ten minutes. Still no luck. Despite Joanna's limited Spanish, they were able to learn from one of the shopkeepers about another approach to their search. If seeking out galleries proved unsuccessful, why not try the state capital where foreigners obtained legal papers to live in Mexico? Perhaps there was a record of Dixie there. Betsy…a gallery…the state capital. Surely one of these would pay off sooner or later.

When they discovered that the last gallery on their map was far out of the city, a place they had passed driving in, they decided to call it quits until tomorrow. That one they would drive to. The rest of the afternoon was going to be—stretch out and rest their fatigued bodies.

When Joanna awoke it took several moments to focus on her watch-face. A quarter of five. She picked up Ana's flyer from the bedside table. The yoga class started in half an hour. Yoga sounded like something new and interesting. Besides Ana's English could be such a help in answering questions about the papers foreigners needed in order to live in Mexico. Jo shouted, "Lauren, ready to wake up?"

The body in the other bed turned in slow motion to face Joanna. A lazy voice filled the room. "Bet you thought you'd make me jump. I'm awake. Did you have a good rest?"

"Yes. I'm good to go. What do you think? Shall we try the yoga thing? We can get there in less than ten minutes."

"Sounds good. I haven't done any for a few months. I sure need to."

Lauren into yoga? That was a surprise. Jo felt like the country bumpkin who had not the faintest idea what it was about? This would be fun.

When they reached the *panaduria,* the upstairs windows were open enough to hear the drift of music, but not wide enough to see what was going on. The pair found the narrow staircase and followed three local young women up and through a hallway to a spacious room, apparently designed for a multiplicity of uses. Oddly placed mirrors hung opposite the windows and amplified the size, despite the poor lighting. They were greeted with smiles from a dozen women of varying ages who sat on rugs or mats waiting for the class to begin. Ana was adjusting the tape player and had her back to them.

"Come on." Joanna tugged at Lauren's shirtsleeve. "I want you to meet Ana."

"Geez, don't bother her now. Wouldn't it be better to talk afterwards?"

Joanna rolled her eyes and snaked around the seated yoga students, not releasing her hold. When they reached Ana, she turned to face them. Her face held a hint of surprise and Joanna saw that same pensive look and gentle smile. This time she noticed the crinkles that radiated from the corners of her eyes and the two frown lines on her brow, the kind that pinch just above the bridge of the nose.

She wore gray tights, long enough to cover two firm calves, and a forest green T-shirt scooped at the neckline, short enough to display skin between the two. Her hair, no longer knotted in the neat bun of the morning, hung in a single braid down the middle of her back. Sturdy and firm, there was a sensuous fullness to her body that Joanna had not noticed in the *panadaria*.

Ana released a plentiful breath and her shoulders relaxed. "Hello Joanna. It's nice to see you." Her voice was melodious and warm. Turning toward Lauren she continued. "This must be the friend you spoke of."

"Ana, I'd like you to meet Lauren, one of my best friends. A gal who has been an important part of my life since sixth grade. And she knows about yoga. Not like me."

Ana gave her that hooded-eye look Joanna remembered seeing earlier. "So, you are the one who is helping Joanna search for an artist friend?"

Lauren cocked her head. "Well, it's not someone we know. But?..." Lauren's expression was questioning.

Joanna cut in. "She's someone...I lost long ago."

"It would be interesting to know the story. Perhaps another time?" Ana raised her wrist to check her watch.

Joanna bit her lower lip, suddenly feeling flustered. "We're taking your time. Sorry. We did come for yoga."

Ana adjusted the music and waited for Lauren and Joanna to remove their shoes and spread their towels in an area toward the back. Ana's mellow voice sounded familiar somehow. *The same serene quality of her own mother?* They began with centering breaths in a prone relaxation pose, arms to the side, palms up, breathing with slow gentle inhalations and exhalations through the nose. "Allow your abdomen, not only your chest to fill. Pay attention to its rise and fall. Now breathe naturally, letting your mind be free."

Ana led the group through several repetitious movements. To Joanna it felt like her whole body moved in perfect unison through something viscous-like honey, quite different from the aerobics she was accustomed to. As Ana instructed one pose, then the next, Joanna listened to the careful instructions, a blend of Spanish and English, as they did various spine twists, downward-facing-dog, bridge, sun salutation, mountain, eagle and triangle poses.

Throughout the routine she found Ana's prodding soothing. "Be fully awake to your body. Hone your sense of focus and concentration. Listen to your internal voices. Let your bodies connect with the meaning and purpose of your life. You can be at one with the universe. We work toward a comfortable balance—bodies, mind, spirit. Now clear your mind from conscious thought and allow thoughts to come voluntarily."

During the final relaxation Joanna was aware of her steady breathing. Sitting erect, her legs crossed, she focused on the full moon of a poster hanging at the front of the room. Its roundness brought to mind circles. The circles floated before her like translucent bubbles that delight children as they are blown into the breeze. To Joanna the bubbles carried goodness and power and she wished them into the world, spreading joy when they burst upon whomever was nearby. It was a pleasant peace and mellowness.

Then in a jumble the good wishes she sent to the winds were replaced by all that she could *not* push aside. Visions of the adoption box, the mother she carried in her heart, the agonizing memory of her father, her precious longtime friends from childhood, Tony, Manuel, the mother she sought. How did they all fit in? Where did she fit in? Was this the way that letting thoughts come voluntarily was supposed to work?

Joanna was relieved when Ana broke the silence. It was like a light switch, the jumble stopped. "When you are ready, take a few deep breaths." Ana waited, then continued. "Then we'll come together. I like to end each lesson with some words of wisdom or affirmation. And for those who are new, we conclude with hands together in a prayer position and acknowledge each other with *Namaste*. The meaning is difficult to put in words, but it's like saying 'may the best of me honor and greet the best of you'. Is there someone who would like to lead in the affirmation today?"

A graying woman toward the front volunteered and shared a closing. "May the blessings of God rest upon you. May God's peace abide with you. May God's presence illuminate your heart, now and forever more. *Namaste*."

And they nodded to each other sharing the word, *Namaste*.

CHAPTER 29

"So, you think we should forget the trip to that other gallery today?" Joanna spoke to her friend as she set two bowls of cereal on the cozy table of the Roadtrek and Lauren poured steaming water into mugs and dipped a spoon into the instant coffee.

"Geez Jo, if we don't, we'll never make it back to meet Ana at her place by 10:30. I'd say we ought to take advantage of her day off. Who knows? Maybe she can help with some other avenues in our search. We may need to go to the state capital."

Jo smiled at the 'our search' part. She was grateful that Lauren was a part of this expedition. She would have felt so alone otherwise. "Time is running out Laurie Mac. I need to get you back to the airport in four days."

"We'll work something out. I can take a bus back to PV while you stay here. Better yet, I'll cancel my trip home."

"Never. You can't abandon your folks. They'd never forgive me. When their daughter's ready to be a star? We need to step up our pace."

They had an hour before they were to meet Ana, and Jo wanted to check the e-mail on the way. She had spotted several Internet signs along the main spine of the city. At the last minute, Joanna snatched Dixie's painting of 'The Laundress' from its tucked away corner. She was proud to show it to Ana and maybe it would mean something.

At the Internet business Lauren saw an idle machine. "Think I'll send a note to my honey. I miss that handsome hunk. Probably nothing from him. He prefers the phone."

"Can you reach him during the day? You could call, you know."

"Not really. Never know where he'll be during work. Maybe I'll try tonight, but just in case I miss him, I'll whiz him an update over the wires."

Joanna found three messages. Those from Amy and Janene were short. Each wanted to know how Lauren's visit was going and wished that she could join the pair on the beach. Janene added that Tony's dad had improved, but no other mention of Tony.

She was surprised to hear from Tony. After his 'let's put this relationship on hold' message and the brief follow-up she expected no more contact. His dad's progress was slow yet encouraging. There was no mention of Nene. He hoped that all was well and that she and Lauren were enjoying their time together. Work was much more gratifying than he expected, and he was definitely needed. He had no idea what Mario thought about his role in the business. Tony gave his father details each day, trying to encourage some fight in the man. The reaction continued to be a vacant glare. He thought he saw a faint glimmer yesterday and a wobbly smile. There were no plans to return to Bucerias. The cyber cafe was prospering under Jesus' management, so things could stay that way for now.

She stared at the computer screen. It was all so confusing. He signed it, *Keep me posted. Love, Tony.* Her fingers flew as she keyed a combined message for all three. There was much to tell. None of them knew about the trip to Guanajuato. She closed several pages later and clicked on send for Amy and Nene, then added several lines for Tony.

It seems like ages since we had time together. It's not easy to say all I want to say online. My heart goes out to you, your mom and especially your dad who I remember as being so full of life. It must be heartbreaking to see him otherwise. I am happy that there is some progress. That must give you all much hope. I would have liked to talk with you about my dad, too. You have such a good listening ear.

I detect a different Tony, not the one who was adamant against being a part of the family business. Surely your father approves, and appreciates what you are doing, but can't or won't let you know. May you resolve the differences from the past. My dad and I won't have that opportunity. My best to you.

Love, Jo

Ana's directions were complete and led them directly to her door. They had passed the place before. It was near the little plaza where they had found the dimly lit gallery the first night. Around the *plazuela* stood the gallery and other *tiendas* selling women's clothes, baby furniture, snack foods, bridal goods, and pizza. Three walkways extended spoke-style from the plaza, and Ana lived on one of them. Her place was the first upstairs unit. The two climbed the steep open stairway and felt her friendliness when Ana greeted them and invited them inside.

The living area, deeper than it was wide, held a small kitchen, a small dining table with two chairs, plus a wooden couch and its matching chair bearing bolsters covered in an Indian print in reds, rusts, yellows, and browns. A gaping hole was fixed at the back of the apartment. Multi-paned doors stood open to the balcony in front, which overflowed with plants that spilled into the room. Was there a fragrance of jungle?

Ana produced a tray of limeade, little sandwiches, and wide, flat cookies, placing it on the long table squatting in front of the couch where Joanna and Lauren sat. "Please have whatever you'd like." She sat on the matching side chair. "I don't have visitors too often. Nice to have you come." She appeared ill at ease.

Lauren looked around. "I like your place. Convenient location. Have you been here long?"

Ana leaned forward to pluck a cookie for herself. "Couple of years, I guess. Other than my plants, it's a little barren. Somehow, I haven't worked at decorating. Thought I might put up some curtains, but I like the light from the French doors and the neighbors aren't directly across from me, so it really doesn't matter."

"I like it, Ana. It's pleasant here." Joanna swallowed and continued. "I enjoyed your yoga class. A few more sessions and I could be hooked. I don't know why, but I didn't think about people in Mexico doing yoga.

"It's quite popular in the bigger cities. And I've seen it benefit people of every age and ability. Glad you liked it? Teaching helps me be more committed to keeping healthy, myself."

Lauren gestured toward Ana. "I've had several instructors. You're good. Think you could ever make it full time? Or do you want to?"

"No plans there. Actually, I enjoy the bakery, too." Ana tucked her shoeless feet beneath her. "Enough about me. How about you two? What's this mission you're on?"

"Well, I think my birthmother, Dixie Donovan is here somewhere and we're trying to find her."

A shiver slithered over Ana, and she rose to close one of the French doors. "Excuse me. Sometimes that north breeze swoops in here. What makes you want to find her? So, you're adopted, huh?"

Joanna recounted many of the events of her life with her mother, father and her three friends, then the loss of both of her parents. She was brave and kept the tears at bay but could see that Ana was touched by her story.

Ana rolled her lips together, sighed a little sigh and asked. "What led you to Mexico, to Guanajuato?"

Joanna did not rush telling of Ellie, her courage, her family making a Christmas, her gift to Joanna, her death. She told of the time the bracelet was almost lost, the woman with the prayer, the comfort in wearing the ring. Joanna glanced at Lauren beside her and saw glistening tears one by one roll over those high cheekbones.

Joanna fought to continue. "Then I found Dixie's mother...my... grandmother in Arizona. She invited me to come. She gave me..." Joanna lifted the painting propped at her side and unwound the wrapping and held it proudly..."this painting. Isn't it magnificent? Such passion in her work. I have another one. A church in San Miguel. So that's where I went first. Through some miracle, I found someone who knew her. I know she is real. I've come this close." Jo pinched her thumb and forefinger together.

Tears squeezed onto Ana's cheeks and her face twisted. She eased herself from the chair reaching her hand out, as if to quiet Joanna's words. "Excuse me. I'll be right back." She retreated through the black hole at the back.

Lauren attempted a smile and leaned to hug her friend. "I love you, Jo." And the words caught with a sob.

The two held each other fast and Joanna whispered, me too."

When Ana returned, she held a painting before her. The same hues, the same setting, the same translucent profile, but a different pose. Signed Dixie A.

Joanna sat stunned, staring into the tear-stained face. "You know my mother." It was not a question.

"Yes." Ana set the painting aside, crossed the room and seated herself in the side chair and leaned toward Joanna. No one spoke. Lauren pressed one hand to her heart and covered a gaping mouth with the other. Joanna's eyes locked with Ana's and she felt the back of the sturdy couch cradle her and keep her from falling backwards.

A wide chasm of time elapsed before Ana spoke. "But it's not what you think." Ana took her time forming her lips around her next words.

"I not only know your mother, *I am* your mother. *You*…are my Cara."

No one moved.

CHAPTER 30

I t was a sobering tale Ana told—a life foreign to both Joanna and Lauren. It was a difficult telling as well, torturous for Ana to talk of the secret hours of sexual molestation and threats by her father. Admitting mistakes that followed was equally difficult. Naiveté, uncertainty, neediness—all contributed to a life of reckless abandon.

Ana met Buddy in Aspen after she ran from the torment of leaving little Cara behind. He was an aspiring musician living a fast life and she became his girl, joining another pair, Pike and Nicki and four other band members. They rubbed elbows with stars and other musicians who came to the beautiful Rockies for skiing and living high.

In time the band split and she with Pike, Buddy and Nicki left for California. The new group struggled to build a name, hoping to cut a record deal. They lived on the meager earnings brought in by Ana and Nicki. Finances became tight; disagreements heightened; desperation took over. Ana was dragged along in the robbery decision. The first two went off without a hitch. Not the third.

Ana continued her story. "It was much later when I learned all that had happened. Buddy said there would be no guns, only the threat of one. Pike, the hotheaded drummer, was not about to be told what to do and took one anyway. That night, the cashier reached under the counter and pulled his own gun. Pike went crazy yelling for him to drop the weapon and shot a warning when he didn't. Everything escalated from there. There was more shooting and, in the end both Buddy and the cashier were left in pools of blood while Pike and Nicki ran."

In disbelief Joanna asked, "Buddy was killed?"

Ana shook her head. "Fortunately, both recovered. However, it was touch and go, I guess. Buddy did the time though. Fifteen years. I hate myself for that part." Ana looked toward the floor, ignoring their eyes.

Lauren tried to defuse the guilt in Ana's voice. "But you were just the driver. You weren't even inside for the shooting." Ana waved her words away and Lauren continued. "Pike. What happened to him? He was the shooter, wasn't he?"

There was silence before she continued. "Yes, he was the shooter. Nicki, Pike and I escaped to Mexico and roamed around for a while. It was summer and the weather was warm enough and we threw a bedroll out at night. When our money ran low, we headed to Mazatlán and got jobs cleaning rooms and bussing tables at a hotel. We stuck by him, but Pike got more and more out of control, using pretty heavily, though Nicki and I had stopped. We knew the damage that drugs and booze had done to our lives.

"One night Pike got some bad stuff. We buried him the next day."

Joanna had so many questions. How did she start painting? What happened to Nicki? Buddy? Why did she say her name was Ana? Did she see the ring and bracelet when she was at the *panaderia*? If so, why didn't she say something then, and why did she send them on a wild goose chase all over the city?

Much of the day had gone and they all felt drained, and it was time for the two young women to leave. The questions would have to wait. Lauren went on out while Joanna and Ana lingered in the doorway. Then Ana reached her arms around her daughter and held her tight. She said simply, "I never believed I would hold you again."

The return trip to the hotel was mostly reflective. Lauren started. "It's interesting that she calls herself Ana. Do you suppose it was her way to leave the molested Dixie behind? After meeting her as Ana, it's hard to imagine her as the Dixie we have been searching for."

Joanna responded, "I'm sure you are not far off on the name thing. I've been calling her my Dixie Mother for so long, that it's hard for me to see Dixie and Ana as one and the same. She doesn't fit any of the images from my imagination. After meeting her, I can't picture her as

Dixie. It makes me sad hearing more about her life. It could have been, it should have been so different."

Lauren slowed her pace as she said, "Yet, if Dixie had not been molested, if she had not run away at seventeen, if she had not been a confused teenager, there would be no Joanna."

"My dear philosopher friend—ever reciting the mysteries of the universe. I am grateful for my life. I may even tell Ana. It may relieve some of her guilt. It depends on where we go from here."

This time Lauren stopped her walk and looked at her friend. "I remember my dear grandmother again. She said that the most important part of Christmas was the planning, the anticipation, and the hope that the gifts you chose would bring pleasure. She said that the few minutes of opening and watching, followed by the aftermath of clutter could leave one empty and let down. It could be much the same—finding Dixie, Ana." Lauren's eyes looked into Joanna's, questioning.

Her response was thoughtful. "It is much the same. Before she was found, the anticipation and curiosity was compelling. It is wonderful to find her yet, there is that feeling of being let down, of so what! After Christmas, it's the cleanup and then back to life. Will it be that way with Ana and me—it's been nice, now back to life?"

"After the shock, the high and the letdown feeling, the full realization will kick in and you'll both know the right way to continue this relationship." They began to walk again, and Lauren's voice grew mischievous. "It doesn't look like I'll have to scrape you off of the payment and you won't have to tell Ana what a jerk she is."

Joanna smiled and the two were silent. She wondered about her future. Here? Where? An image danced in her thoughts. *Instead of Leticia's clattery typewriter a shiny new computer stood in its place. Joanna crouched in concentration over a newly installed system, organizing reservations and financial information for the campground sites and bungalows. Manuel in his winsome way poked his disheveled head in the doorway, grinning at her, saying, "Ana just stopped by. She sold another painting and is taking us to San Pancho for dinner tonight. Is that OK?"* In time would her life take such a turn? Near the mother she was now learning to know?

The two young women could not pass the opportunity to explore more of this interesting city while they were here. Before their meeting with Ana, they had decided to take a city tour tomorrow morning. Since Ana would finish at the bakery about two, they stuck to the plan. Joanna and Ana would share a late lunch and Lauren would find something else to do so the mother and daughter could be alone.

Near the hotel, Lauren stopped at a phone booth. "I think I'll call Greg. What about you? Do you want to talk to Janene, I mean Nene, and Amy?

"I don't think so. Not now. I'm spent. I know they'd like to hear. Would you call for me?" As an afterthought, she said, "Have Nene call Tony with the news. Tell them I need a little down time."

Lauren hugged an arm around her friend and responded, "Sure. After all the calls, I'll pick up a pizza at that shop around the corner. See you later."

After such an emotional day Joanna was surprised to sleep so soundly. She was dreading the city tour. There was so much more on her mind. For her friend's sake she vowed to put on a good front.

She needed not to have made the vow. There was so much history in the area and four hours would barely scratch the surface. Fernando, a charismatic young man who had picked up some English, was their guide. They began driving near the sprawling University of Guanajuato, which had been operating for some two hundred and sixty-five years. Nearby they heard the blending tones of the University band and saw the brightly colored uniforms columned before a massive stone structure.

Neither one would have chosen *El Museo de las Momies de Guanajuato*. However, it proved to be most educational and fascinating. Apparently, the soil, temperature and humidity of the area enabled buried bodies to naturally mummify. As mausoleums were vacated when space was needed for those who recently expired, the mummy museum displayed the specimens for all to see.

Lauren and Jo browsed through room after room, noting how the dead had been buried, most in prone positions, but some sitting cross-legged. Though the inner organs and tissues had atrophied, leathery skin stretched over the form-giving bones. Dark hair draped across skeletal heads with empty eye sockets and gaping mouths, some revealing a few oddly spaced teeth. Most had outlasted their clothing and lay without any. Some wore socks or leather boots that comically covered their feet. A few necks and fingers were adorned with rings or other jewelry looking oversized and out of place.

La Boca Mina was the next stop. Descending sixty meters below the earth's surface, they found the mine cool and dank. When the guide extinguished the meager bulbs, which had lighted the way, the darkness was unfathomable. They listened to the story of the mine workers who from the mid 1500's toiled in near darkness, lighted by oil lanterns which might bring about explosions when the conditions were just so. They learned of the children who were taken into labor when a relative was killed in a mining accident to replace the lost worker and how they carried jugs of hot water into small corners so that cracks could be expanded and chiseled more effectively.

The next stop verified the many hardships and evils of the past and Joanna found herself wishing that the world was a different place. No doubt some of what they saw at *Galaria Subteranian* persisted in other places even today. Recently discovered and unearthed, the underground dungeon was a site of torture in the 1700's. A cruel inquisitor, whose job seemed to be to assure proper behavior, snatched people from their lives for refusing a certain marriage proposal, for aiding the poor, for praying the wrong way. They endured water torture, body stretching, head presses, or lived in cages strung from the prison ceiling until they confessed or paid for their misdeeds. Many died at this evil man's hand under the guise of religion, much like the Salem witch hunts.

Next Fernando drove into the nightmarish maze of tunnels beneath the city. Bus drivers tromped their gas pedals and shot from unseen side streets. Cars, trucks, and motored cycles belonging to shoppers and workers doing their business above ground, parked alongside, leaving just enough room for vehicles to swish by each other. Their guide found his own parking place and the group climbed the stone steps to the network of alleys that came together.

Fernando explained in a blend of English and Spanish, "Heer ees importante calle, *el callejon del beso*. Ees good luck to kees heer." He pointed to the third step.

Joanna had read that at this spot the balconies across from each other angled so that people standing on them could touch. Legend maintained that two lovers, defying family disapproval, stood on the balconies to profess their love. Joanna positioned herself on that third step at the 'alley of the kiss' imagining the couples who had kissed here to ensure their own happiness.

Lauren turned and peered behind them. "How charming! Look at those critters!"

Sure-footed, yet gaunt and too heavily burdened, three burros one after the other, wound their way along the zigging street. Each carried several sacks, most probably filled with corn, draped across their backs. What a blend of quaint and modern this place was. The pair watched and listened as the clip-clop echoed through the canyon-like *callejon* long after they had disappeared.

Quickly the four hours were over. They had missed seeing the *Alhondega de Granaditos*, the famous granary that *Pipila* had stormed during the revolution. It was now an anthropological, art and historical museum. So much to see and not enough time. Joanna anticipated the rest of the afternoon with Ana. It was far more important, and Lauren could explore the granary on her own.

A spring in her step Joanna virtually loped to Ana's place. The leaden sensation she had after listening to Ana was beginning to dissolve. They greeted each other comfortably and decided to order from the deli in the plaza near her flat. Seated outside at one of the several tables they could talk the whole afternoon if they wished.

Ana told Joanna about Nicki's return to the states to start a new life after Pike died, while she remained in Mazatlán and learned to paint. "It was ten years," she said, "before I thought I could make a living on my art. I was selling some, but I needed to be near a better market, so I moved to Mexico City for five years. I made some good money, but I really didn't like the city. San Miguel was much smaller and a good place for artists, so off I went again."

"Then you left San Miguel. From what Oscar said it was rather sudden."

Ana gave Jo a surprised look. "You met Oscar?"

"Well, it was Nene that found Oscar and he led us to Fred."

"Amazing. Mary, Oscar's wife, and I were very good friends. Oscar's a sweetheart, we didn't talk a lot, but he was always fixing something when I needed him. What a loving and gracious pair."

"Did you know that Mary died?"

"No. So sorry to hear that. What a sad loss. About my leaving San Miguel. Buddy was with me for a while. After prison he took whatever day job he could find and tried to get a band going again, enough to put food on the table. That worked for a while, but Nicki said he seemed to be spiraling down, so I convinced him to come to Mexico. When I learned that my father was dead, Buddy and I went back to the states. I decided to see Darlene after all those years. You met her Joanna, what did you think?"

"She's lonely even with the social life at her club. She wants to see you. She wants your forgiveness."

Ana's voice had grit in it. "That's hard to believe. Darlene's a hypocrite. I'm not ready to talk about her."

"So, Buddy stayed in the states?"

"We're not a couple, Joanna. We will always care about each other. I wanted to see him go on with life. The last I heard he was a janitor at some school and the kids loved him. He'd been doing some work with the musicians there on the side. He's still a kid at heart. He'll do well there."

"Why didn't you return to San Miguel?"

Ana thought a moment. "No reason to return. Guanajuato held a certain charm for me. I already knew Jane who had the yoga classes here. We had studied together in Mexico City, and she asked me to take over some of her classes. I needed something. I was through being an artist."

"Why? Your work is beautiful."

Ana shrugged. "No desire, no inspiration. It's part of my past."

"You've not done one painting since?" Joanna could not imagine giving up such talent and ability.

"Not one."

"What about your name change? More severing the past and denying the connection to Darlene?"

"Exactly. I took my middle name Anne and used the Mexican form, Ana with the ah sound. That's who I am."

Around them pigeons displaying their exquisite iridescence and with their cocky boldness pecked at fallen morsels, then fluttered when a curious child ventured too close. Music sounded from one of the balconies. The peace and beauty of the place filled Joanna. People on their way to and from somewhere slowed their pace as they entered the plaza. Young or old painted, read or shared in conversation. Though all were oblivious to these two, intent on learning of each other and sharing themselves, Joanna felt connected to the humanity around her. This connection propelled her to search out the answers to her questions.

"When we met in the *panaderia*—you knew then didn't you?" Joanna asked.

"Yes, it was quite a shock seeing the ring and then the bracelet. A woman seeking an artist. It had to be my little Cara."

"Then why did you send us on the wild goose chase all over the city?"

"I'm sorry about that. It was cruel. But I needed time. I didn't know what to do. I suppose it was a risk, but I knew where to find you."

"So, you thought about letting me go on without finding you?"

"There was that thought, but it was only momentary. I would not let you get away from me after all those years."

"Did you wonder about me? Would you have ever searched?"

"Oh, yes. I wondered. On your birthday, I imagined you wide eyed sucking the frosting from the ends of extinguished candles. Did you like school when it came? I always enjoyed learning. What about my little Cara? I hoped at thirteen, at sixteen, you had the innocence I never had. Oh, how I hoped your parents deserved you."

Joanna wanted to reassure this newly found mother. "I had a wonderful childhood. I've already told you, my mother Allison, was the greatest." Joanna breathed in deeply and dropped her eyes. "I have great sorrow about my dad, but you've heard that story."

Ana's eyes held a tenderness, but the shadow of their first meeting lingered. "I am so sorry you have lost both of your parents." She looked directly at Joanna. I can see pain, but there is strength, too. The perseverance your mother taught has brought you here. I am proud to have carried you and to have given you life." Ana paused and bit her lip before she continued. "But I never thought seriously about finding you."

"But why?"

"I didn't deserve you. Wasn't good enough. I couldn't burden you with my tainted past. Besides, I had no right to intrude in your parent's or your life."

"Surely you don't feel that way now."

"Not exactly. But as my mind was going in circles last night, I came to one conclusion." Joanna waited. "For my own self *and* so that I might deserve you in my life, I must right my past."

CHAPTER 31

I t was a different anticipation that Joanna and Lauren experienced leaving Guanajuato. Lauren had volunteered to take a bus to PV so that Joanna could spend more time with Ana. That would come later, she told her friend. She would not miss their last few days together. It might be months or even a year before they saw each other again.

"Well, what do you think of her? Is she anything like you imagined?"

Before she responded Joanna smiled at that easy drawl she was going to miss. "Ana seems to be a combination of wounded deer and wary, steel-eyed mountain lion. The mountain lion part enabled her to survive her mother's denial, her father's abuse and other men who used her. I think it gave her the power in her painting."

"Did she feel used by your birthfather? What did she say about him?"

"All I know is that his name was Ben, that he was married and had two kids and their fling lasted two weeks while he finished some training program. For sure he used her. She was only seventeen."

"Would she help you find him? You have some siblings out there somewhere."

Joanna thought a moment, then shook her head. "I'm not interested."

Lauren did not ask why. "And the wounded part of Ana? What do you mean by that?"

"The way she looks at me with those tormented eyes. I sense a deep wrenching and discontent in her heart. That comes out in her painting, too."

"She seems so together, just the opposite of what you are saying.

"I could be wrong, but I don't think so. She's hurting inside. Unresolved turmoil from the sexual abuse and maybe some of it is the guilt. The drugs, the wild life, the robberies, then running off and leaving Buddy to take the rap."

"*And* giving up her precious daughter."

Joanna thought about that. She could never give up a child. Yet she understood. "Well, Laurie Mac, what do *you* think about her?"

Lauren pondered before she spoke. "I would describe her as 'Mother Earth', an earthy sensual woman who has buried some of that sensuality and is just waiting to allow it to fruitinize."

Joanna burst into laughter. "Fruitinize? I've never heard of such a thing."

"You know like come to fruition."

Grinning, Jo glanced at her friend, shook her head, then nodded. "Yes, 'Mother Earth'. It does rather fit Ana."

Waving excitedly Toad and Vera were the first ones to spot the Roadtrek as it stopped in front of the office at the Bucerias campground. Several sites were now available, and they chose the one nearest the office and the swimming pool. Jo decided that staying closer to the Puerto Vallarta Airport would be the best choice. The two women would have all day tomorrow and half of the next before Lauren took the flight to Colorado. Both looked forward to enjoying the warmth of the sun and relaxing near the soothing surf, having been on the road or tromping all over Guanajuato for the last six days.

Once settled in, they joined the campground residents on the beach for their nightly ritual of drinks with the sunset. In celebration of Joanna's return several brought trays of food to pass. As day turned to dusk, Barney and Barb hauled out sticks, chunks of wood and palm fronds crisp with dryness for a beach bonfire. Soon flames fluttered and flicked the air. Once the remarkable story of Joanna's birthmother was told and the trays and glasses were empty and the hypnotic flames had turned to glowing embers, one by one the group disbanded. Joanna and Lauren were left alone in the darkness.

"Lauren I'm still trying get a handle on *la espina* in my own life." Joanna had told her the story of the weaver. "Have you ever had a thorn in your heart?"

"Oh, yes. That is part of life. But there many kinds of thorns."

"What do you mean?"

"Some puncture you for life and though there may be healing, they never leave. I think that is what you see in Ana. She was scarred for life. La espina may never leave, but she goes on and makes of life what she can."

"And other kinds of thorns?"

"My grandmother talked about the sticks and stones and the clouds and sun of life. She said that living was a roller coaster ride. We're on top for a while—in the clouds and the sun. Things are good, life is a breeze, relationships are smooth. Then we hit a rugged place—sometimes unavoidable and other times brought on by our own ignorance, stupidity, selfishness. She called this the sticks and the stones. Sometimes we bottom out, we're out of sync, often loneliness builds, frustrations or uncertainties take over, disappointments pervade. It's when we feel stabbed in the heart. This type of la espina is like hitting a rough place, but when the thorn festers it can be washed away."

"So, you think I've hit a rough place. That is my thorn."

"Well, you've had several thorns to deal with, don't you think?" Lauren went on. "Another thing my little grandmother said, was 'don't let yourself stay in the sticks and stones too long, it has a way of hardening the soul, but appreciate and be grateful for them. Without them, the clouds and sun would not be so fine.' But there will always be thorns, Joanna."

Prior to leaving Guanajuato, a place that would hold the dearest memories, Joanna and Ana had decided to return to the states together, where Ana hoped to square herself with the law. It would take a week to pull things together, then Ana would take the bus to Lo de Marcos. The idea of resettling in Mexico after Joanna's birthmother cleared her name, had been left dangling.

Snaking her way along the winding highway Joanna contemplated having a few days with Manuel before her new-found mother arrived. She tromped the gas pedal and imagined the intriguing smile of the handsome Mexican and wondered if she had a future there.

Peaceful and sunny, it felt like coming home as she drove into the campground. The office door was open, and she poked her head in hoping not to disrupt Manuel's mother in her daily record keeping.

Surprised, Leticia blinked at Joanna. "Hello Joanna. It is good to see you again. Did you have a good trip?"

"Thank you, Leticia. Nice to see you, as well. Yes, it was good. Lauren and I found my birthmother."

Leticia's gaze sharpened. "Unbelievable. You must be thrilled."

"Yes, it is unbelievable. She's coming here in a few days. Then I'll take her back to the states. Do you have a place for me?"

The space she had before was available, the one across from Manuel's shop. She completed the papers and paid the fee. A shape filled the doorway casting a shadow on Leticia's face. When Joanna turned, Manuel's flashing eyes linked with hers.

He glanced away before he spoke. "I am surprised to see you, Joanna. In my mind, you did not return."

"Well here I am. I have a lot to tell you. Save some time for me this evening. OK?"

He appeared to consider the question, then nodded in an assured manner and walked away. Leticia handed Joanna the receipt and leaned forward on her desk casting Joanna a look of caution. "If you need anything, please let me know." An eyebrow arched when she continued. "Angelica arrives here tomorrow. She and Manuel have not seen each other for almost a year. Perhaps you know about Angelica?"

A scorching rush flushed through her body. She hoped her face did not reflect the heat. "Oh, yes. Manuel talked about her." Joanna tried to remember if he had been wistful in the telling. Perhaps the indifference in his attitude was a mask that hid his regret of their breakup. "I look forward to meeting her."

Dumb thing to say, but she couldn't think of anything else. She remembered the serenade and his scorching lips. They would need to talk tonight for sure. What an awkward time for her to come, just when Angelica was arriving. If she was returning early, if she was coming here, not staying in Guadalajara, there was reconciliation on her mind. Joanna was certain.

There was fluidity in the afternoon as she walked the beach and inhaled the salty mist. In her hand she cradled a bronze box embossed with entwining vines and leaves. She had no idea where she was going and was not at all disturbed about it. She thought about the poster, *If you don't know where you're going, you won't know when you get there.* So what! She had always been goal-oriented, yet those goals did not seem so important now.

Mother—she held the box before her—you always said, *In life you put one foot in front of the other and pretty soon you're there.* That's what I intend to do, Mom. I just don't know where I will end up. I found my birthmother and now it is time to put you to rest. I love you mother. No one will ever take your place. You will always live in my heart, wherever I am, whatever I do. You loved your visits to the ocean and your adventure in Mexico. I hope you approve.

Joanna walked into the sea as the waves swished around her. She lifted the cover to the box and cast it's contents into the air. They settled on the water and Joanna beheld their iridescence, gleaming and glittering until finally the waves took them away.

Night came and with it a grinding sound from the workshop where she knew Manuel was working. Too often relationships hung in the air, and each waited for the other to make a move. She had been in that situation numerous times and rarely made the first move. Tonight, would be different. That smoldering fire they both felt had not had a full chance to ignite. The smoke needed to be cleared, even if this intriguing Mexican was destined to be tucked into her memory and not a part of her life.

The moment Joanna stepped into his domain, the grinding ended, an echoing twang hovered, then silence. His sideward glance was playful as he spoke. "Oh ho! The Gringa with the yellow bikini, the yellow butterfly returns."

"To face *el zorro*, the fox. Right?" Joanna traced a finger along the counter feeling the gritting filings and flung and oily cloth she grasped with her other hand toward his chest.

Without a flinch he grabbed it from the air and twirled it overhead, fanning her face with each rotation. "You make a man forget he has work to do, little Gringa."

She stood chuckling and shaking her head at his "Gringa" reference. "And I thought you were always Mr. Serious."

He tossed his head back. "Oh no. There is much you do not know about me." Growing solemn, he stared a moment at the ceiling. Dropping his glinting eyes to look into hers he opened his arms wide to take her to him. A gentle voice nestled in her hair. "In another life, perhaps we will meet. Thinking of you will always make me smile, *chiquita, mi mariposa amarilla.* You see, Angelica and I go way back. Anyway, I hear that you leave with your birthmother in a few days."

Tomorrow she would greet Angelica pleasantly and be inconspicuously absent when the party was held. Ana would arrive the next day and they would leave that afternoon. Tonight, was for good-byes.

Manuel reached above to pull the light string and the pair stood in the darkness among greasy, metallic smells and a hint of sawdust. They held each other swaying lightly and murmuring admiration for each other. Their lives had quietly been enriched in the short time their hearts had touched and each hoped for wonder and happiness for the other.

Ana

There is magic in the air. And my new life has become a part of it. That moment Joanna stood before me at the *panaderia* is frozen in my memory. Uncertainty gripped me the moment I saw what she wore—my grandmother's ring and the bracelet I had designed for Ellie, who was so good to me. It's a wonder I didn't go to pieces on the spot. *And she was looking for an artist. It had to be me.* The overwhelming shock at seeing my precious Cara, all grown up and beautiful, gripped me. So close that I could reach out and touch her. Yet something cautioned. *You cannot reveal yourself. She deserves better.* I needed to square myself with the world. Then I might deserve her.

Leaving Mexico in the little Roadtrek a healing and bonding began for both of us. Joanna struggled to resolve the joy we felt in finding each other and the disloyalty she felt to her adoptive mom, whom she fiercely loved and admired. I am ever grateful to Allison for raising such a fine woman and vow never to rob the memory of Joanna's 'real mother' from her.

A plea bargain and an understanding judge in California helped to close the early chapters in my life. The six months in jail gave me a chance for reflection and there I started painting again. My most powerful work hangs in a prominent place at the jail. My hope is that it is an inspiration. My attempt was to show that demons could be cast away. Unbelievably I am being allowed to finish my year of probation here in Colorado.

It is a pleasant place I have. I live over the hill and around the corner from the resort where I worked that season so long ago—that time when I carried the babe that in her adulthood was brave enough to search for me. I have been working to make my little cabin cozy and warm for the winter. There is plenty of space in my roomy living room, the corner flanked with windows, for easels, paints, brushes, and canvasses. I am experimenting with new techniques. The days melt together. I am pleased with the outcomes. Three times a week I lead a group in yoga. We are becoming quite proficient. Wonderful friendships are coming to me. Joanna affectionately calls me her earth mother. I'm very OK with that.

It's been one joy after another. I keep telling myself that I deserve them. Perhaps I'm coming to believe it. So far, my proudest moment was in November escorting my lovely daughter down the aisle. It was a simple, yet elegant affair and everyone was touched by the beauty of the vows the wedding couple wrote for each other.

Though they were three weeks away from wrapping up the movie, Lauren sneaked away to be there. I've grown to love Joanna's three friends. It is nice to know of the special relationships that were a part of her childhood. Naturally, they acted as bridesmaids and when Joanna could not choose one to be her honor attendant, they ended up drawing straws. I was silently thrilled when Lauren pulled the long one.

And the groom with his groomsmen. Even an oldie like me had stars in my eyes. Of course, once I met Tony and saw the two of them together, I was confident that this would be a good match. Tony had the maturity to put their relationship aside while he faced what he called his own demons of the past, surrounding his father and their relationship. Certainly, life will be lively with two strong willed partners locking horns from time to time, but I've seen the commitment and pride in their eyes. They'll be fine.

It was a touching moment when Joanna urged Mario to his feet for the first dance. His shuffle was awkward and unstable, but one would have thought he was a grand duke the way Joanna carried it off. I virtually floated in Tony's arms delighted to be his choice for the first dance. His eyes had sparklers in them as he chatted on and on about his new bride. I wore an uninterrupted grin.

Darlene, I don't know if I can ever call her mother, was at the wedding. We are talking some and forgiveness is coming. Joanna used her travel benefits to surprise Tony with a honeymoon trip to Italy where they found a cousin who helped search the burial grounds for Mario's parents. It was a touching time for Tony especially. Some meaningful roots were established.

That was three months ago. Joanna continues to be busy at the travel agency and Tony is president of the newly formed Angelino Construction partnership, while Jesus has taken full responsibility for the cybercafe in Bucerias. Tony and Joanna are excitedly awaiting the completion of their new house.

I'm holding on to a bit of a secret. Perhaps at the right time it will be revealed. I discovered where Joanna's birthfather lives and if she wishes to seek him out, I will help her. So far, any mention of him brings indifference, so I will wait.

Oh, and the other thing. Phil came by a few weeks ago. He continues to heal from the loss of his fine wife, Ellie. He helped with some paneling and replaced the doors osn my kitchen cabinets. Tonight, we are going to the movies. It is the first night of Lauren's film and has been getting good press. Also, I have some exciting news to share with Phil tonight. He is thrilled that his son and daughter-in-law, Rod and Sally, are expecting in four months. Today, I learned that I too am going to be a grandmother.

Is it no wonder then, that *la espina* which so long carried the anguish in my heart has vanished?